Dear Gerard,

We live forever through our sto...

I hope Augustine's speaks to you.

NAGALAND

With my very best wishes,

A LOVE STORY FOR MODERN INDIA

BEN DOHERTY

P.S. Happy Birthday!
(March 2018)

WILD
DINGO
PRESS

Published by Wild Dingo Press
Melbourne, Australia
books@wilddingopress.com.au
www.wilddingopress.com.au

First published by Wild Dingo Press 2018

Designer: Debra Billson
Editor: Catherine Lewis
Chapter graphic: Tracey Small
Print in Australia by Griffin Press

Doherty, Ben, 1981- author.
Nagaland / Ben Doherty.

 A catalogue record for this
book is available from the
National Library of Australia

ISBN: 9780648066378 (paperback)
ISBN: 9780987381354 (ebook: pdf)
ISBN: 9780648215943 (ebook: epub)

Praise for Nagaland

Delightfully engrossing page-turner that provides a fascinating insight into *Nagaland*, its rich tapestry of legends, history and culture. Ben Doherty's intimate understanding of the Naga people is evident in the flair and passion of his writing. A riveting and poignant read.

– Nim Gholkar, author

With echoes of Rushdie annd Garcia Marquez, *Nagaland* takes the reader on a lyrical exploration of person and place. This enchanting work of fiction explores a lesser known corner of India through the protagonists' gripping and wondrous journey, while revealing Doherty as a writer with serious talent.

– Nick McKenzie, *The Age*

I have come across some extraordinary real life stories of inspiration, love, and tragedy with my travels in India as a journalist. But *NAGALAND* is exceptional. Ben's skilful storytelling engages emotionally in the life of an amazing man, his defiance for the sake of love, and his devotion to place and to culture. In my opinion, it is a must read.

– Som Patidar, journalist

ACKNOWLEDGEMENTS

I am the messenger of another's story. As such, there are many, too many, people to thank for the existence of this work.

I offer my deep and abiding appreciation to those many and varied folk who have supported this story along the way. To the late and beloved Michael Gordon, to Anthony Sharwood, Favourite Aunty Pauline, Dan Street, Laura Doherty, Kath and Cam Deyell, Stephanies March and Convery, Nim Gholkar, and Paul Wilson for reading early drafts and offering their feedback, criticisms, and encouragement.

To Andrew and Susan Cowell, to Tom Cribb, and to the Codrington Library at All Souls College for—at various times—a quiet place to write and re-imagine.

To Margaret Gee for her early faith and guidance. And to Jody Lee and Nadine Davidoff for their insightful assistance. This work is better for all of your contributions.

My immense thanks to Katia Ariel, who seized the essence of this story immediately, to whom Augustine spoke intuitively and for whom Nagaland resonated in all its complexity and colour. You found the soul of this story, and unveiled so much of Nagaland's hidden beauty.

I owe an enormous debt of gratitude to Catherine Lewis, Alex Cseh-Scurry, and all of the team at Wild Dingo Press for their immense leap of faith, taken in me and in this story. Catherine found me in the long, long grasses of storytelling and—somehow—brought forth this tale you have before you. I hope this work, in some small way, repays the faith you have shown.

My undying love and gratitude go to my wonderful wife Kim, who believed in this story from the first word, who read it over time and time again, and who always encouraged me to keep going. And to Molly, for simply being the sweetest, most gorgeous girl imaginable.

But my greatest thanks must go to Augustine, his family, friends and community, for allowing me a glimpse into the majesty of Nagaland, its history, its tribulations, and its indomitable spirit. Thank you for allowing me to be bearer of this tale.

In the green-grey hills of your land Augustine, you told me: 'we live forever through our stories'.

This is yours…

Ben Doherty
February, 2018

EIGHT WORDS

The diary arrived addressed to me.

Wedged into my letterbox, its battered yellow envelope carried no sender's name, no return address. Ends crudely wrapped in sellotape, the package was postmarked with a single circular stamp bearing a date—19 December 2015—and, in tiny letters: Republic of India: Nagaland.

The diary itself was a small book, bound in brown leather and held closed by a long, thin twine wound tightly around its middle. Its creamy pages were filled, overfilled and seemingly without order, with drawings of birds and mountains and flowers; with hastily drawn maps and tightly scrawled verses of poetry—song-lyrics-in-progress perhaps—all written in the same shaky hand.

A feather—white with a dark brown, almost-black, horizontal stripe, I recognised it to be from a hornbill—served as a bookmark, attending the penultimate page. Now unbound, the book fell open in my hands here to reveal what appeared to be a journal entry. The script was Roman, written in the careful cursive of one writing something important, something permanent, but I could make no sense of it. To my inexpert eyes only a handful of words were familiar: enough, only, to recognise the language as Tangkhul, one of Nagaland's myriad dialects.

But at the bottom of the page was a single sentence written in English. The letters ran haphazardly across the page: set down, evidently, in haste:

We live forever through our stories. Tell ours.

I recognised the plea. Instinctively now, I knew to whom this diary belonged. So why was it now here with me, on the other side of the world?

TABLE OF CONTENTS

Part One

WALK WITH ME	5
THE VILLAGE AT THE END OF THE EARTH	10

Part Two

THE UN-NUMBERED BUNGALOW TWO FROM THE VERY TOP	20
YARHO	29
THE SONGS A FATHER SUNG	37
INDIAN HISTORY	44
THE NUMBER 4	55
THE BOY WITH THE BIRTHMARK	63
BUSINESS IN BURMA	75
GOLDEN	88
BOMBAY BY BICYCLE	97
THE LILIES OF SHIRUI	110
THEJA	121
THE SOLDIER WITH THE SHINY GUN	138
ZAKI	151
IN MY ACHING BONES	160
TICKET 161	172
SUNSET	184
THESE HILLS	191
A TRAIN AT MIDNIGHT	204
KANCHAA AND COWARDS	216
SECHUMHANG	223
GRACE	234
THE HORNBILL	247
NIDO	254

Part Three

SUKHAYAP	266

Part One

WALK WITH ME

WALK WITH ME

'We live forever through our stories,' Augustine said, running a testing thumb over the newly sharpened edge of his *dao*. He turned to look at me, swinging the squat knife to his shoulder, the blunt edge coming to rest on his collar bone, the acute glinting in the weak sun of the mountains. 'That's why this is important, that's what you must understand.'

Augustine had never spoken like this before: so expansively, so easefully. We'd met almost three years earlier at the height of India's cruelly hot summer of 2011, and in the time since, we had slowly built a friendship in instalments—parties of mutual friends, gigs of bands we'd wanted to see, long drives stuck in Delhi's unrelenting traffic. But little was simple, was predictable with Augustine. He was a person comfortably silent a long time, and guarded when he did speak. His was a character revealed by adumbration. Augustine would vanish often and without explanation even when he returned, weeks later. He'd simply been 'busy' or 'around', offering no clue as to where he'd been, no real concession he'd ever even been gone. Yet return he would, always.

He would appear on his terms. When I was struck by dengue, delirious with the break-bone fever and able to find a tiny measure of comfort only by lying in strange contortions on the cool stone floor of my house, he materialised without notice, carrying a dark-green concoction made of papaya leaves and myriad undeclared spices. 'My *Ayi's* recipe,' he said. It popped and bubbled in an old Coke bottle.

'How did you even know I was sick?' I asked him.

He shrugged. Augustine stayed, for days it seemed, silently pressing upon me another sip of the foul-tasting potion during my half-lucid moments of wakefulness. When I awoke properly after nearly a fortnight, well again but weak, he was gone. I wouldn't see him again for two months.

Now, it was 2014, and we were in Augustine's homeland, the land of the Naga. India's brief-but-sharp winter had settled all over the north of the country, but it lay most heavily here. The fierce winds carried flurries of snowflakes too fragile to settle on the ground, but enough to dust the eaves of the houses and the branches of the trees.

We sat in the hard dirt outside Augustine's ancestral home in the village of Ukhrul, high in the mountains of far north-eastern India, that forgotten teardrop of brittle, unyielding land wedged between Bangladesh and Burma. It was here, despite the cold and the wind, that Augustine felt most comfortable, felt most himself. Here he held court.

'These are not just stories we tell our children and grandchildren; these stories are who we are.'

He paused and lowered his voice. 'You are a journalist. You call them legends. But to us they are truth, they are history. They are destiny.'

Augustine was not usually like this. In low-lying Delhi where we had both lived, a few suburbs and several worlds apart, he was quiet. Not sullen, but cautious, almost timid. In the city, he spoke only when he had to, and as much as he needed to. And he spoke quietly there, so quietly he could barely be heard in that noisy place. He moved cautiously in the big city, walking with his shoulders hunched and his head bowed slightly, as though he felt he took up too much space in the crowded capital.

Here though, in Ukhrul, he was different. I have noticed it on each visit to this place. Here among his own people, he stood far taller, with his shoulders back and his chin lifted. He spoke power-fully, and laughed readily. He smiled so I could see his teeth.

Augustine and I met when our rock bands played together at the same New Delhi pub, one of the few that existed, and one of the fewer still that had live music. Augustine's band was on before ours, but it should have been the other way around. They were much better than we were. Three-quarters of the crowd were Naga, like Augustine, and they'd come to see him play.

I wasn't in India to play in a band. I was a journalist, a foreign correspondent with an Australian newspaper, on my second post-ing in Asia, and forever racing over a roiling, restless region—the far-distant corners of Pakistan, Afghanistan, Sri Lanka, Bangladesh and Burma. Mine was the impossible task of 'covering' a home to one-and-a-half billion people.

When I was here, in this country, 'India Rising' was supposed to be my story. The emergent behemoth, with its tens-of-millions-strong middle class, the coming global superpower: that was the assignment from my editors. But inexorably, almost subconsciously, I found myself drawn to the fringes of India, the ragged, inchoate edges, the parts that remained fuzzy to understanding even as the rest of the country swung into the sharp focus of global view. I found myself filing stories on the disappearing language of Toto in the remote jungles abutting Bhutan, on a baby girl in Madhya Pradesh who couldn't grow because she was born when the rains didn't fall, and on children digging shiny stones out of mines in Meghalaya.

The more I learned over my years in India, the more I realised how little I knew. Everything that was true about India was also inescapably false. India was gloriously uncategorisable, proudly defiant of generalisation or stereotype. The more I grasped for its essence, the more it eluded me. There was no one India. The difference of India—that's what staggered, what captivated, me. Its divergence and dichotomy: from the hard-scrabble stone villages of Kashmir in the north to Kerala's tropical fecundity in the south; from the river deltas of Gujarat in the west to the grey-green hills of the Naga, where I sat now, in the far, far east. The difference was akin to that of Scotland to…Poland. Everything was different: the languages people spoke, the food they ate, the crops they grew and the houses they lived in, the gods they worshipped and the clothes they wore while doing it. The time people got out of bed in the morning was different; so too, the movies they watched, the music they listened to, their politics and their histories. Their interest in cricket—surely, I thought, India's one unifying factor—I discovered, waxed and waned across this land, the barren plains and the fertile river valleys, the coarse-sand beaches and the jagged mountains.

For all of India's diversity, Augustine was something different again. Nowhere in my travels through India or across the region, had I seen anyone like Augustine. He was unmissable. He wore his hair long, falling in a straight ponytail halfway down his back, but the sides of his head he kept closely shaved. His angular face was carefully inked in tattoos, three horizontal lines across the bridge of his nose and a vertical pattern that ran from his lower lip down his chin to his neck. These were the traditional markings of the Naga people, the tattoos of the headhunter. But now, even among the Naga, they represented a custom that had almost entirely died out. Only the oldest men and women in the villages looked like Augustine did. Of his generation, only he was marked in this way.

Despite his ancient adornments, Augustine dressed in modern clothes, head to foot in black: long flowing shirts that draped formlessly across his lean body over jeans, and heavy boots. And he wore a feather—the white feather of a hornbill, with its single dark stripe—pointing straight up from the back of his head.

◈ ◈ ◈

'We live forever through our stories,' Augustine's voice brought me back to the here-and-now, to the cold dirt outside his home. He was still running that thumb along the sharp edge of his *dao*. Augustine had never done small talk, but both he and I recognised the unspoken significance of my visit to Ukhrul this time. What we had was ending. A month earlier, Augustine had suddenly announced—a declaration in itself was unusual enough for him—that he was moving back to his village to live in these hills and the house he called Sechumhang—No Man's Land—halfway down the valley. At the same time, my posting in India was almost finished. I would be replaced, in the way of correspondents, and leave soon for Australia and its distant familiarity. I had returned to his village to say good-bye, to Augustine and to these hills. But I had come back, too, to know that Augustine was okay, and to seek to understand what it was that had pushed, or pulled, him back to this place. I sensed not trouble, but disquiet in him. It might be a long time before we saw each other again.

'Come,' Augustine said, again, too-casually swinging that blade, this time to point straight at me, and then out over the mountains. 'Walk with me.'

THE VILLAGE AT THE END
OF THE EARTH

Augustine and I walked west, downhill along the same dusty streets, barely changed from those he'd known as a child. We passed the vaulted roof and the spire of the chapel his family still attended each Sunday morning. The Shimrays' pew was on the gospel side, five rows from the front. Ukhrul boasted two churches, impressive stone Baptist houses that stood, like gleaming white sentries, at either end of the village. Two churches gave the town a sense of grandeur, either past or impending, though there was no suggestion that these halcyon days were either particularly recent or in any way imminent. The churches, their stone courtyards and statues of Christ—graphic, agonised representations of the final moments of his crucifixion—were kept spotlessly clean, washed every day as if to further accentuate their piety in comparison to the remainder of this fusty, faded place. 'My father,' Augustine said, 'used to say these were the grandest buildings in all of Ukhrul'. The blasphemous mutterings were lost on the child. 'I was much older before I understood what he meant.'

Augustine's attendance at church services was, these days, sporadic at best, he confessed. There were reasons he didn't go much anymore, memories that lived in that place. But as a child he liked visiting church, the familiar drone of the incomprehensible hymns, the colourful kaleidoscope of light from the stained-glass windows swirling across the spotless marble floor. Just being at church was an occasion. 'Nobody we knew lived in a house made of stone or brick.' Homes in Ukhrul were all just like his, he said, unpainted wooden bungalows with dirt floors and low ceilings stained black with the soot of the fireplaces.

Ukhrul is an emaciated village, strung narrow as it descends west along a nameless mountain ridge, below and around which the Langdangkong River curls on its languid way to the plains below. Augustine and I turned to look back uphill: we could see the school buses wending their lone route, up and down the main street that was the only sealed road in these hills. People built their modest homes along narrow alleys that ran off this street, steep passages that plunged from the ridgeline into the forest below, spindly capillaries to the town's lone artery. From east to west the town fell nearly forty metres, and the villagers divided themselves into Upper Ukhrul and Lower, defined by which church they attended. The *maidan*, a grass-starved public square that doubled as a football field and a place for teenagers to hang out after sunset, was the dividing line. The distinction, Augustine said, was not a spoken one, rather it was felt, almost by instinct. Up or down. There was little hostility to it but everyone had to, in the way of small places, belong to one or the other. The Shimrays' house—we could see it now—sat atop a small rise about halfway down the town, but the Shimrays belonged to Lower Ukhrul. That's why they went to church where they did.

We stood unmoving as sunset's momentary brilliance, those final few minutes of glittering defiance, faded, and the dusty town was returned to its unremarkable brown hue. The dark falls quickly in the mountains and we looped around the sparse few houses at the bottom of the village, above the place Augustine called No Man's Land. We stared down into the valley. The next ridgeline was an indistinct grey smudged into the dark sky above it. The ranges beyond blurred one into another. Everywhere here, in every direction, were mountains. The ground was hard and unyielding. What little farming land there was, by the rivers in the valleys, was over-worked and barely subsistent, let alone profitable. It was that time of year now, Augustine said—the time between the rains and the harvest. Ukhrul knows the hungry season. We started back up the hill towards the light of the fire that had appeared in the window of his family home. There would be food there.

We were not the only ones walking. Farmers carrying tools had made their way up the mountainside from the paddy fields, saying hello to Augustine as they passed. Women bearing shopping were less inclined to stop, too busy corralling meandering children home before dark. From behind us, out of the gloaming, came the sound of a measured, careful tread. Augustine did not turn around, but muttered only one word: 'Rifles'.

Just beyond the lower western end of Ukhrul stood an imposing military base. From almost any vantage point in town, one could see its floodlit whitewashed walls, wreathed in rolls of razor wire. The base thrummed to the vibration of generators 24 hours a day. It was the only place in the village where the electricity never went out. This was the garrison of the Assam Rifles, the Indian government's oldest paramilitary police force. The Rifles were, in fact, older than the country they were paid to protect. The British, in the days of the Raj, established the Cachar Levy, as the regiment was first called, to protect white settlers from the raids of the 'bloodthirsty' headhunters who lived in these hills.

While the Rifles were separate from the army, they were, to anyone who saw them, indistinguishable from soldiers. They wore khaki and neat moustaches, carried ranks on their shoulders, and assault weapons in their hands. They saluted. Their symbol was two crossed *kukri*, the curved fighting knives most famously carried by the Gurkhas of Nepal. In full parade dress, each Rifleman bore one on his belt.

Augustine ignored the two riflemen, but I turned to look. They weren't marching, but out of habit their feet fell in perfect unison, their black boots crunching noisily on the gravel of the road. In the dusk, the men were barely distinct until they were almost beside us. The riflemen didn't look at Augustine or at me, and offered no acknowledgement we were there. They wore camouflage pants and green army-issue t-shirts, the fronts of which carried their unit's motto 'Friends of the Hill People', a bleak misnomer. The hill people of Ukhrul and the Rifles didn't talk much, and they certainly weren't friends. The Rifles looked different from the local people, being plainland north Indians or darker-skinned Tamils from the south. These men were not happy about their posting, Augustine said. They were a long way from home, it was cold in these hills, and the chance for proper soldiering—the adventure they signed up for—was limited. 'In a strange way, they are a good fit,' he said. 'The Naga don't want the Rifles here, and the Rifles don't want to be here. On that, we agree.' We watched the two men stalk off into the night.

'The Rifles are told they have two jobs: watch the locals, and watch for outsiders,' Augustine said cryptically once the men were safely out of earshot. Manipur had, for decades, been gripped by a secessionist insurgency, an ancient grudge that, most of the time, bored most of the people, but which every few months broke to some violent new mutiny. The insurrection was the work of a left-wing guerrilla outfit called the National Socialist Council of Nagaland, whose declared aim was Naga self-determination, a free nation for the Naga people. They were Baptists; some people called them 'Christian extremists'.

'It was more active when I was small,' Augustine said. 'I didn't really know what they were talking about, but I would always hear the adults talk about "the NSCN" or "the Underground", and when they did, they kept their voices low.'

The NSCN was weaker now, its campaign wearied by internecine conflict and the creeping corruption endemic to any long struggle for freedom yet to yield any appreciable liberty. But it loomed large still in the psyche of the people of these hills. Once, it was rumoured the NSCN had 10,000 fighters in the mountains and valleys of Nagaland and Manipur, but no one really knew how many there were, or how many remained. 'But we would know when they were close,' Augustine said. 'I would hear someone at my mother's shop say, "they are back from the hills".' Invariably, a few days later, trucks would begin blowing up in the marketplace: small bombs, but enough to kill a few blameless vendors and their customers, so everyone was again exercised by the terror that walked among them. But each time, a few weeks would pass without event, and the shopkeepers would return—someone always in the lost person's place—and everyone would resume their unworried routines. There were still bombs now, but not so many, Augustine said. The Rifles occasionally made a few arrests, always loudly trumpeted in the local newspapers, but the insurgency seemed undiminished by their attention. It was as though a certain amount of rebellion was permitted, and the Rifles were there just to make sure it didn't get out of hand.

The Assam Rifles' other task was the nearby border with Burma. Both they and Burma's Tatmadaw patrolled these hills, even though there was not much of a border. There was no fence, no boundary posts controlling movements, just a few stone cairns on a ridgeline marked out decades ago by some forgotten cartographer. People walked back and forth unhindered, crossing with the seasons, herding cattle from one country to another, or working land on the other side from their homes. People here weren't Indian, or Burmese—those were labels that mattered in Delhi and Rangoon. No one here had passports, or ID cards. Nationality was just another marker of dislocation, another category into which people didn't comfortably fit.

It was the same even inside India. This was the state of Manipur, but Augustine and his family were not Manipuri. Those people were 'meitei', plainland people. The Shimrays were Naga, people of the hills. Their homeland, rightly, should be part of the state immediately to the north: Nagaland. 'The British draw lines on other people's countries,' Augustine said as we walked back up the final dusty rise to his family home. 'Now we are told what is our place by some faraway Delhiwallah *babu*[1]. We don't worry about such things. We have been here much longer than that.' As if in evidence of that truth, Augustine's grandmother, here long before the bloody birth of the modern nation of India, was waiting for us at the front door. She leaned on its handle, her back bent, it appeared, from decades stooped over the same fire we could see burning low

---

1 *Babu:* a Hindi term, literally *Mr* or *Sir*, but used most often as a noun to refer to a government bureaucrat. Often, though not always, it is used disparagingly, to describe a person who is officious or pedantic, or obsessed with hierarchy.

behind her. Wordlessly, she motioned us inside with her arms. 'Sorry *Ayi*,' Augustine mumbled, but she was smiling as she ushered him in.

That night, there was mutton for dinner; I couldn't tell if this was usual, or an indulgence by virtue of my visit. I worried it was the latter, but it was an impossible question to ask. Augustine's family sat cross-legged by the fire as the food was placed before them. As the guest, I was impressed upon to sit nearest the fire—'the seat of honour', Augustine explained. He translated his statement into Tangkhul for his older relatives, who smiled and nodded. Grace was said in English, hands held. Augustine's *Ayi* pressed a heaving plate into my hands, gesturing with her fingers for me to eat. The meat was rich, marbled with fat. 'Very good,' I said, eating, to the same nods and smiles.

◈◈◈

After dinner, Augustine and I took a small brazier and coals from the fire and walked to the roadside to stand outside the now-closed shopfront. Augustine rolled and lit a cigarette, then offered it to me. I declined. As the darkness closed in, he talked idly of the families that lived in the houses we could still see, his features lost to the tendrils of smoke that escaped into the cold night air and the uncertain light of the flame.

'You're more at home here. I can see that,' I said at last. 'I can see why you've come back to this place.'

'No, you can't,' Augustine replied forcefully, more forcefully, I think, than he intended. He softened. 'I mean, it's not…there is more to it than what you can see from the outside.'

'Than I can see from the outside?'

'Than anyone can see from the outside.'

'Then why did you come back?' Finally, I asked the question that had hung between us since I'd arrived. The one question Augustine had been both anxious for me to ask, and fearful that I would.

'It's a long story. And it doesn't make sense unless…' Augustine stumbled, 'unless you understand it all.'

'Start from the beginning.'

'Well,' he said, 'it really starts on that day.'

'Which day?'

'The beginning, the first day I can remember.'

Augustine hauled himself up to sit on the bare wooden counter of the shopfront.

'Here,' he said, patting the bench with his hand, 'this is where I sat and waited for my father that night: the night after the day my sister was born.'

Part Two

THE SONGS
A FATHER SANG

Augustine arrives at the riverbank before Akala. It is less than ten minutes since he'd received her text; she'd still be coming down the hill. But he is worried. Someone might have seen her; her father might have caught her leaving, or maybe her brothers would know where she was going. He drums his fists against his thighs as he paces back and forth. He doesn't want to sit, he can't stand still, or think clearly. He wants her to be here.

❖❖❖

Akala arrives within minutes, sobbing. She carries nothing but her *chonkhom*, red too, for Tangkhul, but decorated in the women's style with brilliant, angled stripes of electric green. She wears it pulled tightly over her narrow shoulders, as though the threadbare shawl has some power to protect her. She scrabbles up the rocks the last few metres to where Augustine stands in the shade of the trees. 'No one saw me leave,' she says, pre-empting his question. They stand at a distance from one another, momentarily shy. Then, Akala falls into Augustine, collapsing in his arms, crying. She is normally shy about touching, but now she clings to Augustine tightly and howls. He holds her as her body shudders against his. Only now does Akala realise, and now he does, too, just what it is they've done.

'How did your father find out?'

'I don't know,' Akala says through tears. 'I came home to find my mother crying. She handed me my phone that I had hidden in my room, and she told me my father had found it. He had gone to see Atsu's family, fearing they would find out I'd been seeing you, and would call the wedding off. He was going round to beg them to honour our engagement; and was going to offer more money, like a disgraced man, on his knees. My mother told me to wait for him.' Akala is in hysterics at the thought of her father, humiliated and pleading for a wedding she doesn't want. 'My mother kept asking, "Lord, where did I go wrong?". I started to cry, so she sent me to my room, but I was still holding the phone. I texted you and then. When you replied, I escaped out the window. No one saw me leave, but I have, no money, no clothes, nothing...'

Augustine has little more, but he has what they need. Before he left Sechumhang, he wrapped a shawl around his shoulders and pulled his father's old air rifle from the eave on the back stoop. There was ammunition in a small leather pouch by the door that he now feels in his pocket along with matches and a mug, and a small cloth knotted at the top, holding a handful of rice. Augustine feels his *dao* too, the sheathed, sharpened blade pressing against the small of his back. They will need it where they are going. Only his diary is missing, but Augustine is comforted by the knowledge it has been dispatched to safety, far away. Further than he has ever been in his lifetime.

Augustine doesn't have a plan, not yet. He just knows somewhere else, anywhere else, will be better than here. He holds Akala and allows himself a moment where he doesn't have to think, just feel. Her heaving, racking breaths settle. They hold each other's hands a minute longer, heads bowed close.

'Come on. We have to go now,' he says.

The easiest path out is back up towards Augustine's village, but that is impossible, as is walking back towards her home. In the other direction, the valley falls towards the plainlands. They know they cannot make their way there, either, without being discovered. They must climb. 'This way,' Augustine says, pointing north. 'Above these trees is a trail out; I know it from hunting with my father. We can get out over the plateau at Phangrei. It's not too hard.'

'We go together?' Akala says, half-questioning, half-insisting.

'Of course.'

THE UN-NUMBERED BUNGALOW
TWO FROM THE VERY TOP

In a high, forgotten corner of India in a village at the end of the earth, Augustine Shimray formed his first memory. Two memories. He fell off a chair onto his head, and his sister was born. He was five.

Climbing on a chair at school to open a window, Augustine fell and gashed his forehead. It didn't hurt, but the amount of blood was immense. He blinked hard, in shock as much as discomfort, as it ran into his eyes and down his shirt. The overwrought teachers at Little Angels, the modest primary school at the lower end of Ukhrul village, didn't want to deal with a mischievous kid who wouldn't sit properly on his chair and was now covered in blood, so the principal, Madam Soso, sent him home with a note to his mother that he might be concussed. The letter was handed to Augustine in an envelope marked with the date—October 31, 1987—and addressed: 'To the family of Augustine Horchuingam Luiyainao Shimray'. Augustine couldn't read very well yet, but he recognised his own full tribal name when it was written out, so he knew he was in trouble. People only ever called him Augustine.

He walked slowly home, alone, up the hill to the un-numbered bungalow two from the very top which commanded views down the valley and to his family's land by the river. Unusually, for his was a house where people congregated, there was no one out in the street. Nor was his mother behind the counter of the single-room shop that she owned and ran on the roadside outside their home. The shop, nameless and unadorned save for a single, unreliable light bulb hanging from the front awning, was a slouching edifice with a dirt floor inside and a low bench for customers at the front. Typically, the shop's regulars would sit on the pew for hours talking to his mother, she relaying to them the gossip of the last visitors, they, in turn, listening, adjudicating, and adding their own. Together, they knew all of Ukhrul's business, and kept watch on the world passing by.

Augustine loved the fact that his mother owned a shop. But he didn't love the shop itself. It was an uncomfortable place to spend any length of time, at any time. In summer, the dust whipped in from the street and coated everything inside in grit despite the near constant attention of Augustine's mother's feather duster. In winter, the cold wind exploited the lack of insulation and the cracks in the timber walls. The shop sold, to Augustine's comprehension, anything and everything imaginable. In reality, it was anything and everything Augustine's mother, Likoknaro, could source. Its offerings varied with the seasons and the markets: tomatoes in spring, rice in the weeks after harvest, chips and lollies and hair oil and razor blades year-round, batteries if they could ever be found for a reasonable price.

Now the shop was open—Augustine only ever knew it to be closed on Sundays—but empty. He slid underneath the counter, and from the unguarded plastic tin on a low shelf, he helped himself to a *heingar*, the sickly-sweet discs of confectionary his mother made from desiccated coconut, sugar and water. Breaking it in half, he stuck the larger brown ellipse in his pocket, the other sticky piece into his mouth, and walked inside.

He stopped suddenly as he stepped through the door into the front room of his home. Before him was a tight gaggle of busy women—most of whom he recognised—and in the middle of them, his mother. His aunties were all here, and he knew, though more vaguely, the women from church who were fussing over his mother and the fire and the food, but he was nervous with their crowded presence in his home. He ran to his *Ayi*—his father's mother, Changsonla—who stood in a corner, and wrapped himself in her skirts.

'Come,' *Ayi* said to him gently, 'there is someone you must meet'. Augustine's grandmother guided him to the middle of the throng. There, his mother was holding a baby he'd never seen before.

'Augustine,' she said, 'this is your sister. This is Maitonphi.'

Maitonphi had been born an hour before, at home, just as her siblings had been. She was sound asleep. Augustine was intrigued by the new arrival, but hardly overwhelmed with curiosity. He had understood enough to know a new baby was coming, but the mechanics of it were beyond him, and besides, there were kids all over in this street, and new ones all the time; another one was not especially interesting. Still, he wanted to hold her all the same. His mother told him he was too small, but he could 'very gently' stroke her head. He roughed up the mess of soft black hair on her head. Maitonphi slept on. He liked her straight away.

'Augustine, I must stay with the baby,' his mother said. 'Could you take care of the shop for me, just until your father gets home?'

The note from the Madam Soso was still burning a hole in one shirt pocket, the contraband *heingar* the other. Augustine had been worried he would be in trouble, but no one seemed to notice, let alone worry, that he was home in the middle of the day, his blue school shirt splashed with a deep crimson stain. Even at the age of five, Augustine was wise enough not to offer the principal's missive unprompted.

He nodded to his mother and patted his sister again—still no reaction—and walked back out to the shop. Taking another *heingar* from the tin, he sat down on the low wooden stool behind the counter. Augustine was short for his age, and slight. Sitting in the cool of the dirt floor, he couldn't be seen by customers who arrived at the counter. Instead, he watched through the gap at the bottom for the arrival of legs. Whenever someone came, he would clamber up onto the counter to ask what they wanted. It wasn't a taxing or even a crucial, job. Customers were few in Ukhrul, and the Baptist values of honesty and fairness ran deep. Usually, in the moments when Liko was drawn away from staffing the shop, people would leave their handful of coins or notes on the unattended counter, carefully doling out the right amount, and confident the rupees wouldn't disappear in their absence. This afternoon it was quiet.

Augustine sat, tracing his fingers through worn patterns in the dirt of the shop floor as he waited for his father. His father's traditional Naga name was Luishomwo. In Tangkhul it meant 'the reliable harvest': he was born in a season of solid rains and subsequent plentiful crops. More commonly, his father went by the Christianised, Luke. Luke himself was not someone to be relied upon, to be punctual, or for anything really. Augustine knew he could find his mother, anytime, at the shop, or at home, or at the church. He wouldn't know where to begin looking for his father. Even at his young age, Augustine understood his mother was the one on whom he could depend. He waited.

Tired of having sat still for so long, Augustine climbed up to sit on the shop counter, and gazed down at the farrago of houses that seemed to tumble down the hill away from him, their patchwork silver tin roofs slowly turning a seamless gold in the afternoon sun. This—Ukhrul—was Augustine's world. The town limits were the boundary of his lived experience; beyond was a world he knew only through stories. He knew there were other villages like his—he had heard his father talk about them—perched on ridges like this, the ridges he saw now stretching grey-green to the Burmese border. He knew, from his father too, that for as far as he could see in any direction, the land belonged to the Tangkhul, his people, one of the multifarious Naga tribes of the north-east. And further, he knew from the teachers at school that he lived in the state of Manipur, one of the 'seven sisters' they called it, using the collective appellation for the far north-eastern states of India. Augustine knew all of this, but only because people had told him it was so. Ukhrul was the limit of his lived experience, the knowledge he knew for himself.

◈◈◈

Augustine willed his father to be home, as he stared down the road, desperately hopeful Luke's form would suddenly materialise out of the silent dark. Hunger gnawed at him now, though he knew instinctively, there would be food before bed. His mother never sent him to sleep hungry. The Shimrays had more than many in Ukhrul. Their shop, run in genial competition with a few neighbours' further down the hill, was stocked most of the year; and the family had rice paddies that were well-watered, and forest in which they could hunt without fear of infringing another clan's claim. There was enough. Augustine knew families in Ukhrul regarded as rich by local standards. The Shimrays were not that. But they had more than many. Augustine had recently been bought his first-ever pair of shoes, to start school. He hated them initially as they felt heavy and gave him blisters, so he would take them off and put them in his bag to walk home. But he was also glad to have them—plenty in his class came barefoot. Even at five, it was a distinction keenly felt.

Still Augustine's father had not come home. Now Augustine longed, more in raw hope than any expectation. The stars were out, and it was getting cold. There hadn't been a customer for over an hour, and there were no *heingar* left. His younger brother Alex, still a toddler, had wandered into the shop for a time; he liked to be part of whatever his older sibling was doing. But he was soon bored, and as night fell, he went back to the warmth of the fire. Augustine could see the lights inside his home were on now—they always drained the amps and dulled the bulb outside the front of the shop. The electricity might hold for an hour or two more.

'Close the shop and come inside,' came a voice. Augustine's mother had suddenly appeared in the rear doorway, still with her newborn who was soundly asleep. Liko had wrapped Maitonphi tightly in a blanket and secured the infant to her body, in the Naga style, with a shawl knotted around her shoulders. 'Dinner is ready.'

The church women and most of the relatives had left Augustine's home now. But the inconvenience of giving birth had not deterred Liko, helped by Augustine's *Ayi* and a couple of aunts who remained, from cooking dinner. The women were wrestling the blackened pot of sticky rice from the fire and cleaving off chunks for people's plates. There was chicken, boiled in a hot, watery curry, and a spicy chutney. Over it they crushed heads of *yongbah*, a grass whose grainy flower served as a garnish. Placed on the floor, the plates sat untouched until the women had finished serving everyone. Liko reached out for Augustine and Alex's hands and bowed her head.

'For what we are about to receive, may the Lord make us truly thankful.'

'Amen.'

Liko picked up her tin plate and began eating, her fingers swiftly transferring chunks of broth-stained rice to her mouth. Alex, too young, pushed his chicken around the plate, occasionally finding his mouth with a stray grain of rice as he licked his fingers. Augustine didn't eat, his hunger displaced now by concern his father was not yet home. Luke had not yet seen his daughter.

'Why is she called Maitonphi?' Augustine asked pointing to the baby. The infant lay in a woven cradle hanging from a hook high up and to the side of the fire. The air in that corner was warm, but not smoky. The crib rocked gently back and forth.

'Maitonphi was my grandmother's name,' Liko said.

'Was she nice?' Augustine wanted to talk, not eat.

'You never met her, but she was very beautiful, and very kind,' Liko replied. 'When I was a girl, my aunties were strict and would make me stay inside to do chores, but my grandmother let me play outside or go to the forest with the other children.'

'Why was she called Maitonphi?'

'The name means "gentle one". My grandmother was like that. It is a traditional name, very old-fashioned.'

'From the old ways, the Hao, like Dad talks about?'

'Haa,' Liko answered 'yes' in Hindi, rather than Tangkhul, their mother tongue. Her voice had noticeably stiffened at the mention of Augustine's father. Augustine recognised the tone, a sign that Liko considered his line of questioning extinguished and the conversation over. Liko didn't share all of her grandmother's easy-going nature, but she had inherited no small amount of her aunties' rigour.

'Shouldn't we wait for Dad to come home?' Augustine pushed his luck. He was still wearing his school shirt, stained red with the blood from his own head. He put his finger to the gash on his hairline, it wasn't bleeding, but it felt swollen, the flesh around it tender. No one had noticed, or if they had, hadn't felt compelled to ask what had happened. Hours ago, he had torn up the note from Madam Soso and thrown it in the gutter outside, where it vanished amongst the other rubbish. Augustine wanted his father home, his family felt incomplete without him. He had waited all afternoon for him. Maybe his father would ask about his head, and Augustine could tell him about his accident.

'We should wait for Dad to come home,' Augustine said, pushing his plate away, 'otherwise he'll have to eat dinner alone'.

'Eat,' Liko told Augustine, putting down her own plate to force his into his hands. 'Your father can eat whenever he chooses to come home to his family. You eat now.'

❖ ❖ ❖

Augustine leads Akala from the grove of trees. He marches quickly to begin with, allowing too much of his anxiety to manifest. But the still of the midday forest is calming, and conscious that Akala does not know these forest trails, he slows his pace, helping her where the path becomes steep. Akala is determined to show she can keep up, as though any hesitancy, she fears, he will read as reluctance and try to send her back. Augustine knows she can't go back, however, just as much as he cannot. But as if to prove her commitment, she shuns his help more often than she accepts it, reaching past his outstretched hand to grab the rock face and haul herself up.

In an hour and a half, they have reached the southern edge of the Phangrei plateau. There are few trees on the broad, windswept grassland. It is not a place where people spend much time or cross without reason. At the far end from where Augustine and Akala stand now, Shirui Peak rises imposingly from the plateau, curling up into the sky. Today the mountain's summit is lost among clouds: Philava, the Goddess of the mountain, is home. But the plateau itself is flat, and despite the altitude and the wind, the walking here across grassland is easier. As they thread their way between the waist-high tussocks, they can see Augustine's village, Ukhrul, perched on the headland of a short, steadily rising ridge to the east. On the flank of the closest valley west stands Akala's village, Tiya. Their homes are separated by barely two kilometres, and the river. No two villages are closer. None are further apart.

Augustine has been here dozens of times, but as they walk now, he looks more closely at his village, perhaps for the last time, and at Akala's. Ukhrul appears much larger than Tiya. The vegetable market in the middle of town is attended by tall street lamps, and the neat file of power poles and their wires can be seen charting the course of the main street, even from this distance. Tiya has none of those things. There is no main market, just a couple of roadside stores. There are barely a dozen families in that place and only one church.

The people of Tiya are Tangkhul too. They share the language and celebrate the same festivals. Their dress is similar enough that only those from each village can tell each apart. Most of the Tangkhul tribes, in these days of Christian fraternity, are on good terms, further bonded by families that weave in and out of each village, putting down roots and sprouting new shoots across the valleys and the ridges and the rivers. Clan names are common across the tribes; markers of the familial journey. The old women in the villages know who has married whom and from where, and it's they who dictate the unions of the next generation, keeping names and bloodlines alive.

But proximity breeds contempt.

There is bad blood between Tiya and Ukhrul. In each generation, men have died. The feud between the two villages has its origins here at Phangrei, over the plateau on which they are now walking.

The plateau runs south to north: Tiya stands guard on its western flank, Ukhrul on its east. Neither is closer than the other, and both make equal, singular, claim to it. Land, and its control, is the fundament of power to Naga tribes. Villages that control large territories seek more, always, while those with little, do all they can to defend what they have. To allow another village rights to land is to cede one's own sovereignty, to be weakened, to surrender without honour.

But it's an old fight. There is no real reason for the rancour between Ukhrul and Tiya, only stubborn old-world pride. Perhaps pride is enough. No one, on either side, is prepared to concede. And it infects everything. People from Ukhrul do not speak to those from Tiya. They don't hunt together or farm the same fields. They don't allow their children to marry. There is rarely anybody on Phangrei plateau. Save for Augustine and Akala, there is no one here now.

On Augustine's part, it is all unintended, he hasn't had time to formulate any real plan, let alone a gesture of grand symbolism. This is just a way out.

YARHO

The house was asleep when Augustine's father finally came home. But he was singing, so soon everybody was awake. Luke had the fire going, and the radio, he thought softly, tuned to a station playing the latest Bollywood bubblegum pop. The static would come in waves, overwhelming the lyrics, but Luke would fill in the gaps with the right words or the wrong. It didn't matter, the songs were all the same.

In his right hand, he held a bamboo cup half-filled with *zu*, a homemade beer made from rice and typically fermented in someone's illegal still, hidden in a paddy-field shack. Luke had spilled some of the viscous white brew down his forearm where it had dried in clumps. This was not his first cup. His hair was wet and slicked back. He'd walked home through the rain. Now, his noise woke Maitonphi, not yet a day old. He fetched her from her crib and sat by the fire holding her, still singing. Gradually, with the noise apparently unlikely to abate, the rest of the family joined him at the fire. Liko awoke, groaning in annoyance, and tried to take Maitonphi back to bed.

'She needs her sleep.'

'No, she's my little Naga, my little Tangkhul. She stays with me.'

Her husband was not in a mood to be argued with right now, so she put a kettle on the fire: tea would help him—his morning hangover, at least. She stoked the fire and turned off the radio. Luke began to sing, in Tangkhul, a lullaby to his infant daughter, who had fallen asleep in his arms. It was a sad song, one sung by farmers to encourage the rains in times of drought.

My father was a cloud of the heavens,
My mother was a wind from the sea,
They are gone from me now, and the tears that I cry
Fill the earth that nourishes me.

Augustine and Alex came to sit next to the fire, draped in the blanket from their shared bed. Alex leaned drowsily on his sibling, but he didn't want to miss out.

Their father's singing came to a quiet close. 'Have I told you the story of Yarho?' He addressed the question to Augustine. The baby was asleep and Alex nearly so. Liko had her back to Luke, making no attempt to hide her displeasure at his intrusion.

'You told me, but tell me again,' Augustine answered.

'You're not too tired?'

'No.'

'Okay.'

'It happened down past Yao-yi,' Luke began, 'near our fields, but a little further downstream. There, by the same river that flows past our land, a Tangkhul family had their house and their paddy fields. They were good fields and the family was a good family. They had only one child, Yarho; the name means "only son". One day, the wife fell sick with fever. The husband looked after her as best he could, but she was too ill, and she died soon after. The husband was sad for a long time. He stopped going to work in the paddy fields, and he stopped eating. He didn't talk to anyone; he just lay in his bed, looking out at the mountains. Soon he died, too, of a broken heart.'

Augustine could hear, faintly, the rain outside, a little heavier now. He stared at his father. Luke's eyes appeared impossibly bright. They shone, a heady combination of the beer, the light of the fire, and his own enthrallment, even at a legend he'd told a dozen times before. Luke was never more alive than when he was telling a story, when he had the floor and an audience captive. And Augustine never loved his father more than when he was like this. Liko took back the baby, who was awake again now and mewling with hunger. Luke gave her up without a fight, his attention was elsewhere.

'Yarho was too young to live alone, so his father's younger brother, who had no land, came to his house to work in the paddy fields. His uncle was a good man and he worked hard. But the uncle's wife did not like Yarho. She wanted him to leave. When the uncle was home she was pleasant, but when she was alone in the house with Yarho, she was cruel to him. She would beat him and told him he was stupid. She made him pick up hot sticks from the fire, and laughed when he was burned.

'Upset, Yarho would leave the house and would run up and over the hill and down to the bank of the river, to the bend where the birds would gather on the branches of the mahogany trees. There he would sit and cry, for the longest time, but always, that place made him feel better. It was quiet, and he felt safe. Nearby, there were fruits in the trees and the water from the river was cool. He spent more and more time in that place.'

Absent Liko's ministrations, the fire had died down, leaving the room in almost total darkness. Despite her annoyance with her husband, Liko had come to sit next to him to listen. His charisma had won once again. She'd heard the story before, countless times, but Luke's tales were always evolving: he'd add a plot twist or a turn, a new character or a song. He'd blend old legends together, or weave ancient with new. Each iteration of Luke's stories offered fresh meaning, every telling revealed a new shade of his soul.

Luke had put down the bamboo mug. He spoke with his hands and his eyes as much as his voice. 'You know the place, Augustine. We have been there together.' Augustine nodded.

'Yarho would gather the feathers that fell from the bodies of the hornbill birds who rested on the trees. The feathers were very beautiful, long and white, with a brown stripe. Yarho would watch the birds. They would sit peacefully on the branches, but when there was a noise in the forest, they would instantly rise up together and fly away. Sometimes they would be gone only a few minutes, sometimes for days, but always they came back. And wherever they went, they were always together.

'Yarho wished he could be like the hornbills; he wished he could leave whenever he wanted, to fly all over the land, to be free. And he wished he belonged somewhere. He used to belong to his family, but his parents were dead, and his uncle worked in the fields all day. His aunt did not want him. Yarho felt he belonged with the hornbills, so he gathered up all the fallen feathers he could find, and he began to weave. He tied the feathers together with grass and used fallen branches as frames to make himself wings. When the hornbills saw what he was doing, he thought they would laugh. But they didn't. Instead, they sat above him and furiously beat their wings against their bodies, shaking free the feathers that were loose. The feathers fell down gently onto Yarho for him to use.'

Alex was awake now too. Augustine could see, as his little brother clung to his arm, that Alex didn't understand much of the story, but he knew about hornbills, and he gasped and giggled in the right places in imitation of his elder sibling: the thrill of the late-night communion with his brother and father enticing him.

'Yarho would go home each night where his aunt was cruel or kind, depending on if his uncle had come back from the fields. His wings, Yarho left hidden in the hollow of a tree near the river. In the morning when he returned, there'd be new feathers left for him by the birds. For weeks he worked every day, until he had woven two strong wings as long as his arms: broad, smooth arcs like a hunter's bow, just like the hornbills.

'Now, he put the wings on. Attached to his arms they felt light, but strong, and when he waved them, he felt the air move underneath. He could sense the power they held. Flapping his arms fiercely, and jumping as high as he could, trying to take off, he ran and leapt into the air, pushing down with his wings. Nothing. He tried again, but he tumbled to the ground, crashing hard onto the stones, and covering himself in dust. He fell again, and again, and again. The blood on his knees and his elbows mixed with the dust clotted darkly on his skin. He couldn't do it. He would never fly. He would never be free like the hornbills. Slumped on his knees, Yarho cried.

'Suddenly, beside him were two hornbills—tall, strong males, nearly as tall as Yarho. They lifted him up, and standing on either side of him, put a wing each underneath his body. Each flapping their single free wing, they leapt into the air and surged upwards, flying higher and higher on an updraft. Yarho was scared, he was high above the river now, over the hills and his home. He clung tightly to the bodies of the birds, fearing they would let him fall. But they told him not to be afraid; they told him to stretch out his arms and to feel the air against his wings. Slowly...slowly, the boy released his grip and stretched out his arms. He felt the warm current of air pushing up, up against his chest, filling his wings. In an instant, the two hornbills that were holding him were no longer there but were flying far below. He saw the crude sticks that held his homemade wings together tumble towards the ground. But Yarho didn't fall. The feathers were his now—he had grown wings of his own. He was flying.'

It was morning now, and the first wan rays of sunlight were breaking through the cracks in the wall and underneath the door. The fire was out. Alex had fallen back asleep and Liko had got up to fetch more wood for the fire and had begun making breakfast. Augustine was exhausted. He was struggling to keep his eyes open, but the story hadn't finished.

'What happened after that?'

The magic of the nighttime was gone. Luke was prosaic, standing and stretching as he answered. 'The boy soon learned to fly well with his new wings, and from that day, he lived with the hornbills. But he would return often to his village where he would sit with the elders, and they would ask his advice. Hornbills are wise birds because they fly so high they can see everything all at once. Yarho became a magistrate for his village. He could change form—from boy to bird and back—but he lived with the hornbills, he was one of them now...'

◇◇◇

'Augustine, it's time to go.' Augustine had fallen asleep by the fire, curled up next to his brother who clung to him for warmth. Their blanket from bed had been laid across them. His father had gone. 'You have school,' his mother bristled. 'Now eat up.'

Augustine rubbed his eyes. His mother handed him a plate from which he absent-mindedly began to scoop rice into his mouth, still half asleep. From where he sat, he could see his father's form lying in bed. One arm hung listlessly from underneath the red shawl that rose and fell with his steady breathing. The energy and the magic of the nighttime were gone.

Augustine yawned as he walked to school. His father liked a good time, 'too much', he sometimes heard Liko whisper, not always under her breath. But her opposition was never any stronger than this, a muted undercurrent of discontent. Augustine liked his father's good times too. He could see, better than his mother could, that the firelight and the friends, the beer and the bonhomie, were Luke's nirvana. And the stories. Telling stories. That was when his father was closest to his true self.

Augustine walked to school imagining Yarho, the boy who became a hornbill. 'The stories of our people are real,' Luke would always insist at some point, but his father's fantastical stories felt hollow, almost comical, under the scrutiny of the light of day. But Augustine would cast his gnawing doubts aside: he believed, willing his father's stories to be true.

◈ ◈ ◈

'I need to rest,' Akala says suddenly. They have reached the northern end of the plateau where Shirui Peak begins to rise, and have cut right following a path that leads beside the mountain through a pass that will take them into the valley beyond. They can stop now. On Phangrei plateau they were exposed; any pursuer could easily see them. But they are sheltered here. They've been gone now nearly two hours. Long enough.

Their villages would be searching for them by now.

'We'll stop down there,' Augustine says, pointing to a clearing below.

Instinctively, Augustine wants to keep moving but he knows, too, that without rest they will barely make it out of the next valley, worn down by the terrain and the heat. He sits on a rock and, with his hand shielding his eyes from the sun, he looks across at her. Akala sits with her back against a tree facing him, her face in the shade, her legs still in the sun. She is 24—half a decade younger than him—but she looks even younger. She could still pass for a teenager. And the fear in her eyes is that of a child.

The first time Augustine saw Akala was at the river. Not at the spot from where they'd just come, but further upstream, towards Augustine's village. There, the river is broader and moves more slowly, and there is sand on the banks. Akala had come down to wash clothes. She walked down to the river, to the bank opposite the Ukhrul side, almost directly across from where Alex and Augustine, and a few of their cousins, stood. The brothers were at the river to collect water for their households, to fill the bulbous pots of the kind that stood at kitchen doors of all Naga houses. But they'd stayed down at the bank to swim in the shallows. Akala crouched at the water's edge. The clothes she carried in a narrow wicker basket were hanging on her back, held by a woven strap that ran across her forehead. Full, the *sop*[2] was heavy and it pulled her chin up- wards in a pose that looked, from a distance, like pride. She didn't look across.

And no one looked at her. Except for Augustine. He had noticed her as she walked down the hill, and had stopped swimming with the others. Why did he watch her? Was he captivated? Curious? Augustine's brother and their friends carried on without him. None of the boys could swim very well, but when it was hot they liked the shallows: the game they played was to push each other deeper and deeper into the river, closer to the channel they knew ran through the middle, where the water was darker, and flowed dangerously fast. There was no one else on Akala's side of the river.

Akala emptied the *sop*, and filling two buckets left on the riverbank with water, patiently soaked the clothes. Augustine watched her: her quick, precise movements, her head so still. Even as she concentrated intently on the changeless work in front of her, she seemed to him, dis- engaged from it. She seemed to float above it as if it wasn't really her, or that this was nothing more than a tired ritual, faded of any meaning, but one she felt obliged to uphold. She wasn't really there.

---

2   *Sop:* the Naga word for a wicker basket as described here.

Was she beautiful? Augustine caught himself thinking. She was slight, almost childlike, and couldn't be said to be classically beautiful. Most Naga women wore their hair long, but hers was cut short above her ears, her fringe swept upwards, further accentuating her sharp, high cheekbones. Crouched, her eyes were hidden from Augustine. She kept them on her work. He wondered what colour they were.

On the smooth-worn rocks at the river's edge, Akala scrubbed the clothes piece by piece. This river was drinking water downstream, and it irrigated the paddy fields, so she was careful to keep the soap from the current. She threw the used water up above the bank on a bare patch of earth above the highest waterline. Augustine didn't know her name, or to which family she belonged. But he knew from where she had come: she was from Tiya.

Walking from the shallows of the water to the bank, Augustine called over his shoulder to his brother that he'd had enough swimming for today. He knew he couldn't stay, standing, watching her. To have been caught staring would have been a grave offence. He stayed on the bank, deliberately not looking in her direction, but he was drawn to her, even when he wasn't looking at her. From the corner of his eye he could see where she was, he knew what she was doing. For all her work's mundanity and her apparent disinterest, Akala brought a rhythm to her every motion, a grace that held Augustine's attention. He crouched on a stone at the river's edge. Now he was captivated.

After rinsing the clothes twice, Akala expertly twisted each piece before beating it against a flat rock near the water's edge. Each item, close to dry now, was then folded and put back in the *sop*. She still hadn't looked up.

Augustine was shocked from his reverie by a push in his back that sent him sprawling into the water. He lifted his head out, hands still in the mud of the river bottom, to the sound of Alex and his cousins laughing at him. Augustine's absence had been noted. 'I don't want to play your stupid game,' he told them, but laughing as he dragged himself up.

'You have to, the game is always on,' his brother said.

Augustine turned to see Akala. But she had gone.

THE SONGS A FATHER SUNG

In the summertime, Augustine turned six and Luke chose the milestone to begin drawing his son further into his own world, into his existence beyond his home and family. Luke took Augustine to his paddy-field shack where he had, unbeknownst to the rest of the family, begun to brew his own *zu*. The crude rice beer was fermenting in green plastic rubbish bins, their lids kept shut with heavy rocks. As well, he was making *kui-kok*—'bald head'—the fierce spirit so named for the smooth round pot with ear-like handles it was typically kept in. 'The *zu*...sometimes you can have a small-small taste. But this one,' Luke said to Augustine, picking up the gourd of *kui-kok* and taking a swig, 'this one is not for children'.

Manipur was a dry state, so his father's homebrews were, technically, illegal. But here, it was a prohibition rarely enforced. Augustine was old enough to understand the mechanics. Money rarely changed hands; bootlegging was less an industry than a way of life and taking it away would have caused more problems for the police than it could ever solve. Anyway, Augustine wasn't worried about the police, but rather, his mother finding out. His mother or the church. The church railed almost every week against the evils of 'strong drink', and the lost souls it claimed. Augustine was quietly thrilled to be drawn into his father's confidence but frightened of his complicity if it were uncovered. He felt compromised, and feared accidentally giving his father up; he didn't want to betray him. But Luke wasn't scared. Nothing, Augustine knew, scared Luke.

Down in the paddy fields, father and son would sit and speak as men. Just the two of them. Luke would talk. Augustine would listen. Sitting down in the evenings, by the fire if it was cold and dark outside, on the back stoop of the single-room shack that stood in the middle of their fields if there was light still, Luke would remind Augustine that he, like Augustine, was the eldest of his brothers. The eldest son of an eldest son of an eldest son, he said. And to him had fallen the family responsibility. 'And so to you, too. You are my eldest son, and there are things you must know, and you must do.'

In Tangkhul culture, his father explained, the eldest boy inherits the family's land from his father. He is charged with keeping it together, with working it and making it profitable, but most of all, with preserving it for the next generation. 'Our people have a saying: "Treat the earth well. You are its steward, not its master".'

'As the eldest son,' Luke said, 'you are in charge of upholding the old ways, the *Hao*, the way the Naga used to live before Christianity and English came to this place and changed everything'. His eyes narrowed. 'Every day we lose a little bit more of ourselves, of the life my father knew, there is less and less to leave to you.'

In the Naga tradition, the eldest boy is in charge of the stories, his father said. He is responsible for knowing and preserving them, with keeping them alive and with adding to the canon. The eldest needs to know the songs, too, and when they should be sung. The Tangkhul had songs for *Manei Phanit*, the blessing of the weapons of the hunt and the tools of the field, and they sang ballads of protection when the warm air at the end of winter brought with it the risk of epidemics. There were songs that had to be, but could only be, sung at funerals, and joyous songs for weddings and to celebrate new children.

There were festivals to know, too, that marked the passage of the seasons: the *Luira* forecasting the sewing of the seeds, and the *Chumpa* giving thanks for the bounty of the harvest. Luke was enthused by his curriculum. 'I will teach you, too, the stories of the

Goddess of Shirui Peak who lives on the mountain and watches over her chosen people to keep us safe, but who exacts a tribute from her villages as well. All of this you must learn; you are old enough to know now.'

Luke taught Augustine about *Kazeiram*, the afterlife that the Naga believed in before the imposition of Christianity's dichotomous heaven-and-hell. *Kazeiram* wasn't good or bad like those places, Luke said, and unlike those places it belonged to the earth. You could, if you really had to, reach *Kazeiram* while you were still alive, but only if it was truly necessary. Then, you were guided by your instinct to walk into the forest where you would find *Kazeiram*. You couldn't stay, but there, all of the souls of the dead would walk past, so you just had to wait for the person you needed to see. You could speak to them, Luke said, 'but you cannot bring them back'.

'Is Kazeiram real?' Augustine asked his father.

'Of course, it's real.'

'Have you been there?'

'I have not.'

'Do you know anybody who has?'

'No. Not from this village. Not from any village I have visited.'

'What about heaven, like they talk about in church? And hell? Don't we go there when we die?'

'You believe in these places, but no one you know has ever been there,' Luke said emphatically. '*Kazeiram* is more real than those places.' His tone did not brook argument.

And because Luke believed, his son did too.

But Luke's education of his eldest son was typically shambolic. Perhaps twice a week, he would come home late at night and wake Augustine, taking him to sit by the fire, as the rest of the family slept. Not willing to risk the pique of Liko, he would recount legends in a bare whisper.

'Dad, when did these stories happen?' Augustine asked one night.

'Some of them happened a long time ago, in the time before your grandfather's grandfather. Some of them I remember happening when I was a small boy. But some of them are stories that haven't happened yet. They are stories for the future. They will happen one day.' Augustine couldn't understand how his father knew of events that hadn't yet occurred, but he enjoyed his secret, late-night conclaves with his father too much to question it further. The next day, he would yawn through school, earning him the wrath and the strap of his teachers. But he endured their punishments gladly: Maths and English lessons were dull compared to the magical tales of his father.

Always now, with his father's lessons, there was drink. It hadn't always been so, or perhaps it had simply been better hidden before, but Luke was cavalier these days. Almost invariably he would arrive home carrying a gourd of beer, and occasionally, when he was sure Liko was asleep, would give his son a small sip. The *zu* was sweet and faintly fizzy, stronger than its pale colour suggested, much stronger than the lemonade Augustine occasionally requisitioned from the shop, again, when he was sure his mother couldn't know.

Too much *zu*, Augustine found one night, gave him a headache and made him sleepy. But the rice beer invigorated his father. He seemed fuelled by it, almost dependent. When he drank, Luke was inspired to a bombastic nationalism, a belief in the inherent greatness and destiny of the Naga people. His lessons, then, became an amalgam of legend and politics. 'The Naga believe in "a chosen one"—that someone will come one day to lead our people to freedom. The chosen one will unite us and give us back our soul.'

Luke would quote the speeches he had learned from his own father, addresses to the Naga people by Phizo, the Naga's quixotic independence leader from the 1950s: 'We shall not go down in history in shame or live in sorrow or disgrace as victims of Indian imperialism'.

He would delve further back into history. He would recount the life of Haipou Jadonang, the 'Messiah King' of the Naga, who believed in Makam Gwangdi, an independent Naga Kingdom, and who was hanged by the British because he was a threat. 'Our day will come,' his father said, quoting himself now. Late into the nights, keeping careful still to be quiet, Luke would stand to re-enact the heroics of the Naga warriors in battle against other tribes, and hunting the tigers that once prowled these forests. The fire cast grotesque and terrifying shadows against the walls of the house. Illuminated, Luke's eyes shone.

One night, however, Luke's eyes were dull. Augustine lay in bed as his father told him a story, but the words were slurred, and he kept confusing the characters. The fraying thread of the plot seemed always just beyond him, and Luke reached clumsily for it, his mind and tongue grasping. Yet it was always just too far, lost among tortured spasms of heaving breath. Eventually his father gave up trying to talk at all, and just stared, silent and dazed; for hours, just sitting - awake but unseeing.

In the darkness, Augustine gazed back at his father. Something was different tonight; something was changed in him, and altered between them. In the quiet, Augustine lay in his bed watching his father and waiting for him to come back from wherever he'd gone. Luke did not move. Augustine fought sleep, but the blackness of the night poured over him, and tiredness overwhelmed his fear. In the morning when he woke, his father was gone.

◈◈◈

Augustine and Akala have left Phangrei plateau and are walking through the quiet of the daytime forest. There are few birds or animals around now, so no one hunts. For as far as Augustine can see or hear, they are alone. They walk low in the valley, following the small streams, tributaries to the Langdangkong River: their river, the river they've left behind. This water will ultimately flow past his village, and past hers, past the spot where they first met. Augustine wishes these waters could take them back to then.

They are walking north, but indirectly, following the contours of the river along the valley floor. Staying low means they have to walk further, and the forest is dense here, but it keeps them safe. The Naga build their villages on top of hills, a legacy of the days when clans were almost constantly at war. Defending a home from *dao*-wielding headhunters was easier from above than below, and the Naga believe it to this day: the low part of the forest is good for hunting, and the floodplains of the rivers are fertile land for crops, but they are not safe places to stay.

Augustine and Akala are tiring. The sun is high above their heads, and even in the shade there is little respite from its muggy oppression. The forest sweats around them and shimmers in the heat. Augustine feels suddenly drained: the adrenaline of that first impulsive decision to flee has faded now to the dull dread of its consequence. They can never go back. They both know this, though neither has said it. They don't have the words for it, but that doesn't make it any less real. No village will accept them now. No place in the land of the Naga will bear their disgrace. They walk on, each step committing them to the next. Each step taking them further from their families, but closer to each other. They come across another stream. They are a little higher up now, this one is narrower, but fuller than the last. The water rushes in swift contortions over the rocks. 'We should rest here,' Augustine says.

Akala slumps against a tree, her familiar pose, legs stretched out in front of her, and looks down, not speaking. Augustine walks to the smooth stones by the edge of the stream, and crouches to drink deeply from the fast-running water. Cupping his hands, he carries water back to her. 'Akala, lift your head,'. She raises her chin and, wordlessly, begins to drink. She leans back, short of breath from the effort. There is still far to walk.

'Don't worry, we can wait here,' he says. 'It will...'

He was going to say 'it will all be okay', but he stopped himself. He doesn't know what it will be, but is sure Akala can tell what he was going to say. She doesn't press him for a promise she knows he can't keep. They wait in the still and the cool of the shade. The sweat grows cold against Augustine's back. Akala has her eyes closed, not asleep, but daydreaming. Perhaps in her mind, she isn't in this forest anymore.

'Come on,' he says, gently shaking her, 'a little further before we rest for the night'. She opens her eyes, and suddenly sobs, burying her face in her hands, howling like an animal in pain. 'What have I done?' she wails, her chest heaving.

Crouching beside her, Augustine holds her, saying nothing for a full minute. 'It will be okay,' he whispers finally. He allows himself the lie now. What harm can it possibly do?

'I'm all right,' Akala says, wiping the tears from her eyes. 'We'll be okay.' For her too, perhaps, the comfort of deception is respite from the enormity of the reality. At least for now. 'We should go.'

NAGALAND

He waits a little longer, then stands and offers his hand. She refuses it. She still feels the need to prove she is capable, and perhaps more than that, committed. They walk on, Augustine leading. In his right hand, he carries his *dao*, but he barely needs it here, a hunters' track runs beside the river. Augustine starts singing, a song his father sung. It's a slow, sad song. A song of mourning.

> *This morning I trekked with my beloved*
> *To cross the flooded Kenro.*
> *The water too swift, too high, too strong,*
> *My lover, my hand, she let go.*

Behind him, Akala joins in. She knows the song too. Her voice is breathy with exertion, but it is haunting and beautiful.

> *Those moments I wait for my love to emerge*
> *Through the dark of the eddies and swirls.*
> *Those moments they last now forever for me,*
> *Forever I search for my girl.*

INDIAN HISTORY

Fridays were the longest days at school. The weekend beckoned, and the students chafed against their final few hours of confinement. Augustine was in third class now, for six and seven-year-olds, and every Friday afternoon they studied Indian History. It was always called that—Indian History—a far-off place as well as a far-off time.

Augustine knew he was Indian, he just didn't feel it. It was a common Naga problem. To begin each history class, he and his classmates were made to sing the Indian national anthem, mumbling over the unfamiliar Bengali words, meaningless to most. They had to copy long passages from the blackboard about the Indian heroes of independence, the country's glorious history and its struggle for freedom. But the 'Indian' heroes Augustine learned about at school, the 'Father of the Nation' Mahatma Gandhi, the first Prime Minister Jawaharlal Nehru, the 'untouchable' Dr Ambedkar, didn't look like him, or anyone he knew. They had strange names, and everything they said was written in Hindi, a language he was passably familiar with to speak, but that he barely understood when it was written down. These foreign old men were his people, he was told. Their country was his, and his, theirs.

The teachers at school, too, impressed upon their charges India's bright and brave new future. Indians would go into space, they said.

Their nation would soon be a superpower, whatever that was. India would rival America. Augustine didn't know much about either place. To him, they felt as foreign as each other. And he didn't much care. His place was Ukhrul village and the rivers and fields and trees of his people's land. Beyond was all somewhere else. Augustine's world was these hills, and Friday afternoon lessons kept him from it.

Friday afternoons also felt longest because Friday evenings were when Augustine's father taught him to shoot. Augustine was stronger now, still lean, but he had grown several inches over the summer, leaping from being one of the smallest in his class to the second-tallest.

'It's time the boy learned the skills of his people,' Luke had announced solemnly one evening, to Liko's weary acquiescence. She saved her resistance for battles she might win, and Luke's determination, combined with her son's enthusiasm, were signal enough that this was not one of those. Luke had procured—he never said from where—a .22 air rifle for Augustine's practice. It was old and underpowered, but the weapon had been cared for, the action was smooth, and the sights were straight. Friday afternoons after school, Luke would walk with Augustine—Augustine proudly carrying the weapon bent over his arm—down to the family's paddy fields. There, Luke had set up a crude target hanging by the wall of the wooden shack. The target was a discarded plough blade he'd painted with black concentric circles.

Luke had taught Augustine to stand to shoot, straight-backed with his legs apart, knees slightly bent. The butt of the rifle, Luke pressed hard into Augustine's shoulder. Although Augustine found it uncomfortable, he didn't protest, and brought his finger to rest on the trigger.

'Squeeze, don't pull,' Luke would say, 'squeeze, don't pull'. He repeated the words softly and rhythmically, his incantation as Augustine would line up his shot.

The gun was heavy for Augustine to lift at first, and unwieldy. He could barely keep it on the target for more than a second. But he soon learned how to smoothly draw the barrel to the height needed and squeeze—never pull—just as his lungs emptied of air. The pellets made a satisfying 'ting' on the plough blade when they struck. Five shots, and then he would go searching in the dust for the shot pellets so that he could fire them again.

'You're a natural,' Luke would say proudly grinning, as he swigged another mouthful of *zu*. Augustine beamed.

One Friday afternoon, having spent Miss Angela's interminable dissertation on India's magnificent Nehru-Gandhi dynasty gazing out the window, Augustine raced up the hill to home.

His father was waiting.

'No practice tonight,' he said. 'Tonight, you come hunting for real.'

Luke always hunted with his younger brother. Simeon lived further down the valley, in a small house close to the family's paddy fields at Yao-yi. It was near, too, to the river and to the forest where they hunted. These hunting trips didn't start until the sun had almost completely disappeared, and ran deep into the night.

Late in the afternoon, Luke retrieved his shotgun from its resting place under the eave of the back wall and began his careful preparations: checking its barrel and sights, patiently oiling its bolt. He prepared an immodest stash of ammunition, taking more bullets than he needed. The cartridges sold in town were not powerful enough, he said, so, having shot them, he would find the spent casings and repack them with more gunpowder and larger pellets. 'More bang for your buck,' he would say grinning, as he filled his pockets. The red casings could be used over and over again.

Luke wore dark pants and a camouflaged overcoat. The ammunition went in one pocket, and in another was a wedge of dried goat meat, heavily salted. That was dinner, unless and until they shot some more. He carried no water. The stream ran close by where they were going, and besides, it was cool in the forest and they wouldn't be thirsty. As the sun fell, he rose and nodded to Augustine, 'let's go,' and to Liko: 'we'll be home tonight. Not too late.'

The sunlight left the valley early, so by the time they reached Simeon's house it was already dark and growing cold. Augustine was glad his father had insisted he wear his shoes. Luke flashed his torch at his brother's window, his silent signal to come out. Simeon's young children were asleep. The path to the forest ran from Simeon's house west, further down into the valley. For the early part of the walk they talked freely. There were no animals here, no birds to scare off.

Placing a gentle hand on his shoulder, Simeon asked Augustine how he was enjoying school. Augustine scrambled to recall something of what he'd heard that afternoon… 'We are learning about India's heroes,' he replied, buying some time. Reaching for the first name he could remember: 'we learned about Jawaharlal Nehru, how he was very clever, and how he went to a famous school in England called "Cane-bridge" and how he became the first Prime Minister of India'.

'Liar!' Luke spat suddenly, scaring Augustine. 'Nehru was a traitor. He betrayed our people. When the Naga declared themselves to be an independent nation one day before India became a country, Nehru refused to accept it. Instead, he sent soldiers in. He started a war with people he said were his own countrymen because we didn't want to live under the Indians' oppression. He wanted India to be the Naga's new colonial ruler, but the Naga said "no".' Luke stopped on the forest trail and turned to face his brother and his son. Augustine recoiled at his father's sudden rage. 'Nehru refused to let the Naga people be free. Free like we'd been before. Do you know what he said? He said: "Whether heaven falls or India goes to pieces and blood runs red in the country, I do not care: Nagas will not be allowed to become independent".'

Luke spun on his heels and walked on, followed tentatively by Simeon. Augustine stood in the darkness, unsure if he wanted to follow. His father's anger confused him. What his father had said was not what the teachers had taught him. Why would he—or they—tell him something that was untrue? Augustine stood on the forest trail, lost in thought. Suddenly, he realised he did not know his way back in the darkness. The noise of the two men walking ahead was faint already. Forced to abandon his doubts, Augustine ran deeper into the forest, following the fading sound.

The two men were still talking when Augustine breathlessly caught up with them.

'The Naga should have stayed and fought,' Luke said. 'They were strong warriors; the last headhunters in all of India.'

'We knew a headhunter when we were boys,' Simeon chipped in, too cheerfully. He was addressing Augustine now, and Augustine understood why. Even at six, he understood that his father's nation-alist obsession was not shared by his younger brother. Simeon was trying to take the edge from Luke's fury, for his own sake and for Augustine's.

'He was an old man when I met him, this headhunter,' Simeon continued. 'Do you remember him, Luke?' His father only grunted in reply.

Simeon turned to face his nephew. 'He lived at the top of Ukhrul, and his whole face was tattooed. The headhunters all had tattoos marking the battles they had fought and won. This man would tell us all about the battles he had fought against Tiya, fights over land, over the plateau at Phangrei.'

Augustine was vaguely aware of headhunting—the blood-thirsty part of Naga history—but not especially interested by it. At the Tangkhul village chief's house, across the road and two doors up from his own home, he had seen the skulls claimed from the vanquished warriors of neighbouring villages, neatly arranged in a glass cabinet in the front room. The skulls were a mottled brown, with huge, gaping eye-holes, most without jawbones. They seemed too small for a man's head, Augustine had thought. His teachers never talked about that history either.

'The headhunters,' Luke agreed, the bitterness faded from voice, 'those men lived free. Like the Konyak do still.' Augustine had heard his father speak of the Konyak before, with an almost spiritual reverence. The Konyak were a warlike Naga tribe, who lived right on the limits of the country, in the dark hills that bordered Burma. They'd not yet been brought to heel by soldiers or religion or the law.

Now father and son walked side by side. Simeon followed behind, chewing betel nut and hawking the bright red spittle that stained his gums. The forest was quieter now. The river flowed easily to their right, silent save for the occasional broken gurgle in an eddy. It was dark. 'Nehru,' Luke said, shaking his head. 'For one short day, all of the Naga were free.'

Simeon shook his head. 'Brother,' he said, gently testing Luke, 'this politics, you should not worry. Free, not free, independent, not independent. There is not one person who will save a whole people. You can only worry about your own people, your own family. Honour your family, and the Naga will be okay.'

'One day,' Luke replied softly, 'a chosen one will come'.

Augustine could more easily understand Simeon's point of view than his father's. He was too young to care greatly about the words and acts of long-dead politicians. They were figments of fiction, neat besuited men in black-and-white photographs, names he had to learn for school. They didn't really matter. They were from another time, another world. How could what they said, so long ago, matter today? Augustine couldn't comprehend his father's roiling anger over freedom. His father was free, was he not? Nobody made him go to school, or wear a uniform. He was free to hunt, to farm, to drink *zu*. What more freedom could he want?

Where was the oppression his father railed against? The police rarely came to Ukhrul, Augustine knew. There was a half-built jail on a low ridge below the northern edge of town, but the government's money ran out halfway through construction, so it was just four concrete walls without a ceiling or a fence, no prison at all. If there was a problem, the police would come, but they didn't want to have to take prisoners all the way to Imphal, and they didn't like the paperwork, so they would just let the families, or the village headman, sort it out. It was imperfect, but it worked well enough.

Augustine saw the Assam Riflemen often enough, and he could sense the Naga people's hostility towards the *jawans* who patrolled the marketplace, but he never understood it. The soldiers never spoke; but they stood, silent and impassive, lazily fingering the black assault rifles that hung on their chests from straps around their shoulders. They wore camouflage fatigues, bullet-proof vests and strange domed helmets that were too hot for the summer sun, but not warm enough for winter. Augustine felt sorry for them. They were Indians, they didn't belong with the Naga.

The forest grew denser and darker. Luke walked ahead of Augustine, Simeon following. They stone-hopped across the narrow creek and headed up a shallow north-facing ridge. This ridge, if they followed it, would take them up to Phangrei plateau, and beyond that to Shirui Peak, commanding views for hundreds of kilometres around. Luke had long promised he would take Augustine to the summit of Shirui, to visit the Goddess who lived there, but he would have to wait until he was older. It was a full day's march for a man to reach the peak and descend, too much for a small boy.

'That's why the NSCN began, because India took away our freedom,' Luke said, filling the quiet that had settled on the three. He couldn't let it rest. 'The insurgency was noble to begin with, they were fighting for Naga freedom. And the Indian army were savage. They came in, with better weapons and more troops, and they killed all the best fighters on the front line. That was okay, because it was a war, but then they raped the women and burned the villages. "Scorched earth" they called it. They torched houses and destroyed paddy fields wherever they went. They wanted us to be Indian, but they tried to chase us out of India.'

Much of what his father was telling him, Augustine was too young to properly understand. But he knew better than to interrupt. He concentrated on the climb, standing in his father's huge footprints, taking two steps to Luke's every one.

'The people supported the NSCN to begin with. They would allow the fighters to stay in their homes, they would hide them and feed them, and give them information about the Indian army troops. But the insurgents grew corrupt. They began fighting among themselves, they forgot about the people and became only interested in their own power. They ate pork every night, given to them by the people who had nothing but rice and salt. The insurgents grew lazy and fat, while the people worked hard and went hungry.

'Sixty years and 200,000 people killed, but still we have no freedom. I want what the fighters want, but all they have brought us is misery.'

The trio cut left now off the ridge and scrabbled their way down into a scrubby grove populated with small alder trees. It was dark, but Augustine could sense it was long and narrow, with steep walls on either side. There was only one way in and out of this grove at each end. It was a good place for an animal to seek shelter and food, and a good place for a man to hunt. 'Here,' Luke said. He stopped and sat cross-legged, on the ground, his gun on his lap. 'We hunt here tonight.' His father took the hunk of mutton from his bag and tore a chunk from it with his teeth, then passed it over. Simeon did the same. Augustine found the meat tough and too salty, but he didn't say anything. The three ate in silence.

Most hunters in Ukhrul went looking for birds, the prey-seeking kites that circled low over these forests at dawn and dusk. But Luke came in the night, looking for boar. The wild boar that roamed these forests were low-slung, well-muscled creatures, black, with small hard tusks. Their meat was good if you cooked it the right way. But the boars were hard to catch, because they were clever and were easily frightened.

Augustine sat and watched his father and uncle prepare, his eyes slowly adjusting to the darkness of the forest around him. He knew these hills. In the daytime they held no fear. But at night, the shapes of the forest took on a sinister complexion. The familiar boughs of the trees moved in the unseen winds, and wreathed in dark contortions in the shadows. Beyond the quiet circle where he sat with his father and his uncle, it felt to Augustine as if the whole forest were alive with extraordinary sounds. He felt ringed by unknown and hostile life, just outside his sight and his understanding. He stayed close to his father.

Luke and Simeon always hunted together, but apart. Tonight, they set up their positions, separated by about thirty metres but facing the same small clearing into which the forest footpads emptied. Simeon lay on the ground, staring down the sight of his rifle, the smooth, polished butt jammed hard against his right shoulder. In his left hand he held a torch, switched off, pressed against the barrel, his thumb on the switch. Luke employed the same set-up, but with his body lying across a fallen log, the torch and the shotgun in concert, held together and pointed at their target. Augustine sat by his father.

In a bare whisper, Luke explained to Augustine that when an animal came into view, the hunter flicks on the torch to stun it into stillness. Almost in the same motion he must squeeze the trigger. It didn't matter who made the kill. Everything Luke and Simeon shot, they shared. It was an unspoken rule they'd silently agreed upon as boys, and observed ever since.

'Quiet now,' Luke said. Augustine hadn't spoken in over an hour. 'No moving.' Augustine sat perfectly still, watching his father, watching the blackness. His father breathed slowly, almost imperceptibly. He never took his eyes from the sights.

It was quiet in this part of the forest: quiet and still. Augustine watched his father. His father watched the blackness at the end of the barrel. Augustine's fears were being slowly overwhelmed by weariness; he had walked a long way, and it was late. How late? he wondered. When would they be going back? Lying down on the cool of the forest floor, keeping his eyes on his father, Augustine wasn't scared anymore; he was a hunter now…the soft earth was comfortable.

BANG!

Augustine woke in a blind panic.

BANG!

Unfamiliar, dark shapes loomed over him malevolently, the trees in foreign silhouette seemed to be reaching down to grab him. That noise. A light…a light moving…the ringing in his ears. Augustine exhaled suddenly in realisation: it was his father's torch. The light was his father's torch, the sound was his rifle. He was okay, he was safe. Augustine fought back tears. Hunters didn't weep. The jolting, restless arc of yellow light was dancing a few metres beyond him. It was soon joined by a second. Simeon.

'Dad?' Augustine asked.

'Augustine,' came the reply from the darkness.

'Did you hit it?'

'No,' Luke said. 'He got away.'

Luke had seen the boar first, but it was Simeon who opened fire. Luke's shot missed as well, and the boar made good his escape into the undergrowth and the dark belly of the valley. Luke began gathering his kit and unloading the remaining cartridge in his rifle. 'Will you stay out hunting longer?' Augustine asked, sitting now, his eyes again adjusting to the darkness.

'No animals will come here for a long time,' Luke replied. 'The noise of the guns will have frightened them away. We are finished for tonight.'

'How long was I asleep?'

'A short time, maybe an hour, maybe a little more.'

'I'm sorry I fell asleep.'

'Don't be. It was good you could come,' Luke put his hand on his son's shoulder as they walked from the gully. Simeon joined them.

'I had a clear shot.'

'Next time, little brother, next time.'

◈◈◈

Augustine and Akala walk steadily, rhythmically now, almost marching, but their progress is determined as much by the forest as their own efforts. They are heading broadly north. It is too far to see from here, but Augustine knows there is a ridgeline ahead they must cross. He hopes to reach it by tomorrow evening. It will be steep there, but not too steep, and there will be paths, usually trodden only by smugglers and soldiers, that can take them across. Those paths will take them down into the next valley, into the valley of the Laplongtang River, below the village of Mimi that his father had told him about. At the end of that narrow river basin stands Sukhayap, the giant cliff and, over the ridge beyond, Burma.

Maybe they can reach Burma? Briefly, Augustine allows himself the indulgence of the fantasy. Maybe they can get over the border and live safely there. They could get to Hkamti, the traders' meeting-point, or a village even further beyond. No one would know them there: who they were or from where they had come. They could make a new life.

Augustine knows it is an impossibility. The Naga villages in Burma, he had learned from his mother many years ago, are just like those on the Indian side of the border: close-knit and familial. Everyone knows every-one, and everyone comes from somewhere. You cannot simply appear without a claim to kinship and expect to be welcomed. The bonds of Naga are tight, so tight it feels that sometimes they choke the chance to breathe free. But they are a safety net too, Augustine can see that now. Cut from those bonds, you flail like a sapling in a storm, severed forever and left to fall. You have nothing and no one. Augustine and Akala walk on. Maybe they can get to Burma. The daydream is persistent.

Years of hunting have given Augustine a keen ear for the sounds of the forest. He has heard nothing, seen no evidence of a pursuing pack. But he knows they will be coming. There is honour to uphold here. Both villages will feel their child's disgrace intensely. The elders had been disobeyed. Akala and Augustine cannot be permitted to defy their families and communities. Augustine wonders whether it will be only the men of his village, or only the men of hers, who will come for them. Maybe, for this circumstance, they will work together for once. Perhaps this union is so contemptible to both that the two villages might agree to co-operate, to momentarily abandon their unreasoned prejudice, so that it can be preserved for the future.

They walk on. It doesn't matter who is pursuing them, it matters that they are. They will be coming; Augustine and Akala have to keep moving. However slow their progress, they cannot stop. To stop is to give up, to abandon all hope of being together, to die. Only the men of the villages will give chase. They will be the bravest hunters and the best trackers; they will be strong, and they will cover the ground quickly. The fugitives just need to keep far enough ahead of them. If they can do that, then maybe they can reach Burma. Burma. Again, the daydream intrudes. Augustine knows that's not where they are going, that's not how this is going to end.

His uncle Simeon is sure to be among the chasing pack. It will be Simeon. He is the one who will put himself forward to defend the family honour, to 'do the right thing'. Simeon will be hunting them right now. And he will know where they are going.

THE NUMBER 4

Augustine couldn't sleep. Alex, insensible next to him in bed, was breathing steadily. It wasn't cold, but Augustine could hear the fire in the main room next door. Not the low crackle of a fire dying on its embers, but the steady rumble of one ablaze. He could hear voices too. He walked to the door which had been left fractionally ajar, and peered through. He could see his mother, putting a pot on the fire to make tea. And he could see her brother, Augustine's uncle Mun, sitting across from her, his round face illuminated by the fire-light. He looked sad.

Mun was his mother's closest sibling. He was a junior minister at the lower Ukhrul Baptist Church, and widely held up by the extended family as the relative Augustine should most seek to emulate. It felt an impossible threshold—Mun was too perfect—but Augustine liked him all the same. Mun called Augustine 'my man' and spoke to him as a friend, not a child. Mun's presence was, ordinarily, unexceptional. He visited often enough to see his sister, but he had been over three times in the last week, each time with the same solemn face that Augustine saw now.

'I'm sorry, Liko,' Mun said. Augustine crouched down, silently, against the doorjamb where he could see and hear the conversation inside, sure that he would not be noticed. 'You're certain?' Liko asked. She seemed reluctant to ask the question, as if it carried an answer she already knew, but didn't want to hear.

'I saw him buying foils from a dealer in town,' Mun replied. 'Needles too, and I talked to some people I know. I think he's been using for months now.'

Seven-year-olds grow up quickly in Ukhrul. Augustine recognised the jargon, the English words dropped into Tangkhul conversation. He knew precisely what they were talking about. Everyone in Ukhrul knew about heroin. Heroin was a huge and sinister problem for the Naga, 'an epidemic' headmen would call it, talking in low voices, at village meetings, 'a scourge' the teachers used to say in their semi-regular 'just-say-no' diatribes. In Ukhrul it was known as Number 4. Augustine had even seen it, wrapped in thin twists of foil, the cheap dirty-brown clumps of heroin that came over the border from Burma.

'My husband,' Liko said in the darkness, 'my husband, the junkie'. The final word she said, not angrily, but with a sense of wearied expectation. Of resignation. Maybe deep down, she had already known, Augustine thought.

Augustine knew that word, too: junkie. In Tangkhul, they were *nisha sikachin mi*, but the English term was more common. He had seen them before, hovering over a strip of foil in an alley, or passed out glassy-eyed with a needle sticking out of their arm in the corner of a field. Junkies were always pitiably thin, and they hunched over so they looked smaller still. Their faces and fingers were scabby, and their eyes watered. They wore billowing old shirts unbuttoned, loose trousers with thin belts, and sandals.

To Augustine, the addicts all seemed the same. They were young men, some only teenagers who were the older brothers of friends at school. He knew those junkies by name, though he always felt awkward talking to them. They were unpredictable. If they'd scored and they weren't slumped against a wall somewhere, they were amenable and harmless. If they hadn't, they were torpid and sullen, or violently raging, spitting, and snarling in the street. They didn't seem to know themselves which to be. They didn't seem to have a choice. Augustine never imagined his father could be one of them.

Augustine was seven. His father was a junkie.

Mun knew what he was talking about. As part of his outreach work, Augustine's uncle spent much of his week in Ukhrul's alleys, pulling wasted men from the drains and the rubbish dumps. He'd clean them up and talk to them, and at least to begin with, listen to their assurances that they'd get clean this time. Then he'd find them the same way the next week.

Mun had seen most of what heroin could do to a person, and he'd talked with grieving families who'd lost sons and husbands to the needle before. But nothing in his clerical training had prepared him for this conversation with his own sister. He began to talk, to fill in the silence, as much for his own benefit as for Liko's.

'I asked a user I know "why"? He was a clever fellow, he'd finished school, but he was a junkie. He kept trying to get clean, but every time, he went back. I asked him "why"?

'You know what he told me?' Mun answered his own question: 'He said: "Number 4 is an easy sell. If you're poor, if you have no land to work and no chance at a job, heroin is easy, and it's cheap". A point of heroin is four hours you don't have to spend thinking about your life. Heroin makes it all go away. For a time.'

Liko shook her head. 'But Luke's life is not like that. He is married, he has a family, children who look up to him, lands to work. He's not like them.' From where Augustine sat, he could see his mother's left side, illuminated by the fire. Her face shone wet with tears. Augustine couldn't remember the last time he'd seen his mother cry. Mun had no answer to Liko's protestations.

'You need to be careful,' Mun said, 'for your own health. When it grips them, they'll do anything. All the doctors' offices get smashed up by junkies looking for needles. They find half a dozen sharps and save them. The same needle gets passed around dozens and dozens of arms. I've seen them, bloodstained and blunt on the side of the road, but someone will pick it up and stick it in their arm.' Mun's voice welled with a rare anger. 'The *nisha sikachin mi*, they all get infected in the end, Liko. They all do. You need to be careful. For you. For your kids.'

Liko was quiet. She didn't look up. Her silence ached inside Augustine. He wanted to run to his mother, to grab her skirts and hug her, to tell her it would all be okay, that together, they would save his dad. But he stayed sitting. Silent. Barely breathing. Mun was discomfited by Liko's quiet too. He kept talking. 'This is really serious, Likoknaro,' he said. 'A fortnight ago, I officiated at a wedding in Yuensang, right on the Burmese border. It sits on one of the main supply routes. One of the aunties there said that the village had had a drug overdose death every week for a year. Even if a junkie is found alive, there is no hospital there, no way to bring them back. They breathe these horrible, shallow, rasping breaths. Until they don't anymore. Everyone there has seen it, but the users keep coming, keep rolling up their sleeves, a never-ending supply.'

'And that's what you think will happen to Luke? That's what you think of him? Another nameless junkie? Another lost soul? Another statistic?' Liko hissed at Mun. 'He's my husband. He's a father.'

Mun was quiet.

'I'm sorry,' Liko said, and after a pause. 'It's not you I'm angry with.' Her eyes were still ablaze. The siblings sat in silence.

Augustine sat in the doorway. He wished he were back in bed; he wished he hadn't got up and heard what he had. Now, in the quiet, he was too scared to move. 'I should go, it's late,' Mun said. 'I'll come down to see you tomorrow. Let me know when Luke gets back.' Augustine realised all of a sudden that his father obviously wasn't home. His absence was not unusual, but it felt sinister now. Mun rose to leave and Augustine used the cover of his noise to creep back to bed. Alex hadn't moved. He was warm.

◈◈◈

Luke wasn't home by the morning; but he was there, sleeping on a *charpoi*[3] by the fire when Augustine arrived home from school in the afternoon. He looked the same. He was the same man, but he was diminished somehow. Augustine had always seen his father through a son's eyes. His dad was tall and clever and brave. He was more

---

3   *Charpoi*, also spelt *charpoy*: a day bed usually made from a bamboo frame and a woven web of rope netting. Literally: 'four-legged'.

of these things than anyone else. He told stories and shot straight. He recognised the sound of every animal in the forest and knew the winds off the hills and the rain in the clouds, just from a glance at the sky. Augustine tried now, as he looked at his father asleep, to recreate that impression. But it had fled; a happy fiction supplanted by a brutal reality he wished he didn't know.

A week later, Luke was home in the evening, and he asked Augustine to come and sit with him on the back stoop. He wanted to talk, he said. Augustine felt a wave of dread rise from his stomach. He knew what this was about. He didn't want to have this conversation. This conversation would make it real, it would mean Augustine knew, and they knew he knew.

Augustine followed his father outside and sat down. It was dark and cold, but clear. The moon was a thin sliver, but in compensation the sky seemed overfull with stars tonight. Augustine wanted his siblings beside him, his brother at least. 'The younger ones are too small,' Luke said, sensing Augustine's discomfort, 'but I need to tell you'. Luke talked. He never explained how he first came to try heroin, or from where, or from whom he got that first hit. He never explained the attraction, or what it felt like. He talked too simply to Augustine, as though he were speaking to a child much younger. 'I took this drug, I took it too many times, and it made me sick,' Luke said. 'But I kept taking it, and I got even sicker. Now I want to stop.' Even to a seven-year-old, it felt far too simplistic. Augustine was angry with the condescension. His father had never patronised him before.

Luke sniffed and wiped his nose on his sleeve. For all his charisma, that liquid tongue that wove fantastical stories out of thin air, he was clearly uncomfortable confronting his own flaws. Augustine blinked hard; he didn't know what to say. 'I'm sorry, Augustine,' Luke said.

'It's okay.'

'I'm going to get better.'

'Okay.'

❖❖❖

Things did not get better. Now that Augustine knew, Luke seemed to care even less about what happened to him. Augustine would wake up some mornings to find his father gone; his mother would discover money from the shop missing. Augustine would ask Liko where his Dad was, hoping for a better explanation than what he knew to be the truth. Liko pretended she hadn't heard. Augustine gave up asking. Sometimes Luke was gone for days. It was always quiet when he was away.

Then suddenly, his father would be home, wearing the same clothes he'd left in, unsteady on his feet, caked with dust and sweat. Occasionally, he would return bearing a gift for the younger kids, holding it out in two hands as though that was what he had gone to collect, and that it made his absence all okay. He'd bring a cheap plastic toy or a ball, but he'd be too tired to come outside to play with it. Most of the time he came back empty-handed. And hungry. Augustine's mother seemed furious behind her tears. She cried often now. But she still fed him, perhaps out of relief he was still alive. He would eat amazing amounts, scooping rice and curry and chutney and chicken into his mouth with his fingers, not talking. Then he'd sleep and sleep.

Then, without warning one afternoon, Liko announced that the family—everyone—was moving to Dimapur, in the state of Nagaland, more than 200 kilometres away. Augustine had never left Ukhrul. 'We leave tomorrow,' Liko said, her tone offering no room for debate. She handed Augustine two cheap carry bags and told him to pack everything he wanted to take.

Augustine understood vaguely that the move was to do with his father, with his addiction, but wasn't quite sure why things would be better in Dimapur. And he only part-understood Liko's attempt at an explanation: she wanted her husband away from his junkie friends, further from the border, in a place where the drugs were harder to get. Liko's sister was to take over the shop, and Augustine was allowed one farewell sweet from its shelves as the family piled into the minivan his mother had hired for the move.

Liko sat with Maitonphi in the rear seat while Augustine and Alex were crammed into the back, atop bulging bags of clothes, and boxes filled with the blackened pots his mother cooked with and the bamboo cups his father drank from. Luke sat in the front seat, sullen but uncomplaining. He sang softly, almost beneath his breath, an old song about an ancient battle. The lyrics were call-and-response, a contest between a man's fear and his bravery. Luke's fear won.

We chose to stand our ground and fight,
But you, you coward, fled.
We said we would defend our land
Or lie upon it dead.
When dao and spears were drawn in rage
And rivers turned to red,
We Naga would call no man King,
You knelt and bowed your head

It took all day to reach the city.

◈◈◈

Akala walks in front now. The afternoon has grown cooler and she, it seems, revitalised. They haven't far to go now. But they are not safe to stay in the valley here, they are too close to two Tangkhul villages, Akiko and Nuro. The villages sit on parallel ridges above them, to the east and west as they walk. Augustine can see smoke rising from a chimney in Akiko now. If they camp here, they risk being discovered by hunters out in the evening twilight or the quiet of the early morning. Akiko and Nuro are part of the Tangkhul tribe, they speak the language. One of Augustine's cousins married into a family in Nuro so they will know what has happened, what they have done. Augustine and Akala cannot stop here and risk being caught. But a little further on, where the river curves around the foothills, there they can rest. There, they will be safe. So they walk on.

Augustine watches Akala's quick, precise movements as she leads further into the forest. She takes small steps, balanced on her toes, moving like a dancer, hands held slightly away from her body for balance, the beginnings, almost, of a curtsy. Augustine feels cumbersome by comparison, his heavy footfall noisily following her soundless lead. He loves to watch her walk, to know she is here with him, but he feels a dread, too. Every step, he knows, is leading them further into trouble, every minute they are away makes it harder to go back. 'Where did I first go wrong?' he wonders. That day he first laid eyes on her, what should he have done differently?

After Augustine saw Akala by the river for the first time—washing clothes on the bank opposite to where he was collecting water—he returned regularly to the same spot, at the same time, hoping to see her again. He was living alone then, in his grandmother's old house, Sechumhang, outside of town, so he was easily able to slip away unseen, and he could walk to the river by himself, just in the hope she would be there.

For two weeks when Augustine arrived, the riverbank was busy on both sides, but there was no sign of Akala. He would wait on the bank slowly filling water pots or swimming quietly in the shallows, before reluctantly making his way back up the hill. He feared that perhaps she was gone, that she had left her village and he would never see her again. Or worse still, that he'd never seen her at all, that he'd imagined her.

Then, on his fifth trip to the river, he saw her, again with a bundle of washing she was wrestling at the water's edge. She was surrounded by old aunties who were nattering away loudly to each other along the river bank, the usual banalities and the withering jokes about their menfolk followed by gales of cackling laughter. Akala was silent, her head down, seemly uninterested in the conversation as it flew back and forth above her head. But this time she saw him, Augustine knew that. It was only the briefest glance, but she lifted her eyes for a moment and looked straight at him, and smiled, before putting her head straight back down, back to her work. But Augustine had seen. He got up to leave. It was enough.

THE BOY WITH
THE BIRTHMARK

The roads were sealed with bitumen in Dimapur, and people lived in concrete houses. There were cars everywhere, and tall buildings, and billboards advertising Honda motorcycles and Thums Up Cola[4]. There were more people than Augustine had ever seen before. Ukhrul suddenly felt small and distant. There were lots of Tangkhul in Dimapur, dozens of previously unmet family, distant members of the Shimray clan. After a few nights at the home of an ancient aunt Augustine had never met before, but who welcomed him and his siblings like her own lost children, the Shimrays found a house to move into. For weeks after their arrival, there was a constant stream of visitors, claiming kinship or some distant connection, bringing food and gossip, and toys for Maitonphi. Augustine had new cousins to play with, and a new city to explore.

The Shimrays' new home in Dimapur was smaller, but Augustine liked it better. Augustine and Alex had a room to themselves, with a concrete floor, and a small window out onto the busy street. Maitonphi slept in an adjacent room. Their parents stayed in the main room next to the fire. It straightaway felt like home.

---

4   *Thums Up Cola:* brand name for a very popular Indian version of Coca-Cola, invented after Coca-Cola abandoned India in the 1970s, when the government tried to force Coke to partner with a local company. Thums Up was later bought by Coca-Cola.

The new house had mains power that ran, with reasonable reliability, between six in the morning and six at night. The neighbours, the Horam family, had a generator which coughed and sputtered and spewed diesel when it overheated; but when it was working, they had electricity all through the night. Their house was bright and warm, and Augustine and Alex found themselves drawn to it. The Horams were Tangkhul too, originally from a village nearby to Ukhrul, and they welcomed the Shimray boys in, as playmates for their only son, Nido.

Nido was two years older than Augustine but looked two years younger; he was slender, almost mouse-like, with a large birthmark on the right side of his face. He seemed less excited than his parents about the intrusion into his home, but at their insistence, reluctantly played host. The thing that did excite him was television.

'You wanna watch TV?' he asked the brothers, removing a faded dust-cover to reveal a large square set sitting impassively in the corner of the living room. Augustine had watched TV before, but only ever at school, or in shops, never a privately owned one. No one in Ukhrul had a TV in their house. Nido adroitly manipulated two wires hanging down from the ceiling into the back of the box. 'Satellite dish,' he said, by way of no explanation at all, pointing up. He clicked a button on the remote control.

A burst of colour and sound filled the room. Suddenly, it felt to Augustine, the whole world had arrived in their little corner of the planet. Nido grinned a toothy, wonky smile. He began pressing buttons on the remote. 'We get all the channels,' he said, flicking expertly through a dazzling array of screens. There were cricket games and spy programs and dramas, and chat shows where beautiful people sat on couches and laughed and talked and people clapped for no reason. Nido came to rest on the BBC, barely intelligible to Augustine with their Queen's English accents. The next channel, CNN, Augustine could understand better. 'American,' Nido said. 'They hardly ever mention India, and when they do, it is only ever Delhi or Bombay, or to talk about a flood or a building collapse somewhere.'

Augustine was hooked. From that day on, he would spend almost every evening, usually with Alex in tow, at Nido's house, crouched or sitting in front of the screen. Nido was scrupulously fair: they took turns to choose which program to watch—Nido, then one of the Shimray boys. Alex happily deferred to his older brother's suggestion every time.

The TV also brought Bollywood. Half a dozen channels were dedicated to replaying its vast catalogue of films, old and new, 24 hours a day. Nido knew all about Bollywood, all the stars' names, the movies they'd been in, the gossip about their private lives. Augustine had heard of none of it, but was captivated. Everything shone in Bollywood. Everything was bright and elegant and exciting. Augustine's Hindi was limited but he could speak enough to follow the simple plot-lines and dialogue. Besides, he watched Bollywood films for the colour, for the music, and for the hundreds and hundreds of dancers, all in perfect synchronisation. Everyone was so happy in Bollywood. They smiled all the time, huge grins that showed off enormous white teeth. No one chewed betel nut, or spat, in Bollywood. No one was ever sad, or drunk, or stoned. It was magical.

Liko was a flurry of activity in Dimapur. She found an unused shopfront at the intersection at the bottom of their street, and soon had it cleaned and stocked and open. The new shop was better than the one in Ukhrul, Augustine thought. It was bigger, its shelves seemingly heaving with an extraordinary array of goods for sale. In reality, it was still a modest operation, the same brands of biscuits and long-life milk, vegetables that cost more because they had to be brought further from the fields to the city. But people in Dimapur had a little more money; Liko could get a better price here than at home.

Alex was old enough for school now so the brothers were enrolled at Carmel School, a brutalist, three-storey concrete building where 900 children were taught, not by gentle young women whom they called by their first names, but by male teachers in long pants and ties and suit jackets. All of them were 'sir'. Augustine had to wear his old uniform while his mother sourced one for his new school, which only made him feel even more of an outsider, but he soon found he could avoid attention by sitting at the back of the class and keeping quiet. There were 63 kids in fourth class and Mr Kumar, a Hindu fresh out of teachers' college, was already overwhelmed by the mass of unruly young humanity in his charge. Lessons were a shambles. Augustine was stunned by the behaviour of his new classmates, who would shout at each other in class, and at the teacher when he tried to reprimand them. Amid the tumult, the quiet new kid melted invisibly into the background.

The education at Carmel School was slavishly focused on 'the fundamentals', as the principal, Mr Jamir, called them. By that, he meant a relentless program of rote learning of times-tables and historical dates, and of reciting every day the few phrases of English he felt were vital in proving his students could speak the language. Mr Jamir would visit each class every day, so every day Augustine was forced to stand and say aloud: 'Good morning, sir. My name is Augustine, my father's name is Luishomwo, my mother's name is Likoknaro. I study in Class 4.'

'Good,' Mr Jamir would respond, moving onto the next student. This went around the entire class, sometimes twice. The principal knew that the district inspector of schools had a standard list of questions he asked every student to assess their English skills: what is your name, what is your father's name, what is your mother's name, what class are you in? So Mr Jamir taught those answers. Nothing more, nothing less. Teach to the test.

Most of the kids in Augustine's class attended church and so were familiar with English, even if they didn't speak it well. But the children who came from Hindu or Muslim families, or from villages too small to have a church, knew no more than these rote-learned passages, and they didn't really understand what they meant. The words sounded strange in their mouths, awkward, meaning-less, syllables rushed together: 'goomuningsirmynaymis...' Still, it was enough to pass the inspector's less-than-forensic examination, so Principal Jamir would proudly declare that all of the children in his charge spoke English. 'One hundred per cent,' he would say. Each morning, Augustine dutifully stood in line awaiting his turn, but his mind ran elsewhere, to Nido's and to television and to Bollywood.

'I'm done with school,' Augustine said one afternoon, walking into the shop from school. His mother was on her knees, stacking boxes of washing powder on a low shelf. 'Augustine,' she sighed, resting her hands on her hips, a tiredness in her voice, 'please don't do this'.

'It's a waste of time; I never learn anything. I could be helping you in the shop, earning money.'

'Please Augustine, your education is important. You know it is. And besides, you're an example to Alex and Maitonphi.'

'They don't care what I do, and anyway—'

'Listen!' Liko cut him off. 'Listen to me: you need to go to school so you don't end up like your...' Augustine knew she was about to say 'father' but caught herself. 'Like me,' Liko said. 'So, you don't have to work so hard like me.' She sighed and rubbed her fingers across her forehead. 'I never had the chance to go to school, and I wish every day I did. I want you to go...' She paused now and turned back to her work, picking up another box. 'I want you to go, so you don't have to work all the time like me.'

Augustine acceded and stayed at school for his mother's sake. He let the charade of the daily English ritual pass him by, and the chaos of the lessons wash over him unaffected. He took to sketching in his school notebooks, a picture of quiet concentration at the back of the room while others ran riot around him. He blended in, expert at hiding in plain sight.

Augustine was working on one of his sketches at lunchtime when a teacher, Mr Sai, walked up behind him.

'That's very good.'

Augustine was worried. 'I'm sorry sir,' he stammered, expecting trouble, 'it's just a small sketch, of a hornbill.'

'Don't apologise,' Mr Sai said, 'it's very good. You should do more.'

'Yes sir.'

Augustine was still unconvinced he was not in trouble. He sat, hand poised over the page, but unwilling to draw another line. The silence between student and teacher grew uncomfortably long.

'I used to teach art,' Mr Sai said after a time, 'at a different school, a larger school than this.'

Augustine was too anxious to respond.

'I would like to draw again. Would you like some lessons?' Mr Sai asked. 'We could practise our artwork together.'

'Yes sir,' Augustine said, timidly, still awaiting the reprimand. 'I would like that'.

'Tomorrow afternoon. We can meet in the maths building. Bottom floor.'

Augustine knew Mr Sai. He was different from the other teachers. He was much older and didn't seem worried about the discipline that so obsessed his colleagues. Oddly, this meant nobody played up in his class. He was so nice that students felt bad about misbehaving. It wasn't an authority but a reasonableness that he radiated. Mr Sai, it was said, never had to raise his voice.

Augustine had never been taught by Mr Sai, but he knew that Nido had, so that afternoon, as the pair flicked through the multitude of channels on the television—Nido was sure there was a new Amitabh Bachchan[5] film playing that afternoon—Augustine asked him to come along too. 'Sure,' Nido said, unworried, 'why not'. Augustine still wasn't certain.

The next afternoon the two friends found Mr Sai moving furniture around a small classroom at the end of the maths block. The room was too small for any of the massive classes at the school, so no lessons were taught here, so it had become a storeroom for broken old desks and unwanted benches. Mr Sai had obviously been moving things about for a while—his face was streaked with dust—but from the chaos he had created a small art studio in one corner of the cluttered room, turning an old blackboard into an easel around which he arranged a handful of small desks in a semi-circle. Another student whom Augustine recognised from a couple of classes above, Vizol, was already seated at one of the desks.

'Shall we start,' Mr Sai said, gesturing with outstretched palms towards the desks. After the children had sat down, Mr Sai handed out one sheet of paper and a pencil to each of them, then took a piece of chalk in his hand: 'I thought we might start with portraiture'.

---

5   The doyen of Bollywood. Amitabh Bachchan is India's best-known and most influential Bollywood actor. Described as a 'one-man industry', he has appeared in more than 190 films over five decades.

Mr Sai didn't teach from any set curriculum, and his classes were unhurried and ad hoc. The lessons fell into a rough routine of Monday, Wednesday and Thursday afternoons—moved from Friday after Augustine explained that Friday afternoons he spent with his father. (Augustine and Luke didn't hunt on Fridays anymore, Luke was rarely even home, but, in a forlorn hope, Augustine maintained the commitment, even only as a fiction in his head). Each lesson, Mr Sai would appear with handfuls of purloined paper, usually old maths forms, and special graphite pencils he kept sharpened with a knife. There were no paints, so he taught drawing, talking about light and perspective and composition. Most of the concepts were beyond his students, but for Augustine, the simple chance to draw whatever he wanted and be encouraged rather than scolded was an enormous attraction.

From the outset, Augustine was Mr Sai's most dedicated student. After a couple of lessons, the lure of television drew Nido away, and the appeal of extra work after school soon faded for Vizol. From then on, it was just Augustine and Mr Sai. Neither minded. Augustine liked to draw birds and worked for weeks on a single massive composition, a picture of a hornbill flying high above the mountains, wings spread wide. Below, a handful of men, rendered tiny by their vast distance from the bird, watched on, mute and helpless.

After class, Augustine and Mr Sai would talk, sitting on the steps to the school, now deserted of children. One afternoon, as they looked out over the dusty forecourt which held assembly each morning, Mr Sai asked about the picture.

'It's Yarho,' Augustine said. He explained to his teacher the story of Yarho, the boy tormented by his aunt, who fled his home to become a hornbill.

When Augustine had finished, Mr Sai said: 'My village tells that same story; it is very beautiful.'

'My father told it to me, he said it happened down from our village,' Augustine said. 'He always tells old Naga stories.'

The pair sat in silence in the cool of the afternoon.

'What do you think is the most important part of that story?' Mr Sai asked.

'I don't know.' Augustine had never considered it: 'that he turned into a bird'.

'Maybe,' Mr Sai said, 'but I don't think so. I always thought that what happened after that was the most important part of the story. That the boy whom no one wanted, became a leader of his people. He solved disputes, gave people guidance, he united people. I always thought that was the crucial part.'

'My father never tells it that way,' Augustine said, 'never told it that way, I mean'. He ventured a belated qualification: 'He doesn't tell those stories anymore'.

'I see,' Mr Sai said, staring out at the vacant schoolyard.

'My father is sick now,' Augustine said quickly, to fill the silence. It felt like a betrayal to offer anything more. Mr Sai didn't ask any further, leaving Augustine wondering if he somehow understood the truth completely, or not at all.

Augustine flourished under Mr Sai's guidance, and even his interest in his other schoolwork improved. All of the Shimrays, it seemed, were making new lives for themselves in Dimapur. Alex was immediately the centre of a gaggle of friends in Class 1. Liko busied herself in the new shop and, when she wasn't there, with the baby Maitonphi. In the city, Augustine's father got a job labouring for a relative who was a builder, carrying bricks on a construction site. He worked hard, arriving home just as the sun went down each evening, caked in sweat and dust and blood from where he'd invari-ably cut one of his fingers again. Liko fed him well, and he seemed happy, even though he was tired.

But it wasn't enough. Not for Luke. Perhaps nothing ever would be. Augustine watched his father unravel, powerless to intercede. He was home the Friday afternoon the boss came round with Luke's salary. Three weeks' worth in cash. That night after dinner, Luke walked out of the house and was gone for four days. Luke lost that job. He went back to work a couple of times, to different jobs, but they always ended the same, and soon he stopped going. Stopped looking. When Luke was home it was worse. Every couple of days, someone, 'a new friend' would come round to see him, and he'd step outside to talk, then just disappear.

Soon Augustine began to stop expecting his father home. Even when he was, Luke wasn't really there. The bedtime stories stopped. His father, the one with the adventures and the shiny eyes, never came home anymore. Nor did anyone else. The cousins and aunties and uncles who crowded their small living room in the first few weeks stopped dropping by. The roaring trade from relatives at the new shop dried to a trickle. People weren't around at mealtimes anymore. It was just Augustine and his brother and baby sister, and their mother, if she wasn't too busy running the shop. The only people who came around anymore were his father's new junkie mates, shivering and thin and covered in sores they were forever picking at. Few others came to see the Shimrays.

◈◈◈

They walk, ever onward. They are too deep in the forest now to be able to gauge their progress; they know only that they must keep going. But Augustine's thoughts are far from these dark trees. He keeps returning in his mind to that first meeting with Akala, that first glance across the river, and the desire, the need he felt to see her again.

He had waited two days to return to the river. He came later this time, in the last quiet minutes before the sun disappeared behind the mountains. Already the hills were hazy in the twilight, one grey-green ridge indistinct from another. And there she was: at the river and alone, right at the end of the bare sandy stretch of river bank. Augustine crouched by the riverbank directly opposite, sitting quietly without speaking. She looked up and smiled. She glanced up the river to see they were still alone and, when she saw they were, she smiled at him again, this time for longer. There was barely 20 metres of water between them, but still they'd made no communication. Tribal tradition forbade them from speaking. Already, just by being here together, they would incur the wrath of the elders should they be discovered.

But more than the inhibition of any societal constraint, Augustine simply felt shy, uncertain as to what came next, by what it would mean if they did speak. Back and forth across the river, their silence, for now, was communication enough: the same thoughts at the same time.

He hadn't thought this far ahead. What would he say to her if he could speak? They sat in silence in the near-darkness. Akala had finished her work, and they would both have to leave soon to make it home before it was too dark to walk on the forest trails.

To Augustine's left, just where the forest began to grow thickly again, sat a huge boulder worn smooth and soft by the passage of countless years, an endless succession of rainy seasons and dry. He picked up a hard piece of shale and began scratching with it into the stone. He wrote his name first, in capitals: A-U-G-U-S-T-I-N-E. The whole process was painfully slow and his face burned with self-consciousness as he carved out the clumsy letters. The last E was misshapen by a bulge in the rock. Underneath he wrote 10 digits: 9-9-5-8-3-7-9-9-9-0. He turned to look at Akala. She reached underneath her shawl, pulling from it a black mobile phone. She had her head down, her thumb working the keypad. She looked up again at the rock, then down again at the screen on her phone. She put the phone back inside a pocket and looked at him one last time. She smiled, and she almost, almost spoke to him. She mouthed the word 'goodbye'. Then she gathered up the clothes before her and turned to walk back up the hill. She didn't look back once.

Augustine was alone now. It was growing darker by the minute, and a handful of lights from Ukhrul, up on the ridgeline, showed him how far he had to go to get home. But he stayed a moment longer in the quiet. Then he got up and, using a different rock, scratched over his name and his number. He took a lot longer this time, careful to erase every detail. When he had finished, the markings looked like a series of mindless scratchings, as though some kid had been using the boulder to sharpen rocks to skim. The weather would take care of the rest. Augustine turned and walked home, first along the river bank, then bearing right up the path which took him to the ridgeline and on to the warmth of home.

◈◈◈

Hours later, Augustine was in bed, almost asleep, when his phone lit up on the low table beside him. He had the phone on silent, but saw the green glow of the screen and the buzzing sent the phone skittering.

A message from a new number: **I am Akala. I am from Tiya. Perhaps I will see you again at the river? Not tmrw, maybe the day after.**

Akala. Augustine was shocked to realise he hadn't known her name. Akala meant 'shadow' in Nagamese. It felt right for her.

But this message was dangerous. Augustine was excited by it, but he could see the hazard that lurked behind. Not for what it said, but for what it was. Mobile phones were a menace in this part of India. The old men of the villages, the fathers, didn't like phones because phones took away their power. Previously, a father could control who his daughter saw or spoke to. He could keep boys he didn't want from his door. But phones allowed a boy to slip into his house without him even knowing. With a phone a girl could contact boys in secret, and they her.

Everyone knew the stories of the fathers who'd discovered their daughters' liaisons. A year earlier, a father in a Meitei village down in the valley had uncovered his daughter's texts to the boy who lived in the house behind theirs. In a rage he walked around to the boy's house, dragged him by the hair into the street, and beat him while the neighbourhood watched on, unable or unwilling to step in. The man punched the boy's face until it didn't look like a face anymore, just a mess of red flesh, telling him with every strike, 'you blackened my good name'. When the boy stopped moving, the man dropped his dead body in the street and walked back to his own home. He took down his shotgun and said to his daughter 'see what you've done'. He shot her in the face before turning the gun on himself. The newspapers said it was an 'honour killing'. Augustine couldn't see much honour in it. But phones were a serious business.

All of this raced through Augustine's head as he lay there in the dark, staring at the phone. He knew that texting Akala back was fraught with risk. Of course, he knew all the tricks to stop the texts being uncovered. He would save Akala's name under a boy's name, or some unremarkable village surname. Or he would commit her number to memory. He would erase her texts as soon as he'd read them, as well as those he sent her. But still, there was risk. Her father only needed to find one. Augustine spent an hour crafting a reply, sitting in the darkness, the only light in the room the faint green glow from the screen. He tried a dozen versions, sometimes writing and erasing the same message three or four times before he settled on a choice of words. Even then, he hesitated. He wasn't sure he wanted to do this. Augustine wished for long minutes she hadn't texted so he wouldn't have to make the decision on whether to reply. Finally, he hit the green button and watched the sending icon stutter through. He fell asleep with the phone in his hand.

BUSINESS IN BURMA

Augustine's mother, it seemed to him, tried desperately to hold the family together while his father did the opposite, choosing to poison himself while everyone who loved him was forced to watch. Luke's helplessness in the face of addiction inspired a quiet sadness in him, but a white-hot rage in Liko that she channelled into ceaseless activity. The further he fell, the harder she worked, until there was not a moment she wasn't wholly consumed. For different reasons then, Augustine saw less and less of either parent. With his mother working all the hours of the day, and his father erratically absent, more and more responsibility fell to him to care for his younger siblings. He cooked dinner, approximating the recipes he'd learned by watching his mother and grandmother and aunties. He washed and ironed his own school uniform and Alex's, and kept Maitonphi dressed and fed and safe.

Luke's troubles aside, Dimapur was good to the family, though Augustine missed the quiet routine and the certainty of the smaller town. In Ukhrul he knew everybody, and everybody knew him, if not by name, at least from which family he came, to where he belonged. By comparison, Dimapur was impersonal and anonymous. Augustine had turned nine, he was in Class 4 now, but he felt small again, as if he'd become somehow younger. In Ukhrul, he was on the threshold of becoming a man, he hunted and learned the stories of his people. Now, there was nowhere to hunt, and his father was too removed, too vacant, for stories.

Luke tumbled chaotically, uncaringly, downhill, though his was not a linear descent. There were weeks, even months he was well, and each time, there was hope in the family that maybe, maybe this time, he'd won the battle against whatever private demons tormented him. When Augustine's father was well, his mother would relax, she would be home more, and the family would be together at meal-times, life would be as it once was. Luke could win forgiveness. He was expert at convincing others, employers especially, that he had turned a corner, that he could be relied upon this time. Sometimes he could even convince himself. He would find work in the city, or would put in long days stocking the shop, filling the high shelves to overfull until it seemed as if they might collapse under the weight of all the exotic goods for sale. Inspired, Luke was a natural salesman. He could be good for business. And on those days, Augustine felt that his family had pieced itself back together.

But it was only ever temporary. Seemingly without catalyst, Luke would disappear again, for days, and Augustine's mother would bury herself in work with a renewed fury, railing to whichever aunty she came across that he was gone again, maybe this time for good. 'I've been abandoned,' she would mourn, her voice high-pitched and thin with anger.

Business was harder in Dimapur. After the surge of early support from relatives while the Shimrays settled in, the shop struggled through the summer. Their shop was a little out of the way for most of their extended family and people were loyal to the places they'd known for years. Liko's, as everyone called it, was too new. But burdened with the sole responsibility of providing for her young family, Liko found a way. She sought out goods that were hard to find or expensive, in Dimapur, and made herself the woman who could get things. She met a man, Sem, who was a smuggler out of Burma. Every month, sometimes every fortnight if orders were good, he would catch a bus to a border town, and then walk the final forty-or-so kilometres into Burma along the high mountain tracks that bypassed the border guard posts. He would walk to the town of Hkamti on the Burmese side. There sat an outsized market, dwarfing the village itself, selling Chinese-made homewares—pots and pans, cups, crockery, shoes, and children's clothes—all for sale at huge discounts from the Indian prices. Goods flowed freely into Burma from China's manufacturing cities of Kunming and Degen. But Chinese goods coming via official channels into India attracted massive tariffs and huge price hikes by monopolistic middlemen. Sem had found a way around. He just had to walk.

It was a clever operation because the goods themselves were completely innocuous and, even if caught, Sem and his band of porters—'my foot soldiers', he called them—could cheaply pay off the border guards, whichever side of the boundary they were on. The guards were after drugs and guns, looking either to make a bust for the benefit of their careers, or for a cut of the action. They couldn't care less about a few cups and saucers. Often enough they knew Sem by sight and waved him on.

After those first few lean months, and with Sem's help, Liko's reputation, and that of her shop, flourished. In Dimapur it was soon known if an item in a store was too expensive, Liko could find it cheaper with a few weeks' notice. She began taking orders, and built up a roster of regular customers, who in turn referred friends and relatives. Liko was reliable and she was honest. That was the word around Dimapur. Business grew. She got a cousin to add a second room onto the shop and even hired an employee. The new girl was a young Naga. Her name was Honlei. She was not from Dimapur either, she was from the hills on the other side of Nagaland, from the Ao tribe, but was living in the city while her marriage to a local blacksmith was being arranged by her family. She was a diligent worker and Liko loved her instantly, for her company as much as her help. Augustine loved her too. When Liko was out, Honlei spoiled him and his brother, allowing them a free run at the lollies in the shop, the ones on the high shelves that Liko fiercely protected from her marauding sons.

Augustine knew the shop was doing well because there was meat at home at dinnertime more often. Not just chicken, but pork and mutton too. Augustine and Alex had new uniforms for school and new books. When the weather turned cold Liko bought them, through Sem, a black duffel coat each, with wooden toggles and deep pockets in which Augustine loved to bury his hands from the wind. He wore it every day. By late November there was snow on the hills that surrounded Dimapur. The mountains seemed to draw closer together in the winter, they hugged the city, and the low grey sky added to the sense of claustrophobia.

His father seemed well again, though Augustine had learned not to trust these false dawns. Cynicism was an uncomfortable fit on his young shoulders, but he'd been hurt too many times. It was safer this way.

One Friday in early December, Augustine and Alex walked home together, as they did on afternoons when Augustine didn't have art classes. Alex clung to his brother's hand as they crossed the busy roads, made more treacherous by the ice that formed in the shadowed corners. They turned left, passing their mother's shop where Honlei stood casually on duty, smiling at them. There were no customers now. Schoolbag bouncing on his back, Alex ran ahead and inside.

'... so I don't know if I can go. It should all be for the children, but every rupee from the shop goes up your arm!' His mother was railing at his father. Liko stood square in front of Luke, close in and leaning aggressively forward, pointing her finger. Luke looked thin and drawn. His father seemed smaller these days, Augustine thought. With his eyes downcast, Luke appeared beaten. Tired. Liko heard the boys come in and was immediately self-conscious. 'Alex. Augustine. Come in from the cold, come and sit by the fire.' The anger melted from her voice. Augustine knew his mother's fury was still there, but she'd packed it away for the sake of the family. These one-sided fights were so common now that Augustine was no longer upset by them. He felt sorry for his father. He could see how much Luke tried, but seemed helpless in the face of a force far stronger than him.

Liko made chai with milk and sugar for the boys, then took their coats as they warmed up by the fire. 'Boys, I am going to be going away for a few days,' she told them. Luke had shrunk to a far corner.

'I need to go and buy some things to sell at the shop. It will be good for the family,' Liko continued, her justification preceding the practicalities. This is what the fight was about, Augustine knew.

'It will only be a few days, four or five days. Your father will be here to look after you.'

Luke nodded in confirmation.

'Are you going to Burma with Sem?' Augustine asked. He'd seen Sem at the shop often and Honlei had explained to him the arcane, not-exactly-legal supply route that he ran. Honlei didn't like Sem, or his method of business, but she was worldly enough to realise that the shop depended on him. And if not him, somebody else would have cultivated the same racket. Sem could be trusted, up to a point.

'Yes, I'm going into Burma' Liko said.

'Will you be safe?' Augustine asked.

'Of course. I will go with Sem. He knows the way, and all the people along the path.'

'How many days?'

'Four or five.'

'How many?'

'Probably five. It depends on the buses and the market when we get there.'

Liko left in the morning, before the boys had woken for school. They got up to find their father cooking rice for breakfast. It was burned black at the bottom by the time he finally pulled it from the pot, and Alex's schoolbag took half an hour to find, sitting, where he'd left it, on the front stoop. The boys were late for school that day, and the next.

Liko was home on the fifth afternoon. She was sitting inside when the boys arrived home. She had a present for each of them, a hard rubber ball for Augustine and a hoop for Alex. Maitonphi got a collection of shiny bracelets, which jangled as she waved her arms in the air, craving her mother's embrace.

'What was Burma like?'

'Burma was fine, Augustine,' Liko replied. 'It was a long way, but we got good prices because we bought a lot.'

'Do they speak a different language in Burma? Do they look different from us?' Alex interjected, tugging at his mother's sleeve.

'They speak Burmese to each other. But they are Naga people like us, so they look the same, and they can speak Nagamese.'

'Will you go there again?'

'I think so.'

'When?'

'I don't know.'

It was barely a fortnight before Liko had built up orders enough to go back. And soon, it became routine. Liko would announce she was leaving in the morning for Burma, and when the family awoke, she'd be gone. They never heard from her while she was away, but each time, she would appear a few days later, weighed down by goods she had crammed into striped carry bags she bore on her back or balanced on her head.

Sometimes she had porters with her: lean men, shirtless and barefoot, who carried enormous loads and never spoke. When they arrived, the porters wordlessly laid down their burdens in the corner of the shop and held out their hands to be paid. Then they disappeared. Where had they come from? Augustine asked Honlei. Out of earshot of the men, Honlei explained that most of the porters were Konyak, members of the fierce martial tribe that lived in the hills of the borderlands. But one man, she said, pointing to an especially wiry, darker-skinned man, was from the Wa, a Burmese tribe from the eastern side of that country. 'The Wa are wild. They don't speak our language. But they have an insurgency, too, called the United Wa State Army,' Honlei whispered. 'It is the Wa who carry the Number 4, the drugs, into India.' Augustine gazed at the man, his young eyes blazing with contempt. The Wa man looked back. He was hollow-cheeked and lean, his eyes were two pitch-black dots that stared unblinking, boring into Augustine's. Augustine looked away.

The goods that came from Burma were simple but highly decorated. To a nine-year-old boy they held an aura of the magical. Instead of plain white plates, the crockery sets Liko brought home were garishly ornamented with dancing, fire-breathing dragons. She sourced girls' shoes of a brilliant red that seemed to sparkle, even in the dull light of the shop. Augustine's sister insisted upon a pair. To Augustine these exotic goods gave the impression that Burma, and China beyond, were mythical, magical lands, just past the hills over which the sun rose each morning. These places were wealthy and colourful. In Dimapur, everything was grey.

'I want to come to Burma,' Augustine told Liko over dinner on the eve of yet another trip.

'I'm sorry, Augustine. I would love you to come, and I could always use another porter, but it's too far for you, and besides, you have to go to school.'

'I'll come in the holidays.'

'It's too far, Augustine. I'm sorry.'

Luke was sitting by the fire. He held Maitonphi in his lap.

'I'll come.'

'What?' Liko asked.

'I'll come to Burma. I can help. Simeon is arriving tomorrow. He can come too.'

Simeon was coming to see his older brother and to look for work. In the depths of winter there were no crops to plant in the fields at Ukhrul. Work in the city paid well.

'Are you sure?' Liko asked. Two more strong backs could be hugely profitable, but in her mind, Augustine could see, she was already weighing up the risks. Taking Luke to Burma, the very place from where the heroin he was so weak for came from, walking the same trails the Number 4 porters trod, was she courting catastrophe? But he'd been good lately, and she'd be there to watch him. And Simeon. Surely, she prayed, it would be okay.

'It's a long way, and it's a boring march. And you can't take guns, no hunting. If you have a weapon, the border guards or the Tatmadaw will shoot you,' Liko said, using the locals' word for the Burmese army.

'I want to come. I want to help,' Luke said.

'Augustine, can you help your brother?' Liko asked. It wasn't really a question. 'Make sure he gets to school every day. Honlei will look after Maitonphi.'

'No,' Augustine replied. 'I want to come with you.'

'Augustine, you know you can't. I'm sorry. One day, I promise, you will get to go there. You can look after your brother?'

'How many days?'

'We will leave in two days, we'll be gone for five. I promise to bring you back something.'

The allure of gifts was diminishing in Augustine's eyes. He didn't want more things from a distant place; he wanted to know the place for himself, to see the lands beyond the hills of his home. But he knew better than to argue with his mother when her mind was set.

Simeon arrived on a bus from Ukhrul the next day. He immediately agreed to walk to Burma; he loved the forest as much as his brother. He led a brief, quiet resistance to Liko's 'no weapons' decree, wishing to hunt as they walked. He missed Luke, he said. Hunting trips back home without his brother weren't the same.

'Simeon, if you are carrying a gun, they will shoot you before you even see them,' Liko said, looking him in the eye as she spoke. Simeon acquiesced, but unhappily.

The trio left the next morning, a Wednesday. Their movement woke Augustine, and he heard his mother still imploring Luke and his brother. 'You need to be diplomatic with these people,' she said in a harsh whisper. 'You can't get angry. The border guards do it all the time: they open fire on smugglers or farmers and then they recreate their murders as "encounters", saying they were "hostile insurgents". It's easy for them to do. They plant a weapon on your body, or a few kilograms of contraband and they just tell their superior "we were fired on first". That's all the higher-ups need to hear.'

'Uh-huh,' Luke sullenly agreed. Whether because of the early morning or Liko's tone, he was clearly resentful.

'And you'll be dead,' Liko said, forcing the point. 'Please, please, be careful.'

Augustine heard them leave. He didn't get up.

At home, little changed. Honlei took care of the youngest child, who passed her days in the shop. Augustine washed and ironed Alex's uniform, though he didn't care if his brother did his homework, and he didn't do his own, save for his drawing for Mr Sai's class. Liko was home on the fifth afternoon, Sunday. Despite the distance and the unpredictability of her sorties into Burma, she always found a way to get home by whichever time she had promised. She willed it. But today she was alone.

'Where's Dad?' was Augustine's first question. Liko was still unloading the masses of bags she carried on her back and head. His mother had not brought the gift she'd promised, but Augustine couldn't care less. He began to tremble with fear at the possibilities: his father had been discovered by the soldiers on the border… he was in trouble… why would his mother not say anything.

'Is Dad okay? What happened?' Augustine pleaded, suddenly in tears.

'Augustine,' Liko slowly stood upright, finally relieved of her burdens. 'Your father is fine.' She sighed. 'He stopped to stay in a village. A place called Mimi on the Indian side. It's high in the mountains close to the border. We were on the way back when we met a man hunting in the forest. He and your father got talking, and he invited Luke and Simeon up for rice beer and who knows what else. Your father will be fine.' Liko seemed not even to be angry anymore. She'd had a day-and-a-half of fury walking home, and she appeared simply weary of it all now. Honlei quietly started to unpack the bags. 'I honestly thought this was going to work,' Liko said to her, not worried that Augustine could hear. 'I thought he could help, but there's too much risk in that place, too much temptation.'

His father's absence still left Augustine with an unshakeable anxiety. He wanted him home. And he didn't want him to go to Burma again. Augustine sat outside on the sill of the shopfront, watching for his father to come up the hill, knowing he could be days away.

❖❖❖

The men arrived home Wednesday morning. Simeon was drunk. Luke was clearly high. Augustine knew the signs now. The men had the goods they had carried from Burma, though not all of them.

'We traded them,' Luke said when Liko challenged him.

'For what?' she asked.

'We traded them,' Luke repeated.

Liko's forbearance evaporated.

'Luke, why can't you understand? People had paid for those things, now I have to tell them I don't have them yet, and I will have to go back to get them. And *I* will have to pay for them.'

Luke cast down the bags he had been carrying. Augustine ran to his father and hugged him, squeezing him around his legs. He knew Luke was in trouble with his mother, that'd he done the wrong thing, but he was just glad his father was home. 'I stayed in a village called Mimi, Augustine,' Luke said quietly, crouching down to speak with his son.

'They live right up high, in the cold, tall hills near Burma. A long way from here. And they told me a fantastic story. Do you want to hear it?'

Augustine nodded, beaming. His father hadn't told him a story for months.

'Here, we'll sit by the fire,' Luke said, pulling up chairs for the pair of them. Alex sat on the floor. The issue of the missing home-wares and of Liko's approbation was, for the moment, forgotten.

'Mimi is a small village, smaller even than Ukhrul,' Luke began. Maitonphi waddled over to sit on his lap. He held her close. 'But before there was Mimi, the families of that place lived in another village lower down in the valley called Tzuru. This is the story of a young couple who lived in Tzuru, of their village, and of a mountain called Sukhayap.' Luke paused. His children sat agape, transfixed in expectation, before him. He smiled and a new tone, resonant and deep, took over his voice.

'The couple were called Shishio and Hatang,' Luke continued. 'Shishio was a very fine young man, handsome and a good hunter, and Hatang was the most beautiful girl in the village. But their families did not agree to their union. He was the son of a chief and she was from a low family with poor lands. The families said they could not marry. The couple resisted and begged for their families' blessing, but the elders said "no". The girl's family found another boy in a nearby village called Betang and arranged for her to marry him, and to move away.'

The old Luke was back, Augustine could see, even if he also knew it might only be for that one brief afternoon. Augustine smiled and moved closer to him. His father's words boomed around their small home, and his eyes shone as he wove his fantastical tale.

'Shishio and Hatang decided to elope, to run away to a place where no one could find them. There was a cliff on the other side of the valley to their village called Sukhayap. No one had ever climbed it. It was so steep and the terrain so difficult, that even the animals never went there. But if they could find a way, they'd be safe there.

'In the middle of the night, they escaped together and walked down the steep path into the valley, across the Laplongtang River, and up the other side. There, they found the base of Sukhayap. Shishio was an experienced hunter and a strong climber. He knew the men of the village would be able to track them, so he had to find a way to the top. They climbed. It took all day: Shishio helping Hatang, Hatang helping Shishio. Low down, when it was steep, the boy used his *dao* to cut down trees to build ladders. After they had climbed them, Shishio burned the ladders and laid false trails back down the cliff to confuse the trackers. That night, they slept at the height of the highest trees.

'Above them was only rock face. In the early morning, they climbed. The boy carried vines from lower down and would climb ahead, tying the vines onto the rocks so that Hatang could climb up behind. They went slowly-slowly. Many times they nearly fell. They cut their hands on the sharp rocks, and they were tired and hungry.'

Weary from his own journey, Luke sat with his eyes closed as he gathered his strength for the story's denouement. The story lived in him; he was its herald. And his belief was irresistible. Even Liko was now by his side, listening to every word.

'They found a way. They reached the peak of Sukhayap. At evening time, they stood at the top of the cliff, looking across the valley to their village below. A few metres down from the summit of Sukhayap, there was a small grotto the couple could climb into, where they were protected from the wind. They spent the night there, not sleeping, but talking about their lives and their desire to be together forever. In the morning, they walked back to the summit to look down at the village again. And then…' Luke faded to silence.

'And then what?' Augustine, misunderstanding the significance, pushed his father for a resolution.

'The men from the village who were following them eventually reached the top of the cliff,' Luke said. 'They saw where the couple had lain together in the grotto. They found their shawls, and the men walked to the very summit. But there was no sign of Shishio and Hatang.'

◈◈◈

Augustine and Akala built a relationship slowly, in secret, and in 160-character instalments. By text message they would arrange to meet, and if they found themselves alone, they could sit on opposite riverbanks and exchange more messages. Really, they were close enough to be able to speak across the river, if they talked a little loudly, but it was too risky if someone came down to the water, on either side, and besides, they felt more comfortable communicating by text. They would sit, in identical crouches at the edge of the water, watching each other and the screens of their phones, smiling at the messages that flitted back and forth across the Langdangkong. Augustine loved to watch Akala type. She was fast, a picture of concentration, and her texts were always flawless. She punctuated. Augustine did not, and he was forever making mistakes.

When Augustine was a child at school, Miss Angela had taught him how to make toy boats from pieces of paper. Stuffed into his pocket, he began to bring pages of newspaper down to the river, to fold into little vessels to send across the water to Akala, parchment emissaries to the unknowable land on the other side. On board his fragile ships he would put feathers he had found in the forest, or pictures he had drawn for her. The boats were of unpredictable seaworthiness. Sometimes they forged straight across to Akala. Sometimes the current turned them around and brought them back to his side. Sometimes they would suddenly take on water and sink in the middle of the river. Akala always laughed, but it upset Augustine when they didn't make it across. The boats that did reach the far side, Akala always picked up from the water, and folded up to put in her pocket. If there was a feather on board, she would take it and put it in her hair. If it was a folded-up picture, she would flatten it upon a smooth stone and carefully study it, sometimes for minutes, before gently re-folding it and putting it in her pocket. 'Thank you,' she always texted.

They met six times over the next month—Augustine counted—but they never really met. Always, the river was between them, the conduit that brought them together, the barrier that kept them apart. Were their clandestine meetings discovered now, they could expect their families to be furious, perhaps to send them away as punishment. But if they were caught together, on the same side of the river, it would be so much worse. The violence of the old days would be revisited, their villages would be at war again, and it would be their fault. Augustine didn't care. The generations of hostility meant nothing to him, and he felt a recklessness about Akala. She felt dangerous, but it only added to her allure. Akala. A shadow. Untouchable, unknowable, unobtainable, always just beyond Augustine's reach, flitting from his grasp just when he felt she was his.

GOLDEN

Augustine was ten now, still just a boy, but he felt overwhelmed by the tumult of the world around him. Everyone seemed to be in the grip of something: nationalistic insurgent fever; a ceaseless drive to make money 'for the family'; drink; drugs. Everyone was in thrall to a power stronger than themselves. His father was disconnected from everything and everyone. For all of his family's efforts—the move, his wife's beseeching, his children's distance—nothing could reach him. He grew steadily sicker. The drugs held him ever tighter. He was home less and less.

Augustine's mother kept working, kept walking. At least twice a month now she would leave home in the dark of the early morning, headed for Dimapur's main bus terminal and whichever vehicle could take her east towards the foot-trails that ran east over the border. The family had been made comfortable by her enterprise; they would never be rich, but Liko was not motivated by avarice. Rather, it seemed to Augustine, she seemed enslaved by an irrational belief that the harder she worked, the better her husband would be, that her work ethic would somehow win over his addiction. It made no sense, but she remained seized of it just as intently. She walked into Burma and out, time and time again.

Liko still carried the household goods and clothes she always had, but she would return now wearing, too, gold bangles and necklaces and jewel-studded earrings she'd never had before. She never mentioned them, but they were conspicuous. She'd never worn much jewellery before, and never anything as ostentatious as this. The precious rubies in her ears glinted in the sun. But Liko never had the jewels longer than a day or two, then they would disappear as mysteriously as they'd come. One night, an hour or so after Liko had returned from yet another journey, Augustine asked her.

'Where did they come from?' he said, pointing at a pair of hooped gold earrings, each adorned with a small shining gem.

'Oh, these are old, Augustine,' Liko answered, brushing aside the query. 'I just don't wear them very often.'

'They look new. And I've never seen them before,' Augustine replied, the incredulity clear in his voice. Liko looked at her eldest son. They were alone in the kitchen.

'Augustine,' Liko said, 'can you keep a secret?' He nodded.

Gold, Liko told her son in a conspiratorial whisper, was cheaper in Burma too. Much cheaper. 'And if I wear it when I walk out, the soldiers never think to ask about it. They don't realise that that's what I'm bringing from Burma. It's simple, see?' It didn't sound simple at all. Smuggling gold sounded much more dangerous to Augustine, but his mother appeared blithely unconcerned. Now informed, Augustine became aware of the transaction around the precious jewels. Usually the morning after Liko returned, a man they never saw at any other time, would come to the shop and stay a long while, talking to Honlei in a loud voice as he bought biscuits and soap and bottles of soft drink. Liko would hear him would suddenly bustle into the shop with a confected air of busy-ness and distraction, asking Honlei if she could go into town on an errand. Honlei knew what was going on, but kept up the pantomime. She would absent herself, telling Liko she would stay for lunch at her fiancé's home. Shop empty, Liko would close the front awning. This wasn't business to be done in the street.

Liko would then remove the jewellery, piece by piece. Anything she wasn't wearing at the time, she kept in a black velvet bag. She handed it all over. Augustine would watch through a crack in the back wall of the shop. Usually, the man paid in cash, peeling off golden 500-rupee notes from a roll in his top pocket. Sometimes, he paid Liko several thousand rupees, often more than she would make from all the other bulky goods she had to carry. But sometimes, Liko chose instead to keep a bracelet or a pair of earrings in lieu.

The world was too much, Augustine felt. There was too much of everything: too much money, too much work, too many drugs and drinkers. Sensing his mounting anxiety, his mother encouraged him to take guitar lessons, 'you like music, you should learn to play'. The first week was fine, the cool young teacher with the nylon string guitar and a Guns N' Roses T-shirt taught him a few chords. Augustine was in love with the instrument, with the idea of being a musician. But when he returned for his lesson the next week, the teacher was slumped, drunk, in a corner, an empty bottle of whisky at his hip. He swore at Augustine when he arrived, and when Augustine picked up the guitar to practise, the teacher lashed out, slapping him hard across his face. Augustine dropped the guitar and ran. The teacher threw the bottle at his retreating form. Augustine never went back. He told his mum he didn't like the guitar any more. She didn't push it.

Although, Augustine liked living in Dimapur, it wasn't the same as Ukhrul. The city was uncertain and unpredictable; he couldn't trust anything to stay the same. He grew quiet, at home and at school. He sensed it happening, but it didn't worry him at all, he just didn't want to talk. He wanted to listen, and to observe. His homework came back affixed with notes of concern. Words like 'withdrawn' and 'uninterested' peppered his teachers' comments. Alex complained to his mum that 'Augustine doesn't like to play anymore'. Augustine wasn't sad; he didn't mind school, he just didn't care for lessons. And he loved his little brother. He just wanted quiet.

But the exam results that came home at the end of the year were another trial, another source of exasperation for Liko. Luke was holding court this afternoon, in one his rare moments of presence and lucidity at home. He was expounding dramatically '…what the Naga people need is a leader, someone to unite us,' when Augustine walked in ahead of his brother. Liko had only been half-listening anyway, but now, pulling out and reading the crumpled report card Augustine had attempted to hide in the bottom of his schoolbag, her distraction was complete. Liko knew what she was looking for. She had known it was report day from the other mothers in the street.

'Augustine,' she sighed, scanning past the Ds and Cs for the teacher's notes below. They contained the faintest of praise enthusiastically damned with comments like "must apply himself", "uncommitted", and, at the very bottom, "limited educational capacity".

'What do they mean by that?' Liko turned to Luke, who was suddenly silent in his corner, sulking at being interrupted.

'He's a small boy,' Liko continued. 'How dare they tell him he has "limited capacity"? What do they mean?' But Augustine, and his parents, knew exactly the meaning behind the teacher's coded message. Education was a numbers game: the number of children starting school in a place like Nagaland was halved by the time primary grades ended. One in ten could expect to finish high school and Liko could count on one hand the number of children she knew who had gone on to university, down in the valley in Imphal. Even among ten-year-olds, the teachers were sorting the educational wheat from the chaff.

Luke answered quietly. 'The boy will be okay,' he said, as though their son wasn't even there. Liko turned her attention back to Augustine.

'You're a clever boy, I know that. And I know you don't believe me, but your schooling is important. I wish I could make you see that. I wish you would trust me.' Augustine was silent.

Liko wasn't finished.

'I asked next door about Nido,' she said, now addressing both Luke and Augustine, both of them wishing her harangue was over. 'He was the topper again, first in sixth class.' Augustine kept his eyes down, but Luke looked up. 'First?' he asked, a little colour returning to his voice.

'First,' Liko said.

'I knew that boy was clever,' Luke said. 'Perhaps he is the chosen one. Maybe he is the leader the Naga need, the one to unite us.'

'Oh, shut up about that,' Liko snapped. 'Be a father first, not a politician, not an insurgent.'

Augustine's solace was art. He remained Mr Sai's only disciple. The pair spent long afternoons sitting side by side in the cluttered, dusty classroom, working on their respective projects. Mr Sai would occasionally glance over and offer suggestions, but Augustine learned better, they both felt, by trial and error. 'There's no such thing as a meaningless piece of art,' the teacher said. 'They all say something, they all teach you something.'

Mostly, the pair talked about family, and poetry and songs. But, days after the report card had passed from his mother's temper, Augustine remained distracted by it, and his father's reaction, much more than his mother's. He and Mr Sai discussed his marks.

'My mother is disappointed,' Augustine said. 'She says I don't try hard enough.'

'Do you think she is right?'

Augustine ignored the friendly interrogative.

'Nido was topper in his grade. My father and mother think he's wonderful. My father thinks he is the chosen one, the one who could be the saviour of Nagaland.'

Mr Sai was silent, picking up a knife to carefully hew his pencil to a sharp new point.

'Nido is too young, he can't save Nagaland,' Augustine said hurriedly, all of his insecurities about his father's flippant comment tumbling out. 'Not him. It will be someone older, someone who is wise. I think it will be you.'

Augustine stopped. He was suddenly embarrassed. His affection for his teacher, so obvious to both of them even undeclared, sounded childish and needy when spoken aloud. Mr Sai sought to minimise Augustine's discomfort. He sighed, and kept drawing, then spoke casually, as though discussing the weather.

'I agree with your father that the Naga need a figure to unite them, but I don't think it will be me. You say Nido is too young, but boys grow to become men, just as he will, just as you will, while we men will only grow old. I have great hopes for the young generation; I have been too often disappointed by mine.' Augustine didn't know what he meant. The pair sketched on in silence.

◇◇◇

One afternoon in December, Mr Sai arrived at class carrying a thin metal box under his arm. 'Come, see,' the teacher whispered, almost reverentially, to Augustine, laying the box down on the desk to open it before his student. Lifted, the lid revealed sixty-four coloured pencils of every colour Augustine could imagine, graduated through blues and greens, reds and oranges, yellows and white. The pencils were brand new, each exactly the same length, and perfectly sharpened. Augustine could not remember ever seeing something so beautiful. The unabashed colour was almost shocking, made all the more stark by its contrast with his surroundings: the box was like an exotic bird, caged in this silent, colourless classroom, this forgotten place, deserted of children and piled with old furniture.

'A friend of mine brought them from Delhi. A gift,' Mr Sai said, smiling. He was almost as excited as Augustine. 'Go on,' he urged, 'draw'.

Augustine knew immediately what he wanted to draw. He sketched a broad sweeping horizon through the middle of the page, and set to work. He drew for three straight lessons, without showing his teacher. By the next week, Augustine was ready to reveal his work. It was a waterfront scene, in the late afternoon. On the foreground shore, Augustine had sketched a host of people dressed in bright, almost luminescent, clothes, dancing on the grass. Behind them, a setting sun laid a shimmering golden path across the water. 'Bombay,' declared Augustine. 'Beautiful,' said Mr Sai.

It wasn't like that in Dimapur. In the wintertime, the hours of sunlight were short, and the days felt enveloped in a kind of double-ended gloom. The hills nearby carried snow. Augustine's father withdrew further, more mirage now than man. Liko busied herself in furious work as if to pretend none of it was happening.

❖ ❖ ❖

Augustine wanted to meet Akala properly: to talk to her, to hear the sound of her voice, to see the rise and fall of her chest as she spoke. He wanted to touch her, to know she was real. He wanted to see if the excitement that welled within him when he saw her, lived in her as well.

Augustine still didn't know. The fear of being caught, of all the ramifications that would surely follow, he didn't care about anymore. He texted her: **Tmrw, meet by the river? 1 km downstream is a place we can go. I will show you.**

Akala was late, arriving out of breath with the effort of walking quickly to the river. They each stood in their respective positions, on either side of the water. Happily, they were alone, otherwise they would have had to simply turn around and go home. Akala smiled at Augustine, and he smiled back. He pointed left, and mouthed the words: 'this way'. They set off walking, Augustine on his side of the river, Akala on hers. On his side, there were boulders and screes of loose rocks. It would have been easier to walk up higher, away from the bank, but he wanted to stay by the river where he could see her. He clambered over the stones. On her side it was easier. The riverbank was flat and there were few trees.

The river dropped over a series of rapids before it reached a wider section where the water was still. There was a sweeping bend here, and above, on the northern side, a grove of mahogany trees. Augustine's father had showed this place to him; this was where Yarho, the boy who became a hornbill, had found his first feather. This was the place where he had built his wings under the trees where the hornbills nested. This grove would be good for Augustine and Akala too. People rarely visited this part of the river. There were no paddy fields here and the raised, sheltered vantage point of the trees offered a clear view of the valley and the river bend. Behind the trees was a steep hill. Almost a cliff, it was too steep for anyone to approach from, and looking out the other way, upstream and down of the river, they could see anyone approaching from far away.

The trees were on Akala's side of the river, so Augustine crossed where the water was shallow, hopping from one exposed rock to the next until he was on her side. He walked ahead until he was right in the middle of the stand of trees before he turned around to face her. They'd still never spoken a word to each other. Augustine waited... too nervous to utter a word... before, finally, he spoke: 'I'm Augustine'.

'I know,' she said, giggling. 'I'm Akala.' It was the first time Augustine had heard her voice. It was clear and high, and her laugh cascaded like the sound of altar bells. They stood before each other and did not speak again.

Embarrassed by his awkwardness, and anxious to fill the silence, Augustine found words now tumbling from his mouth. 'My father showed me this place. People hardly ever come here, and even if they do, we can see them coming. It is quiet and peaceful.'

'It's okay,' Akala assured him, 'I think it is a fine place. We will be fine here.'

He drew breath again.

They sat side by side in the grass beneath the trees and looked out over the valley. Augustine's wet footprints on the riverbank rocks were the only sign a human had ever visited this place. They watched them dry in the sun.

Augustine willed himself to relax, to be comfortable in Akala's presence, but again, he felt discomfort at the lengthening silence. He had brought her here; he should speak. 'This place,' he said finally, 'this place is special to my village. This is the where Yarho came.'

'Who is Yarho?'

Augustine felt self-conscious all over again. He knew he lacked his father's flair for storytelling, so he didn't try. Augustine told Akala the story of Yarho without embellishment. Simply, he explained that Yarho was a young orphan who lived with his aunt and uncle.

'They lived on land near to this river. The aunt was cruel to the boy. She teased him and beat him, so finally he ran away, down to this bend where the mahogany trees grow and the hornbills nest in the branches. Yarho came to this place because he knew he would be safe here.'

Augustine explained that Yarho was jealous of the hornbills. While he was a boy and they were only birds, they were free to go wherever they wanted, and they lived, always, together. Yarho felt alone in the world, trapped in a place where he was not wanted, where he would never be loved. 'So he began to search for the hornbills' feathers, gathering hundreds that had fallen from the birds' wings, and spending weeks weaving them into wings.'

'And he could fly?' Akala guessed the ending.

'The hornbills taught him,' Augustine said, 'and he became one of the them. He could move between being a human and a bird, but he lived with the hornbills. He flew high over everyone, over his village, over his aunt who had been cruel, but he didn't leave this place. Instead he became a magistrate for his village, the elders would call on him to help settle disputes. My father used to tell me: 'Hornbills are wise birds, because they fly so high they can see everything at once'.'

The footprints that had marked Augustine's passage across the stones in the river had completely disappeared now under the sun.

'We should go,' he said.

BOMBAY BY BICYCLE

Augustine knew Bombay was west, and he knew that there, things were different. Bombay was on the ocean, and the sun always shone there. That place would be like it was in the movies, where no one was unwell or addicted, where no one went hungry or shivered in their beds. He would go there. At ten, Augustine had no concept of how vast the subcontinent was: he figured if he could reach Assam, which he knew to be just over the border from Dimapur, he could get to Bengal and then find his way to Bombay. No one ever called it Mumbai. Augustine understood from his father that India was trying to break free of the impositions of British colonial rule, and part of that meant abandoning the names the British had appended to India's cities. But Mumbai was the name the Hindu National- ists, including the militant Shiv Sena, had given the city, so everyone in Nagaland felt more comfortable with Bombay. It seemed more Christian. Augustine thought he could reach that shimmering city on the west coast of India in a few days. From there he'd call to tell his mother he was okay.

It was lunchtime Friday when Augustine decided to go. There was no art class that afternoon, and Augustine knew his father would— again—not be around to keep their Friday evening appointment, only ever observed in the breach now. Augustine walked straight home from class, leaving Alex to find his own way. He gathered the 140 rupees he had stashed under his bed, and took his bicycle from the back of the house. He put a box of matches and some firelighters into a small black bag which he slung over his shoulder. Liko was busy with the shop. Luke was nowhere to be seen. He was wheeling his bike through the front yard when Alex arrived.

'You didn't wait,' Alex said.

'I was in a hurry, sorry.'

'I waited for you but when you didn't come, I walked home alone.'

'Sorry, little brother.'

'It's okay,' Alex kicked at a stone on the ground. 'Where are you going?'

'Nowhere.'

'Then why are you in a hurry?'

Augustine paused. He didn't know what to say to his little brother whom he loved and trusted, and who loved and trusted him back.

'Come with me,' Augustine said, taking Alex by the shoulder and steering him out of the front yard. They turned downhill, back towards school, but only as far as the corner, where a street vendor stood, surrounded by aluminium pots of fried food. Augustine peeled off a ten rupee note.

'Chicken *momos*[6],' he said.

The vendor wordlessly filled the order. Augustine handed the full plate to Alex.

'These are for you, but you can't tell anybody you saw me this afternoon. I'm going away, but you can't tell.'

'Where are you going?' Alex insisted. Augustine could see his brother's first instinct was to want to come, too, but the idea of leaving home frightened him.

'I can't tell you,' Augustine said.

'Tell me or I'll tell mum you're running away,' Alex responded. Bargaining worked better than pleading with Augustine.

'No.'

'Tell me.'

---

6   *Momos:* dumplings, usually with a filling of vegetables or chicken. Similar to the Japanese gyoza, but called *momos* in Tibet, Nepal, and across north-eastern India.

Augustine paused. 'Okay,' he said, grabbing back the plate of *momos*, 'but you only get these if you promise not to tell anyone we spoke about this, or where I've gone.'

'Okay.'

Augustine found he was actually pleased to be able to tell Alex. It made his plan more real when he said it out aloud. And Alex was solid. Alex adored his older brother and would never betray him. Augustine explained that he wanted to see Bombay, he wanted to see Bollywood, so he was going to ride his bike there. He would call home when he'd reached his goal. Alex took it all in quietly. His sense of India's massive geography was even more inchoate than Augustine's. He knew Bombay was far away. But if Augustine said he could ride his bicycle there, it must be possible.

'Eat your *momos*. I'll see you another time,' Augustine said, mounting his bike.

'I'll miss you,' Alex said, through a mouth full of *momo*, waving goodbye.

◈◈◈

Augustine rode downhill, freewheeling behind the laden trucks smoking and grinding their way into the valley in low gear. His heart beat furiously in his chest; he was exhilarated to be free. Augustine knew the road west would take him to the border. The city of Dimapur was tucked up in a tiny corner of Nagaland, so the border to Assam was less than ten kilometres away on two sides. The proximity of the next state convinced him that all of India's states were similarly close. Having no concept of the massive land mass beyond him, he was undaunted by having to cross Assam and Bengal and Orissa and Madhya Pradesh and a host of other states before he reached Bombay. The road flattened out and Augustine pedalled fast, wanting to get as far as he could before his first night.

Augustine rode on, and on, and on. Farther than he'd ever ridden before. The roads were unfamiliar now, Dimapur had disappeared behind the hazy hills. By late afternoon, Augustine had reached Assam Gate. He knew this was the border because of the troops manning the fortified checkpost. They wore different uniforms on the other side of the sandbagged walls and the razor wire. That was Assam. Soldiers on both sides were stopping every car, searching for bombs or contraband and inspecting the licence of every driver. But a kid on a bike was just that, and Augustine didn't stop to attract attention. He felt tired, and hungry, increasingly uncertain his bicycle was the best idea. But he rode on.

As the sun dipped below the horizon, the road turned uphill. Augustine noticed a train line running beside the road so decided he would follow the tracks to the next station. A train would be faster, but he knew a ticket would cost more money than he had. Now he pedalled on, more slowly. By the time he reached the station, it was almost dark. 'Diphu' said a battered blue-and-white sign. Across the road from the train station was a ramshackle bicycle shop. In the gutter outside, a lean, shirtless man in a dhoti crouched, trueing a crooked wheel. Behind the counter sat a heavyset man with a moustache. Augustine presumed him to be the owner. The bigger man wore an open-neck shirt that revealed a heavy gold necklace. On each of his fat fingers was a chunky gold ring. Augustine wheeled his dust-covered bike up to the counter. 'Good evening, sir,' he said, speaking Hindi as the man was not Naga. 'Would you like to buy my bicycle?'

The man appeared stunned by the offer: 'Is it really your bike?' he asked.

'Yes sir, I've just ridden it from my home. I have some money, but I need more for the train.'

'And where is your home?'

'In Dimapur, sir, in Nagaland.'

'I can see you are Naga,' the man said. 'You are a long way from home.'

Augustine didn't understand. Why did this man ask these questions? This was a simple transaction. He wanted money for the train, and he had a bike to sell.

'Do your parents know where you are?' the man asked Augustine. Another question.

'Please, sir, I just need money for a train ticket.'

The man paused. He exhaled. 'Wait here, I need to ask someone if we want to buy your bike.'

The shop owner spoke to the shirtless man on the wheel, barking an instruction in Assamese. Augustine should have been able to understand, this man's language and his were similar enough to be mutually intelligible, but the man spoke so quickly and with such a guttural rasp, that Augustine couldn't follow. The shirtless man nodded and kept working. The man with the rings rose from his stool and waddled out from behind the counter. 'Wait there, my young friend,' he said to Augustine in Hindi, and disappeared into the darkness around the corner.

It was truly dark now. Through the gloom, Augustine could barely make out the station across the road. He wondered when the next train to Bombay was leaving. He hoped he would not have to wait long, it was getting cold. The man with the rings returned. Beside him was a policeman. Augustine's heart sank. He had limited experience with police, but from what he knew of them, and from what his father had told him, he felt sure this man was not here to help. Too late, Augustine decided to run. The policeman put a heavy hand on his shoulder. 'Don't worry, we'll help you get home.' Augustine didn't believe him. And besides, he didn't want to go home. He wanted to go to Bombay. 'Please, sir, let me go. I need to catch the train,' he said. There were tears in his eyes now. The man with the rings had betrayed him.

'It's okay, you're not in trouble,' the policeman said, still holding Augustine. He had him by both shoulders now, and was holding him as gently as he could, while still firmly enough to stop him from escaping. 'You must be hungry,' the officer said, 'Why don't you come with me? We will have chai.'

'Please, sir,' Augustine said, pleading now, 'I have money, I need to catch the train.'

'There are no more trains tonight. You should wait with me.'

Augustine looked at the officer. He was not Naga, nor Assamese. He was Hindustani, young, with a smooth, slim face and a neat moustache. He did not look unkind, he did not look like the sullen police in Ukhrul or Dimapur.

'My name is Pura. You don't need to call me "sir". Come.'

Augustine figured he couldn't run, and if there was no train tonight, perhaps the policeman would let him continue his journey in the morning. He was still too focused on reaching Bombay to be truly worried. The teachers at school had drummed into him and his classmates the perils of 'stranger danger', and their warnings flashed across his mind now. But Augustine's desire was stronger than his fear: he needed to find a way to that city. Pura walked with Augustine, the policeman's hand still on the child's shoulder, past the garishly lit chai shops along the road parallel to the train station. He turned down an alley and found a quieter place with a vacant table at the back. They sat and Pura ordered two chai.

'Now, tell me, what is your name?'

Augustine was reluctant, still, to co-operate. But he had little option.

'Augustine.'

'And where are you from?'

'Dimapur.'

'Dimapur?' the man said with surprise. 'You have ridden a long way.'

'Yes sir.'

'And where are you going?'

'Bombay.'

Pura burst out laughing and slapped the table with his right hand. The chaiwallah arrived with two cups of milky tea in small clay cups.

'Bombay!' Pura said to the man. 'This boy is going to ride his bicycle all the way to Bombay!'

The chaiwallah laughed too.

'Or I might catch a train,' Augustine said. 'If it is far.'

Pura sipped at his chai.

'It is too far, Augustine. I think it is best if you go home to your family. You have a family in Dimapur, I think?'

'Yes sir.'

'I think they will be worried about you.'

'No, they are busy,' Augustine said.

'Too busy to notice their son is missing? I don't think so.'

'I think so,' Augustine said.

The pair sat in silence for a minute.

'Bombay on a bike,' Pura said to himself under his breath. Then he grinned, but in a nice way. Augustine felt more comfortable. The pair sat, their hands clasped on their warm cups of chai, from which tendrils of steam escaped into the cold night air.

'I think your idea to cycle to Bombay is brave Augustine,' Pura said.

'Really?'

'Brave, but not clever.'

Augustine slumped in his seat.

'India is a big country,' Pura continued, 'and it is not safe for a small boy'.

'I'm ten.'

'Dozens of children your age go missing across India every single day,' Pura said, his tone more serious. 'Someone sees them alone, and they will just grab them. They will do whatever they want to the child. We have these cases all the time, but very few of the missing children are ever seen again. I think you have seen them, in the newspapers.'

Augustine knew what Pura was talking about. He had seen the photos, a smiling school picture alongside a few pleading lines from a family desperately seeking information, or a grainy shot of a battered, tiny corpse alongside a police inquiry into their identity. Even in Augustine's limited experience, he knew that few of these cases ever had a happy ending.

'The thieves and the thugs traffic children all over India, sometimes into Bangladesh or Burma,' Pura said. 'They sell boys for mining or for factory or farm work, for girls it is even worse. Often,' here Pura lowered his voice, 'the police and the government officials are part of the racket, so there is no one children can turn to for help.'

Pura's warning was having the desired effect. Augustine felt the faint chill of his sweat-soaked shirt on his back. He knew all of this to be true. Occasionally in Dimapur, one of these unhappy souls found their way home after years and years away. It was always big news, and everybody talked about it when someone came home, because most never did.

'It's not too late for you,' Pura said, draining the last of his tea. 'You should go home, Augustine.'

He waited for the boy to finish his tea. 'Come,' he said, 'it's late. You can stay at police headquarters tonight.' They walked past the darkness of the now-nearly-deserted train platform, empty save for a few families sleeping on plastic mats, waiting for the morning. The police station was a squat concrete bungalow, with a weathered wooden door beneath a blue light and a sign that said 'Police' in faded white letters. Inside was a single room where a lone pole stood from floor to ceiling. Beside it sat a desk, groaning under a welter of cardboard files. And at the back of the room were two cells. It was dark in the cells, but emerging from within, through the thick steel bars, Augustine could see half a dozen pairs of hands.

'The drunks,' Pura said in a voice loud enough for those within to hear, pointing to the cell on the right.

'The real criminals,' he said, pointing to the left.

'What if you're both?' said a voice in the darkness, to laughter.

'Then you sit at the desk.' Another voice. More laughter.

'Augustine,' Pura said. 'I have to go out on patrol now. But I want you to sleep here tonight. You understand?'

Augustine nodded. He had little choice it seemed.

'I don't have a bed for you, and I don't want you to run away again, so I'm going to make sure you stay here.'

Pura pulled out a pair of handcuffs from his belt, and—before Augustine could even think to react—had swiftly clinked them around his narrow right wrist. Augustine was suddenly in tears. The shiny cuffs glinted in the light and they felt cold. Pura snapped the other cuff to the pole by the desk.

'What did the kid do?' one of the voices from the cells called.

'Nothing. He was trying to ride his bike to Bombay,' Pura said, to more laughter. 'Leave him be. Let him rest.'

'I'm sorry, Augustine, but I have to make sure you stay here,' Pura ruffled Augustine's hair and was gone. Augustine sat down cross-legged next to the pole and cried. He felt betrayed by the policeman, a man he thought was his friend. He tugged half-heartedly at the cuff, but it only clamped more tightly onto his wrist. He didn't want to go to Bombay anymore; he wanted to go home. And for the first time, he was scared. The men in the cells saw his distress, and were quiet. Only one called out.

'It will be all right. Soon, the morning will come and you can go home. You get some sleep now.' Augustine lay down on the cold concrete floor, still fighting back tears. His bed at home would be warm. Alex would be next to him, breathing deeply. He missed his brother, but he was tired, so tired that even as he suddenly realised he'd left his bike back at the shop, his head was too heavy to lift from the floor. Within seconds, he was asleep.

◈ ◈ ◈

Pura woke Augustine with a gentle squeeze of his shoulder. It was broad daylight. The sun and the noise of the street outside were flooding in through the open window. Pura was still in his uniform.

'You'll take breakfast with me?' he asked Augustine, as he uncuffed him. At the back of the police station a *peon*[7] had laid out tea and rice. Using his right hand, Pura manipulated the rice into small balls, which he devoured in between sentences. 'I am off duty now. I am going to quarters to sleep,' he said, pointing at the bungalow behind. Augustine hadn't seen the building the night before, but now he saw half a dozen other police, in various states of dress, preparing for, or unwinding from, their days and nights on duty.

'You will have to stay at the station a little longer.'

'Where is my bike?' Augustine asked, again remembering suddenly. He was stranded without it.

'Your bike is at the shop. It is safe. The owner will keep it for you.'

'When does the train to Bombay leave?' Augustine asked, half-heartedly. Deep down he knew he didn't really want to go anymore.

Pura laughed, but kindly.

'Augustine,' he said, 'you cannot go to Bombay. You have to go home to your family. We want to take you to Nagaland, but the road is blocked now. There was an insurgent attack late last night, the

---

7 *Peon:* a low-ranking soldier or worker, often employed to perform menial tasks.

NSCN—you know about them I think?—the insurgents attacked the checkpost. One policeman died, and three or four of their fighters. The border between Assam and Nagaland is completely closed. There is a lot of fighting still. You will have to wait here.'

The Bollywood dream was gone. Augustine was surprised by how unworried he was. The familiarity of home, so constricting a day ago, felt reassuring now.

'There are no phone lines into Dimapur right now, and we cannot send a message through, everything has been cut off. We just have to wait,' Pura said, finishing his rice. 'Come, I will take you to meet Inspector Singh; he will look after you today.'

The Inspector was a Punjabi of the expected girth for a man of his rank. He used his size to intimidate generally, but he looked kindly on Augustine and promised to 'keep an eye on him' until the night shift, when Pura came back on duty. Without hope of reaching Bombay, and unable, for now, to go home, Augustine sat quietly at the feet of the officer and watched the ebb and flow of the life of the station. The inspector didn't get up much. Problems, instead, were brought to him. He solved them without ever really moving, barking orders as he leaned dangerously far back in his fraying leather chair.

Pura came back on duty at sunset, and he and Augustine ate together and talked until the officer had to go out on patrol. Augustine slept again on the floor of the station, this time without cuffs. Pura didn't even mention them. Augustine's ambition of reaching Bombay had been discarded, almost forgotten.

The boy quickly became a part of the landscape at Diphu Police Station. The next day Inspector Singh found him a shirt from an old uniform and cut down an old *lathi*, the bamboo poles police readily use for coercive crowd control. He made a miniature police officer of the interloper, a mascot for the station. 'Constable Augustine', Singh called him, laughing every time at his own joke. The Inspector showed off his protégé to everyone who came in, and Augustine happily played the part, saluting on command. He liked belonging. On the second afternoon, Singh unusually had to leave his desk momentarily. He asked Augustine to mind the station for him while he went around the corner. Augustine sat in the policeman's chair, uncomprehending of what he was to do if anyone turned up. But no one did, and Singh was soon back.

The days were full at Diphu, and somehow, Augustine found himself still there four days later. Each morning, the Inspector would order chai and kiss Augustine's cheeks. 'If your family does not come to collect you, I will adopt you,' he said once.

'Thank you, sir, you are very kind,' Augustine said, but he wanted to go home. Still, he couldn't. Each evening, the station would get a report on the border from the Ministry of Home Affairs. Each day they were told no one could cross, the border was still not secure. There were no phones, no way of getting a message through. Augustine had to wait.

On the fifth day, a Naga man came into the station. He was a journalist who'd come to interview Singh about the fighting on the border. He asked when the road might be open again. When he saw Augustine sitting by the policeman's desk, he asked about him and Singh explained.

'I am going to try to get back to Dimapur tonight,' the journalist said. 'I have some contacts with the NSCN who say they can get me across the border. I can contact his family if you'd like.'

Augustine burst into tears as he relayed his family's details to the man. He told him everything he could remember, his mother and father's names, his address, the names of his aunts and uncles and brother and sister.

'It's okay, it's okay,' the man said, trying to calm Augustine, 'I know this place; I think I know your mother's shop. I will find them.'

Singh held Augustine. 'Don't cry, my little constable, you'll be home soon,' he said, ruffling Augustine's hair.

At dawn two mornings later, Liko appeared at the station, drawn and dusty. She saw Augustine as soon as she walked in the door and burst into tears, running to her son and sweeping him up into her arms. Augustine had been prepared for his mother to be angry, but she only kissed him, and held him close.

'Don't ever leave, don't ever leave,' she kept saying, over and over again, almost under her breath, a mantra to herself as much as an instruction to him. Liko turned her attention to the officers who had cared for her son. She thanked them profusely, offering them money for their 'trouble and expenses'. They politely refused. Pura walked in—one of the officers had fetched him from patrol—wheeling Augustine's bicycle which he'd fetched from the shop. Augustine handed back his *lathi*, and took off his too-large policeman's shirt.

Augustine took his mother's hand. The autorickshaw that had brought her from the border was waiting to take them back. Pura tied the bike to the roof then shook Augustine's hand. 'Good luck, my young friend, I hope you find what you are looking for.'

'Thank you, Pura,' Augustine said.

Augustine and Liko drove for the border, Liko still hugging her son, still weeping. She explained that they thought Augustine had run away to join the NSCN or been snatched and sold to work in a mine in Meghalaya. When the journalist turned up on their doorstep talking about their missing son, she said that they thought he was a kidnapper come to demand a ransom. Liko had threatened to have him killed. But the man explained he knew where Augustine was and that he was safe. Through his NSCN contacts he was able to organise for Liko to cross the border checkpoint—which the NSCN still controlled—and for her to bring Augustine back. 'That man was your guardian angel,' Liko said.

'Pura was my guardian angel, mum,' Augustine said. 'He took care of me.'

'Two guardian angels in one trip. You were too lucky, Augustine. Please, please, please,' here Liko turned to look her son in the eye, 'please don't leave us again. I was so worried. I've lost him,' she said, 'and I thought I'd lost you too.'

◈◈◈

The mahogany grove—Yarho's grove—soon belonged to them. 'Our place' they called it in their texts. They kept it secret, even from Alex, with whom Augustine shared everything but this. Neither Akala nor Augustine ever mentioned that they were going to keep this place hidden; they just understood that this place was for them alone. Sometimes they would meet there two or three days in a row. Sometimes it was a week or more before they could find a way to slip away from their respective families and lives at the same time. They would sit among the trees, sometimes side by side, sometimes facing each other, each resting their backs against a trunk. And they would talk.

They would talk for hours if they had time, for a few minutes if that was all the moment they had. Augustine would reach out to hold Akala's hand. He talked the most. He told stories of the past. He talked about his village and the conflicts it had been through, the families whose histories he knew. He told Akala the old legends his father had taught him, of the Naga people and the ancient Gods of this place, the Gods whose names were almost forgotten now. Akala talked about the future. She told Augustine her family wanted her to study law, not so that she could become a lawyer, but so that she could meet one to marry. "'A girl with education will find a better husband," my father always tells me,' she said. 'That's probably good, because I'm not interested in law.' At this, Akala laughed bitterly, pulling at the grass before her. Augustine felt awkward. Here was he, a boy from the wrong village, with no great name and a patchwork education. He was not someone whose 'prospects'—as her parents would view them—matched those of a lawyer. But Akala seemed unworried.

When it was time to go, they would stand in the middle of the grove and hold hands. They would hold each other close. On their sixth meeting, as they said goodbye, Akala kissed him.

THE LILIES OF SHIRUI

Luke was in Augustine and Alex's room. Asleep. The boys came home from school to find him passed out in their bed. That their father was asleep in the middle of the afternoon was not especially unusual, but he had always stayed on the *charpoi* by the fire, in the main room of the house. 'Leave him be, he has a fever,' Liko said when she found the boys staring at their supine father. But Augustine noticed her eyes. How red they were.

Luke stayed there the night, while the boys slept by the fire with their mother. Alex was young enough for the novelty of staying up late with his family to be exciting. Augustine just wanted his father to be well. This time, and forever. Liko tried to create some normality, she told them a story—she tried to recreate the story Luke had brought home from his single ill-fated trip into Burma, about Shishio and Hatang and the cliff at Sukhayap—but she couldn't hold their attention like he could. Luke lived his stories. Liko recited hers. Augustine watched his mother as she talked. She stared into the fire with weary resignation. The shadows from the blaze danced across her face, the restless energy of the flames in contrast to the impassive features across which they wreathed.

Luke was still asleep in the morning as Liko fed and dressed the boys and sent them off to school. By the afternoon when they returned, Luke was awake, but still in bed, propped up by a stack of new pillows—stock from the shop.

'Is your fever better?' Augustine asked. He stood timidly by the door, afraid to approach his own father in his own room.

'A little, a little,' Luke said. Augustine was shocked by his father's voice. It was thin and breathy: smaller, like his body had become, and it came in rasps, from deep within his chest. The voice that had assumed the characters of a hundred brave Naga warriors, Augustine could now barely hear from across the room. Alex appeared at the door too. Luke waved a hand at his sons, beckoning for them to approach.

'Boys, come and sit with me. I want to talk to you.'

Liko silently appeared from the shop. Maitonphi was with her, holding her mother's hand. The family was not often all together these days. Liko came in and sat on a small stool by the head of the bed, Maitonphi on her lap. The boys sat on the mattress, by their father's thin body—Augustine by his shoulder, Alex his hip.

'Boys, I have to tell you something,' Luke began, weakly.

Augustine's insides froze. He gripped the edge of the bed. Instantly, he was transported back to the conversation with his father about his addiction, back to that lonely evening on the stoop in Ukhrul all those years ago. The agony of dreaded expectation seized all of Augustine's body as he waited for his father to continue. He half-wanted his father to hurry up and just say whatever terrible thing it was he had to say, half-wanted him to be silent forever, to never to say it at all. Luke saw none of this. He was gathering his breath. He looked at neither of his sons, nor at his wife and daughter. He stared off into a dark corner of the room.

'I saw the doctor today. He told me I am very sick. The fever is just a small part of my sickness,' Luke said. His children were silent.

'I have a disease called HIV, and now,' here Luke paused, 'now it has become another disease called AIDS.'

Augustine knew the names of these illnesses. He didn't understand them fully, how one became the other, but he knew they were serious. He knew people died from them. He knew, too, that somehow, this sickness was because of the Number 4.

When will you be well again?' Alex asked. Liko burst into tears. She began howling, her body racked by sobs. Luke put out a hand seeking hers, but couldn't find it. In one hand, she had the baby, the other she held to her face. Luke let his thin arm drop to the floor. Finally, he met the gaze of his smallest boy, who stared at him, eyes large and shining. 'I don't know, Alex. The doctors say maybe I will not get better.'

Alex didn't understand. 'Then what will happen?' He was too small to apprehend this, too young for diplomacy. But Augustine understood it all. He knew what his father was going to say before he said it: 'The doctors say I might die soon'. As Liko howled even harder, Maitonphi began crying too, her mother's overflowing distress seizing her tiny body. Augustine blinked, hard, waiting for tears that wouldn't come. He knew he was upset. He loved his father more than anyone. Luke was the most important person to him in the whole world, the man he looked up to, the man he wanted to be. But this was beyond sadness. This was impossible, too awful to be real, too bleak even for imagining. And yet, at the same time, it felt almost expected, as though he knew this was how his father would end. Needlessly, pointlessly, painfully. Too soon. Augustine sat, unmoving, for long minutes. Alex too. Maitonphi fell back into silence. The only sounds were his mother's weeping, more softly now, and his father's laboured breaths. Augustine sat, barely aware he'd begun to cry too.

◈◈◈

The days and weeks in the house passed interminably. But the world outside marched on unaffected, uncaring it seemed. The darkness of winter gave way to longer, brighter days. For weeks, there were soaking rains, then the sun shone on the mountains, turning them from grey to green. Augustine turned eleven that summer, and the family celebrated with a party. Luke was there in spirit, but barely in body this time and could hardly drag himself from bed for the cutting of the cake. Wanting to include him, Augustine asked his father to help him blow out his candles, but Luke could hardly muster the breath to make them flutter, and the effort sent him into another fit of racking coughs. The birthday boy wished he hadn't asked.

The warm days failed to revive Luke, and the family came to accept his diminished existence. Almost daily, he continued to shrink. Some nights Luke was at dinner, sitting and asking the boys about their days at school, talking endlessly, though it pained him, to disguise the fact he barely ate anymore. Most nights though, he was absent. Through the doorway, Augustine and Alex could see his thin frame laid out on the *charpoi*, shrunken, under great mounds of blankets. The boys had accepted their father was sick, and that he was never getting better. Only Liko seemed to disbelieve it. On days he showed the slightest improvement, she took it as an irrefutable sign he had 'turned the corner'. When he inevitably regressed, she wrote it off as 'a cold that's going around'. 'It's only one local doctor, he might have made a mistake. Maybe you don't have it,' she would say to Luke, as though denying the diagnosis would make it go away. All through that summer, and the winter that followed, Liko waged her battle against the inevitable.

Finally, in April, a government-run mobile health service came to town, setting up in the dusty *maidan* near to the boys' school. HIV had become an epidemic across Nagaland, the macabre corollary of the heroin plague. Most people lived many hours walk from a hospital and even then, the hospital couldn't help. In the city, sometimes it was possible to get the anti-retroviral drugs, but never consistently, and they didn't work if you only took them some of the time. The hospital's stores of drugs were regularly stolen by staff and sold illegally outside the gates. There was a black market in the drugs that gave you the disease, another black market in the drugs that could keep you well. Whilst Liko saw the futility in all of this, she held out still, her shaky, but unsinkable hope. She convinced Luke that he needed to take the test again, to confirm the local doctor's diagnosis: 'If not for you, then for me, and for the children.' Luke went reluctantly. Knowing that he was sick, and that he was going to die, would not change the fact. This time he had the result in two days. Positive.

He walked into the shop clutching the piece of paper. Augustine and Liko were stacking shelves. 'Same as before,' Luke said. Finally, finally, Liko handed herself over to the truth. She collapsed onto the floor of the shop and wept. Luke stood there helpless. He was too weak now to pick her up. It fell to Augustine to pull his sobbing mother from the floor.

There was no serious doubt that Luke had contracted HIV through heroin. Augustine understood this. Needles were a valuable commodity in the alleyways of Ukhrul and Dimapur, and no junkie ever thought twice about plunging someone else's sharp into their own vein. Some of the needles were blunt with blood by the time they found their final user. People would re-sharpen them on rocks, or burn them with matches, in the belief that that made them clean again. But usually they were too desperate, too focused on the hit that was coming to worry about hygiene. Luke told his son he had no idea which needle had infected him. 'All I know is that one did.'

Knowing for certain seemed to make it worse. Luke seemed to give up. Every day, he accepted he was a little sicker, a little weaker. Having fought the disease for so long, having tried each day to live up to Liko's pretence he was okay, having resisted for month after exhausting month, he was drained of all his defiance. Liko shifted her husband into the boys' room permanently. Sometimes he didn't move from bed for days. He was cold often, even though it was warm now. At nighttime, Liko kept piling blankets on top of him. All that could be seen of him now was his sunken, unshaven face, his once sparkling eyes dulled. Alex didn't like going into the room; it frightened him to see his father so ill. But Augustine went every day to sit with him. Even if Luke was asleep, Augustine would crouch on the stool by his father's bed, his smooth young face level with his father's weathered, decaying one; a silent vigil of hope, imagining all the time his father would wake up again and suddenly feel better. That things would be as they had been before.

But Luke, rather than seeking to recapture a past he knew now he'd never relive, had already turned his mind to what was to come. He spoke quietly to his son, a barely lucid stream of consciousness, his voice hardly above a whisper: 'I've seen it happen before, too many times, to too many friends,' he said. The weight loss, the tired-ness, the coughing and the mucus and the blood. The weakness. The slow, steady descent into illness followed by the rapid deterioration of the final few weeks. That's what Luke feared most, even more than

114

dying. It was the constant pain of those last days, a pain that only ever got worse, and from which there was only one escape.

❖❖❖

Luke wanted to die at home, in Ukhrul, and Liko told Augustine she saw no reason to deny him. It would be easier back home, she explained, with more family nearby. She could take over her old shop again and Luke would be more comfortable—he could see the hills of his ancestors again. The bid to keep him well, to perhaps save him, by moving to Dimapur had failed, so there was little reason to stay. Everyone in the neighbourhood knew why the Shimrays were leaving. They didn't say anything, but they understood, and they were sorry to see them go. The Shimrays had been three years in the city, long enough to make a home of the place, long enough to put down roots of a strength that it hurt when they were wrenched out. The family would be adrift again.

Augustine didn't mind. He liked Dimapur, but Ukhrul still felt like the place he belonged, and he hoped beyond reason that his father might, by some miracle, be well enough to take him into the forest one more time. The day-long drive, again packed into a hired van, was quiet. Luke slept the whole way, his emaciated frame bouncing along Nagaland's unsealed roads, the seatbelt wearing a vermillion stripe against the frail skin on his neck.

A succession of tearful aunties was waiting for the family back in Ukhrul, sitting on the back stoop to welcome them home. Awake, but barely, Luke offered a perfunctory greeting to everyone before retiring to a *charpoi* especially set up in the back room. This would become his place in the house, his last place. Where he lay, propped up on pillows, the light shone through the window onto his face, and he could see the grey-green hills beyond. For hours, he just stared.

Liko re-assumed responsibility for the shop. Her trips to Burma were made easier now she was closer to the border, and she recruited a new clique of mysterious porters. Augustine and Alex returned to school, though, using the excuse of his father's illness, Augustine missed as often he attended. Alex, on the other hand, went every day, and Augustine understood why. It was quiet in the house now, and it seemed darker. At school Alex could be noisy, he could run around and play, he could be a kid.

Augustine spent whole days sitting by his father's bedside. Luke would silently stare at the hills out the window, and Augustine would draw, sketching with a pencil on paper he'd brought home from school. He drew a scene of his father—young and strong and well—walking with his rifle up the flanks of Shirui Peak. Despite his promises, Luke had never taken Augustine there. Now, they both knew, he never would.

When it was finished, Augustine showed his father the drawing. Luke was instantly enlivened. He asked Augustine to move his pillows so he could sit up 'to look at it properly'. He stared at the picture for a long time, not speaking. Then he looked out the window at Shirui Peak proper, and Augustine saw the tears in his eyes. 'Let me tell you about the mountain, Augustine,' Luke said, pointing at the peak. It was clear today, and Augustine could see the mountaintop against the blue sky. 'But first,' Luke said, coughing and grimacing in pain, 'I must give you something'. He pointed to the corner of the room, where his *dao*, unused for years now, lent impassively against the corner. 'Bring that to me.'

Augustine silently carried it over. His father held the knife almost reverentially, his hand shaking as he slowly ran a thumb along the now-dulled blade.

'Many seasons ago I forged this *dao* in the fire in this house. But I cannot use it anymore.'

Luke held the knife upright, both hands clasped around the worn bamboo handle.

'I remember the power of this knife. I remember how it felt to swing it. The *dao*'s power is still there. But my strength is gone.'

With shaking hands, Luke presented the blade to his son. 'You must have it. But you must promise me you will look after it always. Never lose it.'

'I promise,' Augustine said quietly.

'Now you have your own *dao*,' Luke said, 'you can explore our lands and visit the mountain, but first you must know the story of that place.'

Talking was an immense effort for his father. Every sentence left him short of breath, rasping for just a little more oxygen so he could continue. It was warm, so he wore no shirt, and Augustine could see each of his ribs in his wasted chest, heaving up and down with the effort. Sometimes, Luke was silent for minutes as he gathered the strength to keep going.

'Our people believe there is a Goddess who lives on the mountain-top, Augustine,' Luke began, 'the Goddess of Shirui Peak, her name is Philava. Philava watches over the people of her chosen villages and protects them and brings them good harvests. It is she who controls the rain and the sunshine and the rivers and the soil.'

Luke paused and drank deeply from a glass of water by the bedside. Even his beloved rice beer was too strong for him now. He gathered his breath and his thoughts.

'All the villages on this side of Shirui Peak are her chosen people. But the Goddess exacts a price from the people she protects. Every few years, she requires one man from one of the villages to leave their place and to go with her, to be her lover. She comes down from the peak and assumes human form, taking over the body and the life of a beautiful woman. She seduces one man, young and strong and fit, and lures him away to live with her amongst the clouds.'

Augustine had heard this part before. When a distant, older cousin had mysteriously disappeared during a hunting trip a few years ago, people had muttered about the Goddess choosing her man. Noklen was handsome and strong and brave. He was promised to a girl in upper Ukhrul. Augustine had wondered why the search for him was so perfunctory.

'But she only takes men from her chosen villages, the villages she favours,' Luke continued. 'The people the Goddess favours are those who can see the white lily when it blooms on Shirui Peak. That is the sign of the Goddess Philava.'

Augustine knew this too. Every summer in June, white lilies blossomed across the peak, and cascaded down Shirui. The bloom was thick, the whole mountain appeared carpeted in flowers. It looked, even though it was hot in Ukhrul, as though there was snow on top of Shirui Peak. The peak was the only place in the world where the Shirui lilies grew, and sometimes the men who hunted there brought the flowers back for their wives to wear in their hair. It had never occurred to Augustine that the flowers might only grow on one part of the mountain.

'The lily only flowers on the eastern side of Shirui, never the west,' Luke said. 'The villages that don't have the lily, that cannot see it from their homes, they are not the Goddess's chosen people. The village of Tiya, that is not a friendly village, they are not our people.' Luke's rising passion had inspired in him a coughing fit that contorted his body and sent waves of pain juddering across his face. Augustine sat quietly, holding out the water for him to drink. Luke pushed it away. 'We don't talk to them, or hunt with them, or trade with them. We don't marry them or go to their funerals. My mother—your Ayi—used to tell me "our blood doesn't match".'

The effort of speaking had left Luke bathed in a thin layer of sweat. It beaded on his forehead and his upper lip. Augustine realised suddenly why he was making such an effort; he understood that he was hearing his father's last story. 'Ayi also used to tell me,' Luke continued, his voice little more than a whisper now, 'that it hasn't always been this way. That once, the flowers bloomed on both sides of the mountain, and in the valleys below. Ayi told me that one day, a man will come who will unite the villages. The chosen one, when he comes to bring peace to the Naga, then, the Shirui Lily will bloom all over the mountain and deep into the valleys. One day.'

Luke closed his eyes and his breathing slowed. It was steady now, and peaceful. He needed to rest. Augustine stood up to draw down the blind. 'No,' Luke said from his half-sleep, 'leave it up, I want to see the mountain.' Augustine left his father, the sun streaming onto his face.

❖❖❖

A week later, the monsoon storms arrived. It rained constantly, and the sky was dark and menacing. It was Luke's birthday, his thirty-third, but the anniversary was barely noticed. Two days later, it was time. Luke knew what was happening. He wanted to be brave for his two sons, the proud Naga warrior meeting his destiny unafraid. But his eyes gave it away. They were animated again, Augustine could see, but this time by fear. The family was in the room, standing silently by the bed. No one had told them, but they all somehow knew. Augustine wanted to tell his father that he was not alone, that they were there with him. But he knew it was not true: to die is the ultimate isolation, and Luke's loneliness wreathed across his face.

Luke's bony, riven hand held Liko's smooth one. Augustine rested his palm on his father's forearm, Alex's hand was next to his brother's. On the other side of the bed, Augustine's Ayi sat with Maitonphi, her chubby, blooming grandchild, in painful contrast to her gaunt, decaying son. Gusts of wind pushed an occasional spray of rain onto Luke's face, but he didn't want the window closed or the blind drawn. He gazed at the dark hills outside. Barely above a whisper, Luke had a final song. Ayi sang with him.

Lightning and thunder of the sky
Is my father, my creator
The gloomy dark below
Is my mother, my creator
Today I will proclaim my grief
Lightning—please help me now that I go

◊◊◊

He'd not seen Akala for a week when the text arrived: 'Today afternoon. Our place?'

'OK' Augustine wrote back.

He was early. He had known something was wrong, confirmed when Akala arrived at the grove sobbing. Her eyes were red and her cheeks streaked with tears. 'What is it?' Augustine asked. He feared the worst.

'I am to be married,' she replied. Akala said it in that strange, formal fashion, as if it were something she didn't quite comprehend, as if it were happening to somebody else. This was worse than Augustine had imagined. 'There is a family in Jessami,' Akala continued. 'My parents have been meeting with his parents. They want me to marry their son. They came to visit the day before yesterday. The son is much older than me: he is an old man. My mother says he is very handsome, but I . . .' Akala was bawling now, her words lost between tears. 'They are a high family in their place, and we are just small people from Tiya, so they are demanding an enormous dowry,' she said. Dowries were illegal in India, but still, no wedding ever went ahead without one. It was one of those Indian laws flagrantly disobeyed, acknowledged only in the breach. Dowries crippled poor families and made daughters their father's burden. 'We cannot afford it,' Akala cried, 'and I don't want to marry him, I don't love him. But my father says he will find the money somehow, and my mother says I will learn to love him.'

Augustine held Akala close.

❖ ❖ ❖

'Augustine,' Akala's voice comes ringing through the memory, shaking him from his reverie. They are not at their place in the mahogany grove. They are here, in the deep forest on the floor of the valley, fleeing together from their own people. This is their reality.

'Augustine,' Akala is pointing, asking a question, 'we go straight ahead?' Augustine can see the river curves east here, but a hunter's trail leads straight into the belly of the dark and narrowing valley. This is where they must go. 'Straight ahead,' he says, nodding. 'We have to keep going.'

THEJA

All of Ukhrul, it seemed to Augustine, came to his father's funeral. In their dark colours, they overflowed the aisles and spilled out the doors to the courtyard beyond. Augustine was happy to see them. For all his flaws, his father was loved, Augustine felt assured of that. He sat in the front row between his weeping mother and his solemn little brother. When they played *Abide With Me* he cried, but otherwise, he was dry-eyed. His tears had come on the rainy afternoon his father died.

It was unseasonably sunny on the day of Luke's funeral, but weeks of rain had softened the ground at the cemetery. The hole for his father's thin body was deep and dark. Augustine stood right at the front at the burial service, in front of his mother, her hand on his chest. He couldn't stop looking at the thick, red soil that would cover his father.

The funeral was on a Friday, but all the relatives who came stayed at the house for the weekend. The women talked and wailed and cooked and fussed over Liko. The menfolk sat silent and still during the day, then headed off into the forest 'to hunt' in the evening. They didn't take Augustine along but he knew what they were really doing. He saw the gourds of *zu* and *kui-kok* they carried, affixed to straps slung casually around their shoulders. Their guns they carried for show. He knew they would come back having shot nothing.

The relatives left on Monday and Liko, tired of so many people in her home, pushed Augustine and Alex off to school. They walked reluctantly, and late, down the hill. At the tall iron gate to the school, his first-class teacher, Miss Angela, met them.

'Alex,' she said kindly, 'you can come in, but Augustine, you are too old for Little Angels now. You need to go to Saviour School, further along. You know the place. Mr Meru is the principal; he is expecting you.' Augustine was instantly angry. He prickled with the embarrassment of being told he couldn't go to his own school, and he was furious with the teacher's caprice. Miss Angela had been at his father's funeral, he had seen her there. She was supposed to care about him, but no one had told him anything, not the teachers, not his mother. Why were they kicking him out?

'No,' he spat at Miss Angela. His voice was vicious and venomous.

'Augustine, please.'

'You can't tell me what to do.'

'Augustine, I know this is a difficult time, I am sorry your father passed away. But you are too old for this school now. You must have known that one day you would have to go to the big school.'

'Come on Alex, they don't want us here. Let's go.'

'I think Alex should stay.'

Now Alex was crying, frightened by his brother's temper. Augustine was sometimes withdrawn, but he was never angry. Not like this.

'Fine,' Augustine said, letting go of his little brother's hand. 'Take him. But I'm not going to Saviour.'

Augustine stalked off, back up the hill towards home, not the school. He left Alex standing there, still crying, with Miss Angela, and walked to the bottom of his street. He could see home from here, and he ached to go back there, to find that everything was as it used to be. He wanted to find his father there, still alive, still healthy, still with those eyes that shone, and with another story to tell. He wanted his mother to be relaxing on the front stoop, not harried and weary and carrying things on her head from Burma. His mother hardly ever smiled anymore. She was too busy, too tired.

But Augustine realised it would never be that way again. His father was dead now. He didn't just die, he was dead now. He hated it when people like Miss Angela said 'your father passed away', like it was something that happened, and it was over now. It didn't stop. His father was dead forever.

And his mother, Augustine thought, if she was home, she'd be working, too busy to talk to him, too consumed by plotting her next expedition over the border. She'd be gone again for days, and come home exhausted. She never used to be so thin.

He turned right, away from home, and walked downhill into the trees and the valley below, to the grove where Luke had first taken him to hunt. He sat in the quiet and tried to remember everything about that night his father first took him hunting: the sound of his father's voice, the slow rise and fall of his chest as he lay in wait, his smell, his broad, rough hand on Augustine's shoulder as they walked home. The boy wanted to feel close to his father again. His real father—his old father—not the wasted husk they had buried under the dark, red earth.

◈◈◈

Over dinner Liko asked: 'How was school?'

'Fine,' Augustine answered quickly. He stared at his little brother to ensure his silence. Alex saw the look and cast his eyes downwards. He didn't speak. Liko looked at her boys but said nothing.

The next day, and the next and the next, Augustine and Alex maintained the charade. Augustine would put on his Little Angels uniform each morning and walk with Alex down the hill. Liko would wave goodbye from the stoop. At the school gate, Augustine would turn towards the forest, while Alex would go to class. When the bell rang for the end of the day, Augustine would be waiting for Alex, and they'd walk home together, Augustine asking questions about Alex's day, but never speaking about his own.

Liko let it run for four days. On Friday morning, she sat down next to Augustine in the kitchen.

'I know you haven't—'

'But—'

'Let me finish, Augustine,' Liko said firmly. Too firmly. Augustine shrank back from her gaze.

'I know you haven't been going to school this week. And that's okay. You don't have to go now. But next week, you have to go to Saviour. I know it's hard, but we have to try to make our lives normal again.'

Augustine stared at the dirt of the floor. He wanted the earth to take him too. He didn't want this new world, this new school, this new 'normal'. He didn't want a world without his father in it.

'Augustine?' Liko asked, more kindly now. 'Okay.' He hated to disappoint his mother.

On Monday, Augustine showed up at the gate to Saviour School. Liko had offered to come with him, but he wanted to show her he could do this alone. Saviour wasn't entirely foreign to him. A handful of the older kids from his street were here—they didn't look so grown up now they were all together—and he asked one of them where the principal's office was.

Mr Meru's door was open and he was sitting at a broad wooden desk, surrounded by precarious mountains of cardboard files on all sides, carefully writing a student's report. Augustine could hear his pen scratching on the card in the silence of the office. A clock ticking on the back wall was the only other noise. He knocked quietly against the half-open door.

'Come in,' Mr Meru said without looking up. Augustine walked to the desk, and the principal raised his eyes to look at him. 'Ah, Augustine, I am pleased to see you. We've been expecting you.' He smiled, genuinely, his kind eyes creasing in the corners. Augustine relaxed.

'Let me show you to your classroom,' Mr Meru said, getting up and putting a gentle hand on Augustine's shoulder. 'I know a new school can be difficult, but we are here to make things as easy as they can be.'

◈◈◈

But things were never easy, or normal again, for the Shimrays. Augustine never felt comfortable at Saviour. Arriving part-way through the year, the other kids already had their friendship groups and were loath to upset the delicate dynamics of those. Besides,

Augustine didn't try very hard to make friends. He was quiet in class. Outside, he preferred to keep to himself, sometimes drawing, but mostly just sitting quietly. The playground felt noisy and aggressive to him. He wanted peace. He had Mr Sai's address in Dimapur, and occasionally, if he was particularly proud of a drawing, he would send it to him. Mr Sai would reply, though it usually took weeks, with the original returned attached to a drawing of his own and a note of encouragement. It should have made Augustine feel better, but it only made him miss Dimapur, and his father.

Liko chafed against the strictures of the old small town again. At night, when the younger children were asleep, she talked to Augustine about the shop and the family and life since coming back to Ukhrul. In Dimapur, her business had thrived on the money and aspirations that washed through the bigger city. People there were prepared to pay for new goods, and a premium for things a little exotic, things others didn't have. That was important to people in Dimapur. But the same philosophy hadn't reached Ukhrul. Shoppers here wanted the same things they'd always had, the same things everyone else did. Change wasn't welcome. Liko found herself frustrated by her old customers' intransigence, their demands for the old things at the old prices, and she found herself longing for somewhere larger again.

The family that surrounded her, and that she needed so much in the final months of Luke's life, now felt cloyingly close. Everywhere were reminders of her dead husband, in pictures, in places, in people. 'When Simeon visits, the way he sits on the stool on the front stoop and drinks rice beer out of Luke's old mugs,' she told her son. 'He even laughs like Luke used to.' The walk to the market took Liko past the cemetery, the bright red earth of Luke's grave a constant reminder of what she'd lost. The grass hadn't grown there yet. It stood out, raised and angry, like a swollen scar.

As weeks rolled into months after Luke's death, Liko felt the walls closing in around her in Ukhrul. Home wasn't home, anymore. Home was too small, too close, insufferably so. 'You can never go back,' she said one night. She wasn't talking to Augustine as much as she was herself, staring off into the distance. 'It's never the same. We should go somewhere new.'

A week later, Liko had her somewhere new. 'Sem'—Augustine had seen him in Ukhrul, and still felt vaguely mistrustful of him— 'has asked if we would like to open a new shop with him. We would be partners… in Kohima.' Liko left the key element of her declaration, Kohima, till the very end. It was not phrased as a question, rather a fait accompli. The children weren't being asked whether they'd like to go to Kohima, they were being told they would be.

'Would you still be smuggling?' Augustine asked.

'Both Sem and I have good contacts in Burma. A new shop in Kohima would bring in good money for the family.'

Kohima was the state capital of Nagaland. Augustine knew of it. The city was famous among Naga for the role it played in the Second World War when the Japanese advance was finally repelled by the British-led forces, including thousands of Naga on the frontline, at the brutal battle of Kohima. Augustine's Ayi had told him the story one night when his father was still alive, but lying stupefied in bed. Augustine couldn't remember—how could his memories fade so fast?—whether his father was high or sick at that point. But he remembered the story. The final battle took place on the hill in the middle of Kohima, across the tennis court of the British Deputy Ambassador. The two armies had fought for months from distant hills and trenches with machine guns and mortars; they'd bombed each other in aeroplane raids, scarring the land with thousands of tonnes of TNT. Now, they were locked in deadly embrace at volleying distance, so close they could almost reach out and touch the enemy.

'The tennis court was where the worst of the hand-to-hand fighting took place,' Ayi said. She was a little girl then, and the story, to her, was proof of the bravery and skill of the Naga warriors. All the might and technology of the British Empire couldn't halt the march of the Japanese, but the resolute defiance of the Naga, fighting with bayonets and bare knuckles, stopped their advance in its tracks.

'That was where the war was turned around, on that tennis court, with the net still up. In the morning after the battle, the whole hill was lined with the bodies of the dead and dying. The fighting was the worst of the war. The Naga lost some of their best soldiers, but the Naga did not forfeit their land. They did not give up.' Augustine remembered Luke smiling weakly from bed at his mother, one clenched fist half-raised in triumph. Augustine understood in that instant that the story had been for his father as much as it had been for him. His father needed to be reminded what it was to fight on, Augustine realised.

The Shimrays moved to Kohima in April. Augustine had to change schools again, and he immediately hated St Joseph's. The kids were all bigger than he was, and they were from the city. Kan-chaa they derided him, an insult that literally meant goat-herder, but was used to mean hick. That he was slighter than his classmates gave them even greater licence to bully. The lessons, too, were in Hindi, a language Augustine spoke only clumsily, and could barely read and write at all. He'd watched enough Bollywood films to understand what was going on around him, but he was constantly frustrated by not being understood. The kids and the teachers thought he was stupid, and they laughed at him when he lapsed into Nagamese, or worse, Tangkhul. Augustine began bringing just one book to class—his sketchbook—and he withdrew even further.

Liko and Sem set up their new shop in the suburb of Mohon Kohla, and instantly, were swamped with commissions. They had more work than they could handle and were co-ordinating smuggling trips into Burma every single week. Sometimes one of them would go with a handful porters under their direction. Other times, so great were the orders, they'd both be gone for days. At those times, Augustine looked after his siblings, getting them off to school—Maitonphi had joined first class and he would walk her to her school's front door—but he all but stopped going himself. He'd show up a couple of times a week to have his name marked off on the roll, but then he'd leave. His teacher didn't care. 'You can't teach the villagers anything anyway,' Augustine heard directed at his departing form one morning, 'they're not capable of understanding'.

Outside of school, there was no forest, no hunting. So Augustine spent his days in town, at the main intersection of Kohima, a mad five-ways of autorickshaws and cars, of motorbikes swerving around prone dogs, and the occasional buffalo meandering with bovine insouciance through gaggles of passing schoolchildren. The intersection was ostensibly overseen by a policeman in a white helmet standing on a raised plinth in the middle of the maelstrom. But in reality, the officer just stood there waving his arms and blowing his whistle—red in the face and angry for eight hours at a time—while everyone around ignored him.

There were jury-rigged shops of all description ringing the intersection, and a group of Tangkhul boys hung out there, trying unsuccessfully, in the way of young teenagers, to cultivate an air of menace. After a few days nervously lurking on their periphery, Augustine fell in with the crowd. They were a little older than Augustine, but not by much, and they liked the idea of having a young acolyte at their beck and call. Augustine would fetch chai for them, or ferry messages to the houses of friends nearby. Augustine liked belonging. He felt more at home here than he did at school. And it was okay, Augustine reasoned to himself, none of these boys ever finished school, and they always had money for chai or samosa. Together, they'd sit at the intersection and talk, making jokes and passing judgement on the traffic cop's ineptitude. They complained good-naturedly to the stall owner nearby that his food was terrible, that it wasn't proper Naga fare. That was another thing about Kohima, people ate plainland Indian food here: samosa and parotha that Augustine found heavy, dripping with oil and ghee.

Augustine admired his new friends, they seemed worldly to him, especially their putative leader, Theja. His Christian name was Thomas, but he preferred the Naga appellation. Theja was rakishly tall, but he slouched always, with his shoulders slumped and his hands in his pockets. His hair was a carefully cultivated mess on his head. Most striking, however was the heavy camouflage jacket Theja wore every day with the symbol of the NSCN on the shoulders. It wasn't his, it belonged to his father, but it gave him status amongst the group.

Augustine had absorbed unquestioningly all the rhetoric his father had sermonised about the National Socialist Council of Nagaland, but to him, the NSCN fighters were an 'other' who existed somewhere else, out in the dark green forests beyond the city. That's the way his father had always spoken about them. But in Theja, Augustine felt he'd found someone who was living, not merely talking, revolution. And in Augustine, Theja felt he had a disciple.

In the quiet moments as they hung out at the intersection, or as they sat at one of half a dozen chai shops the group patronised roughly in turn, Theja would take Augustine aside and talk to him alone about politics: 'the revolutionary agenda' he always called it, using a term he'd heard from his own father. Augustine knew the basics of the guerrilla insurgency: the National Socialist Council of Nagaland was fighting the Indian government to re-unite the Naga people who'd been diffused across four Indian state lines and a national border with Burma. 'Some people say there are 10,000 fighters out there in the hills,' Theja said, sweeping his hand towards the distant grey-green hills. 'But I don't think there's that many.'

'How many?' Augustine asked.

'I don't know, but not that many.' Theja drained his chai, and tossed the tiny clay cup onto the pile of its broken predecessors, where it cleaved neatly in two.

'But that's not the important thing. The numbers are not important, it's what the NSCN does. In the east, the Indian government is weak, and the NSCN controls territory, the villages as well as the forests. That's NSCN land. And in those parts, the NSCN is not just an army, it is a parallel government. The NSCN collects taxes and it fixes roads, and runs hospitals. It is forming an education ministry so children can be taught the proper Naga way.'

'But that's not here?' Augustine said, half in statement, half in question. The Indian Army made its superiority abundantly clear in Kohima—troops were stationed everywhere in the town, in the markets and outside government buildings—and outside the city too, manning road checkpoints on the mountain passes between villages.

'No, that's not here, Augustine,' Theja said. 'Here, they have more men, more money, more firepower.'

With two fingers, Theja tapped at the NSCN logo on the sleeve of his jacket. 'But that's why I wear this jacket.'

'Why?' Augustine asked, confused.

'To show them we are coming. To show them I am not afraid.'

Even to his limited understanding of the political nuance, Augustine knew that to wear an NSCN jacket in the middle of Kohima was brazenly defiant. With so many soldiers around, it made Theja a target. But Theja wore the jacket every day.

Theja, too, reminded Augustine of his father. He called everybody 'comrade' and he talked about the inevitability of a united Naga state breaking away from India. 'One day, brothers,' he would declare, loudly enough for passers-by to hear, 'we will be free'. Theja said that his father would soon grant him permission to join the insurgency in the mountains and fight for freedom. He already knew how to shoot, he bragged, pretending to aim a gun at his friends, and he would take aim, he claimed, at the Indian Army soldiers and at the Naga who failed to support the cause.

One morning Theja arrived at the intersection and whispered conspiratorially to the group that he had something to show them. The gang piled into an auto[8] and rode to a house on the outskirts of town. Theja ran inside for a minute while the auto waited, before emerging with what was clearly a rifle wrapped in a blanket. The covering, a dun-coloured sheet, made the weapon all the more conspicuous and suspicious, Augustine reckoned, but he didn't say anything. Kohima wasn't like home, people didn't carry guns here, these city boys who thought they were tough—like the kids in his class who gave him a hard time—they'd never even held a weapon. At home in Ukhrul, Augustine would think nothing of walking down the main street with an open shotgun bent over his shoulder. You couldn't do that in Kohima, especially if you were a young Tangkhul man. Carrying a gun would get you locked up. Or shot.

Theja wouldn't let any of the others hold the weapon. They rode on to the edge of the forest, where they paid the auto driver to wait an hour for their return. Walking into the jungle, they sought a clearing in the scrub where Theja could demonstrate his capabilities. They

---

8   *Auto:* a three-wheeler with a small single cabin, used as a taxi (they are open at the sides). They are the type seen across Asia. Elsewhere, most commonly called a tuk-tuk, but known in India as an auto or an autorickshaw.

chose an old creek bed that had been dry many years, and set up a cairn of rocks at one end, topped with a discarded Coke can as a target.

Theja made a great show of unveiling the weapon. The boys of the gang were suitably impressed by the long shiny barrel and the smooth polished wooden butt, but it was all Augustine could do to suppress a snort of derision. It was an air rifle, pathetically under-powered, the same model with which he'd been taught to shoot as a six-year-old. The weapon would be lucky to kill a robin. It wasn't going to defeat the might of the Indian army.

'My father said I'm the only one who can shoot it,' Theja stated emphatically, as if challenging anyone else to ask for a turn. He took a pellet from his pocket and dropped it into the waiting barrel, then cocked the weapon, pulled the butt into his shoulder and stared with his right eye down the sight. It was quiet in the forest. Click. A rustle in the leaves as the pellet was swallowed by the forest. The unmoved Coke can glinted in the sun.

'Just a bit to the left,' Theja said, dropping another pellet in. 'I'll get it this time.' Click. The can stood defiantly still, unaffected even by the breeze which wound its way down the glade, its scarlet livery standing as a silent mockery of Theja's marksmanship. Theja's face, flushed with embarrassment, turned a similarly vermillion shade.

After his fourth miss, Theja caught sight of Augustine, with the faintest, most fleeting hint of a smile on his lips.

'You hit it then,' he said, thrusting the weapon into Augustine's hands.

'I thought your father said you were the only one who could shoot it,' Augustine replied innocently. He wasn't taunting him. He still looked up to Theja, and he knew his place.

'I don't care about that,' Theja said, emboldened to cover his em-barrassment.

'Okay.'

Augustine took a pellet from Theja, and dropped it into the barrel. He raised the gun to his shoulder and pressed his cheek to the cold metal. He paused for a second, and the world around stood still and silent. He heard his father's words in his ears: 'squeeze the trigger Augustine, don't pull.'

The 'ting' rang loudly in the quiet forest as the coke can crumpled, rocked backwards, and fell. The boys all, save for one, cheered.

Theja grabbed the gun back. 'I'm going to learn to shoot from the NSCN,' he said too loudly. But Augustine knew his status in the group had been elevated, and for good.

◈◈◈

Spurred by Theja, Augustine's political awakening gathered apace on its own. He found a dog-eared old copy of a book called *The Naga Saga*, about the history of his people and their fight for freedom, which he devoured in four days.

'I've barely ever seen you read before,' his mother said, when Augustine carried the book to the dinner table, still engrossed. 'Now you can't put this one down. Is it an assignment for school?' Liko knew he wasn't going to school, and she tried to steer the conversation back to Augustine's interrupted education at every opportunity. He didn't answer.

Augustine began reading Kohima's daily newspapers, the *Nagaland Post* and the *Morung Express*, which carried densely written accounts, of varying reliability, of the state of the conflict. In recent months there had been a schism in the NSCN, and the papers wrote endlessly of the 'great split' in the insurgent movement and what it might mean. They claimed the organisation had ruptured over peace negotiations with the Government of India. Some of the leaders advocated a political solution, arguing the only way a Naga homeland could be achieved was through negotiation. 'The Indian Army is a million men strong,' they would say. It couldn't be beaten. The hardliners wanted to fight on anyway. 'Nothing more, nothing less, sovereignty,' was their chant. Every day there was a new incremental development in the saga.

'The papers are all wrong,' Theja said, finding Augustine at the intersection one morning, reading the *Post*. 'Do you want to know the real reason for the split?'

Theja didn't wait for Augustine's response. 'Clan rivalry,' he said. 'It is a power struggle between the Konyak and the Tangkhul tribes over who will lead the organisation.'

Theja explained the NSCN was now, in effect, two armies: the NSCN-K, led by a Hemi Naga from Burma called Khaplang, and the NSCN-IM, led by two men, Isak Chishi Swu and Thungaleng Muivah. Muivah was a Tangkhul so Theja—and, by association Augustine understood, he and the others—supported IM. Augustine and Theja sat together in a narrow strip of shade at the edge of the intersection, the rumble of morning traffic steadily building. 'Lately,' Theja said, 'all of the fighting has been between these wings of the NSCN, rather than against India'.

As if to prove Theja's forecast, that summer, Nagaland's fraternal feud grew suddenly and brutally violent. Villages were burned to the ground and bombs set off in markets, the papers reported, while men suspected of sympathising with the rival wing were kidnapped, tortured, and killed. The internecine violence carried a bitter savagery. It was July. The heat rose out of the hard-baked earth and cast a shimmer of ill-temper across the land. The rains would come soon. That might stop the fighting. Perhaps for a little while.

◈◈◈

For the briefest second everything was perfectly quiet. Even the dust filling the air seemed to be falling silently. Then, with a painful rush, sound came screaming back. Over the ringing in his ears, Augustine heard the alarms and the shrieking. The policeman was blowing his whistle even more forcefully now. That whistle, that whistle, it crowded everything else out. He felt himself being pulled up roughly under the arms.

'Are you okay?' a man's voice was shouting at him. The noise sounded far away. Augustine nodded. The man was very strong. He tried to get Augustine to stand, but Augustine's legs crumpled beneath him and he slumped back to the ground. The man lifted him bodily again and carried him across the street. A woman ran beside them, pushing Augustine's hair from his face. Augustine figured he was dying, such was the woman's hysteria. But dying was okay; he was sleepy now anyway. He wished the man would put him down; he was jostling him and it hurt, but he was too tired and his arms were too heavy to protest.

The man slung Augustine down on the front step of a shop in the shade and barked at the shop owner to fetch some water. From a plastic cup, he washed the dust and the blood from Augustine's face. Augustine was suddenly terribly thirsty. The strong man and the shopkeeper stared into his eyes. The woman was still in hysterics nearby. She was speaking on a phone.

'I want to lie down,' Augustine said, his first words since the explosion. 'Sir, I will die just here if that's okay.' He felt the need to speak respectfully to the older man.

'You're not dying,' the strong one who had carried him said, smiling. 'You will be okay. You have a cut on your forehead, and there is some small-small shrapnel in your back, but you're not going to die,' he said.

'I think you were facing away from the bomb,' the shopkeeper said. 'I think that saved you.'

Augustine was suddenly alert. Theja.

'Are my friends okay?'

'The one in the jacket,' the shopkeeper said, 'the insurgent. I think he was the target. I think he is dead. Some of the others are badly injured too. But don't worry about that now. You will be okay. What is your name?'

'Augustine.'

'Augustine. A nice name.'

'Do you have a family we should call?'

Augustine was worried about telling his mother, but he knew that something like this she would find out anyway.

'My mother. Likoknaro Shim—'

'I have spoken to your mother, Augustine,' the woman cut in, her voice suddenly calmer. 'I know your mother from the shop. I am Bhanu.' Augustine didn't recognise her.

'She is coming to fetch you. She will take you to hospital.'

It felt to Augustine like seconds until Liko was there. She grabbed him. Between sobs of relief, and thanking the men and Bhanu for caring for him, Liko was furious. She knew Augustine had been cutting school, but she hadn't known he'd been hanging around with insurgents who wore their revolutionary uniforms in the city. 'How could you be so stupid?' she said, as she piled him into an autorickshaw. The driver saw Augustine's condition and demanded more money for all the blood Augustine would spill on his seats. Liko venomously spat back: 'You should be ashamed. How dare you try to extort my family. We have been attacked.' The driver reluctantly agreed to the standard fare, but he took no extra care on the pot-holed road. The jostling stung Augustine's back. Every part of him was starting to hurt now, and he could feel the blood that caked his shirt. 'Your father,' Liko muttered, looking out at the hills. 'From beyond the grave he is still tearing this family apart.' Suddenly, Liko was bawling, and she held Augustine tight, holding his face next to hers. 'I'm sorry, Augustine, I'm sorry for everything. I thought I'd lost you.' Augustine recognised the tone in his mother's voice: the anger overwhelmed by despair, the sense of utter helplessness. He'd last heard Liko speak like this five years earlier, when he'd tried to ride his bicycle across India to Bombay as a ten-year-old. He remembered now his mother's rush of tears when she rescued him from Assam.

'I thought I'd lost you,' Liko kept saying, over and over again.

Augustine spent the night in hospital, and had to sleep lying on his chest. The doctors had spent two hours pulling pieces of metal—'they look like ball bearings'—from his back. Liko stayed by Augustine's bedside, along with Alex and Maitonphi. They all slept on a mat on the floor. It was crowded in the general ward. There were dozens of patients' families doing the same thing.

Early in the morning, the doctor brought Augustine a newspaper. It had a picture of the aftermath of the bomb blast on the front page. In the foreground was the policeman, face contorted from blowing his whistle. Behind him was Theja. His body was under a blue tarpaulin, but his left arm, in the distinctive camouflage of his NSCN jacket, lolled out on the road. The paper said he was targeted as a payback for something his father had done, an attack he'd ordered on a Kuki village, or something like that: the paper didn't seem to really know, it was quoting 'a source'. Theja was the only fatality. There were some other injuries; one of the other boys had lost an eye, and another had burns to his arm and back. Augustine wasn't mentioned at all. Police said the bomb, wrapped in a shopping bag, was apparently placed behind the boys, by someone walking on the footpath. No one noticed it amongst the rows of motorbikes and the rubbish. It was on a short timer. Time enough for the bomber to get away, but short enough to ensure Theja was still in the same spot.

'Augustine,' Liko whispered, sitting on the side of the bed. The younger children were still asleep on the floor. 'I want you to be safe. I think we should move back to Dimapur.' She had tears in her eyes. Augustine nodded.

◇◇◇

Augustine and Akala have been running a full day now. They've not stopped nor eaten, but still they stagger on, breaths coming in ragged gasps. The forest is thick and unforgiving. Augustine has cut his left hand on a vine. In an attempt to dull the pain, he tore a sleeve from his shirt and wrapped it around his hand, but still sweat runs into the wound and it stings. They are low in the valley; the sun disappeared hours ago and the black of night is closing in all around, depthless and cold.

They've crested a gentle rise to a small clearing, away from the valley floor and the river bed. It is too damp by the water. Here it is drier and the dead trees around offer fuel for a fire. They are a long way from any village and no one comes to this part of the forest. They keep the flames low and the smoke will be too hard to see in the dark. Besides, it is growing cold, and they need to eat.

Augustine drags a knot of dry branches to the middle of the clearing and begins stripping them of their twigs. He is careful of his cut hand. It aches now, and he is sure he can feel the beginnings of infection. He needs it to be okay for only a little longer. He stacks the wood for a fire, then takes some dry leaves from the edge of the clearing and shoves them underneath the kindling. Taking matches from his pocket, he tries to light one. There is no wind, but the matches are damp from sitting against his sweating thigh all day. The first three break without even sparking, the fourth flames out in an instant. He looks into the box. Four matches left.

The next one takes. He lights one leaf, then another on the other side. Soon the twigs above are alight and the fire takes hold. The glow from the flames dances across Akala's face and lights up her dark, liquid eyes. The smoke rises straight up, and Augustine watches Akala from across the fire. She stares into the blaze, then looks up and smiles. They are both too tired to speak.

Augustine has the mug he has kept bound inside the shawl slung over his shoulders which he has carried, along with the square cloth filled with rice, all this way. Now, he walks down to the river in the darkness and fills the cup with water. Back at the fire he uses two stones and half a dozen short sticks to make a small platform over the flame on which he stands the water-filled mug. Then he shakes a handful of rice from the cloth and pours the grains into the water. He sits back in silence, now, next to Akala, as they wait for it to boil.

'I saw some *yongbah* further down,' he says, as the rice swells. 'You like?' Akala nods wearily.

'I won't be long.' He rises and walks back down the path they'd come, holding the *dao* in his uninjured right hand, returning a few minutes later with a dozen stalks of the violet flower. When the rice is ready, he strips the *yongbah* flowers from their stalks, and crushes the small wheaty husks in his hand, sprinkling them over dinner. It is not much flavour—Augustine longs for meat—but it is something. He pulls the mug from over the fire, and rests it on the ground. They eat straight from it with their fingers. They share their first meal together and feel better.

THE SOLDIER WITH
THE SHINY GUN

The move back to Dimapur felt like a return to a world Augustine knew intimately, a place where he belonged and where he was safe, away from the violence and the scheming plots of revenge. He wanted no more part of it; he was not seeking trouble and he was sure it could not find him here.

The family settled back into Dimapur easily. His mother re-established a share in what was now Honlei's shop—she had married her blacksmith fiancé during the Shimrays' time away—and Augustine worked there as an extra hand, in addition to running the household in his mother's absences. He even flirted with the idea of going back to school. He'd not gone so far as to actually turn up at the gate, but he'd been to see his former teacher, Mr Sai, and the pair had recommenced their ad hoc art lessons in the quiet back room at the old man's house. In his oblique way, Mr Sai had proposed, and nurtured, the idea of Augustine's return to classes. 'You have a maturing mind, Augustine, ripe for education,' he said as the pair sat one weekend morning, sketching. Augustine stayed quiet.

'The Class X (Class 10) exams are at the end of the year,' Mr Sai continued. 'You should sit them. You have the potential to do well.'

Augustine knew Mr Sai was genuine, but he suspected his mother's hand in these entreaties too. She was anxious for Augustine to sit the All India Secondary School Examination, the nation-wide 'Class X' test that was the sole determinant of whether or not a student was permitted to continue their education to higher secondary. Augustine wasn't resentful of his mother's, or Mr Sai's, efforts to get him back to school. He knew they meant well, and he seriously considered re-enrolling, but every time, he found—or was able to find—an obligation with the shop or with the smaller children that held him back.

❖❖❖

On the morning of Boxing Day 1996, Mr Sai turned up unannounced at the Shimrays' home, clutching a newspaper under his arm. It was only a short walk from his home, but Mr Sai was out of breath, a thin sheen of sweat across his brow.

'Merry Christmas,' Augustine said, standing in greeting.

'No, it is not,' Mr Sai replied brusquely, beginning to speak even before his pupil had a chance to offer him water and a chair on the narrow front porch.

'Augustine,' Mr Sai said, 'we need to get you back into school.'

'Why?' Augustine said.

'This,' Mr Sai replied, thrusting the paper at Augustine.

The front page of the *Morung Express* carried a massive picture of a bus, torn apart by a bomb, and lying burning in the road. Even in the grainy photograph Augustine could see the bodies of those killed, blackened and twisted in horrible contortions. Augustine scanned the article. The bus that was blown up was carrying the family of a government minister called Niheto. Augustine knew his name. Niheto was from the Sema tribe and he was aligned with the Tangkhuls of the NSCN-IM, though not firmly enough, it seemed. Niheto's sin, the article said, was being too moderate. He had preached conciliation with rival Naga groups and co-operation with the Government of India. To the hardliners, he was a sell-out to the cause, a lapdog of the hated Delhi regime. So, they had come for him.

The newspaper article was full of graphic, lurid detail. The bus was heading home from the Christmas morning church service, carrying Niheto's extended family. The minister had remained at church to speak with some tribal and church elders, but his grand-children were anxious to get home to open presents, and so the rest of the family had gone ahead. The bus had rounded a corner at Arai Mile and begun a slow winding ascent up the hill.

The bomb was buried under clay where a section of the bitumen road was missing. The insurgents, the paper said, had known the bus would come this way, and would be heavy enough to trigger the explosion. A piece of missing tarmac was unexceptional here, long-neglected roads were regularly washed away by rain or the slipping of the mountainside. Makeshift repairs were commonplace. The driver of the bus had not noticed there were no tyre tracks on the clay.

'The explosion rang out through the valley,' the newspaper reported with typical breathlessness. But it was ten minutes before anyone could reach the scene. The bus was burning, and those still alive were screaming. The local villagers left the dead and ran between the passengers they thought they could save, pouring water on their blackened skin and pressing on the broken bones that protruded from their limbs. Mostly, it was in vain. Niheto's wife, daughter, and grandchildren died there on the side of the road. Eleven more people would die too. They would die where they lay, screaming in agony, or they would die later in hospital, as they bled out or infection took hold.

The NSCN-IM, opposed to Niheto's conciliatory approach, had planted the bomb. Niheto had been the target, but his decision not to take the bus had saved his life. He wasn't killed, but perhaps better, he'd been made to suffer.

'I don't understand,' Augustine said, looking up from the newspaper at his teacher. 'What has this got to do with me?'

'Augustine, please,' Mr Sai said, 'this is serious'.

'I am serious. I don't know what this has to do with me.'

'There will be retribution for this attack, Augustine—something in return. This will be the start of a civil war amongst the Naga, where everyone is a target, where everyone has a side. You have a side.'

'Me? But I'm no one.'

140

'No one, really?' Mr Sai said. For the first time, Augustine could hear the concern in his voice laced with anger. 'So why did a bomb go off near your feet?' The old man removed his glasses and looked Augustine in the eye. 'It is a bad time to be a young man of fighting age,' he said.

Augustine was quiet. He looked back at the newspaper, at the horrific picture on the front page. The bodies. The bodies, like Theja's, lying desolate and disfigured in the street.

Mr Sai spoke quietly now. 'If you're back in school, you're safe. That's where you must be.' Mr Sai rose. 'I have to go.' He left his pupil holding the newspaper.

Augustine didn't get up straight away. He understood now: the attack that killed Theja, the bomb that had wiped out Niheto's family, these didn't happen in isolation. They were parts of the same whole. Augustine had been amazed when he had gone back to the intersection where Theja had died, to find it unchanged. In a single day, the acrid smell of the smoke had cleared and the blood had been scrubbed clean. The traffic had resumed its ceaseless, uncaring cacophony. Augustine had stood there watching as the intersection thrummed just as it always had, and the brutality it had witnessed became an unspoken history, another horrible milestone on the continuum of violence. Theja's death didn't start anything, and it finished nothing. The attack on Niheto's family would be the same. All of it, every brutal, callous attack, was just another act of ever-escalating retribution. A bomb explodes, a woman is raped, a village is razed. All of it justified as payback for the crime before, born of the one before that. Augustine had hoped that Theja's death would be the cessation of the violence, that afterwards, things would get better. Instead, he could see now, they would only get worse.

Niheto's moderation died with his family. He buried his wife, his daughter and grandchildren on the same day, New Year's Eve. And on New Year's Day he vowed revenge. He would exact it, he said, if it was the last thing he did on this earth. Overnight, there was no one who could be trusted. Both the NSCN-IM and the NSCN-K had squads of gunmen who ranged between villages or roamed the streets of cities at night, targeting their ever-widening circles of political opponents. The government imposed a curfew, willingly adhered to by a frightened populace, but ignored by those it was supposed to keep off the streets. Under the cover of darkness, with the land to themselves, the thugs went about their work. A cowed police force allowed them to strike with impunity.

Niheto had connections and the IM members who might—this was no time for legitimate investigations—have been connected with his family's death were rounded up. People began to disappear from their homes. Sometimes they turned up again, alive, just. Their bodies were bruised and scarred. They wouldn't talk about where they'd been or what had happened. Invariably they would move, with their families, far away, lost to whichever cause they'd supported. Most of the time, though, people were never seen again, or their corpses were discovered deep in the forest, friends tipped off as to where they could be found. The bodies were bound and bloodied. The fear spread from house to house and village to village, a plague running ahead of the violence that was surely to follow. Nagaland descended into civil war.

Mr Sai's warning rang in Augustine's ears. He could see himself now from the perspective of others. He was 15, Mr Sai was right, a young man of fighting age. He knew he wasn't an insurgent, but that's not how it appeared from outside. It was known that he was in the square in Kohima when Theja died. And that was connection enough. Augustine resolved to go back to school when the new term began.

It was not soon enough. They came for him first. It was early March, evening, and Augustine was at home cooking. His mother was out, he didn't know where, but responsibility for dinner had again fallen, undirected, to him. It was dark outside, and the curfew imposed across Dimapur gave the streets a menacing quiet. As Augustine stood at the kitchen bench chopping onions, he stared absent-mindedly out of the window at the unmoving street. It felt later than 8 p.m. In the darkness outside, a momentary glint of light caught his eye. He looked closer. There it was again, and he saw now what it was: a streetlight shining on the polished chrome magazine of an AK-47. Some boastful insurgent had wanted to make his weapon stand out and he'd found a mechanic who'd indulged him. Augustine watched carefully. He could see indistinct shapes moving in the darkness. Suddenly, the soldier with the shiny gun stepped forward. He'd come into the light now to read a piece of paper. He looked up, straight at the house from where Augustine was watching and nodded. Then he stepped back into the obscurity of the night.

Augustine froze. But the banging on the door that came seconds later shocked him into moving. He slipped soundlessly to the door that led to the main living room. The Shimrays' new house in Dimapur was bigger than their last one. It was a standalone building, the last in a long line of squat bungalows. But unusually, this house had a pitched roof and, Augustine knew, a small space between the ceiling and the roof. Liko had asked Augustine to store smuggled goods for the shop up there before, so he knew there was room enough for a person to hide.

His first instinct was to run into the living room to fetch his brother and sister who were seated on the couch watching TV. But just as Augustine put his hand on the door handle, he realised he risked being seen down the corridor if he stepped into the front of the house. He knew it was him the gunmen were after. The children they would leave unharmed. Augustine willed himself to believe that was true. Surely, he prayed, they would not be touched. And if he was caught, they were all in trouble. Augustine took his hand from the door and turned left into the bedroom he shared with his brother.

Standing on his bed, Augustine pushed the manhole cover to one side, and pulled himself into the void, carefully replacing the cover. The soldiers were banging again on the front door, even more insistent now. 'Open up,' a harsh voice yelled. Augustine crawled quietly along the wooden beams towards the front of the house where a crack in the ceiling afforded him a view of the kitchen— he'd left the stove on—and the living room where Alex and Maitonphi sat.

Alex had heard the banging but he was too scared to react. *Sit quietly*, Augustine thought, silently urging his little brother to be still. 'Don't move.' The TV was loud though. The soldiers must

143

know somebody was home. Suddenly, the sound of wood splintering shocked Alex into standing. The soldiers had kicked the door in and they were marching down the hall, yelling as they went. Augustine watched their leader. He walked with a soldier's confidence and a hoodlum's aggression. His jackbooted feet fell heavily on the wooden floor, and the sound reverberated down the narrow corridor. He strode quickly, unafraid, it seemed, of what might be waiting for him, his weapon already drawn. The man marched into the living room to discover the two small children. Maitonphi screamed and started crying, gripping the sleeve of Alex's shirt with both hands. Alex stood, transfixed. The cartoon they'd been watching blared on, its inanity adding to the sense of horror. Augustine watched from above, and held his breath.

'Where is he?' the soldier demanded, pointing his weapon at the head of thirteen-year-old Alex. Augustine's brother had one hand gripping the leg of his pyjama pants, whilst to his other arm clung his bawling sister. The gunman's comrades had fanned out through the house; they were in the kitchen, and now the boys' bedroom, searching for Augustine. Augustine watched from above as they kicked at the closed doors and turned over furniture. 'Where is he?' The soldier standing in front of Alex was yelling now. 'Tell me!'

'Who?' Alex asked the innocent question. He was genuinely confused. The soldier stared, then, without warning, turned his gun and fired three shots into the television.

The TV was instantly quiet, and the noise of the weapon terrified Maitonphi into silence too. A trickle of urine ran down the leg of her pyjama bottoms, forming a puddle on the floor at her feet. The soldier didn't notice, or didn't care.

'Where is your brother?' the soldier menaced, his voice quieter now, but almost growling with hostility.

'I don't know,' Alex said, his finger still in his mouth. 'He was cooking dinner.'

'Where is your father?' the soldier said. He seemed not to have been briefed fully on this raid.

'My father is dead... sir.' Alex stumbled, pausing before he remembered to add the honorific. How did this man know to look

144

for his brother if he didn't know his father was dead? The soldier took another step forward. The muzzle of the gun was barely ten centimetres from Alex's face. The boy couldn't take his eyes from the weapon he was sure was about to kill him. 'One last chance, boy,' the soldier said: 'where is your brother?' Alex stood perfectly still, he didn't have an answer.

The soldier with the shiny gun walked into the living room. He'd stood guard out the front. It was time to leave. 'He's not here, let's go,' he said, ignoring the two children who still hadn't moved. 'I said, let's go!' he barked again, this time addressing the soldier with his weapon drawn, its barrel still in Alex's face. The soldier turned without speaking and walked out of the house. They left the broken front door hanging on its hinges. The cold night air rushed in.

Augustine forced himself to take five deep breaths before he crept back towards the manhole cover, removed it and swung himself down into the light of the house. Maitonphi had started crying again as Alex continued to hold her. Augustine walked in holding his index finger to his lips, a silent instruction to his siblings they still needed to be quiet. He took Alex's hand, Maitonphi gripped Alex's arm, and the three Shimray children slipped quietly out the back door and down a narrow alleyway. Four houses down was the home of a distant cousin; they would be safe there. Augustine shepherded his siblings inside, explaining in a low whisper to Pfukolie what had happened.

'You must stay here tonight,' his cousin insisted.

'Thank you, and I am sorry to do this, to involve you,' Augustine said.

'It is not your fault, it is the fault of these men. It is the fault of all Naga that we fight like this.'

'I'll be back soon.' Augustine slipped out into the night without further explanation. He stole back home to turn off the stove. Just as he left the house to return to Pfukolie's, he heard a single shot ring out, clear across the valley and the quiet neighbourhood. He wondered if it was the same men.

✧✧✧

Pfukolie brought the news when he returned from the market in the morning. 'Augustine, I'm sorry,' he said, 'your teacher, the friend who taught you drawing, Mr Sai: they shot him last night. They killed him.'

Augustine knew instantly it was the same men. It could not be any other. Pfukolie kept talking. The day was barely a few hours old; Mr Sai was not yet buried, but the market already had the full story, in all its brutal detail.

'The soldier, the one with the shiny gun,' Pfukolie began 'he had walked in first, straight into the house where Mr Sai and his family were having dinner. "You," he said, pointing at Mr Sai, seated at the head of the table, "you are a teacher. Of Tangkhul boys".

'"I teach all students," Mr Sai replied. He spoke calmly to the soldier. He took his glasses off and placed them on the table. "Tangkhul, Konyak, Ao, all of them. I know you; I taught your brother. We are all Naga, are we not?" He spoke as though he had nothing to fear from these men.

'Without warning, the soldier lifted his weapon and pulled the trigger. A single shot, between the eyes. Mr Sai slumped into his food. The rest of his family sat in terrified silence. The soldier turned and walked out the door as the wailing started.'

Pfukolie kept talking, more gruesome detail, but Augustine did not hear another word. Mr Sai had died because Augustine had lived. Mr Sai hadn't run from the insurgents, he hadn't watched them from a hiding place while they terrorised his family. He chose to stare them down, and to speak truth to their faces. And he had died for it. Augustine cried. He cried as he had the rainy day his father had died. In his mind's eye, he kept seeing Mr Sai calmly talking to those irrational, hot-headed soldiers, and he kept seeing the jagged red scar of the earth of his father's grave in the rain in Ukhrul.

Augustine couldn't sleep that night. So, he drew. He took the pencils Mr Sai had given him and a piece of the butcher's paper his mother used at the shop to wrap sweets for customers, and he sat at the small table in his cousin's living room. He drew Mr Sai: he could never draw portraits well, but this time, his teacher's likeness emerged perfectly. The picture Augustine drew was of Mr Sai, himself drawing, seated at an easel. But in Augustine's picture, Mr Sai had turned to gaze out of the page, looking over his glasses, his eyes staring into Augustine's. Below, Augustine wrote a poem he'd known for a long time, but hadn't thought about for years. He couldn't remember now who'd taught it to him—his father or Mr Sai. It didn't matter.

The moon must die, each month it falls,
To be born again in the sky.
But man, when he dies, to the dust he returns,
To the moon, he must say goodbye.

The richest man in the world cannot buy
The moon's life, endless and free.
The most beautiful girl in the village must sleep,
And her breath must return to the breeze.

Augustine worked every day on the portrait of his teacher. He intended to take it around to Mr Sai's house, to offer it to his family, a posthumous thank you to his teacher. Would they want to see him? Was he drawing out of guilt? Out of an impossible desire to bring his teacher back?

The Shimrays stayed at Pfukolie's house a week and a half. They had the door fixed at home. The soldiers never came back and Liko felt it was safe to return. Back at home, Augustine continued to draw. It kept his mind occupied, off thoughts of Mr Sai at his dinner table, and from remembrances of the dark red earth of Ukhrul.

'Augustine,' Liko said one night, interrupting his sketching. He looked up. Her face was tired with worry. 'Augustine, we need to get you back in school. You will be safe there. You must sit the Class X.'

'I'm too old, Ma,' Augustine said, 'I've missed my chance. Concentrate on Alex. Make sure he does his homework.' Augustine was resigned to never going back to school.

'I will find a way,' Liko said cryptically, offering her son no more detail.

Augustine went back to his drawing. He finished his picture of Mr Sai late that night, but he never took it around to his family.

The fire has waned; Augustine keeps it alight, but low. Akala is more awake now she has eaten. 'I am from Tiya,' she says. 'A girl from Tiya should not be out camping with a boy from Ukhrul.' She laughs. Their problems are far beyond that now.

'It's because of Phangrei Plateau,' Augustine says, 'my people and yours, we fight over that. And it's because of the Goddess of Shirui Peak.'

Akala reels, as if in disbelief: 'you believe in the Goddess too?'

'Of course,' he says, 'she is our Goddess, she protects our village'. Augustine relays the story his father told him all those years ago. He can hear Luke's voice in his own: 'The Goddess of Shirui Peak keeps the people of Ukhrul safe. And she protects the neighbours who are friends.'

In return for her protection, Augustine says, the Goddess will occasionally dissemble to take the form of a beautiful woman, and she will seduce one young, handsome village man to take with her to be her lover. This is the exchange, the price our villages are happy to pay for her care.

'She makes the rains come, and the rivers run, and the sun shine. We know we are the Goddess's people because the white Shirui Lily grows on our side of the mountain. The lily grows only for the Goddess's people. It blooms for no one else.'

'You know the story they tell in Tiya?' Akala asks archly.

'The lily belonged to Tiya,' she says, not waiting for a reply. 'The white lily used to grow on the western side of the mountain too, before it was stolen, stolen by a vain man from Ukhrul.'

In the dark, Augustine shakes his head: 'no'.

'Yes,' Akala says, staring across the fire.

'The lily once grew all over Shirui Peak,' Akala says firmly, as if stating an unimpeachable fact. 'Until a man from Ukhrul stole Tiya's flowers.'

Akala speaks plainly: the man from Ukhrul was called Jae, she says, and many years ago he was to be married in the summertime, after the spring harvest, and he wanted to have the grandest wedding the village had known. 'He wanted to show his fiancée how much he loved her, so he wanted to pick one thousand lilies to line the path from their wedding ceremony to their new home together. But more than that, he wanted the flowers to satisfy his own pride so his wedding would be remembered as the most extravagant. But Jae also knew that if he picked all the lilies from Shirui Peak, it would anger the Goddess. She allows a few flowers to be taken for women to wear in their hair, or to decorate homes, but the lily cannot be harvested like a rice crop.'

'Jae was cunning as well as vain,' Akala continues darkly. 'One night, when there was no moon, he walked from Ukhrul to the far side of the mountain, to the Tiya side, and he plucked every single flower he found there. The Goddess was asleep, so she didn't see him do it, but when she awoke in the morning she was furious. She saw the flowers missing from the Tiya side, and she believed we had been disrespectful, so she punished the people of Tiya by never allowing the lily to grow there again.'

Akala has her shawl wrapped around her shoulders, and she stares into the belly of the blaze as she speaks, gazing intently, but as though unseeing, through the flames.

'Every year, a group of men from our village go to the mountaintop to offer gifts to the Goddess to apologise. One day, the lily will grow again on our side.'

Augustine has never heard that story, not from his father nor his grandmother. But he knows, instinctively, why he has not. The Tiya are the 'other' to the minds of his people. This version of the legend requires understanding, requires compassion—something the villagers of Ukhrul are not prepared to offer an enemy.

'Perhaps when the flower comes back, maybe then our people will stop warring,' Augustine says.

'Perhaps.'

The couple speak no more, each lost in their own contemplations. The fire crackles in the night.

'It's not too late, you know,' Augustine says finally.

'What do you mean?'

'You can go back,' He is not talking about the Shirui Lily anymore. He is talking about them, in the jungle, far from home and heading further away.

'But I don't want to go back.' Akala is insistent.

'But you can. I would understand. Tell them I forced you to come, and that you escaped. They would believe you.'

'My father saw the messages.'

149

'Tell them I sent them to you. Tell them that you tried to stop me.'

'No. No more lies.'

The flames burn a little lower now, but neither makes a move to stoke them. They will lie down next to the fire and let it burn down as they sleep.

'Whatever happens,' Akala says, 'I want to stay with you.'

ZAKI

By rights, Augustine was due to sit the Class X exam that year. Born in 1982, he would be sixteen at the end of the year, the final age for eligibility. The Class X exam was the singular goal of the Indian education system, the culmination of ten years of schooling, and all that teachers focused upon. That single paper, that lone result, was the gateway to further education. Students who did well could continue on to upper secondary schooling and university, perhaps a job in the bureaucracy, a life, by any measure, of comparative wealth and security—a life of 'success'. But if you failed the Class X exam, your education stopped stone dead the instant you walked out of that room, and with it, went those chances.

Augustine was too late to sit the Class X exam. He couldn't enrol now because the paper was in a few weeks, and his Hindi reading and writing was woefully inadequate. Much of the exam was in India's de facto 'national' language, and he would barely understand the questions. Ambitious parents often sent their kids to sit the Class X exam a year or two early, almost as practice runs, because you couldn't sit the test late. No exceptions. Once you'd had your sixteenth birthday, the test was gone. Augustine's final chance was about to disappear.

Besides, the Class X exam came with enormous pressure and months of preparation. Parents had been harrying their children for two years in exam preparations, borrowing huge sums to pay for tutors and practice papers, paying even more for stolen copies of the paper ahead of time. There was an air of foreboding that came with Class X; its name was almost whispered among parents. Mothers went on long fasts in the hope of appeasing the Gods, praying for a good result. Those three hours would determine the rest of your life.

Augustine had resigned himself to its passing him by. But Liko had a plan, and already it was in motion. She came home from the shop one evening bearing a pale yellow envelope that she handed to her son: 'Your new papers'. Augustine pulled a handful of forms from it. They were identity documents, all complete, signed and stamped with official-looking seals. And it was him. All the details were correct: his name, his father's and mother's names, everything was right. Except his birthdate: 24 June, 1985. Three years to the day. Three years had just been erased from Augustine's existence. He now had another three years to finish school. 'We don't have to wait three years,' Liko said. 'This year we are too late. But the exam we can pass next year. These papers give you more chances.'

Augustine's mother had clearly paid a huge sum of money, at serious risk, to give him this chance. Now he had to sit the exams, and he had to do well. For all the inherent pressure of the Class X, this was more expectation again.

'I'm never going to catch up. I won't pass. I've missed too many years.'

'I have that organised as well,' Liko said. 'When the exam comes around, you will not go to Kohima to sit it. I have arranged for some-one else to sit it for you.'

'Who?'

'That doesn't matter.'

'It's my exam. Who is it?'

'Nido.'

'From next door?' Nido didn't actually live next door anymore. He had a scholarship, boarding at the famous Sainik School down in Imphal, in the plainlands, though his parents were still in the same house. They were nearby still, though the Shimrays, with their departure and return, were no longer immediate neighbours.

'Yes, Augustine,' his mother said. 'He was a topper on the Class X last year, and he has agreed to sit it again next year. As you. I have worked it out.'

'Is that allowed?' Augustine didn't know why he was asking the dumb question. He knew the answer. Arrangements like these were so common as to be unremarkable, everyone knew they happened, but this didn't mean they were legal.

Liko was exasperated now. 'Augustine, I have worked it out. But you must attend school next year. Otherwise the plan will not work.'

Money had obviously changed hands here as well, some to the student, and more, probably, to a mid-level *babu* somewhere in the arcane corridors of the education department. He would ensure Nido could sit the exam in Augustine's place.

'Okay, I'll go.'

◈ ◈ ◈

Without the impending pressure of the exam next year, Augustine found himself looking forward to going back to school. With the plan settled, his mother was happy enough to reveal how she had engineered his re-birth as a younger student. 'Sem found a way,' she said. Through his byzantine networks, Sem had found a man who could get new identity papers. They were not cheap; there were several, substantial, payoffs required along the way, but these papers were legitimate, they weren't rough copies or even good forgeries. Sem had a man inside who could put you in the system.

Augustine went back to school in the new term. His mother, keen to encourage him to stay and to study, bought him new shoes and books and a schoolbag. It made Augustine feel small again, a sense exacerbated by the fact he was among classmates younger than he. But he soon settled into the routine of school, and the age gap was forgotten. He found schoolwork easier now; he was good at maths and science and English, and the best in his class at art, but his Hindi reading and writing remained weak.

Winter passed into summer and back into winter again. Augustine was still at school, preparing for the exam he would not sit. The memory of Mr Sai still caught Augustine at unexpected times: as he sat in class, or knelt quietly in church, the drone-like familiarity of the service taking him back to the painful near-past. Despite the assurances of his own family and Mr Sai's that he was not, he felt responsible for what had happened. Mr Sai had died because he had lived. No assurance from anybody could change that fact. That wound was raw still, but he felt, at least, by going back to school, he was paying tribute to his teacher's memory in some small, quiet way. The remembrances of Theja, and of the insurgency, were faded far further. One thing had led to the other; Augustine understood that. But one memory he wanted to honour, one he wanted to forget.

Without warning, Augustine had a new sister. Of sorts. The previous May, Augustine's mother's youngest sister, Rhutaruh, had given birth to a baby girl, in noisy good health, at the family home in Ukhrul. Zakiezhuu was a strong child, lean and long, and with the broad features that cast her as unmistakably Naga. She was beautiful, everybody said so, and they called her Zaki. Zaki's father was an Ukhrul man, a hunter and a farmer named Khietso. He was from a good family, a family that in previous generations had provided chiefs for the village and, all were sure, had designs on similar prestige again.

But Zaki's birth was not one celebrated. There was no feast, no thanks offered to the Gods to mark her arrival. The baby was kept secret from those outside the home, so even Liko, Rhuturah's eldest sister, only discovered the child existed through the informal web of gossip that spanned the Naga communities. Zaki was born out of wedlock, and Khietso's family would not accept Rhutaruh, nor her innocent daughter. They were not allowed to live with Khietso's family, nor even were they permitted to visit. Doors in Ukhrul were never closed, not to anyone in the village, but Rhutaruh arrived to find them shuttered to her and her infant. Every day she would go to see the girl's father. Every day she faced the humiliating walk home through the village, alone, save for the sleeping infant in her arms. Khietso never acknowledged the girl was his.

To be an unmarried mother in Ukhrul was a debilitating affliction. Rhutaruh's situation was soon made the subject of the small-minded scandal that dominated the marketplace and the *maidan*. Veiled but pointed sermons thundered from the pulpits of both churches. They were tirades masquerading as homilies, admonitions on the sanctity of marriage and the dangers of straying from 'that holy path'. No one ever mentioned Rhutaruh by name, but the moralisms were clearly directed at her, cast in the form of a salient warning to any other poor woman who might find herself similarly burdened. There was nowhere she could escape judgement. Rhutaruh loved her daughter. But others did not. Rhutaruh's daughter made her unwelcome.

Unhappy months passed. Liko was kept informed of developments with her sister and her baby, but she was not invited to Ukhrul to meet her niece. Augustine and Alex and Maitonphi were never asked to visit their newest cousin. In the autumn, a husband, of less exalted position but willing to accept her, was found for Rhutaruh, and the couple was married almost straight away. The ceremony was a discreet affair, befitting, it was adjudged by the still-gossiping townsfolk, of its circumstance. There were no guests, no celebrations. For Rhutaruh, marriage re-established a level of acceptance in the place where she had to live, and a measure of security. She would not be alone. She would not starve.

But her new husband refused to acknowledge her child, and his family made it a condition of the marriage that Zaki was never to enter their home. Rhutaruh faced an invidious decision, but one in which she felt she had no true choice. She railed at the injustice. She lay in the dirt at the family home and beat at her breast with her fist, but ultimately, she did as she was expected. Zaki was cast out. Rhutaruh left her baby daughter at the door of the church-run orphanage at the upper end of Ukhrul. The child, who had one person in her world, now had no one.

This latest development—Zaki being left at the orphanage—was relayed to the Shimrays by Simeon who had come down to Dimapur from Ukhrul to work for the month of December. Out of obligation—it felt that way to Augustine—he stayed a night at the house of his late brother's widow, and saw his niece and nephews, grown again now: 'almost like men,' Simeon said of the two boys.

Augustine was initially excited to see his uncle. Simeon reminded him of his father in every way: his deep eyes, his lean hands riven with sinew, the way he spoke, the way he ate, the way he moved. Augustine wanted to talk to his uncle about the hunting trips they had shared with his father. He wanted to bring his father back to life, even if only for a fleeting moment of conversation. He wanted his father in the room again. But Simeon did not. He bluntly steered the conversation away from the subject of Luke every time Augustine mentioned his name. 'That was a long time ago,' Simeon said after Augustine again brought up their hunts, obliquely dismissing his nephew—and the memory of his own brother—before moving on to some other asinine matter of small-town scandal in Ukhrul.

Last of all, he relayed the news of Zaki's abandonment. He spoke dispassionately, as though the child were some piece of land or livestock to be bartered and traded, or, as she had been, rejected as unsuitable. Zaki was no blood relation to Simeon at all, but Liko's marriage to Luke had made her family, and by extension, Rhuturah and Zaki, too. He felt he had a right to pass judgement. 'The situation of this baby,' Simeon said firmly, 'was handled right. The family's honour was protected, and that is most important. That girl was not one of us.' Liko sighed and stared hard at Simeon across the fire.

'Not one of us,' Simeon confirmed his point, returning Liko's stare.

Liko wasn't there in the morning when Augustine woke up, but he guessed instantly where she'd gone. Simeon packed moodily and left, barely acknowledging his nephews and niece as he stalked from their house towards the bus stop. He, too, had guessed where Liko had gone, and figured he'd be blamed for her interference. Augustine let his uncle leave unchallenged. He agreed with his mother. It seemed to him savagely unfair that an infant should suffer for the supposed sins of her parents, moreover for the prejudices of her people. The one blameless party in Zaki's birth had been left to bear all of the burden of some ancient ideal of propriety. Augustine knew that baby would be forever marked in Ukhrul, her beginnings the preface to any conversation about her, the caveat to anything she did.

Augustine knew Liko would want Zaki out of Ukhrul. So he was not surprised when his mother appeared back at home that night carrying the child. Liko had hired a car and a driver to take her from Dimapur straight to the chained gates of the orphanage, where she demanded entry of the chowkidar at the gatehouse and marched straight into the building, insisting she be allowed to see Zaki. Sweeping the infant into her arms, she declaimed, 'The child will live with me, as my daughter.' The orphanage's supervisor did not protest. Liko then drove to the family home on the top of the hill, the house where all of her children, and Zaki too, were born, to inform her mother and sister of her decision. She was not seeking permission. Rhutaruh's eyes were red from crying, but she kept them downcast. Her daughter was taken from her without protest. It was just before Christmas. Zaki was not yet a year old.

◈ ◈ ◈

Six months after his new sister arrived, Augustine's results in the Class X came in. His proxy Nido had scored well. Not quite a 'topper', for that would have aroused suspicion, but well enough for Augustine to be able to continue his education. Augustine was unaffected by the news. His mother wanted to celebrate his success, but she was sick. She found caring for an infant tiring this time. Zaki slept poorly, and Liko suffered for it. 'I am old,' she would say to anyone who would listen. Liko grew steadily worse with the strains of motherhood re-imposed for a final, wearing coda. Her illness lingered, hinted at improvement, and then plunged suddenly worse. She swooned in fever. Day after day, Augustine sat mopping the sweat that ran in rivers across his mother's febrile forehead. He prayed for her to be well again. Liko was weeks in bed, then confined to the house as she slowly regained her strength. Running the household fell to Augustine, his brother and sister. They cared for Zaki. Their 'new sister' took her first halting steps on June 21, the longest day of the year, collapsing into Augustine's arms as Liko, pale and weak, watched on from bed.

◈ ◈ ◈

Without speaking, they prepare for bed. Augustine and Akala have walked to the point of exhaustion today, but tomorrow they must go

157

further again. The terrain from here will be more difficult. The jungle will be denser, the hills steeper, and there will be fewer paths to guide their way. Augustine lays his shawl on the ground by the fire. He and Akala lie side by side upon it, facing each other, and pull its edges up over their bodies, wrapping themselves in a tight cocoon. They pull her shawl on top. They will not be able to sleep long. By morning the dew will begin to soak through. But they will have to be up then anyway. They will have to be walking.

All around, the forest is deathly quiet. Usually, Augustine knows, the night forest is alive with the sounds of animals: their movements and calls. Always, there is wind in the leaves of the trees. But tonight, here, there is nothing. Beyond the low murmur of the fire, all Augustine can hear is her breathing and his own. He holds Akala close.

In the darkness, the fear of his pursuers is visceral, it pounds in his chest and shortens his breath. The shadows cast by the flames behind Akala take horrifying form, grotesque caricatures of the men Augustine knows are chasing them. He imagines he can see their cold eyes staring at him from the dark: unblinking, uncaring. He knows what is coming.

Suddenly, Augustine hears the voice of his father in his head, finding comfort in its familiar tones. The legends of his childhood swirl around his mind, each one offering a fanciful escape from the unremitting dread of their current predicament. But he wants to take Akala from this place too. 'Do you remember the story of Yarho?' he asks, barely whispering. The fire is low now, he can hardly see Akala. Her face is in darkness; all he can see is her mouth moving when she speaks.

'Of course, the grove where we met, that was his place before it was ours,' she says. 'But tell me again.'

The story is easy to summon. Perhaps out of a desire to be back there, Augustine dwells on the physical, on the landscapes of Yarho's blighted childhood. He describes Yarho's small family farm, his mother's death and his father's broken heart. He details the cruelty of his aunt, but focuses on the beatitude Yarho found being in the grove, on the peace that existed there, a peace that they shared for a time but now know they will never revisit. As he retells his father's legend, Augustine revels most in the moment when Yarho realises he is flying, that he is no longer being carried, but that the warm current of air pushing up against his chest and filling his wings is allowing him to soar all by himself. For the briefest moment, Augustine is there, he is a hornbill flying on a summer wind in the bright sunshine. He is free, and Akala is beside him.

Then the story is over.

They lie still in the darkness. The fire is almost out now. The wild shadows of the forest are lost to the broader blackness. The men of Augustine's imagination have retreated for the moment, waiting.

'I love that story,' Akala says. Augustine kisses her, deeply, on the lips. After a second's shock, she passionately kisses him back. Locked in their embrace, he traces his fingertips down Akala's cheek and throat. He kisses her neck, and as his hands caress the smooth skin of her stomach and hips, his lips find her collarbone and her breasts. He pulls her body closer still. Akala exhales deeply. She runs her fingers through his long hair and across the tired muscles of his back. The fire extinguishes into blackness. They are warm together under the thin blanket.

'IN MY ACHING BONES'

Augustine's mother was persistently unwell. Where once she was first up every morning, coaxing reluctant children out of bed and corralling them off to school, now she slept the longest of anyone. Her emergence each morning was announced by an uncontrollable coughing fit; hacking heaving breaths that sent spasms of pain coursing down her body, lasting anywhere from ten minutes to half an hour. She lay contorted on the *charpoi*, seized by paroxysms, unable to stop them or move. Winter settled in, and Liko suffered further. The grey sky was low overhead, almost grazing the mountains now dusted in snow. Sleet scudded up the street, and whipped through the cracks under the doors. It was a hard season, dark and relentless. This time Augustine knew before the doctors did, before Liko herself did.

His mother had been infected by Luke. God knows when, and it was hardly important. Nothing could be done about it. Ever since Luke's diagnosis, it had been a fear, but just like Luke, Liko hadn't wanted to know. Denial was a powerful force, and knowing changed nothing anyway. But it was a spectre that felt inescapable all the same. Over this place, this family, it loomed always.

There were government signs painted on walls all over Dimapur city, warning people of the dangers of HIV, especially if a relative was already known to be positive. The signs were a grim reminder of Luke's pained existence, and his potentially deadly legacy. Liko said she couldn't see the point of getting tested. If she knew, she'd still be sick. The drugs she needed to combat the virus could not be found in time or in the quantities that might save her. Some government health officials sold the white boxes of Zidovudine from the back door of their offices. The patients who couldn't afford them despaired. And died sooner.

For months, Liko would shrug when Augustine looked at her concerned or asked how she was. Her shoulders were so thin now, her collarbones stood as stark sentinels against the bright gold jewellery she still wore, shiny markers of the weight and vitality she'd lost. Her hair turned grey and came out in clumps when she brushed it. Liko had resisted the disease as long as she could. But she was weakened now, by the physical loads she had carried back from Burma, and by the weight of a family that had depended on her for so long. Liko had known this was her destiny, and she seem to have accepted it with a weary fatalism.

The first test held false promise. Augustine took his mother to the Nagaland State government-run clinic in the middle of the city. It was a foreboding grey building, perennially attended by a long queue of unwell, unhappy people. Liko and Augustine joined the back of the line early in the morning and it was not till evening time that they had progressed to the front. They were hastened before a young Punjabi Sikh doctor, wearing two pairs of white surgical gloves, one pulled on over the other. He performed a perfunctory physical examination on Liko and chastised her for a having a poor diet. 'You need to eat more meat,' he said.

'Meat is expensive, doctor, and I can't work often now, so we cannot afford it. Often, I am not hungry, anyway, and my children need it more than I do.'

'Your children need you,' the doctor said, suddenly kinder. The harshness in his voice evaporated, and he smiled at Liko. He was not an unfriendly man, but he appeared tired. 'Your children need you to look after yourself,' he said, nodding towards Augustine. The doctor motioned with his gloved hand towards the door. Liko's time was up.

But Liko needed to know. She hadn't waited all day to be told to eat more. She hadn't eaten all day while she waited for the doctor. 'Please, sir,' she said. 'I would like a blood test. For HIV.'

The doctor stared. He was affronted by the old lady's question. Doctors demanded, and were afforded, extraordinary levels of respect in India, particularly by the low-caste or by tribals, the large amorphous demographic into which the Naga were heaped. Doctors were gods. They were never questioned, and patients didn't make requests. They were simply dictated to about what was wrong with them, and what they must do. They were expected to humbly receive whatever medicine or advice the doctor deigned to grant them, and they were expected to be profusely thankful, whatever the outcome.

'Why do you want this test?' the doctor said when he saw Liko would not withdraw her request. 'It is expensive.'

Liko had been staring at the floor, her hands tightly clasped in her lap in nervousness. Now, she lifted her eyes to meet his.

'Sir, my husband died of AIDS. I think I have been infected. I need to know. For my family.'

The doctor was silent a moment. 'Okay. The nurse will take you for your test.' He pressed a button on his desk. 'You must return in four days for your results.'

The nurse who took them to another room was kinder. She was Naga, young, with a smooth face, and large brown eyes that appeared even more prominent under her starched white cap. The nurse explained to Liko that the needle would only hurt a little, and only for a short time. When she was finished, she gave her a ball of cotton wool to press onto her arm.

'Good luck,' she said, as Liko rose to leave. 'Come back next week.'

'God bless you,' Liko said.

The results were negative. Liko was instantly relieved, but not as much as she thought she might be. 'In my aching bones,' she told Augustine, she could feel she was dying. She wore a happy face for her children, for a day, but the nagging doubt remained. Slowly, she came to believe the test was wrong, or, more likely, her negative result was a forgery, that no test had ever been done. The Nagaland government had no interest in discovering the true extent of its HIV epidemic. The more positive tests there were, the greater the pressure to do something about them. Every positive result was another person the government had to find money for, find drugs for; another person whose life would end, soon enough, taking up a hospital bed. The fewer positive tests, the less of a problem the Naga government had on its hands. Bureaucrats had discovered, too, that AIDS patients rarely died 'of AIDS'. They contracted pneumonia or hepatitis or a fever whose symptoms were close enough to those of dengue. Their deaths were attributed elsewhere, and the AIDS problem stayed 'under control'. HIV was a handy disease that way.

Augustine, too, was convinced the test was a fraud. He knew this disease too well; he had seen it all before with his father. So, when the Republic of India government—so often at odds with its Nagaland state counterpart—brought a 'mobile medical van' to Dimapur, Augustine insisted his mother line up to be tested again. The Government of India van was parked in Dimapur's main square. The van had a massive tricolour flag and the lions of the Indian government logo painted on its side—pointed ripostes to the separatists of the city. The Government of India was trying to show it did care. And the health workers were dedicated people: they went out to the slums, vaccinating children against polio and seeking out the weak and elderly who were too feeble to come to town. Their care was free for anyone who needed it. So Liko lined up in the square. Inside, she was directed left to the women's clinic. Again she asked for the HIV blood test. This time she was unquestioningly obliged. After her blood sample was taken, she left, clutching a piece of paper scrawled in illegible blue ink, and was told she was to bring it back at the end of the week.

Friday was the day for the return of all blood test results. Augustine worked late at the shop that night, but Liko was still up when he walked in the door. She was sitting in a corner, staring at a red form that sat on the table, a crude scarlet scar against the dark wood. No one else was up, and there was no sound coming from anywhere. Augustine looked at his mother, and then at the piece of paper. He didn't pick it up. He didn't need to. He knew what it was, and what it said.

'Mama?' he asked.

'Yes, Augustine,' she said, in answer to the unasked question.

'Mama, I'm so sorry.' Augustine rushed to his mother and hugged her. She stayed seated, but clung to him tightly.

'What happened,' Augustine asked.

'Oh, Augustine, it doesn't matter. They gave me the results. Most of the women got blue forms, but mine was in another pile. Mine was red. The nurse handing me my form said *"main bahut maafi chahti hu"*,[9] so I knew straight away.'

His mother paused a moment and wiped the tears from her eyes with her shawl.

'They told me to line up in a queue with all the other women with red forms. Some of the women couldn't read them, they didn't know what was happening. Other women were crying and talking on their phones. One woman was rubbing at the ink of doctor's handwriting, like it was some kind of mistake, like she could rub away the disease. It was horrible. We stood in a line, a line of condemned women waiting to die, and every now and then a door would open to the doctor's room at the front of the queue and a woman would come out clutching a white bottle of pills, and another woman would walk in.'

'What did the doctor say to you,' Augustine asked.

'I didn't see him, Augustine,' she said. 'I couldn't stay there. I felt ill, I felt all the blood rushing to my face. I thought I was going to faint.'

'So, what happened.'

'So, I ran.'

'You ran?'

'I just ran out the door. No one chased me. They just let me go. They just let me...'

Augustine could see his mother had been holding it together, in the silence of that house. She had held the fear and the pain and the sadness captive inside. But saying it made it real, and the tears came now, in ragged, pained breaths. Liko broke down and sobbed: for the family she'd fought so hard to preserve, for the children she'd sacrificed everything for but knew now she would never see grow up.

---

9   Hindi phrase meaning: I'm very sorry.

Neither spoke. Every question that raced through Augustine's mind, he already knew the answer to. He didn't need his mother to say any of it. They both knew what would happen from here. Liko eased her embrace. Augustine stood.

'So you don't have any of the drugs, like they gave Dad?' Augustine asked.

'They had them there, but I just wanted to get out, Augustine. I just wanted to leave. And besides, what difference could it...' Liko trailed off.

Augustine blinked hard as he looked at his mother.

'Okay,' he said. 'Tomorrow, I will line up for you. I will get the drugs.'

He took the red form and thrust it into his pocket. Then he helped his mother to bed, Liko clinging to his arm as she slowly shuffled to her room.

Liko managed her illness as well as she could. She didn't tell the smaller children, but they sensed her 'colds' were part of something more serious. Alex, in particular, had seen this trend before, and he knew how it ended. He watched his mother's deterioration with fear in his eyes. He held his own breath whenever hers was cut short by fits of coughing and wheezing. But, with his assistance, Liko tried to maintain some semblance of normality for her children. 'My youngest daughter especially,' Liko said, referring to her niece, Zaki. 'Make sure she is okay, Augustine,' she pleaded, on the days she was bedridden.

For Liko, part of the normality was an insistence that Augustine stay in school. Her final intervention into his haphazard education was to find a place for him at the National Open School, a private school on a hill at the far end of Dimapur. Liko got Augustine a place through a distant great uncle who taught there, but whom Augustine had never met. She didn't ever reveal how much it might have cost in addition to the clanship claim, but Augustine was sure it was a substantial sum. Regardless, he liked his new school without the pressure of Class X exams looming over his head, and enjoyed the chance just to go and be a kid again. He passed Class XI with better than expected grades; his Hindi reading and writing was now 'very good' and 'good' respectively. Liko beamed from her bed when he brought home his report.

But the new year brought new suffering. January was especially harsh, and the wind off the snow-covered hills snaked its way under doors and through the fraying window jambs. Liko shivered, and no number of blankets could make her warm. Her weakness forced her to loosen her grip on the business. She understood that her illness meant she would never go back to Burma. Sem found more porters to help him with the loads, and the day-to-day running of the business fell solely to Honlei. Sem and Honlei were still not friends—Liko was the conduit between them—but somehow, they managed. It was harder now though, and the shop missed Liko's managerial skills. Staff hired to help were paid too much, and were lazy. Money was getting tight. Augustine offered to say back from school, but Liko was adamant he keep going. 'It is too important. You are doing well, and besides, we've paid too much money.' Augustine hoped it was for the former reason, not the latter, that she was so intransigent. 'Things will get better. In the summertime, things will get better,' Liko said.

They did not. The custom that went elsewhere in the winter stayed there. People didn't abandon Liko out of cruelty, only thoughtlessness. The shop stayed afloat, but most weeks it only just broke even. There was still food on the table, but often not much, and rarely now was there mutton. Dimapur was more expensive than Ukhrul, and the family had no land here, so they couldn't grow their own rice or vegetables. 'For everything here, you need money,' Liko would say to Augustine in quiet moments at home. She missed Ukhrul. Ukhrul was home.

Through the brother of a friend at school, Augustine found a couple of shifts a week working as an autorickshaw driver, plying the streets of the city Wednesday and Thursday evenings. Augustine didn't have a licence, but the man who hired him never asked. He just said Augustine couldn't wear his school uniform while he drove, and the police didn't seem to care—they just moved him on whenever he parked too close to an intersection. Driving an autorickshaw was considered a lower-class job, but for a sixteen-year-old, the money was okay if you drove ferociously, which Augustine happily did.

'Aspirational-class' by Naga standards, Augustine had known where he stood in the schema of Naga society. But he was astounded by the change in people's attitudes toward him, just because he was sitting behind the handlebars of a three-wheeler. People got in and barked directions at him, almost without acknowledgement that he was a person, rather than simply a means to an end. Those who did acknowledge him did so disparagingly. When they spoke, they used the lowest form of 'you', usually reserved for small children or animals. They bargained with him ruthlessly over the fares, disputing even a single rupee, and accused him of cheating them, by driving too slowly, or for stopping too long at red lights.

Occasionally, someone he knew—usually a teacher or an elder from the neighbourhood—would climb in. Before they realised it was Augustine, they would talk with dismissive casualness, instructing him to drive with a wave of a hand. At some point during the journey, they would catch sight of Augustine's face in the mirrors. 'Augustine, I had no idea it was you, I'm so sorry,' one of Alex's teachers said one evening, his tone instantly transformed. Augustine was one of 'them' again. 'Why are you doing *this* job?' The accent on the 'this' was a note of thinly-veiled disdain. Augustine heard it.

'Pocket money,' Augustine replied in half-truth. Satisfied with that answer, the teacher chatted happily all the way home, the normal order of things re-established. Augustine was resentful of the discrimination, and fumed at the casualness of the cruelty. But there was a solidarity amongst the drivers that Augustine enjoyed, a camaraderie in a hostile world in which they had to be constantly on guard. The police, the passengers, the public on the roads— they were all invariably allied against the drivers, so they relied on each other.

Late one Thursday, an Assamese man swung himself into the carriage and demanded to be taken to Assam Gate, the border with Nagaland's neighbouring state. It was the same gate Augustine had cycled through on his ill-fated attempt to ride his bicycle to Bombay as a child. Autorickshaws were not permitted across the border, so Augustine could take him only as far as the checkpost. On the other side, there'd be an Assamese auto to take him into town. The fare was usually 20 rupees, but after 8 p.m., the chances of getting a passenger back the other way were limited, so the fare was raised to 30 rupees. It was standard, and it applied on the other side too. People who made the trip regularly knew about it and didn't contest it. Augustine mentioned the late-hour surcharge to the man: 'you know it's 30 rupees at nighttime'. The man only grunted in reply. Augustine felt the familiar resentment rising in his chest. But he stayed silent.

Augustine watched the man in his rear-vision mirror, who continued to ignore him. The man was well dressed, with smart leather brogues and a checked buttoned-up shirt, the type of which you couldn't buy in Dimapur. That sort of shirt came from the other side of India, from Delhi or Bombay. The man stared out at the hills as they drove. He hawked noisily and spat, aiming at the road, but a fleck of it landed on the pillar of the auto. Although the man saw it, he left it there, sliding down the metal rail. Augustine's face prickled with anger, but he drove on without speaking. The floodlights of the border checkpost loomed ahead and Augustine pulled up in front of the bored, fat policeman on duty. 'Thirty rupees,' Augustine said, turning around. He had won, he had kept his anger sheathed.

'What did you say?' said the man, immediately aggressive.

'The fare is 30 rupees, the night-time rate,' Augustine replied as flatly as he could. He was anxious to stay calm, despite his contempt for this man.

'You cheat! That's too much,' the man said. 'I'm not paying that. Shame on you!' The shame comment was designed to get Augustine to back down, to negotiate.

'The fare at nighttime is 30 rupees. I told you that at the start. You can ask anyone.'

'Officer,' the man said, gesturing towards the policeman, 'this driver is trying to cheat me. He wants 30 rupees for the fare.' The feckless policeman wasn't taking sides. He shrugged indifferently and looked away, saying nothing.

'I'm not paying 30 rupees,' the man said.

Why is this such a big deal? Augustine thought. *Thirty rupees is nothing to this man. He will spend 500 tonight on his dinner, 1000 maybe. It's 30 rupees.*

'You have to pay. That's the fare,' Augustine said. He was calm still, but resolute.

The man reached into his front pocket and pulled out a coin. 'You will have five, because you are a cheat.' He spat the words at Augustine, and threw the coin at him.

Almost before he knew it, Augustine was in the back of the auto, on top of the man, furiously punching and scratching at his face. Augustine was surprised by his own anger. Everything was moving in slow motion, external to him, as though this was happening to someone else, as though he were a spectator to his own rage. His right fist connected with the man's nose, and he felt the cartilage crunch and flatten. Augustine had surprised the man and had the upper hand initially, but the man was powerful, and he gripped Augustine in a painful, choking headlock. He dragged Augustine out of the auto and, grabbing him by the hair and savagely kneed him in the face. Reality came rushing back into Augustine's head with the pain. He felt his brain being jolted against his skull, and for an instant he thought he'd been blinded. The man kneed him a second time, and Augustine dropped to the ground. He felt the blood gushing from his own nose now. It, too, was broken.

Drivers and passengers rushed to intercede on their respective sides, dragging the man and the boy from each other. The policeman, whose job it was to keep order, hadn't moved. A passenger from a nearby auto held the man by the arm as he looked as if he wanted to rush back in and keep fighting. A couple of auto drivers, both in the standard uniform of a brown polyester shirt and matching pants, helped Augustine to sit up. The five-rupee piece the man had thrown at Augustine lay between them on the ground, glinting in the bright white lights of the border post. The man bent forward and picked up the coin, holding it out in front of Augustine, mocking him. 'You will have nothing, because you are a cheat,' he said. He put the coin back in his pocket. Augustine tried to stand in protest, but he couldn't. His legs weren't working, and the drivers gripping his shoulders urged him to 'stay down, stay down'. The man spat, a bloody, phlegmy globule, at Augustine's feet, a final insult. But looking up from the dust, Augustine saw, to no small satisfaction, the man's own blood staining the front of his expensive shirt. One pocket was torn too, right through. Augustine could see the man's chest, bleeding, underneath.

When he awoke the next day, Augustine's nose was swollen and bruised, his eyes blackened. The nose was straight though, so there was nothing anyone could do about it. Liko tended to the wound on his forehead. 'What happened?' she asked.

'Nothing. It's fine,' Augustine said.

'Okay.' Liko didn't push it. Augustine was worried she would stop him from driving the auto. She didn't, but he noticed that from then on, she never slept until he'd arrived home each night.

◈ ◈ ◈

'Lights.'

Akala stops dead in her tracks. For the past few hours, she has led steadily on, but now she stands still and points.

'Straight ahead.'

Augustine comes to stand beside her.

'We're here already,' he says. 'We've come further than I thought.'

He knows this place. He'd not seen it before, but he knew it was here, down here somewhere. He hadn't expected to come across it so soon. The hydro-electricity plant is the only thing that lives in the bottom of this valley. The Naga villages are all up high, but this thrums with life and light twenty-four hours a day down in the darkness. The mountains are high and close here; they lean over, grey and foreboding, from both sides of the narrow river basin. The sun rarely reaches, the forest floor is in near-permanent shadow, but the mill lives in its own circle of light in the deep, broad shade.

The hydro-electricity plant sits at the fine end of the valley, at the confluence of two rivers that spill down the mountainsides behind— where the water rushes most quickly, and most consistently. Its turbines whirr without pause, producing monumental amounts of power. Not that the people of Nagaland ever see it. The plant creates round-the-clock electricity, but the villages nearby live by firelight, or are dependent on an unreliable connection, augmented by noisy, smoky generators. The vast majority of this power is sold off to neighbouring states that

170

can afford to pay more for it, or to Bangladesh where, it is judged, it is needed more. The plant stands, vital and potent, bathed in white light, while the rest of the valley is still, and nearly dark, nearly all of the time.

The plant is of little interest to the travellers, beyond confirming, after two days of walking, that they are on the right path. Augustine knows from the stories his father told him, that there is a mountain path behind the power plant which climbs between the two rivers, up and out of this basin. They must find that path, for beyond is the final valley they must reach. It is mid-afternoon, the hydro-electric plant never closes, but it would be busy now. It will be guarded, but not with any intensity. And besides, they don't want to break in, they just want to get past undetected. They will give it a wide berth. The powerful white floodlights of the plant illuminate like day the edges of the dark forest, but they cast an arc only just beyond the wire fence. Augustine and Akala will stay in the shadows. They belong to the darkness now.

'This way,' Augustine says, pointing right of the plant. From here, it appears an easier path. An unsealed road loops around the end of the valley above the power plant, the route to villages further east. But the road is higher on the right side. He figures they'll be further past the plant when they have to risk the moment of exposure crossing it. Their chances are better this way.

They skirt past what appears to be a workers' dormitory, a long, squat building, standing on short pylons to keep it above the damp ground of the clearing. Through the windows they can see ceiling fans switched on, their casual, lolling loops doing little to disrupt the muggy air. There is only one dormitory. Only men work at the plant. At a distance from the dorms, closest to them, is a larger, standalone house. Augustine suspects this is the manager's accommodation, to judge from the air-conditioning units sticking out from its walls. They tread carefully past, keeping away from the light, keeping to the shade and the safety of the trees.

TICKET 161

Liko's health steadily worsened. She caught every illness that swept through their claustrophobic neighbourhood. Her skin turned yellow and her teeth fell out. She'd never eaten enough, but now it was all Augustine could do to get her to swallow a handful of rice at dinner. Augustine paid hundreds of rupees—more than the shop brought in in a week—to a local doctor to pay house calls. 'There's nothing I can do,' he would declare, baldly still demanding full payment. 'This woman is dying. Perhaps one of the big city hospitals, NCMI in Delhi, could help. They have the drugs to treat her. But not in Nagaland.'

It was decided that Augustine would take his mother to NCMI—the National Capital Medical Institute—where the best doctors in the country worked. NCMI alone could save Augustine's mother. Alone, he would take her there. Augustine's school principal was understanding. Alex and Maitonphi would stay in school. Liko asked a relative in Ukhrul to look after Zaki, but she refused. The animus would not die. Zaki was no niece of hers, she said with contempt. Honlei agreed to take care of the baby; she moved into the Shimrays' home.

The train ride to the capital was dispiriting. Augustine and Liko sat for thirty-six long hours, cramped in the airless third-class compartment—a carriage full of men of a lean and hungry look. No one travelled third-class by choice. The hard wooden seat pained Liko's body, but she could barely move from it. Every time she got up she returned to find it taken by somebody, or by something: luggage, rice sacks. Once she returned from the fetid bathroom to find her spot taken by a cage of live chickens. Each time her seat was stolen she had to plead to get it back. In tears she would explain she was a sick, old woman, that she was travelling to hospital and she couldn't stand. Augustine never asked for his mother's seat back; he demanded, and threatened to call the train guards if he wasn't obeyed. Augustine spoke with a hardness in his voice, he spoke with the surety of a man. Each time, his method worked better than hers. But even with her seat grudgingly returned to her, Liko was never comfortable. Her thin body felt every jolt and jar to Delhi.

The capital was covered in a thick layer of winter fog and pollution when their train pulled into Old Delhi Station. It was early morning, but the air was already thick with the acrid smoke of the city's heavy industry and its incessant traffic. Liko's chest heaved in hacking coughs, as spasm after spasm gripped her body. The decrepit station was in the old part of the city, where an impossible number of people, most of them migrants to this part of India, lived crammed in roiling, restless cacophony. Augustine and Liko were anonymous here. People, if they'd bothered to look, would have seen and known they were from the north-east, but no one was much interested from where they'd come, or to where they were going. There were Indians of every inflection here. Kashmiris in beards and kurta pyjamas on their way to Jama Masjid, broad-shouldered Punjabis in tightly-wound turbans. There were Tamil men wearing lungi, and Bengali women adorned with over-sized bindis. Everyone here was from everywhere else. Here felt like nowhere.

The noise of the station was deafening, and unrelenting. Augustine had to shout to be heard by his mother. He had been warned of the thieves at Old Delhi Station, so he held the bag they'd brought close to his chest. But no one on Platform 16 seemed to notice him, let alone appear interested enough to rob him. Perhaps they could see he'd nothing worth taking. No one cared that Liko could barely walk. Instead, they pressed claustrophobically close, forcing their way past, uncaring of who or what was in their way.

Augustine was tired and hungry from a day and a half on the train, and he could see in his mother's eyes that she was exhausted. He suggested they find a small hotel room to rest. But she insisted they go straight to the hospital. 'The sooner I go, the sooner I am better, the sooner we can go home,' she said. She believed she would be cured here, and Augustine believed in her belief. They found the rank of green-and-yellow autos queued up outside. Augustine knew NCMI was close to the station, but no driver would take them for less than 80 rupees. Reluctantly, Augustine agreed to the fare.

Were he not so tired, and his mother not so unwell, Augustine might have been intrigued by the capital. He might even have enjoyed it. He'd never seen so many people in his life, nor roads so wide, so full of snarling, belching traffic. The whole city seemed entrapped in an eternal gridlock from which it could never begin unravelling. Augustine could barely comprehend the apparently endless city. The sky was a featureless grey, low above his head. There were buildings of brick and concrete—once whitewashed but now all a uniform mottled grey—stretching as far as he could see in any direction, and a seemingly limitless number of people. Around every corner there was more of everything. Old Delhi defied order and understanding. Everywhere Augustine turned was chaos.

But as they progressed through Darya Ganj, Augustine began to see slivers of life in the cold, impersonal city. They drove down tiny alleyways, just big enough for the auto, and even when a cart, or cow, or stone deity, blocked their path, they found a way past. Augustine glimpsed into the darkness of the tiny homes, and saw where people might find respite from the relentless outside. In a narrow side alley, just big enough for a man to walk down, and cast into permanent semi-darkness by a massive knot of illegally rigged electricity wires overhead, an old man with a beard sat on a chair. Behind him, stood a man with a pair of scissors, cutting his hair. From their little alcove, together, they watched the world pass by. On the next corner, a blacksmith crouched by his pit in the street, hammered at the glowing red iron before him, sweat glistening on his brow despite the cold day. He shooed his infant daughter away from the dangerous, but enticing, heat of the fire. Here is where people made their lives.

Augustine had seen on a map he'd found at school that the route from Old Delhi Railway Station to NCMI would take them through New Delhi, the 'Lutyens Delhi' he'd learnt about in class. This was the Delhi the British had built in the days of Empire, and Augustine and his mother suddenly found themselves in its epicentre. The auto careered around a corner into a new road and, without warning, Old Delhi was behind them: here was all broad boulevards, grassy round-abouts, and perfectly sealed roads. The footpaths were neatly paved and empty, the kerbs all painted in thick black-and-yellow stripes. A team of workmen on the side of the road were refreshing the paint by hand as the autos sped past. The houses here were hidden behind high stone walls. Augustine saw only the whitewashed top floors of the grand manors beyond. Old evergreen trees brought dappled shade, but the streets, save for the armed *chowkidars*[10] who peered out from little huts built next to the gates, were deserted. Augustine had never seen such opulence. There was not one house in Dimapur as grand as the smallest of the fifty he'd just driven past. Could this be the same city as the one he'd left behind just a few seconds prior, the same country?

Suddenly, without looking or losing any speed at all, the auto hurtled out into six lanes of untrammelled chaos that arced around a massive park so large Augustine couldn't see the other side. In the park's middle was a grand stone arch. Augustine had learned about this, too, at school. 'India Gate,' he said to his mother, who barely had the energy to turn her head. As they curved around the imposing arch, Augustine looked beyond, down the broad boulevard towards North and South Block, the two imperious sandstone buildings that housed the Indian Government. They were indistinct through the fog, but this only added to their distant, unshakeable grandeur. He didn't say anything to his mother, who had her eyes closed and her head slumped to her chest.

---

10 *Chowkidars*: watchmen or gatekeepers, posted outside a business or private home.

The auto skidded out of the roundabout into yet another traffic jam. Surrounding cars and buses heaved hot smoke into the open-sided vehicle, setting off Liko's cough again. Each vehicle edged forward impatiently, aggressively protecting its space and cutting off anyone who might be seeking even the slightest advantage. No one was let in, to everyone's disadvantage.

In his tiredness, Augustine found himself absent-mindedly looking into the auto beside him. The driver had gnarled bare feet, with thick, filthy nails. His hands were browned and spotted by the sun. Half asleep, Augustine gazed out, not looking at anything, not seeing. 'What are you staring at?' the driver barked, offended by Augustine's apparent scrutiny. His tone snapped Augustine out of his reverie. '*Kan-chaa*,' the man said. Slowly, deliberately. That word again. That hated name they called him at St Joseph's in Kohima. Augustine received the insult as it was intended, as a racist slur, a contempt from a man of this city, to one who was so clearly not from here.

Augustine's newly shorn temper took hold again. He leapt from his seat and smacked the man hard across the face. Augustine's hand stung, but he could see, instantly, a red welt forming on the driver's cheek. The traffic suddenly shunted forward, and the object of Augustine's attack throttled his machine, bursting through a gap that appeared in front. Augustine found himself standing, still roiling with rage, as the cars and trucks began to judder into life around him. He stepped back into the auto. '*Chalo*,'[11] he waved to the driver. Liko didn't open her eyes.

◈◈◈

In Augustine's imaginings, NCMI sparkled, pristine and new, with smiling doctors who would welcome his mother and show her to a comfortable room with a bed. The doctors would know exactly how to treat Liko's illness, and though she'd feel immediately better with the proper medicines, they'd insist she spend a few days convalescing. The reality was different. The NCMI building was a monolith of brown brick, surrounded by an intimidating steel fence, with sharp

---

11 Hindi word meaning 'go' or 'let's go'—often used as an instruction: 'Go'.

points along the top. The main gate fronted onto a busy road, where thousands of people stood in a tight crush, pushing towards the tiny perspex window of a booth built into the fence. Those closest to the window had their hands stretched out at a woman who was frantically, and seemingly without any order or design, handing out yellow tickets.

Augustine and Liko stood on the side of the road. Next to them, sat a man in the gutter accompanied by a pair of warped crutches he'd clearly relied on for years. The crutches had been repaired with tape and wood apparently innumerable times, and the bolts were stuck fast with rust. The man had thin, wasted legs: polio, Augustine presumed. Augustine crouched down and asked the man why the tickets were so sought after. 'That's how you get into the hospital,' he explained. 'The ticket gives you a number. No number, no entry,' he said.

Augustine sat his mother next to the man. 'Wait here,' he told her, 'I will get you a ticket.' He asked the man if he would watch his mother, and he nodded his assent. Augustine joined the crush, pushing his way under the outstretched arms towards the front. The closer he got, the more violent the endeavour around him. Many of those in the crowd were young men like him, robustly healthy, and obviously seeking a ticket on behalf of a sick relative. But many of those caught in the crush were the sick themselves. They wailed in distress. One woman had a gaping, bleeding wound on her leg that was clearly infected. Bourns of blood and pus ran through the fraying bandage, and she gasped in pain every time someone kicked it in their effort to get past. A thin old man with a beard and rheumy eyes was clearly too weak to withstand the pressure of the crush. He was powerless against the sway of the crowd, and kept being swept from his feet, stumbling into those around. Without warning, he suddenly vomited all over himself and the backs of those in front. The man had clearly soiled himself too; excrement was leaking from his pants, and he was crying out, holding his bony right hand in the air. Finally, too weak to stand up, he collapsed into his own foul-smelling mess. The man's groans, and those of the people around him, ensured everyone noticed, but no one stopped. People just stepped over, and on him, to get a little closer to the front. Augustine knew he should have stopped to help, but he, too, was too focused on a ticket. He elbowed his way forward.

Liko was ticket 161, a grubby yellow slip with the NCMI logo and the harried scrawl of a *babu* in some office within to show it was legitimate. As Augustine and Liko sat in the gutter, a boy, not older than seven, walked past. He was barefoot and carrying a hessian bag, dragging it along the ground behind him, clanking the coke cans he was collecting inside. As he walked past Liko he reached out to snatch the ticket from her. He grabbed it, but Liko's grip was stronger, and she pulled it away. The boy came away with a corner of it, but the number was still in Liko's fingers. Augustine got up to give chase, but the boy was already gone, swallowed by the crowd. Liko put the ticket in her bag, which she hugged to her chest as she sat.

A hospital employee in a white shirt stood at the gate calling for patients with tickets. They allowed ticketholders, accompanied by one family member, through in lots of ten, so Augustine and Liko kept their seats next to the man with the crutches. He had ticket 43. It was cold in Delhi, so mother and son sat close together, underneath Augustine's shawl. Liko slept, her head on his shoulder, but Augustine stayed awake, waiting for their number. Just before lunchtime, the boy called out, in English, '160 to 170'. Augustine and Liko hurried to the gate.

Inside, Augustine's heart sank again. His mother tried, unsuccessfully, to suppress a cry of anguish. Within the grounds now, their ticket was only a pass to yet another queue, one that seemed to snake for hundreds of metres, looping across and around the dusty grounds to the main door of the hospital. The ten additions allowed through the gate rushed to the back of the queue, but their presence made no appreciable difference. And the queue was no queue at all, it was a self-selecting hierarchy as new patients pushed in where they felt they were entitled. A couple of young Delhiwallahs walked the queue with a proprietorial air, always with a nervous family following behind. 'Here,' one would suddenly thrust his arm in between two people waiting in line. 'You must wait here.' The sick person and their family member would squeeze themselves in without apology or acknowledgement of those they were displacing. The queuewallah would hold out his other hand—keeping lookout for anyone in real authority—a handful of small denomination rupee notes passed over to him, and he would walk off. Each time, he'd return within minutes with another customer. The queue was a malleable entity. Every hour or so, a hospital official would hustle out of the building and start moving people as well. His manoeuvrings were unapologetically bigoted, and the order was apparent to all who stood waiting, relegated or promoted on the whim of the man with the clipboard. There were few obviously high-caste Indians here, but they and mid-caste Hindus were seen first, followed by backward castes and untouchables. Then tribals: north-easters like Naga and the other ethnic minorities who existed on India's fringes, outside of the Hindu hegemony. The only people forced to wait longer than tribals were Muslims. Nobody complained. That wouldn't help. This was the order of things, so everybody just waited.

It was just before 6 p.m. when Augustine and Liko climbed the steps and were pointed immediately to a small consulting room off the main foyer. There were perhaps a dozen doors down each side of the long corridor, all of them with patients shuffling in and out. A doctor sitting at a desk, a stethoscope around his neck, pointed at Liko as she sat and said, 'It is you?'

'Yes,' she replied. Liko was clearly exhausted. She'd barely eaten all day, and the hours standing in the queue had left her dehydrated.

'What is the nature of your medical condition?' The doctor spoke in English, quickly.

'Please, sir, I have HIV positive,' Liko replied, clearly nervous. 'And now AIDS. Please, sir, I need medicine for my sickness.'

'There is no cure for your disease,' the doctor said bluntly. 'I am sorry,' he said, though he didn't sound it. 'There is no medicine that will make you well again. The drugs that help to control the disease are very expensive, and you have to take them every day, for the rest of your life.'

Liko didn't say anything. NCMI was supposed to cure her. This man was supposed to make her well again.

'How much money do you have with you?' he asked.

'Four thousand rupees,' Augustine said. Liko was still too stunned to speak.

'That will buy you only one month of antiretrovirals. After that you will be sick again.'

'Can you not do anything for my mother?' Augustine interjected.

'What is her worst condition now.'

'She has a cough, very bad, every morning and every night.'

'I think she has pneumonia,' the doctor said, without looking up. 'I will prescribe her an antibiotic.' He scrawled on a notepad and handed the script to Augustine.

'This will help her cough.' He gestured with his hand towards the door.

Liko stood and started to walk to the door, shaking her head. Augustine could see the tears in her eyes. His mother had just been told to go home to die. Augustine turned to say something to the doctor, but the doctor's head was down. He was writing something else, this time in a thick, green journal on his desk. Augustine leaned forward and put his palms on the doctor's desk. The doctor appeared not to see; he did not react. There was nothing Augustine could say. He turned and walked out behind his mother. A small Bengali woman, the next patient, pushed past him, anxious for every second of her consultation. Without speaking, mother and son walked out of the hospital grounds and across the road to a row of pharmacies. Augustine handed over the script and 100 rupees. He took the small, cardboard carton of tablets, and his change, and stuffed them in his pocket. Then he thought about the doctor. He'd have seen four more patients by now. He'd have written identical scripts for most, if not all of them. Liko's illness, the illness that would kill her, was forgotten to him now. Augustine realised with a jolt the doctor had never even asked for his mother's name. To him, it didn't matter; the script was a scrawl for an anonymous woman who would soon be dead.

Augustine swung into the nearest auto, Liko following him more slowly. She winced in pain as she sat down. 'Old Delhi Station,' Augustine said wearily. He didn't bother to ask the fare. It didn't matter now. He hadn't the energy for the fight.

The train left at midnight. The locomotive shuffled through Uttar Pradesh, and Liko slept, but not well. All the next day, as the train lurched on across the flat countryside, she sat without speaking, staring out the window as India passed her by.

❖❖❖

Augustine leads now. From a distance, the whirr of the generators and the thrum of the wires is the only audible sound. But as they draw closer, they can hear the roar of the water as it tumbles down the hillside and into the turbines. Augustine's fear of being heard subsides. No one could hear anything above that sound.

But they are heard.

From underneath the manager's house, a dog comes barking, charging towards the fence in their direction. It is only a small dog, a pet, not a guard dog. It doesn't know what it is doing, but it has heard them and knows that there is something unusual out there. It bounds towards the frontier of its territory, looking for the intrusion. Augustine is not worried. The fence, he figures, will stop it. But the dog gets to the barrier and starts pawing at its base. The fence is old and ill-maintained, and clearly the dog has escaped in this fashion before. Within seconds, it has its paws under the wire and is pushing its way under. It stalks, half in aggression, half simply in excitement, towards where Augustine and Akala stand in the darkness. Frozen to the spot, they dare not move.

The dog finds them in seconds. Its mood is not one of menace. This is a puppy, and it gambols around them in excitement. Augustine tries to reach out to calm it, but the dog is too worked up to be appeased. It retreats a few metres, still barking loudly, making enough noise to disturb anyone who might be asleep in the dorms, or even at work inside the plant. It won't be quiet, and Augustine and Akala can't make it be so.

They are a game to this animal. The dog has its targets cornered against the thick undergrowth of the forest. It moves in closer, wagging its tail and skipping from side to side, still barking. Each time Augustine or Akala puts out a hand to calm it, it jumps away again, still barking. They stand still. They don't want to give it any more reason to make a noise, or make any themselves. They can't run—anywhere they go the dog will follow. Soon, someone will hear the barking and wonder what is out here. Soon, someone will pay attention. Augustine bends down into a crouch.

Over his shoulder, Augustine pulls the air rifle he has carried from Ukhrul. Without speaking, he loads the weapon with a pellet from the pouch in his pocket. He will have one shot only. Augustine brings the weapon to his shoulder, staring down the sight. The dog is still barking, still skittering. It is only ten metres from them, but it won't keep still, it won't be silent. Augustine stares down the sight at the dog's neck. 'Squeeze, don't pull'. Click. The dog drops.

It isn't dead, but it isn't moving. The dog tries to get back up between laboured, pained breaths. It isn't barking anymore, instead it is whimpering with the distress of being suddenly paralysed. The fugitives know they'll be discovered in a minute if the dog starts howling. Augustine is still kneeling. Suddenly, he feels his *dao* being drawn from its scabbard on his hip. Akala has taken it in her left hand and she walks to the stricken dog. She holds the sharpened blade to the dog's neck. 'I'm sorry,' she says, as she pulls the animal's head back and, without pause, draws the *dao* deep through its throat. Akala braces, holding the dog tightly as a final kick of resistance courses its body. She bleeds the animal out. Thick, crimson blood pulses from the wound onto the earth. The forest is quiet again.

The dog can't stay here, they both know that. Soon, someone will realise it is missing and someone else will remember they'd heard it barking over in this part of the forest. A dog found killed by a boar was one thing, a dog shot and then left with its throat slit was another. They do not need more people in their pursuit.

Akala wipes the *dao* on the ground and walks back to Augustine, replacing the knife in its sheath. She gestures to a banana palm behind him. 'The leaf,' she says, pointing at the largest one. 'Wrap the dog in that. I'll find a vine.'

They move quickly; they need to be away from this place, and soon. Augustine pulls the leaf from the tree and spreads it on the ground next to the dog. He rolls the animal backwards onto it, exposing again the massive gaping wound in its throat. The animal's mouth is contorted into what looks like a final ghoulish grin, frozen in the horror of its last moments. Akala returns with a vine. Together, they wrap the leaf around the dog and tie it tightly. Augustine takes his red shawl and winds it lengthways around the dog, making a sling he can tie around his shoulders, heaving the grisly parcel onto his back. 'We have to go,' Augustine says. Akala nods. She holds her hands to her face. Augustine can see the tears in her eyes, and he can feel them welling in his own.

SUNSET

Augustine brought another parent home to die. His mother, like his father before, insisted that she pass away on Tangkhul territory, surrounded by her own people. The Shimrays packed up once more from Dimapur—Augustine was used to upheaval now—and moved back into the family home at the top of the hill in Ukhrul. There, Liko took up residence in front of the fire. She didn't like to lie in the room where Luke had died, with the view outside and the mountain air coming in through the window. It was too cold there, and Liko, as she always had, wanted to be in the middle of all that was happening.

Zaki was too young to understand, but Maitonphi, now a teenager, comprehended the reality that her mother was dying. They spent silent hours sitting by the fire together, Liko lying with her head in Maitonphi's lap, her daughter stroking her mother's hair. They barely spoke, but seemed somehow complete in each other's arms, a perfect cocoon of grief. Alex, too, was more affected this time. He felt guilty he hadn't mourned his father's passing more deeply, and he would spend hours at Luke's grave, now settled into the earth, talking to the weathered headstone that bore his name.

Augustine sought to reassure him. 'You were very young when he died. But you're grown up now. Now you can say the things that you never could before. And he can hear you, I promise.' Augustine talked to Alex about Kazeiram, the afterlife where, the Naga believed a person went when they died. 'Dad is in Kazeiram and he is listening. He knows you miss him.' Alex did miss his father. Almost more now than when he first died.

Kazeiram was a real place, Luke had told Augustine. And you could visit the Naga afterworld when you were alive, if you knew where to go. No one Luke had ever met knew the way. But if you really needed to find Kazeiram, you could. That's what his father believed. But Augustine didn't know anyone who had been to Kazeiram, and he heard about it less and less these days. It didn't accord with the Christian notions of heaven and hell. But it didn't mean he believed in it any less.

Of course, Augustine wanted Kazeiram to exist. Even if he never did see his father again, he wanted to believe the possibility existed. Losing Kazeiram meant losing his remaining link to his father, but it also meant losing some of his own Naga-ness, a piece of his identity. When he believed, Augustine felt more Naga, as though holding on to this faith made him more of the man he wanted to be. Kazeiram was nowhere, but believing in it connected him to his land, to his people.

Liko had been impossibly strong all of her life. She had been famously indefatigable, running the shop, marching into Burma, marshalling her family amidst Luke's indifference, then incapacity, then absence. Now, it felt as if she'd burned too brightly through her days too soon, and the illness had stolen her strength to carry on. Where once she had fight, now she was listless in the face of this unconquerable disease. She had nothing left. Each day was a supreme effort to reach sunset, to stay awake for the end of the day. As she watched the afternoon light through the window slowly fall—from white, to gold, to pink—her head sank a little lower in the pillow in relief. She loved the sunsets, she said. Another day received, another breath granted.

Unable to offer meaningful assistance, well-intentioned relatives laid more blankets on top of her: the massive pile dwarfing her body, rising and falling with her tortured breaths. The aunties cooked mountains of food that lay in bowls uneaten next to her head. Liko became too weak even to shoo away the flies that came to feast in her neglect. She was in pain almost all of the time, and lay in strange contortions on the hard floor, seeking any position that might stop the needles of agony coursing up her back. Her whole body shook with racking coughs, and the mucus she expelled was flecked with bright red blood.

Someone, somehow, sourced a bottle of morphine. From where, no one would admit. But Liko flew into a rage when it was offered to her, her vitality momentarily revived. Her eyes flashed with the life they used to always hold. 'That drug,' she hissed, pointing a bony hand. 'That drug! That's what started all of this. That drug is why my husband is dead, and why I soon will be too.' Maitonphi burst into tears. Liko followed her.

Liko died early in the morning, by the fire. Everyone knew, without being told, that this day would be her last, and they all woke early to sit by her bed, silently marking the final, peaceful breaths of a furious existence. Liko knew too. She knew she would not see the sunset that day, that she had watched the sky fall to pink and to gold for the last time. The dusk would settle on her first today, before it came to her land. The sweet red earth would turn to darkness after her. But she was not afraid. She was quiet. Speeches of valediction were beyond her, and besides, aggrandisement did not befit her. She would not have known what to say. Instead, she held her children's hands in turn—Augustine, Alex, Maitonphi, and Zaki—and smiled at them through eyes that glistened with tears. 'I love you,' she said to each of them, so faintly they could barely hear. The children nodded dumbly in return. They understood there was nothing more to say.

Augustine stared at his mother. Even in her illness, even in her wasted, wizened state, he wanted to burn into his memory the way she looked, the way her mouth moved when she spoke, the way her eyes found his and connected in understanding. Already, his memories of his father were fading. They were fuzzy around the edges, and the details that made him his father were being lost, daily, from his mind. Augustine was determined the same would not happen for his mother. He wanted to preserve everything. Even through this disease's grotesque denouement, his mother shone through, still. Augustine could see it, and he wanted to keep that forever.

Liko looked at her four children, and spoke to them collectively. 'I am so proud of all of you. You make me happy and I will miss you all so much. Grow up good.' She exhaled and sank a little more heavily into the pillow. Her mother-in-law, Ayi to the children, came and sat beside her and ran a hand gently across her hair. The older woman had buried a son, now she must say goodbye to the woman he loved, the woman he wronged, the woman he had condemned to the same anguished fate as his own. Ayi sang quietly to Liko, so softly that everyone else in the room had to strain to hear.

> It's evening time, it's time to rest,
> The work in the fields is done,
> And the sun has sunk below the hills.
> There is no conflict with those whom we fight,
> Everyone is quiet now,
> Let me be at peace too.

Augustine and Alex sat with Maitonphi and Zaki on their laps, listening to their grandmother sing goodbye to their mother. Ayi repeated the last line three times, each time a little more softly, each time holding the last note a little longer, still gently stroking Liko's hair. Liko listened too, with her eyes closed. When Ayi had finished singing, Liko was gone. She was at peace.

❖❖❖

Augustine and Akala walk quickly, away from the plant and up to where a road has been crudely carved into the mountain. It is safe enough to cross. Few cars ever pass here; the Naga of these parts make their way by foot, and the timber trucks bound for the forest beyond they would hear coming for miles. They cross to the high side of the road and climb back into the safety of the jungle. They are exposed for barely five seconds before vanishing again, swallowed up by the shadows. As they make their way west towards where the footpad should be, Augustine can see the two rivers tumbling down the mountain. Akala and he are above the confluence now, so they should, if his father's story is correct,

187

only have to cross the eastern tributary before they will find the path that leads up through the middle of the steep valley, the mountain trail that will take them from here. The body of the dog is warm still, and uncomfortably heavy; Augustine shifts it against his back.

Where Akala and Augustine find the river, it tumbles down the mountain, sluicing haphazardly down rocks kept slick with moss, perennially wet. Just below, the water launches off a precipice and tumbles out of sight. They cannot cross here, and they do not want to lose altitude again. For one, it takes them back closer to the road and the power plant. But just as importantly, every metre they fall is one they will have to climb again. Augustine is exhausted, and he can see in Akala's eyes— the way she closes them for long seconds in the moments when they are not walking—she is too. From here, if they are to make it, every step will matter.

He scrabbles higher alongside the river, slowed by the weight of the animal on his back. They need a flatter spot, where the water moves more slowly, but is not too deep. They need to find a way across soon. For nearly half an hour, they track higher, hauling themselves up through the forest and the scree. The river still offers no obvious route across. Finally, they stop at a small clearing, where the pitch of the mountain momentarily flattens. The river here looks too deep still, too fast-flowing, to cross, but it will have to do. They are running out of energy, out of light, and out of time. 'Here,' Augustine says, breathless. 'I'll make a bridge.' He dumps the dog's body onto the ground.

'I'll get vines,' Akala says, retreating a few metres back down the hill.

Augustine finds two saplings tall enough to span the river and hacks at them with his *dao*. They fall easily and he drags them back to the clearing where Akala waits, holding a vine in each hand. He kneels down and, taking one vine from Akala, uses it to lash the two trunks together. This will be their bridge.

'I wish we hadn't killed that dog,' Akala says suddenly. She is looking at the lump of animal hidden beneath the shawl on the ground.

'I wish we didn't, either,' Augustine replies. 'But we had to. We would have been found.'

'I know,' Akala says.

Augustine's eyes remain on his work. 'It was the dog or us.'

Their makeshift bridge is finished, and they stand it upright at the edge of the river. Slowly, Akala and Augustine let it lean, trying to control its descent down to the other side. Halfway down, though, the weight is too great, and it carries too much momentum. They let it fall with a crash. But the trunks hold fast, and with his foot Augustine pushes the base further into the earth on their side. He ties the second vine at shoulder height to a nearby tree. This, he will carry across and tie to the other side. This will be the handhold. He leaves his gun, his *dao* and the body of the dog for the moment while he tests the bridge. Should the span break he hopes he can swim out against the current, but he knows he could not weighed down by a weapon or a carcass.

Unburdened, Augustine shuffles onto the branches. They are young, green trees and their trunks bow under his weight. But his weight forces the ends into the mud, and they don't shift. He shuffles, left foot in front of right, arms extended like a tightrope walker, step by step to the other side, relieved when his feet feel the soft earth of the river bank. The bridge is imperfect, but it will hold. He hurriedly ties the vine he carries to another tree. 'Your turn now,' he calls, standing with one foot on the edge of their makeshift construction. Akala stands, seemingly paralysed, on her side of the river, staring at the bridge and the dark water below. In her eyes, he can see her fear.

'No,' she says, shaking her head.

'Akala, you have to,' Augustine says. 'There's no other way.'

'No,' she says again. 'Augustine,' she says, finally lifting her eyes, 'I can't swim. I will drown.'

'No, you won't,' he says. 'I will help. I won't let you.' Augustine edges his way back across the bridge. The trees bow a little further. By a third of the way across the trunks have flexed so far as to dip below the water line, a thin, cold trickle runs into his shoes. He tries to keep his balance as the gentle recoil of the trunks to his steps, almost impercep- tible at first, develops a rhythm and a momentum. By the middle it has becomes an unmanageable bounce. He staggers the last three steps, falling onto the bank at Akala's feet. She looks down at him, her face frozen in panic.

'It will be okay,' Augustine says, getting up. He doubts his own words. He is not sure the bridge can handle two people on it at once. But they are running out of time and out of daylight to get across this river and out of this valley.

'I promise,' he says, as much to convince himself as her. He holds out his hand. Akala gives him hers but it is clammy and shakes uncontrollably. Her chest heaves with shallow breaths.

'Slowly, slowly,' he says, holding tightly her right hand in his. With his left he finds the handhold, edging backwards onto the bridge, always looking at her. 'Please Augustine,' she whispers, 'don't let me fall.'

He steals backwards, barely moving, but this keeps the oscillations of the trunks under control. Akala stares at her feet as she inches forward. Water begins to flow over her shoes. 'Augustine,' she cries out, 'Augustine, I'm going to fall.' She is in a blind panic now, squeezing his hand, pulling him towards her. He resists, keeping her moving towards him. Slowly shuffling. 'Almost there,' he says, his voice calmer than he feels. Akala is past halfway and still the bridge holds. 'You're doing well,' he says. 'You have to trust me. I won't let you fall... I love you.' Akala stops moving. She lifts her head and looks straight into Augustine's eyes.

The final four steps with she takes confidently, then collapses into Augustine with deep relief, throwing her arms around him. Her face is wet with tears, her mouth finds his and she kisses him deeply. She kisses him again and pulls his body to hers. He can feel the beat of her racing heart pounding in her chest. They stand, embraced in silence, for a full minute before they gradually release their hold on each other. 'We have to go,' Akala says, slightly awkwardly. She'd been swept up in the moment, overwhelmed and now, momentarily, she can't look Augustine in the eye.

THESE HILLS

Augustine walked outside to a rudely bright morning. All around, Ukhrul was waking up, beginning the morning with its usual rhythms, its agonising indifference. As his eyes adjusted to the light, he could see tendrils of the early white smoke from fires lit for breakfast, wending their way straight up from chimneys. There was no wind. It seemed bewildering that the rest of the world could carry on living while his mother lay inside dying. No, no longer dying. Dead. He dreaded another funeral, another house full of aunties and uncles—well-intentioned, but intently focused on their grief and on his. He just wanted to be left alone.

Augustine walked out of the gate and turned right, striding downhill in the direction of the family lands by the river and the forest beyond. He caught sight of Alex standing in the doorway watching him leave, but did not acknowledge his younger brother, and Alex made no effort to call out for him to stop, nor to follow him. Augustine walked on, past the quiet homes and down the empty streets, without pause, and without a sense of where he was going or why.

Past the fields and the hunters' tracks that were familiar, he found himself walking deeper and deeper into the forest, now over hills he'd not climbed before, and into valleys where he recognised nothing. He did not know where he was, but neither did he feel lost, as he strode on, deeper into the unending forest, each step feeling strangely more certain than the last. Augustine walked as if by instinct, guided by an unseen force he could neither conceive of nor question, but which knew where he needed to go. Somehow, at every juncture, he understood which way to turn without hesitation. Then, without warning, Augustine stopped.

It was dark where he was, the gnarled trees of the gully swooped and dived in their search for the light, drawing a canopy tightly over Augustine's head. Only the narrowest shafts of light found their way down through the leaves, and the edges of the clearing were indistinct, lost to the darkness. Augustine could tell only that he was low down, close to the level of the rivers, and he sensed, without seeing, that this place was bounded by hills on both sides. Nothing, not man nor beast, nor sun nor rain, reached here easily. Augustine did not know what time of day it was, nor which direction home; but he wasn't worried, and he wasn't tired. He just stood calmly in the middle of the clearing. And then he saw.

From out of the dark trees at the end of gully, a man was walking slowly towards him.

It was Luke.

Augustine recognised his father immediately, and he stared as the man who'd been dead almost a decade, walked slowly, almost casually, towards him. As Luke drew closer, Augustine could see this was not Luke as he last remembered him—the wasted, coughing shadow of a man confined to bed—but the father of his childhood. It was Luke when he was well, his face smooth and his mouth filled with strong, white teeth. Luke's gait was unburdened. One arm swung easily by his side, the other hand held a *dao*, resting jauntily on his shoulder. Luke's bicep bulged where it cocked to hold the knife. His clear eyes stared back into Augustine's.

Face to face in Kazeiram, neither man spoke. Luke kept walking towards his son. Augustine's mind reeled with the thousands of things he wanted—needed—to say. He settled on the most immediate.

'Mum,' he said. 'Mum died this morning.'

Luke nodded as if to say 'I know', but he did not speak and he did not stop walking. For a moment, Augustine felt an urge to shout at Luke, to tell him it was he who had killed Liko, he who had given her the disease that slowly sapped her spirit and dulled her body, draining her until there was nothing left. But Augustine knew his father understood this. Nothing he could say now could change that.

'It's just me now,' Augustine said, instead. 'There's Alex, and Maitonphi, and Zaki, and…there's only me to look after them now.'

Finally, his father spoke. The voice was instantly familiar to Augustine too. It was the voice of a thousand late-night sagas, the voice of Naga kings, of warriors and wise men. Luke's voice was clear and rich and resonant: 'It will be enough'.

Again momentarily, Augustine flashed with anger. It felt like another of his father's glib answers, a feckless evasion. But he held his tongue.

'What do I…' Augustine hesitated as his father drew level with him. Still, the older man did not stop walking, ushered on, it seemed, by an unrelenting ethereal hand. Augustine asked again: 'What do I do now?'

'Put your trust in the chosen one,' Luke said obliquely. His eyes were fixed resolutely forward, as though he wasn't addressing his son at all, as though Augustine was no longer there.

Augustine turned to walk beside his father, who looked still rigidly ahead.

'Stay,' Augustine said, railing against Kazeiram's strictures of time, though he knew instinctively nothing could be done. This wasn't enough: he needed more time with his father, more answers. 'Stay,' he urged again.

Luke didn't turn to look at him again.

'Please stay,' Augustine was pleading now, 'I need you here'.

They had reached the end of the clearing now. Augustine's hands met the cold leaves of the copse of low trees that blocked his path. His father strode on. And disappeared.

Augustine slumped to the ground, staring at the unmoving trees into which his father's phantasm had just vanished. He pressed his palms to his eyes, willing himself to remember everything about the encounter, every flicker of emotion on his father's face, the weight on every syllable of every word he spoke, each trace of empathy and understanding he could draw from those familiar eyes. For what felt like hours, he stared back at the far end of the gully, hoping his father might reappear. But Luke did not come. And nor did anyone else.

Augustine felt the dew start to settle damply on his hair and his back. He rose and walked out of the gully, again, simply sensing the direction in which he should go. Suddenly, he was exhausted, his back ached and his legs coursed with pain. He stumbled now on the unfamiliar ground. It was hours before he saw the lights of Ukhrul again. By the time he reached home, it was dark and everybody inside was asleep. There was a plate of food—left obviously for him—by the low fire, but Augustine was too tired to eat. He crawled into bed and fell into a dreamless sleep.

◈ ◈ ◈

Waking early, Augustine walked outside to sit on the stoop and watch the sun rise steadily above the mountain ridges. After a few minutes, Alex joined him, blinking in the light. He made no mention of Augustine's absence the day before, and Augustine chose not to reveal that he had seen and had spoken to their father. One day he would tell Alex. But not yet.

'We should remember this time,' Alex said, turning to his brother, 'we should do something to remember Mum and Dad.'

Augustine nodded, but he kept looking out, over the hills, searching for a clue as to where he spent yesterday, for any indication of the way back to Kazeiram. 'That's a good idea,' he said.

'This evening.' The brothers, lean and broad-shouldered in their young men's bodies, stood quietly together. In the distance, a hornbill climbed on an invisible current unfelt on the ground. The boys watched it intently for a minute. 'Up high, there is wind,' Augustine said.

Their *Ayi* had appeared at the door. 'Come and eat now, boys. Breakfast is nearly ready.' Inside, Liko's body had been moved to the bedroom. Augustine saw through the door that she'd been covered with a traditional red shawl; it was a large haorah, a man's shawl, and Augustine thought it looked like one of the ones his father used to take hunting.

The day was consumed by numbed familial obligations. Having given the immediate family a day's grace, a steady stream of relatives came to pay their respects. Augustine and Alex greeted those who arrived, and ushered them in to see Liko, but stayed, themselves, out of the room where their mother's body lay, instead, they helped *Ayi* make tea. There was little to arrange for the funeral. In control to the last, Liko had planned every detail: she had dictated that she wanted to be buried next to Luke, packed into the same red earth as the husband who had put her there.

It was sundown before Augustine and Alex were alone together again. Alex was sitting on the back stoop when Augustine walked out carrying a nine-volt battery and a sewing needle. 'I know something we can do to remember Mum and Dad,' he said.

'What's that?' Alex asked.

'Tattoos.'

'How?'

'Some friends in Kohima taught me,' Augustine said. 'I will tattoo you, first.'

'Okay,' Alex replied, apparently immediately comfortable with being irrevocably marked.

Augustine laid the battery on the ground, then picked up a rock and violently smashed the battery open. Spilling out was a purple-black ink that caught and reflected the fading sunlight in tiny swirling rainbows.

'This is how they used to do it in Kohima,' Augustine explained.

He took the sewing needle and dipped it into the ink and held it up to Alex's left arm. 'Lift up your shirt.'

Alex winced as the needle bit at his flesh, but he did not cry out. Haltingly, Augustine inked a thin band around his brother's bicep. He marked a second line about two centimetres below. Painstakingly, he connected the two with a series of diagonal strokes.

'The top line is our father,' Augustine explained as he worked, 'the bottom line, our mother. And they are joined, you see, connected. Forever.'

Alex had silently borne the pain for more than an hour. Now he looked at his arm, holding it up and wiping away the spots of blood where Augustine had pressed too deeply.

'I like it. I will do the same for you.'

'You should choose your own design for me,' Augustine said.

'And we will do it in the morning when there is light.'

At dawn the next day, Augustine woke his brother, careful not to touch his arm where he'd been tattooed. It was red and swollen, and Alex slept with it held awkwardly across his body, as though it pained him, even in his sleep. The brothers took another battery from the shop, and smashed it open for more ink. Augustine sat in the cold under a shawl, with just his arm exposed, as Alex set to work. Alex was a more gifted artist than his brother, and he found the needle a natural tool of expression. This was a Naga art form, like the tattoos of the headhunters of generations before, and it came to him without effort. Like his brother's design, Alex drew two bands around Augustine's left arm, but he connected them instead with a series of arcing lines.

'Like the wings of a bird,' Augustine said, finally looking at his arm when his brother was finished.

'Like the wings of a bird,' Alex repeated quietly.

◈◈◈

Augustine finished school in the winter, but it gave him no cause to celebrate; the days only seemed longer now without the structure of lessons and bells and homework. Bored, he chafed against the restrictions of the small town, and the overweening care of the never-ending stream of grandparents and aunties and distant cousins. They meant well, but their cloying attention was suffocating. Occasionally, he would overhear relatives, when they thought they couldn't be heard, using the word 'orphans' to describe him and his siblings. This too, felt oppressive, immutable and weighed down with pity.

Home didn't feel like home with both his parents gone. The raw, new sadness for his mother merged with the ancient grief for his father. More intensely, more savagely than ever, he missed them both. He would give anything, any amount of money, any possession in the world, to have them back, even just for a day.

Augustine had learned the lessons of his father's weakness. He would never touch the Number 4. But in a macabre nod to Luke's grand, destructive indulgence, Augustine found solace in the needle.

He asked Alex to mark him with another tattoo, this one a flower, a lily on his chest. Then he asked for another, a hornbill feather on his back. The sharp, focused sting of the needle relieved some of Augustine's broader pain, just for a moment. Perhaps that was it, perhaps that was the attraction for his father. Over weeks, new ideas spawned new tattoos. Alex was an inspired artist and in Augustine's body he had a ready canvas. Augustine willingly submitted to his new designs, which Alex sketched out in pencil on paper before reproducing them on his brother's skin. The images grew manifest, from fleeting to forever.

'We've got to get out,' Augustine said one morning, sitting on the stoop as Alex wrought a swirling sun across his left shoulder. The weak spring light glinted as it burned off the last of the night's frost.

'Out of where?' Alex was lost in concentration. He'd been etching for an hour and his hand shook with tiredness.

'Out of Ukhrul.'

'I want to go too,' Alex said, finally engaged in the conversation. 'I need somewhere I can breathe again.'

'How do you mean?'

'I can't breathe in this place,' Alex burst forth, the grief of the past months, and the pent-up frustrations of the close, small town spilling out. He didn't want to be surrounded by melancholy aunts who smothered him and talked non-stop about Liko, he said, using their curious Christian euphemisms of having 'gone to a better place' or 'being with God now'.

'I know my parents are dead. You don't think I think about them every single minute?' Alex asked rhetorically. 'I don't need to be reminded of it by every person I meet. Mum and Dad are every-where in this place, especially now they are gone.'

Augustine was silent.

'We will need money to go somewhere, or a job,' Alex's mind had already turned to practicalities.

'I have an idea.' Augustine had been thinking too.

❖❖❖

Simeon rejected Augustine's proposal cold: rupees 1.5 lakh[12] for the paddy fields Luke had owned, and which were now, technically, Augustine's property. Simeon wouldn't buy the lands he already worked. He rejected the deal not because of the price, but because it was not a transaction to be contemplated. 'Treat the earth well,' Simeon told his nephew. 'You are its steward, not its master.' Augustine knew the saying from his father. Simeon sounded just like him when he spoke in old proverbs, Augustine thought.

'I can't buy your land from you,' Simeon said, 'because it's not yours to sell'.

Augustine knew the arguments of the old ways. As an eldest Naga son, it was his duty to preserve the family's land for future generations, for his own son and the sons to follow beyond. He knew that this sale, even though it was within the family, would be a scandal in Ukhrul. People would talk. But they talked anyway. And besides, Augustine felt he'd been abandoned, and any plan of succession long ago corrupted. His father had died nearly a decade ago. Long before his time, long before Augustine was ready to take over. Was the chain not broken then? For all of Augustine's reverence for the Hao, the old ways, he was also a young man living in a modern India, a country, he kept reading in the newspapers, transformed, one on the threshold of being a global superpower. The world wasn't like it was before. How long could they hold onto the old ways? Land was the old currency. Currency was the new currency. Land tied you to a place, money bought you freedom.

And 1.5 lakh was barely a sale price anyway. It was a lot of money for a man like Simeon living in a place like Ukhrul, but the land was worth far more than that. There were plenty of property sharks washing through the village looking to buy up land—outsiders with plenty of cash. They'd offer Augustine a good deal. More money for the fields was tempting, but Augustine couldn't contemplate

---

12 A *lakh* is 100,000, usually written in India as L or 1,00,000. It's the most common unit for measuring large numerical amounts. Rupees 1.5 lakh is 150,000 rupees, but it is almost always said the former way, rupees first and then as a multiple of lakhs (it's a formal measurement, but used in vernacular speech too, the way English speakers might use 'a grand'). The next unit up is the crore, which is 1,00,00,000 (10 million).

selling the lands outside the family. Selling to his uncle felt a tolerable compromise. He would sell the land below its value, but the fields would stay in the family, and he would retain a connection. The price needed to be one that Simeon could afford, too, otherwise there could be no deal.

Augustine spoke with his *Ayi*. She was the closest he had to a parent these days, and the last living link to his father. The old woman's back was bent with age now, and she rarely left the warmth of the fire, even in the summer. But she missed nothing. She understood the transaction he'd proposed, and she knew Augustine felt he could not make it without her imprimatur. She needed to approve, and he feared she would not.

So, Augustine was surprised to find his grandmother immediately supportive. 'You need to go away, I can see that,' she said. 'You are a young man, and things are different now: the world has come to Ukhrul.' Here she pointed at the mobile phone sitting beside her grandson, as if to illustrate her point. 'You must go out into the world.'

Augustine nodded, solemnly.

'Besides, there is too much sadness here for you now,' his grandmother said. 'But you must promise that one day you will return, that you will come back to your people, and back to your place.'

She paused a moment.

'And even while you are away, will you come home for Christmas, for me?'

'Yes, *Ayi*,' Augustine said, and he meant it. He ran a gentle, testing thumb along the dulled edge of an old *dao* leant casually against the wall.

'Simeon's,' his grandmother said, nodding towards the weathered blade: 'you have your father's, I think'.

Augustine nodded.

'Keep the blade sharp, Augustine,' his *Ayi* said. 'It is all we have left of him.'

Augustine nodded his assent again: he had and would. But still he didn't speak. There was quiet between him and his grandmother, together but alone, lost in private memories of a shared loss, an ageing remembrance of a father and son.

Augustine's *Ayi* broke the silence: 'I will take care of the girls'.

In conversations between Augustine and his grandmother, it was always she who dictated their direction and subject matter. But this was what Augustine had been waiting for her to broach, for he could not himself. While Augustine was concerned that Maitonphi should be cared for, she was a teenager and a capable young woman. Augustine was most anxious for Zaki, still a child, with even less of a family than she had before. Zaki was no grandchild to this woman, no relation at all.

'I will care for them as my own,' Augustine's grandmother said. 'Both of them.'

◈◈◈

Augustine went to see Simeon again at his small house by the fields. They sat outside in the warm summer air, and in the soft evening light, they could see Augustine's father's paddy. His dad had been dead a long time. He'd missed many seasons, many crops, plentiful and poor. Augustine had owned these lands for years now, but strangely, he never thought of them as his. To his mind, they were his father's still. Were it not for the siren song of the needle, Luke would still be here, ploughing these fields and harvesting them, celebrating the rains, cursing the droughts and the blights.

When he was well, when he was clean, Luke was a wise farmer. He knew the capability of his land, and he cared for it. He didn't plant too large a crop, or try to pull too many yields a year from the same patch of earth. 'It's not just this harvest, it's the next one, and one after that,' he would say. Like his brother, Simeon had been good to the land. These fields were fertile, and Simeon kept them well-watered. He had put the buffalo through the muddy paddy only today, he said, churning up the soil in readiness for the next rice crop. This land would provide for generations. Simeon had worked since Luke's death in the service of the family. Augustine wanted the fields to be his. But for that, he needed a way out.

Simeon brought two bamboo cups from inside, along with a gourd of *kui-kok*. He poured Augustine a cupful before pouring his own.

'This land is really yours anyway,' Augustine said. Simeon appeared transfixed by the remains of last night's fire, not yet re-lit. He turned over the cool ash with his dao. Augustine continued: 'You work these fields every day, you know them better than any man alive. This place should be yours.'

'The most important thing is to do the right thing for the family,' Simeon said firmly. 'Honour the family. Taking this money and leaving this place, the place where you belong, will bring dishonour.'

'But I hardly know this place anymore,' Augustine said. 'We moved around so much, for Mum to work, for Dad to stay healthy. I'm not of this place anymore.'

'You will always be of this place,' Simeon replied, but then, with acquiescence in his voice: 'I can see you have lost your connection to the land.'

The sun dipped below the mountain range, and darkness began to settle on the valley. Simeon gathered the half-charred wood from last night's fire, Augustine fetched some kindling from the forest nearby. They lit a new blaze.

'I can't stay here, Uncle,' Augustine said as the fire took. 'There are too many memories here, too much sorrow in that house.' Augustine waved his hand in the direction of the darkening hill behind him. The family home was one of the lights on that hill. 'I want know the world outside this place.'

Simeon refilled his cup with *kui-kok*. Like his brother, Simeon drank fast. Augustine had barely touched his.

'Are you sure you know what you want, Augustine?' Simeon asked, looking directly at his nephew.

'I'm sure,' Augustine replied.

Simeon sighed, and stared into the flames. He wanted it known this was against his better judgement. 'Okay,' he said, 'I'll buy the land. I can see you need to go away from this place, and I don't want the family to lose our fields; we've worked this earth since before memories began.'

Simeon turned his gaze from the fire to look directly into Augustine's eyes.

'But know this: you won't be away forever. These hills will call you back. I'll see you again in these mountains.'

Augustine creeps back across the wearying bridge, more slowly now, but he figures it will hold. He gathers his gun and his *dao*, and considers what to do with the dog. The chances of it being found here are slight, but if someone finds the place where the dog was slain, they might be able to track it to here from the spots of blood that have seeped through the leaf and the shawl, marking their progress along the forest floor. The river will break the trail. Augustine considers throwing the dog into the river, but he worries it will be pulled over the falls and end up down near the plant again where it might be found. He will take it with him. Besides, he has another idea for the body now. Augustine slings the animal over his shoulder and knots the shawl in front of his chest. He shuffles his way back across the bridge, the green trunks flexing perilously deep under his weight. But they hold, and from the bank, he turns and kicks the bridge into the river. The trunks swirl in the eddies, before disappearing over the edge of the escarpment and plunging into the forest below.

'There's a path up and over this ridge,' Augustine says, pointing uphill, 'it will be here somewhere'. There is no sign of it in the thick undergrowth, so Augustine carves a way forward, upward and west. 'We'll cross it soon.' It is half an hour before they find the footpad, narrow and overgrown. Few people come this way, it seems, and twice, as they climb in the fading light, they have to retrace their steps to pick up the lost path. They press on. Steadily, more calmly now, they will themselves to the top. By dusk, they reach the ridgeline, and stand for a moment looking back towards home. The hills take on a uniform hue from this distance. It is too dark to see properly, but, almost as far south as they are able, they can make out Phangrei Plateau—a scar of pale yellow against the dark green of the forest. And they can see Shirui Peak, dominant over all.

To the east of the mountain, Augustine and Akala can see the lights of Ukhrul village coming on as evening falls. To the west, a singular yellow glimmer marks Tiya. Augustine wonders whether the lone light shines from Akala's own house: a signal all would be forgiven were she to return, a guide should she wish to find her way home. He looks into Akala's eyes and, for the briefest instant, sees in her a moment's hesitation, a wavering. Right here, right now, the call of home is strong, and Augustine imagines he can see it too: her mother, sitting beneath the solitary bulb at the front door, watching darkness fall on the hills that hold her daughter. The sky above them is not yet black, but its blue is darkening, decorated by a handful of faint stars. They turn and walk on.

The pair plunge into the forest on the northern side of the ridge. On tired legs, they stumble into a clearing that is open to the sky and bathed in moonlight. The exposure doesn't worry them here. On this side of the ridge there are no villages for miles. Akala slumps to the ground. Augustine quickly lights a fire, only small, but enough to keep them warm. He notices Akala starting to shiver, the sweat soaked through her shirt cooling against her body.

Akala has the same idea for the dog's body as Augustine. He wasn't sure how he would say it, but he doesn't need to. As Augustine works the fire, Akala takes his *dao* again and drags the dog to the edge of the clearing. She calmly skins the animal and slices four thin steaks from its hindquarters. It was a lean dog—there will not be much meat—but they will eat properly, a warm meal, tonight, and sleep with full bellies. Tomorrow, they will have the smoked pieces cold as they walk.

Augustine pierces the steaks with a thin green branch which he holds over the fire. The meat cooks slowly, dripping blood which sizzles in the flames. 'I wish the dog didn't have to die,' he says to Akala. She nods in agreement. But they are hungry and they eat.

A TRAIN AT MIDNIGHT

Each day in Ukhrul Augustine found a constriction, a slow suffocation.

Initially, he wanted to reach Bombay. He wanted to actually see the bright lights of the city he'd tried to ride his bicycle to when he was ten. He wanted to know if it really looked like it did in the movies, and he wanted to see, for the first time in his life, the ocean, to look out over a sea that appeared never to end. But in the end the decision on where to go was made for them. Nido Horam, the Shimrays' next-door neighbour from Dimapur had just won another scholarship, this time to the prestigious Indian Institute of Technology in New Delhi. He would be starting classes in July. The scholarship was news all over Nagaland. The Chief Minister held a ceremony to congratulate him, and his picture was on the front page of the *Morung Express*. 'The future of the Naga,' the headline called him. The article speculated on his political ambitions, though Nido himself seemed ambivalent—'I don't know, maybe one day,' was the quote—but that didn't stop the paper forecasting him as the leader of the next generation of his people. Augustine saw the paper, and he called Nido to congratulate him. Nido didn't like the photo, shot from the right under a bright light, his birthmark proud and prominent, an almost angry scarlet.

'And, I don't know about Delhi, Augustine,' Nido said, 'I've never been, and I don't know anybody there.'

'Well, Alex and I will come,' Augustine replied, committing himself and his brother before he'd really thought about it, or even asked Alex. 'Then you'll know two people. And we'll know someone too. There'll always be someone you can speak Tangkhul to.'

The decision was made.

Augustine and Alex moved quickly. Almost as soon as they'd made up their minds, they began to tell people of their plans, as much to commit themselves to going as to inform their village. While the land sale had been controversial, once it was done, most people in Ukhrul understood their decision and were supportive, offering what contacts they had in the big city. The brothers boarded the bus armed with half a dozen phone numbers and addresses to call on, 'if you ever need help'. Alex thought they should call some of the Naga already living in Delhi as soon as they arrived. Augustine disagreed. He wanted to prove they could make it on their own.

Boarding the bus in Ukhrul, a moment of angst coursed through Augustine's body, a fleeting instant of hesitation. *What am I doing?* he thought as he inched his way along the crowded aisle. But he knew there was no going back now. He could not retreat on his word. He'd made the decision he had to, and the deal had been done. *What have I done?* he thought as he sat down.

As the bus juddered out into the street, Augustine felt inside his jacket. The first of the money from Simeon was burning a hole in his pocket. Not all of it, but nearly half a million rupees; the rest would come when it could. The money, in 500-rupee notes wrapped tightly in rubber bands, was more than Augustine had ever held in his life, and right now it felt like an endless pool that could never be exhausted. But he knew life in the city would be different, would be expensive, and he wanted to make it last as long as he could. Alex had to go to school. Augustine had promised this to his *Ayi*. Alex had passed the Class X exam himself; he'd done well and Augustine had vowed to look after his little brother, to give him the opportunity at the education that circumstances, and his own reluctance, had denied him. It was an extra responsibility for

Augustine, but not a burden. He was glad to have the person who understood him most by his side. He could support Alex, he would find a job, doing something, doing anything. They would make it work.

In Dimapur, Augustine and Alex swapped the bus for an over-night train leaving at midnight. From their seats in the second-class carriage, they watched the sun rise twice over India, arriving in Delhi in the middle of the morning. It was the second week of July, and the rains were late. The air in the capital steamed, and pregnant grey clouds hung low over the city, bellies full of rain. As Augustine and Alex walked from the station into Old Delhi, the monsoon finally broke. Rain teemed from the sky and pounded menacingly on the station roof. Fleeing the deluge, the brothers took a room at the first hotel they found in Pahar Ganj, directly across the road from the station. It would do while they found a flat to live in. The hotel block was old and rundown, the paint peeled from the walls, and the ancient eaves rattled and hummed under the sudden pres-sure of the downpour. But the place felt friendly, full of young people from every corner of the land, today huddled tightly in the lobby to escape the storm.

For four days, the rain fell solidly and washed the colour from the city. Everywhere was grey, save for the gutters which ran to overflowing with muddy brown water all day and all night. The brothers spent their first days exiled in their charmless room, poring over maps of the city, working out where they might find a place to live. Augustine sat by the window and looked down onto the street: even in the driving rain, it was crowded with thousands of scurrying bodies. There were people everywhere in this city, and everybody seemed to be from somewhere else, seemed to be going somewhere else. Just like them.

On the fourth morning, he woke early to the absence of a now familiar noise from the city. The rain had stopped. Alex slept on. Augustine walked quietly to sit at his same spot by the window from where he could watch the sun slowly rise, feebly fighting its way through the still-heavy clouds. Augustine could see Old Delhi railway station, even at this hour disgorging passengers by their

206

thousands. The newcomers carried bags on their heads, and boxes tied with string under their arms, or they outsourced their luggage to the red-shirted coolies, who touted for business on the platforms. Delhi already groaned under the weight of its unmanageable, restive population. But still more came, and now Augustine and his brother numbered two of its innumerable, anonymous mass.

The migrants to this city came from everywhere, every day: poor Muslims from Uttar Pradesh looking for labouring work, any work in fact, that they could find so as to send money to their families back home; Bihari women who came to toil on building sites, carrying columns of bricks on their heads from morning to night to feed the maw of the latest rising apartment complex; Kashmiris fleeing the violent insurgency in their homeland; and north-easters seeking the quasi-mythical chance to 'make it' in the promised India Rising they'd heard so much about. Somehow, the overfull city swallowed them all up, adding them to the swollen, ragged, underclass of the capital.

Under the pretence of finding a place to live, Augustine and Alex explored Delhi in every direction. They had been warned about the locals—Delhiwallahs—told that they were arrogant and ruthless, and that the capital was a city that didn't care. The brothers were also warned that plainland Indians were mistrusting of north-easters. Augustine's only previous experience of the capital had been when he had brought his mother here on their ill-fated, worthless visit to the hospital. He tried to shake the prejudice of that experience from his mind; he wanted to approach his new city with an open mind. For days, he and Alex walked, searching the city in every direction. They sought out, and found, the good and the beautiful in the place: the faded grandeur of Lal Qila, the green serenity of Lodi Gardens, the easy fraternity of the Muslims gathered at Nizamuddin's Tomb on a Friday night. The brothers wanted their new home under their skin, they wanted it to feel familiar, to feel comfortable. But they felt they only ever discovered pockets of the city, thin slivers of the place. Delhi was too large. The city stretched on forever it seemed, spilling over the capital's border into the neighbouring states—a limitless concrete jungle. Unconstrained by a coastline or a mountain range, Delhi ran on and on and on, dust-brown suburbs stretching off into infinity.

Alone, Augustine visited Nido at IIT in Hauz Khas, a middle-class suburb in south Delhi. People lived behind large iron gates here, and they took walks at the same time each day along the narrow concrete paths that ran around the perimeter of the threadbare parks. There was order here. 'It's nice,' Nido said, over chai, as they sat by the roadside. 'But these people aren't like us. We don't fit in here.'

'Come with me,' Augustine said, finishing his tea and rising. He did not tell his friend where they were going. They boarded the underground Metro, emerging from Chandni Chowk station in the most ancient part of Old Delhi. The place was noisy and restless, driven by the energy of a million manic aspirations. To Augustine, it felt alive. He saw past the crowds and the chaos, he saw the delicate balance of the place, how every person was a tiny cog in a massive, complex machine. Everyone found a role, a place, a purpose here, however lowly, however far removed from their ultimate grandiose ambition. 'This, I like,' Nido said, standing at the top of Chandni Chowk and smiling at the disorder. The crowd buffeted the two Naga men as they stood still. Augustine could see the drive of this place connected with Nido's own ambition. Nido's scholarship gave him a certainty, gave him a place. He knew who he was, even here, far from home. Now Augustine wanted to know how *he* would fit in, what *his* purpose was, what *his* role would be.

◈◈◈

The Shimray boys' search for a flat to rent was dispiriting. Augustine had been warned that in Delhi, anyone outside of the Hindustani hegemony was considered an outsider. Sometimes the discrimination was subtle, sometimes it was overt. Augustine was apoplectic with the first landlord who said to his face 'no north-easters', when he knocked on the man's door in answer to a newspaper advertisement. Alex was more sanguine: 'Anger only lasts so long'. But Augustine indulged his anger, letting it burn within him, undimmed by time.

They could no longer afford the hotel, so, having resisted as long as they could, they started calling the numbers they'd been given.

Now, they were received without question. He and his brother
drifted around the city, finding small communities of north-easters
who accepted and assisted them. They crashed on couches and in
tiny cramped bedsits, imposing on those who were already painfully
short of space. Augustine felt as if he was living in hiding, an exile in
his own land. As the weeks became months, Augustine's perspective
changed: Delhi felt hard and uncaring.

Finally, through a Naga contact, the brothers found a small,
crumbling apartment in Munirka, a suburb in South Delhi, really
just a narrow scrap of land abutting the roaring freeway to the airport
on one side and a foul-smelling sludge of a river on the other. The
brothers inspected the third-floor apartment in the morning. Black
mould grew in sickly spines up the walls to the ceiling, and cardboard had been jammed into a window where the glass pane had
been smashed. But the boys would have a room each. More importantly, they could afford it, and besides, no other landlord had even
allowed them inside. Alex nodded and Augustine agreed to take it
on the spot. They moved in that afternoon.

Munirka was a maze of tiny alleys and densely populated apart-
ments built in the 70s and barely touched since, but there was
a community of north-easters here—Nagas and Assamese and
Tripuris—jammed in amongst the others of India's multifarious
tribes. Life was low to the ground here, crowded and noisy and
intense. When it rained in Munirka, the drains backed up and
overflowed almost immediately, and the dusty streets turned to mud.
There were fights often, fuelled by cheap whisky and the bootleg
moonshine that did a roaring trade most nights. Augustine could
sense the brawls coming, even without looking, from his room. He'd
hear voices raised in some inconsequential point of argument before
the sound of breaking glass or a hand brought hard across a face.
Nothing ever came of these affrays, the police rarely came to this part
of town, and they certainly wouldn't be exercised over something as
minor as a fist fight. And no one, it seemed, was ever seriously hurt.
By morning, all was okay again.

More occasionally, a building would collapse, an overcrowded
and ageing apartment block, usually illegally extended by several

floors, giving way and tumbling into the street. Once people had died, the police turned up, and government officials would promise a crackdown on the slumlords whose properties were unsafe. But then the rubble would be cleared and everybody in the neighbourhood would turn out for a memorial service—people's funerals were always held back in the victim's home village, no one was ever 'from' Munirka—and the suburb would soon return to normal.

But Munirka's geographic oddity, wedged into an unwanted sliver of land caught between nothing and nowhere, cultivated a solidarity amongst those who lived there. Its isolation inspired people to look out for each other. When an old woman who lived alone at the end of Augustine's street fell ill with appendicitis, the entire block donated money to pay for her operation. She recovered slowly, and in the division of labour that was devised along the street, it fell to Augustine to fetch her milk each morning from the Mother Dairy[13]. Augustine would deliver it at breakfast time, and stay to make her chai; they'd sit together, she with not much to say, he with nowhere to go. It reminded Augustine of sitting with his *Ayi*. For a moment, it was peaceful in Delhi. To the people of Munirka, it felt as if the rest of the world was against them, but they were there for each other.

Now they had an address, Alex could enrol in school. He was accepted at Vasant Vihar High School, one suburb east and close enough to walk each morning. Alex resisted momentarily, worried at the burden of school fees and uniforms and books on the finite supply of money they had; not to mention the potential income lost.

'I could get a job too,' he told Augustine. 'I'm nearly 18.' Augustine insisted—'You promised *Ayi* and so did I'—and Alex, his brother suspected, was secretly happy to go. The strictures of school every day gave his younger brother a routine, something both boys craved in a new, anonymous place that otherwise held no boundaries. Augustine had nothing like that. 'Free to roam,' he boasted to his brother, in a vain attempt to mask his gnawing sense of dislocation.

---

13 Mother Dairy: an Indian company that specialises in dairy products. They have little corner shops—marked by blue-and-white signs—in most neighbourhoods selling milk, ice-cream, paneer, and ghee.

Each morning, Augustine woke early and walked the city: the slums and the suburbs and the industrial districts. He found the street where the Muslim butchers slaughtered animals early in the morning, the flower market awash with fantastical colour, the bridge under which the paperwallahs folded catalogues into the morning's newspapers before delivering them by bicycle. He toured the tiny little alleys that held the art galleries and restaurants and temples and brothels, and he discovered a tattoo artist who admired Alex's work on his back and shoulders. In the third week in their new place, Augustine walked into a graffiti-daubed cafe in Shahpur Jat—a decaying, ancient part of the city that was slowly gentrifying as a hangout for musicians and designers and artists. Augustine liked the cafe. None of the chairs matched, and ancient Bollywood film posters crowded over each other on the walls, covering the chipped paint. He lingered over a chai, talking to the manager. He played up his experience working in his mum's shop, and was offered a job waiting tables on the spot. Within a week he knew the names of all the regulars.

The patrons were young kids with money, but they weren't typical high-caste inheritees. They weren't interested in flashing around the red, impractical 1000-rupee notes—useful for paying for almost nothing because no one ever had change. They didn't loudly insist on drinks from the top shelf; they didn't wear suits and shiny shoes or talk about 'making it' in business. They didn't drive Audis, but dinked each other on beaten up scooters, which they were forever crashing at low speed. They were north Indians and south, but the Aryan-Dravidian divide, so often imposed on India, seemed erased with them; they didn't mind where you were from. Augustine felt his lack of money keenly, but they seemed unworried by it. They asked questions of Ukhrul and of Nagaland, and they fussed over Alex when he came to visit after school. Alex would sit in the corner of the cafe that caught the sun if it could ever find its way through the grey clouds or the smog, and pretend to do his homework. He just liked being around his brother.

Still, Augustine felt a nagging unease: caught between two worlds, with a stake in each, but belonging wholly to neither. The alienation from his homeland wore at his soul. He had always been a proud Naga, and his father's influence, for all its faded distance, still loomed large. But, as he learned the ebb and flow of his new city, he thought that that was there, that was then. It would be different here, it must be different now. The sadness and the tumult of the past needed to stay *there*, locked away in those grey-green mountains and in his memory.

And yet, it never felt right. Removed from his home and his people, Augustine knew in his bones, in the sinuous arrows of his tattoos, that he could not live without either. He didn't need to be there, with them, but he could not bury them either.

❖❖❖

The Sarakuladzu Valley narrows around Akala and Augustine as they walk. They move slowly, careful to choose each step for fear of a wrong one, careful to preserve what little energy they have left. Fear is their constant companion now, beyond the simple exhaustion of their odyssey. They sense what lies beyond the tiredness. The foreboding that has waxed and waned over the past three days, now rests upon them without pause. The forest feeds their black mood. The tall trees, in their fight for light, have grown in great arches that block the sun, so that light never reaches here, and people never come. The fugitives press on. Where the ground is clear, they walk side by side and hold hands, but there is little joy to it. Just a need to feel close.

They have reached the border of Nagaland, the very edge of India, a place that feels like the end of the earth. At the farthest part of this deep basin, Augustine can see where they need to go. There, the two flanks of the valley rise in parallel into worn limestone cliffs, ascending straight from the forest floor, soaring above the trees, up until they are lost in the sky. The two rock faces are close together, so close, that from here, they appear as one great, monolithic barrier to halt their progress. But the cliffs are not yet their concern. As they walk north, they are looking for a cave on the western bank of the river. There, they must turn east, and climb the side of the valley opposite. Augustine knows now what they are looking for, and where they will find it.

Raneakhun Cave is black and forbidding, a yawning maw at the base of the cliff worn by the casual corrosive drip of water over countless thousands of years. A few bats lazily flap out, forward sentinels in the late afternoon light. In another mood, Augustine might have been inclined to explore, but today, this is just a marker, and they have precious little time left.

Turning off the path, they hop from rock to rock across the small stream. Using the cave as their point of reference, they must climb straight up from here. Augustine takes his *dao* from its holder and cuts into the undergrowth. They scrabble up the mountain face, and as they climb higher, signs of a track emerge, although they can see that no one has passed this way for many years. Hints of former habitation, stone cairns dotting their passage up, or more occasionally, a carved step concealed under vines, are indication of lives once lived here. But the forest is doing its best to keep its history a secret.

Akala and Augustine press higher and higher.

They reach Tzuru in the hour before sunset. The afternoon sun shines straight up the valley and casts the abandoned village in a hazy golden light. But no gentle glow can hide the sadness of this place. Tzuru had been hastily abandoned, and long ago: the scattered tools here and there, pots turned over and left—the discarded accoutrement of a forgotten community. The few houses that still stand are not far behind their fallen fellows. They are black with moss and heavy, leaning in on themselves. Collapse appears imminent, and will come, it feels to the visitors, as a welcome relief to the ancient homes, weary of waiting for inhabitants who will never return. Tzuru is the abandoned village Augustine's father told him about; this place was the beginning of the story his father had brought home from his ill-fated smuggling trip to Burma, which lies just beyond these hills. Looking up, he can see the final ridgeline of India to the north-east. That is the border. That is out.

They find Tzuru just as Augustine's father had described it, quietly resisting being swallowed up by the jungle. But the jungle will soon win, they can see. Akala and Augustine are safe here for the moment. No one ever comes to this place and neither of them is really sure why they have come here now. But Augustine had felt compelled to visit this village, drawn to a place he'd only heard about in a story. He wanted to see for himself the things his father had seen when he had come. It is possible that not one person had visited since then, for there was no reason to come. Standing among the vines and the vestiges, he feels viscerally close to his father, connected to a man who'd been dead half a lifetime, in a place they'd never been together.

Augustine knows that a few hundred metres above them, perhaps an hour's walk, is Tzuru's successor village, Mimi. Tzuru had been abandoned by its inhabitants for Mimi three generations ago. Under ceaseless attack from neighbours, the villagers here had decided to climb higher, to the very top of the ridgeline, where they might be safe from predation by hostile villages.

At the back of the village, carved into the hillside, are half a dozen deep gouges in the limestone. They are long, narrow scores, man-made fissures perhaps two metres long, and just as deep. Each is about half a metre high. In the days before Christianity, the Naga buried their dead above ground in hollows like these where they could be visited. The bodies were lain next to clay pots that contained food and water to sustain them on their journey to Kazeiram. Bones were never moved, and the larger clefts became family crypts: newer generations interred alongside old. There are no new bodies here—Augustine is sure there had not been for decades. 'Let's go,' Akala says. Augustine wants to move on too. The living are already in their pursuit; they do not need the dead to join them.

Despite their resolve, Augustine and Akala find themselves drawn, walking along the corroded limestone wall, peering at the ghoulish quarry held within. The skulls in the first tomb leer back, disrobed and decaying in the darkness. It is clear that they have lain undisturbed for generations. The next two hollows are the same. But the fourth tomb is entirely empty, either never used or long ago emptied. Empty, save for two identical items: the two tail feathers of a hornbill, sitting side by side at the edge of the hollow. How had they come to be here? Deposited by a freakish breeze? Left intentionally to be found? Perhaps those were one and the same. Augustine stares at the feathers a long time.

Then he picks them up and puts one in his hair. He turns to Akala, standing beside him, and pushes the other into hers. The plume stands straight up from her head. Neither says anything, but they look at each other in their Naga regalia and smile. Then they turn and walk on.

Akala and Augustine pick their way through the tumbling mess of the former village, and find a similarly overgrown footpad leading down from its boundary, opposite to the path by which they'd come. They force their way downhill, Augustine, in the lead, hacking at the vines with his *dao*. Lower down, the pitch of the hill eases, and the forest opens up. Before them stands a clearing that holds the intersection of half a dozen hunter's trails criss-crossing their way down into the valley. Augustine hesitates.

'This one,' Akala says, already walking ahead on the least-travelled of the roads. It follows the ridgeline downhill. 'We want to be able to see down the valley, to see anybody coming.' Akala's newly-asserted confidence is a relief to Augustine. He has been plagued by doubts he'd dragged her unwillingly into this, that she'd felt coerced. Her resolution is assurance she wants to press on, wherever that takes them. Akala leads. The path is steeper and more obscured here, but that will make it harder for those following. Nearly halfway to the valley floor, the path suddenly flattens out, arriving at an abrupt halt before an escarpment that plunges to the forest floor below.

'I think here is good,' she says.

They make their camp back from the precipice, and sit by a low fire as night falls.

KANCHAA AND COWARDS

W eeks in Delhi rolled into months, and the boys settled into their routines: Alex at school, Augustine at the café. Life in the capital developed its own rhythms; Friday and Saturday nights were the brothers' nights out with Nido, exploring the city. But Sunday they were home, always together, just the two of them. Ukhrul was cast into the background, but always, always it was there. With a growing realisation, Augustine began to understand that he was nothing if not his past, nothing if not a product of his people. Augustine was Naga. The two were indivisible, and he was incomplete without it. In his homeland, he had never needed to demonstrate his cultural identity, or to seek it out. It was unchallenged there. Here, in the capital, he felt compelled to broadcast who he was, to tell others, and remind himself.

In June, Augustine turned 21. His father, he knew, was 21 when Augustine was born. Augustine couldn't imagine being a father; he felt too young still to not have a father of his own. And this would be his first birthday without his mother. Liko had always made a fuss of his birthday, even when she was sick, even when he, as a teenager, sulkily protested he didn't care. But he cared now. In his parents' absence, *Ayi* sent a card and a small gift. It was a journal, bound in brown leather and with thick cream-coloured pages. Inside the first page, she had pressed a single hornbill feather. 'With love, from the forest near my home, from Sechumhang,' she had written.

Augustine took to wearing the hornbill feather in his hair every day, stuck straight up at the back. He wore his hair long, but shaved the sides of his head, like the Naga headhunters of old. He pierced his ears, pushing curved boars' tusks through the holes, and asked Alex to tattoo his arms with the traditional designs they remembered from the old men in the village. He dressed all in black now, and struck a striking, even fearsome, figure. Far away now from the hills of his homeland, he had become a Naga warrior.

Free to nurture his Naga core in the creative nest of the cafe, Augustine would serve drinks, singing the ancient Naga songs his father had taught him; songs he thought he'd forgotten in the dark years since his father had been gone. He began to write down the lyrics he remembered, and to write his own. He learned to DJ from one of his friends at the cafe, and became the regular Thursday and Friday night host. He wrote poetry, and he drew again. He didn't sketch out of sadness for Mr Sai anymore; he drew because he felt he had something to say. The world had taken so much from Augustine: his parents, his teacher, his land. But he was still here, still with a pen, and a mind, and a heart. Still with a voice.

The Naga stories of his childhood, the fantastical tales Luke imprinted on his impressionable young brain, began to resonate with him again. From this distant place, they returned him to the grey-green hills of Nagaland. At least once a week, late at night when the cafe had closed, he and Alex and whoever was still hanging around for a drink, would sit on the fraying couches in the back corner of the cafe and talk. And every time, the night would finish with Augustine holding court with another Naga legend: the story of Yarho, the tragic tale of Shishio and Hatang, or the history of the battle of Kohima. The stories came easily, almost unconsciously, to Augustine, the characters and their voices, their trials and triumphs, emerging from somewhere deep within his soul. In those moments, Luke lived on in him again.

But the comedown always left Augustine feeling hollow. Invariably as they walked out, someone would put a hand on his shoulder and tell him well-meaningly, 'what a great story', or 'you told it so well', and the illusion would be shattered. Augustine could not comprehend why people would not understand. These were not just 'stories', these were not simply entertainment to him. The legends he told were who his people were, the markers of their history and the proof of their existence. Augustine and Alex would walk home through the dark of the sleeping city without speaking. The magic was gone, and they were just empty streets again.

◈◈◈

In November, Delhi shook off its monsoon and the skies cleared and grew cold. Winters were short in the capital, but sharp, and the Shimray boys shivered through the nights in their draughty flat, ill-equipped for the cold season and where there was no place to light a fire. For all of Augustine's new-found sense of connection to his people, home felt far away.

He also found it harder and harder to ignore the hostility to his presence in certain parts of Delhi. At restaurants he'd arrive with friends, only to be told the place was full, even though they could see spare seats and others walking past to sit down. At these times, he would feel the familiar rising of his temper. Most of the time he bit his tongue; occasionally he unleashed a torrent of invective. But he kept his fists by his side.

Once, he was booked to DJ at a hotel nightclub in Chanakyapuri, Delhi's diplomatic quarter, only to be turned away when he arrived at the front door. 'Not your kind, not in here,' the bouncer said pointing at Augustine and Nido.

'But I'm working. I'm doing the music.'

'Then the club will be quiet tonight, because you're not coming in.' The man stood in front of the doorway and crossed his arms.

Augustine's fury rose instantly and he shoved the bouncer in the chest as hard as he could. The man didn't budge. He glowered at Augustine. Nido grabbed Augustine by the shirt and dragged him away. He would lose, Nido told him. 'You can't do anything about it.'

'That's why I hate it,' Augustine spat back, stalking off into the night.

Nido and Alex chose the path of least resistance to the bigotry they encountered. They despised the racism, they were offended and felt demeaned by it. But they had to find a way to live in this place. They were a minority, a visible one, and this was their lot. Retaliating wouldn't achieve anything, and would only make their lives harder. Augustine couldn't make that rationalisation, instead he grew increasingly angry, and increasingly resolute. He looked for discrimination now, he sought it out so that he could oppose it. Where once he'd kept his fists by his side, hostility now often spilled over into violence, and often the escalation was Augustine's.

Almost always, it was the same: a group of young men, out together, looking for women, or trouble, or both. If Augustine had been drinking, he was only too happy to grant them the trouble. 'Kan-chaa,' they'd say, or 'Chinky'. The Punjabi boys, away from home too, and adrift from the social mores that confined them there, were the most aggressive. Most of the time it was minor: some harsh words, and a brief scuffle, a torn shirt or a bloody lip. That was enough to end it, for both sides to feel they'd made their point. But one night in November as Augustine walked home late from work, a young, clearly drunken Punjabi broke off from his group of friends and began dancing around in front of Augustine, pulling at the corner of his eyelids with his fingers, mimicking Augustine's Mongol appearance. His five mates—Augustine did a silent count as they circled him—laughed and clapped. It was a quiet street, and there was no one around. This time, Augustine didn't say anything. He just smashed his fist into the boy's face.

It was a set-up. In an instant, Augustine found himself on the ground, boots and fists raining down on his body. He curled up into a ball and protected his face as best he could, so his assailants kicked at his kidneys and his ribs. Someone with steel-capped shoes kept thrashing at the back of his head. The assault only stopped when Augustine stopped moving altogether. Fearful they'd killed him, the boys ran off down the street, their panicked footsteps ringing on the cobblestones, the sound bouncing off the walls, until it faded to silence.

Augustine lay on his back in the road. The concrete was wet and cool. *I could just lie here*, he thought. Blood began to well up in his throat and run out the side of his mouth. A coughing fit brought him back to animation. Augustine had been drinking—he would not have thrown the first punch had he been sober—but he wasn't so drunk as not to realise he was seriously hurt. Rolling onto his front, he dragged himself onto all fours and shakily to his feet and walked slowly home, careful to avoid main roads where the police might see him. He didn't need their interference tonight. They'd blame him for what had happened. Opening the door to the flat, Augustine tried to be quiet, but Alex woke up with the light that spilled in behind his brother. Augustine stood, in silhouette, bent over and in pain as his brother came to his aid. 'Indians,' he said. He still did not regard himself as one, and nights like this affirmed the apartheid in his mind. 'They don't fight fair. Never one-on-one. They are cowards.'

Alex knew where the roll of money from Simeon was kept, and he grabbed from it a handful of notes over Augustine's feeble and fading protests. They took an auto to Max Medical Centre, the private hospital two suburbs away in Saket where he paid to have Augustine admitted immediately. It wasn't like the last time, with Liko. With money, access wasn't a problem. Augustine spent two days in hospital, pissing blood, before the doctors sent him home with orders to rest. By the first of December he was out of bed, and elt sufficiently recovered to fulfil the promise to his grandmother to go home for Christmas.

❖❖❖

There is meat left over. They warm it over the flames, eating with their fingers. 'My father told me the story of this place,' Augustine says, gazing at Akala. She is watching the fire through tired eyes, staring but not seeing. She turns deliberately to look at him.

'Tell me.'

Augustine points back up the hill from where they've come. 'Many years ago in Tzuru, there was a young couple, very much in love.' As he speaks, Augustine is transported back to his childhood. He is nine years old again, sitting close to the fire in the family home, listening to his father hold court. He can hear the sound of his father's voice, and finds Luke's words rising in his own throat. The story is no longer Augustine's.

His father is speaking now: 'This is the story of a young couple who lived in Tzuru, of their village, and of a mountain called Sukhayap'.

Darkness has descended, but Augustine points out into the black-ness, gesturing over the unseen river valley towards the invisible cliff face beyond. 'There is Sukhayap.'

Akala nods. Augustine is the herald, now, of his father's message. The words that have lain dormant but burnt in his memory for years, spill easily, almost unconsciously, from his mouth.

'The couple were called Shishio and Hatang,' he begins. Slowly, using Luke's words, Augustine tells Akala of the couple and their families, of their midnight escape and flight to the top of the mountain, of their village's pursuit. He reaches the couple's final walk to the precipice.

'In the morning, they walked back to the summit to look down at the village again. And then...'

'Stop,' Akala interrupts him. 'Listen.' Akala has her head cocked on an angle, her index finger in the air, as though trying to locate the source of the sound. Augustine holds his breath and listens.

There is nothing.

Then, straining, he hears it too. The sound is frustratingly faint, just on the edge of his hearing. But it is unmistakable.

'Hooo-yaaaa, Heeeeyyy-yaaaa,' the lead voice.

'Hooo-yaaaa, Heeeeyyy-yaaaa,' many tongues in reply. It is a Naga war cry. Specifically, it is the cry of the Tangkhul. The men of their villages are out hunting. Hunting them. Akala reaches out to hold Augustine's hand. For a minute neither of them speaks. They listen. The voices keep coming: 'Hooo-yaaaa, Heeeeyyy-yaaaa'. Over and over and over again.

Augustine used to love the sound of the Naga war cry. He thought it romantic when his father would imitate the hunters of old. But he'd never heard it sung for a real war, though. Now, the sound is sinister and cruel. Now he understands what it is like to be the hunted, to know they are coming for you.

In the days of the Hao, Naga war cries were designed to intimidate. Powerful tribes feasted on their reputations for ferocity, using their chants to terrorise opponents. Many conflicts were won long before tribes ever reached the field of battle. The fear carried by the voices ringing through the jungle and the promise they held of the merciless bloodshed to follow, reduced waiting armies to terrified, trembling supplicants. Augustine hears the power of the Naga voice now. The men of Tangkhul are coming for him, and for Akala.

But Augustine and Akala know they have time enough. The men have gained ground, but they are still far away. The high-pitched cry of the Naga carries a long distance in the jungle, and the sound the fugitives hear now, they can tell, comes from the bottom of the mountain. The men cannot climb in the dark; they will have to camp on the valley floor tonight. But the pursuers will begin their ascent early, and they will find easily the tracks Augustine and Akala have left. Augustine knows his uncle will be in the pursuing group. He suspects Simeon will be leading it. Simeon will have made it a point of honour. 'To do the right thing by the family,' he would have said. Simeon will know, too, where Augustine and Akala are going. He can take the men right to the spot.

The fire burns low, but it is warmth enough. Augustine lies down next to Akala, his chest against her back, watching her shoulders rise and fall with steady, deep breaths. She rolls over to face him. As her lips find his, he feels her face wet with tears. They kiss.

'Will we make it?' she says quietly. He understands her question instinctively.

'We have enough time,' he says. 'Just.'

SECHUMHANG

Home for Christmas, Augustine was surrounded by the warmth of family, but the town of Ukhrul felt inhospitably cold. Snow lay thick upon the surrounding hills and dusted the main road. In the gutters of the streets, and the eaves of the houses, it gathered in hard frozen clumps and turned brown with the dirt. The sun set early in the afternoon, and the wind blew all day and all night. Again, Augustine felt constricted by the town. There were too many people here who knew him, and the tragic story he couldn't leave behind. His father and mother were here, but they were beneath the earth, side by side in the cemetery. The snow rested upon them too.

He found the family home at the top of the hill, the house that was once his, too full of relatives, and too full of memories. Each time he walked in, he saw, still, his mother and his father lying under sheets by the window in the bedroom. He couldn't stay in this house. He drifted, gradually, over the course of his weeks at home, out of town and down the hill to his *Ayi*'s house at Sechumhang. It was a slow move—first a few hours each morning, then whole days, and finally, he just stayed. He went up the hill for church and for Christmas Day, but otherwise, he stayed away from the town. Alex came to visit, too, but remained living at the house at the top of the hill.

Ayi lived in a three-room house halfway down the ridge on the northern side of Ukhrul which Augustine and Alex called Sechumhang—No Man's Land—because it was precisely that: land for no one, a place between, neither in town, nor down by the river where the crops grew. No Man's Land: it seemed, too, an appropriate place for a boy who'd sold his father's fields, who no longer had a place he could call his own. The house was surrounded by deep forest, and removed far enough from Ukhrul township to be without electricity. Augustine's grandfather had built the house himself with timber he'd cut from the family's forest. That was many years ago now. His grandfather was long dead—Augustine could not remember him—and the house now slumped with inattention. Despite entreaties from the family to move up the hill, *Ayi* had stayed, maintaining the place as best she could. In the wintertime, the uninsulated home was cold and the icy winds slithered their way through the gaps underneath the doors and between the cracks of the ageing wooden walls. In the summer, the bushfires roared through the parched yellow grasses, and *Ayi* would stand at the back stoop with a wetted hessian sack, beating back the flames. Every summer, at least once, the fires came close. *Ayi* would force them back every time. Just.

Augustine loved the quiet of his grandmother's creaking old house, and she was grateful for the help, and for the company. There were no neighbours, and the only footprints in the dust on the path outside most days were their own. Occasionally, a hunter would walk past—it was so quiet, Augustine could hear the footfall of every passer-by—and he would go outside to talk about the weather and the catch. But, mostly Augustine liked the quiet here, stranded on a ridge halfway down into the valley. No Man's Land—the name was only half in jest. After the mania of Delhi, Augustine embraced the beatitude.

Christmas passed and Ukhrul's New Year celebrations were typically rowdy, but Augustine stayed away. On his last morning in the village, as he packed in preparation to make the walk to the bus depot, *Ayi* came into his room. She grabbed him by the shoulders and hugged him tightly. Augustine had told her the night before that it would be two years this time before he would return, explaining that he needed to make a life in Delhi, he needed to be in that place. Unspoken, but understood, was: 'I need to be away from here'.

'Maybe I hold you now for the last time,' Augustine's grand-mother said, not wanting to let him go. 'Be good. Be you.'

It was January 15 when Augustine stepped down from the train at Delhi Station. The city was shrouded in cloud, shivering through its brief but biting winter. Delhi was where he lived now—he had a house and a job and friends here—but his time home in Ukhrul had shown him, too, that the city could never be his home. The money from the sale of his land had allowed him to escape, it had given him the chance to travel; but Augustine saw the transaction differently now. He understood Simeon's disquiet, and he saw, now, what it was he had really sold, beyond the soil that was his birthright. He'd given up his connection with the place that should always have been his, no matter how far away he went, or how long he stayed. And he'd done it for something as base as money. Now he found himself returning, time and time again, to the small corner of his soul that regretted what he had done.

On the streets of Delhi, Augustine continued to be treated as an outsider. People hesitated, unsure of which language to speak to him. They talked loudly at him, and gestured wildly with their hands, as though he was simple. He lacked his brother's equanimity, and was riled by the smallest, even unintended, slight. He was tired of being marked as a minority wherever he went. The awkwardness of the 'other' stayed with him long after it should have faded from care.

But in his neighbourhood, Augustine and Alex found their niche. Augustine brewed rice beer in a tub in a corner of the apart-ment and Nido would come round from college on Friday nights. They sat drinking: Augustine would tell Naga legends, while Nido would talk about the pretty girls in class he was too afraid to speak to. Augustine had known Nido so long, he barely even saw his birthmark anymore. But Nido was acutely conscious of it, especially with new people. 'That's what they see: a north-easter, and a boy with a birthmark,' he would say.

The Shimrays' modest apartment was a sanctuary. There, all three could relax; they settled in for the longest time they'd known away from their family and disconnected from their homeland. At Augustine's rice-beer-inspired instigation, the brothers and Nido formed a band, coming up with the name—'The Featherheads' in honour of the hornbill of Nagaland—before they even had any songs. Augustine sang and played guitar, while Alex played bass. Nido bought a drumkit and found a tutor at university who was willing to teach him to play. The boys practised in a spare class-room on campus, late at night when only the cleaners could hear them. Over months, they worked up a set-list, and once Nido overcame his nerves about playing in front of an audience, started gigging at Augustine's cafe and anywhere around town that would have them.

The songs came from Augustine and Alex, a blend of the old spirituals their father had sung to them as children, and the rock songs they'd discovered on MTV. The boys never wanted to be famous, but Augustine liked the feeling of being on stage under lights, and the centre of attention, singing songs in his own language. He wrote his lyrics in the leather-bound journal his *Ayi* had given him for Christmas. He wrote for his family, to the memories of his father and mother, and in epistles, speaking to his grandmother far away. He wrote his lyrics in Tangkhul, the mother tongue in which he felt best able to express himself. Often, he, Alex, and Nido were the only ones who understood what was being sung. He wrote choruses that were Naga war cries, words without meaning, only intention: 'Hooo-yaaaa, Heeeeyyy-yaaaa'. He liked the shape of the sounds in his mouth, and their weight as they fell upon the ears of his audience.

Alex had graduated from school with passable, though not exceptional, marks. He had known for a long time that his school-ing would stop here. Even with the money from the land, Augustine couldn't support him through years of further education, and it didn't feel right to Alex to impose that on his brother, not now that Augustine was the only breadwinner. Besides, Alex wanted to get out into the world. Augustine took his brother to see the tattoo artist he'd met in his first week in Delhi, taking his shirt off to showcase Alex's abilities: his back was his brother's CV. The owner offered

Alex a three-month trial on the spot. Strictly speaking, Alex was an apprentice, but he quickly progressed from inking simple motifs to taking commissions and creating his own designs. Customers liked his work, but Augustine was still Alex's favourite canvas, willing as he was to experiment with his own skin.

❖❖❖

One night in March, Augustine walked into Alex's shop late, just as his brother was closing up. There was no one else around. 'I have a design I want you to do,' Augustine said to his little brother.

'Sure,' Alex said.

'I want you to tattoo my face.' Augustine said. 'I want a traditional Naga tattoo, like the old men of the village.'

Alex hesitated. 'Are you certain you want this?'

'Yes,' Augustine replied.

'People will stare. No one has tattoos on their face anymore. Even back home, it's only the very old people, and they will be gone soon. People here stare at you already, and you hate that.'

'That's why I should do it. People stare at me already, so why don't I just be who I am. I'm proud to be Naga. Why should I be ashamed? This is what our people do.'

'Used to do,' Alex said, but quietly.

The art of facial tattoos was disappearing among the Naga people, faded with the influence of Christianity. The priests saw facial tattoos as a link to a barbarous past, and while their campaign was assuredly won, they still thundered regularly from the pulpit about the incivility of defacing the soul's earthly vessel. In a way, they were right. Historically, Naga men were only tattooed once they'd been into battle for their village. Special markings were reserved for those who had claimed an enemy head. Tradition dictated they would present the head, holding it by the hair, to the village chief who would grant his assent, allowing the warrior to be inked. It was considered a great honour. Women were tattooed when they were married, or bore children, as a signal they were full members of their clan. But this hardly ever happened anymore. Augustine and Alex only knew a handful of ancient men and women who were tattooed, the deep blue ink faded and lost in the creases of their wizened faces. They were proud of their tattoos, those old people, but they were a tiny minority now.

'Let's do it now,' Alex said, seizing the moment and Augustine's present conviction. Augustine's design was simple. Horizontally across the bridge of his nose, he wanted three short, straight lines. 'To symbolise our father, our mother, and our people. All the Naga, all together,' he explained. On his chin, he asked Alex to ink a traditional Tangkhul warrior's motif: a broad, braided middle line running from his lower lip down to his chin, flanked by two thin lines running parallel on either side. It was simple work for Alex's skilled hand, but he moved slowly—Augustine was sitting in the chair nearly two hours—bearing the needle's pain in silence.

'You've done well, little brother,' Augustine said as he looked in the mirror.

'You're a real Naga warrior now,' Alex said, smiling.

'Hooo-yaaaa, Heeeeyyy-yaaaa,' Augustine's Tangkhul war cry rang out through the deserted shop.

'Hooo-yaaaa, Heeeeyyy-yaaaa.' Alex offered the traditional call-and-response reply. The brothers laughed delightedly. They walked off into the darkness of the night after Alex packed up, and the brothers walked off into the night, Augustine rubbing at his chin where the mark of the needle's passage still stung.

The tattoos on his face brought Augustine even more stares on the streets of Delhi, but he felt instantly emboldened. He felt like himself, a more authentic representation of the man he wanted to be. If people chose to stare, so be it. He was who he was. He was Naga, and he felt it even more intensely now, not only in his outward markings, but in his heart and his limbs. The end of the year approached, and the brothers spent their first ever Christmas away from Ukhrul. Nido stayed in the capital, too, and the three young Naga held their own Christmas lunch in Augustine's café. In the afternoon, Augustine wrote a long letter to his grandmother, telling her he loved her and he missed her. He wrote to his mother and his father too. These final two letters he never posted, instead, carefully folding and slipping them within the pages of his journal.

The next year passed with unexpected ease. Augustine knew the rhythm of his adopted city—its pitfalls and pressure points—but more than that, he felt more assured in himself. Alex, too, liberated from the constraints of schooling, felt a more equal partner in his alliance with his brother. The money he was earning eased the pressure on the steadily eroding funds from the sale of their father's land. Nido continued to shine at university. He'd topped his class in his first year, prompting more adulation back home and the accompanying speculation on his untrammelled political potential, in the *Morung Express*: 'The Chosen One,' it said.

❖ ❖ ❖

For Alex's twenty-first birthday, Augustine brewed a tub full of rice beer, and got his hands on a gourd of *kui-kok* through a Naga source. The boys invited everybody they knew to a party, got drunk and sang tribal songs loudly late into the night, until the neighbours complained, and even the landlord drove from two suburbs away—having been phoned with protestations—to tell them to shut up. But he was good-natured about it. He stayed for a drink.

'This has been a good year,' Augustine said to his brother as they reluctantly dragged themselves to bed, just as the sun was coming up.

❖ ❖ ❖

Augustine and Alex arrived home in Ukhrul a month before Christmas, 2011, fulfilling the promise to their grandmother that this year, they would spend the holiday in their homeland. *Ayi* would have the chance to hold her grandsons again. It had been two years, but little had changed in the town. There were a few new buildings, but the old ones were unchanged, save for the dusty dispirit they wore a little more heavily than when the brothers had last seen them.

Everyone was gathered at the home at the top of the hill when the brothers walked up from the bus depot just before lunchtime, tired and dusty. Maitonphi hugged Alex as he walked in through the door first. She squealed when she saw the tattoos on Augustine's face, but hugged him as well. His grandmother ran her fingers over the brands and smiled. 'They make you handsome,' she told him, 'like a real Naga'.

The brothers greeted their aunties and uncles and cousins in careful order, paying due respect to the elders they'd not seen in months.

'Where is Zaki?' Augustine asked after several minutes, unable to see the girl his mother had adopted and whom he regarded as a sister. He received no reply.

'Where is she?' he repeated more forcefully, suddenly anxious at the silence.

'What's happened?'

'She's okay.' Simeon spoke from the doorway where he'd just walked in. He'd come up from the fields by the river. 'She has moved to a home in Rajasthan, a Christian home, where she will be cared for and where she will get a good education.'

'When did this happen?' Augustine turned to his *Ayi*. 'How long has she been gone?'

Simeon answered the question not directed at him.

'About three months.'

His uncle's tone was suddenly more conciliatory. 'Augustine, you need to understand, there was no one here who could care for her. She was an orphan, and you and Alex were gone'—here, a note of accusation returned to his voice. 'Your grandmother is too old, and besides, the child is not your father's child. It is not her duty.'

Rhuturah, Zaki's birth mother, was still in Ukhrul, Augustine knew. But she was a member of her husband's family, now, and she almost never saw her blood relatives, despite living only at the other end of town. She had had two other children since, but she did not acknowledge Zaki as hers. Even if she had wanted to, her husband's family would not allow it. Liko had taken on the responsibility for Zaki, and now Liko was gone.

Augustine turned to stare at his uncle, but said nothing. Simeon continued. 'A man came from the Grace Home for Children, in Jaipur. It is a Baptist home, run by a pastor called John Jacob. The man said the home was trying to help orphans and children from poor families who couldn't get an education. He said John Jacob was a Christian man, and would take care of Zaki.'

'Why didn't you tell me?' Augustine demanded.

'You were gone.'

'She is still my sister.'

'Not by blood,' Simeon said, needlessly diminishing the relation-ship.

Augustine looked around the room in silence. His relatives sensed his anger, not only with the decision, but with the secrecy around it. He felt betrayed.

'We are sorry you weren't told,' Augustine's grandmother said. 'We did what we thought was right.'

Augustine pressed on with his interrogation. Simeon seemed the one most willing to talk. 'Uncle,' Augustine said politely, 'who was the man who came to take my sister away?'

'I know the man. His name is Chan. He is Tangkhul, from Lumbhi, further down the valley. He is a Christian and knows Pastor John. The pastor helps many children, and the home is sponsored by international charities. It is a good place: he showed us pictures of where the children sleep, and eat, and go to school.'

'When did you last hear from her?'

'She called a few days after she left to say that she had arrived and she was happy. We got one letter, from Zaki, but written in someone else's hand, a few weeks later. Since then, we have not heard. There is no phone number to call.'

'There is no way to call this place?'

'No.'

'Is she coming home for Christmas?'

'We don't know,' Simeon said. 'We don't think so.'

'She's six years old.'

Augustine looked around the crowded, but quiet room. He continued: 'Grace Home for Children in Jaipur?' He was already fomenting a plan.

'It is the best place for Zaki,' Simeon repeated. 'She will have good food and a good education there. She was made an orphan very young, and we wanted her to have a good life.'

◈◈◈

To this place, come the desperate and the damned. From where he lies, without lifting his head, Augustine can see the river. At the very edge of his vision is the sweeping bend where the water is shallow, just below where his village stands. He can't, but he wants to believe he can, see the smoke of the early morning fires, and the women walking to fetch water, barefoot and stooped, their woven *sop* baskets held by a strap to their foreheads. They'd be talking about him. About what he had done.

On the other side of the river, almost hidden from view by a broad, grassy plateau, is her village. From this distance the two places appear almost identical, to outsiders, perhaps two neighbourhoods of the same community, two halves of the same whole. If only it were so. The river separates his home from hers. It was the river that brought them together, the river that kept them apart.

Akala is not awake yet. She is in his arms still, her head tucked under his chin to escape the cold and the wind. He can feel the rise and fall of her chest in slow, even breaths. Akala looks even younger asleep, curled up tightly under her red-and-green-striped shawl. She is naked underneath it, with the blanket pulled tightly over her narrow shoulders. It's cold so high up, but they can't risk lighting a fire. Not here. Not now.

The darkness, so comprehensive last night, is softening now. As Augustine looks towards his distant home, the sun climbs above the hills sooner than he expects, more quickly than he'd hoped. Akala awakes and sits up without speaking. She strokes Augustine's hair as he lies, resisting the obligation to rise, and she smiles. Finally, he lifts himself up to kiss her.

They dress and gather what little they've brought. There is a little meat left over from last night which they eat quickly, for they must soon be walking. Today will be their final climb.

A faded footpad takes them off the escarpment, plunging them back into the forest towards the valley floor below. There, they cross the river for the final time. It is shallow and broad here, flowing easily over smooth stones. They walk west, following a hunter's trail where the path is easiest, side by side. For half a kilometre or so the trail slopes gently and is wide enough for them to hold hands, but the forest grows thicker as they head uphill. Single file now, Augustine at the front; they tread deliberately, steadily. Here, there are still signs of occasional visitation: a run of snapped branches alluding to a path; a crude step hacked into

232

the mountain trail—markers that this, still, is country the locals know. Akala and Augustine turn north, up and away from these signs.

And climb. Here, the jungle is untouched, unvisited even by the hunters of these parts of Nagaland. The short, pale trees grow straight, straining for the sun, their run upwards almost in concert with the hillside now, so steep is its pitch. The mountain sweats with humidity. Akala and Augustine carry no water. She slicks an unruly sweep of fringe against her head. His torn, black shirt is shiny with wet. Their progress is numbingly slow.

For each step of gain uphill, every metre of altitude, Augustine has to hack a path with his father's *dao*. He swings hard at the vines and at the branches, but they fight back, scratching at his hands and his face and back. The two force their way on.

They are beyond tired now. Augustine is weak with hunger and his arms shake with fatigue from the effort of forging a path forward. His breath, in the still, quiet forest, comes in noisy, ragged gasps. In a rare arc of shade he slumps to the ground, back against a tree.

'You should go back,' he says to Akala. 'You can turn back. It's okay.'

'No,' she says. Akala is standing still. She appears serene in comparison to Augustine, almost preternaturally so. Her breathing is calm and measured.

'It's the best thing,' he says. 'Tell them that I forced you to come with me. They will believe you, and you won't be in trouble. It will be okay.'

'But you didn't force me,' Akala says firmly, her voice steady. 'You didn't kidnap me.'

'I know. But that's what you should say.'

They are silent. Augustine blinks away the sweat that has run into his eyes.

Akala breaks the quiet.

'I'm not going back. I want to go with you.'

GRACE

Augustine woke Alex early. 'Come,' he said, shaking his sibling, 'before the others wake'.

He had packed a small bag and walked with it, dragging his still-half-asleep brother, confusedly pulling on clothes, out the door and into the half-light of the early morning.

'Where are we going?' Alex asked, rubbing his eyes.

'Rajasthan,' Augustine said. He strode down the hill, back towards the depot where the buses sat unmoving in the dawn.

It took the brothers three days to cross the Indian subcontinent again. Rajasthan was desert country, on the western side of the Indian plains. At its border, across the Thar Desert, was Pakistan. They wouldn't have to go that far, Augustine thought as they sat, again, in a creaking train carriage rumbling across the countryside, but to go to Jaipur, the capital, was to go deep into that unknown place. The brothers barely spoke on the journey across the plains; Augustine knew he didn't need to explain what they were doing.

Dusted in its famous pink, Jaipur appeared as it had in every picture and movie of the place Augustine had ever seen. But he was uninterested in the majesty of the old city. At the end of Johari Bazar Road, masses of tourists, Indian and Western, shuffled off buses to look at the Hawa Mahal, the 'Palace of the Winds' from where, historically, the ladies of the royal court would watch the street scene unobserved. The tourists, ill-dressed and overweight, dutifully took pictures of the buildings and of each other, and stared at the roiling, chaotic city around them before quickly retreating to the air-conditioned sanctuary of their great sleek coaches. Augustine and Alex barely noticed, as they strode past. Augustine, hands thrust in his pockets, walked quickly. Alex had to trot beside to keep up.

On the train, as Alex slept, Augustine had spoken with an off-duty policeman who was returning to Jaipur after a training course in Delhi. The policeman had heard of Grace Home—'Pastor John is well-known'—and directed Augustine towards Malviya Nagar, an upper-middle-class suburb south-east of the city.

Augustine and Alex hailed an auto and found themselves driving around the neighbourhood, each street as unremarkable as the next. They drove on and on, unsure of where to go. The auto driver was losing patience; he could make more money collecting other fares in the busy city, not driving endlessly up and down the same roads on the sleepy fringes. Augustine quieted his grumbling with the promise of more money. They drove on.

They found it, eventually, in Sector 4 of Malviya Nagar. A faded sign on the high concrete fence announced: Grace Home, A Sanctuary for Children. There was a picture of a rainbow on the sign and, beneath, in small letters, 'In the Care of Pastor John Jacob'. It was a residential street, the homes here being indistinct from those in any of the streets down which they'd driven. But this place was the exception. An unpainted brick wall ran all the way around the property, topped with broken glass set into concrete in jagged barbs. The only break in the wall was a solid, black-metal gate topped with spikes. The gate was large enough for a car, but had a secondary, person-sized door set within. Both were padlocked with thick chains. No other house in the street had such fortifications.

Augustine paid the driver, too well, to judge by the haste with which the man gunned the engine and disappeared. The brothers stood in the empty street. Augustine hadn't considered the plan beyond getting here; he had figured he would just ask at the front door to see his sister, and take her home to spend Christmas with her family. But there appeared no obvious way in. No *chowkidar* posted outside, no doorbell to ring.

But someone was obviously watching them from inside. As they walked towards the gate, a thin panel in the smaller door slid back. A young man's eyes appeared at the opening.

'You don't have an appointment. You can't come in,' he said quickly in Hindi.

Augustine was affronted: 'how do you know we don't have an appointment?'

'No appointments today. Goodbye,' the man said, beginning to slide the panel back across. Augustine reached out to grab it, and forcibly held it open.

'Please *ji*,' Augustine used the respectful Hindi honorific, despite the fact the man was clearly younger than he was. 'I have travelled a long way to see my sister. It is Christmas and I have not seen her for many months.'

The man was unmoved. 'You have no appointment.'

The man pulled hard on the panel, breaking Augustine's grip. It slammed shut, and Augustine heard the click of a lock on the other side.

'How can I make an appointment?' Augustine called out. He received no reply. He knocked politely on the metal gate. '*Ji*, how can I make an appointment?'

Still nothing.

Augustine felt the familiar flush of his rising anger. He was tired, he was hungry, and this man's uncaring disrespect was infuriating. He banged noisily on the gate with his fist. 'Are you there? Answer me!' Augustine kicked at the gate. He got only a pathetic wobble in response. Nothing moved beyond.

Alex grabbed Augustine's hand and dragged his brother away.

'They won't give us an appointment,' he said. 'They just wanted to get rid of you.'

'They are not going to give Zaki back,' Augustine said. 'We are going to have to take her.'

The brothers stood, scanning the impassive fence. There was no obvious way in. And besides, they could clearly be seen from here.

The man behind the fence was watching them still, surely.

Unlike most Indian cities, which were a hodge-podge of tight, winding alleyways, built to no plan and seemingly without any order, this part of Jaipur was a neat grid of wide streets of careful design. The pair walked around the block to an apartment building they figured backed onto Grace Home. Looking down the narrow walkway at the edge of the apartment block they could see the same fence, still crowned with shards of broken glass, running behind the children's home.

'That's our way in,' Augustine said, grabbing Alex by the hand and dragging him down the street.

There was a market in the middle of Malviya Nagar they'd passed in the auto a few blocks back, which Augustine led Alex to now. They walked to a carpet shop in the middle of the square.

'I need a carpet,' Augustine said to the somnolent Rajasthani seated behind the counter. 'An old one is fine, and thin is okay, but long'.

'We have many fine carpets, many fine colours. For what do you want this carpet?' the man asked slowly.

'It doesn't matter about the colour, I just need a carpet.' Augustine was anxious. He was too eager, which disquieted the man. The carpetwallah was more used to the subcontinental way of slow nego-tiation, offers put back and forth over bottomless cups of chai. This foreigner was disrespectfully hasty.

'I can't know which carpet to show you, if I don't know what it is for,' the man said shrugging.

Augustine pointed to the faded blue-and-white rug beneath his feet. 'Yehe,'—'this'. Half the carpet was lost to the dirt piled at the front door, and parts were worn threadbare in the suffering of a dozen summers on the stoop.

'For what do you want that one? I have many fine new carpets,' the shopkeeper said.

'How much for this one?' Augustine asked, still pointing, and tapping his foot now.

The carpet was worthless to the shopkeeper, he could never sell it, and he'd have to replace it soon anyway. '2000 rupees,' he said.

'750,' said Augustine.

'1000.'

'Achchaa,'—'good'—Augustine answered. He handed over two 500-rupee notes, and began rolling the carpet himself, even as the man was still holding the golden bills up to the light—checking for counterfeit—before folding the notes and pocketing them.

'Do you want it wrapped?' the shopkeeper asked. He rose from his stool, sparked out of his torpor by his intrigue at this decorated, impatient fellow.

'It's fine,' Augustine said, hoisting the dusty rug onto his shoulder, 'but thank you very much.'

He walked off into the street, Alex alongside.

◈◈◈

The brothers jogged down the alleyway beside the apartment block to the back fence of Grace Home. 'Grab the end,' Augustine said to Alex, offering him the most worn end of the carpet. Alex held on as Augustine threw the other end over the fence. The rug unrolled in flight and lay now across the wall, a crude pathway over the broken glass. A sufficient barrier, Augustine hoped.

'Boost me up,' he said.

Lacing his fingers, Alex hoisted his brother's foot up, and Augustine, grabbing carefully at the edges of the wall, pulled himself to the top.

'Now you,' he said, thrusting a hand down to Alex. The younger brother clambered up too. The pair dropped noiselessly into the backyard, leaving the rug where it was. They might need it to get out.

The backyard of the Grace Home for Children was no backyard at all. It was a rubbish dump. The entire quadrangle was stacked with broken furniture and rusting cars. There were piles of filthy, discarded clothes and rotting garbage crawling with mice, stacked against the rear of the building. The yard buzzed with flies in the still air. It smelled of decay. There was no one here, and it appeared, no one moving inside the house. In half-expectation of a guard dog, Augustine bent down to pick up a discarded cricket bat. Half the blade was missing, leaving a sharp, jagged edge. Augustine held it out in front of him as he and Alex picked their way through the mounds of garbage towards the house.

Just before they reached the back door, it suddenly flew open. It was the young man from the front gate. 'You cannot be here!' he yelled, one hand on the door. 'You do not have an appointment!' Augustine charged, and was upon him in an instant and stood directly in front of the man, the bat in his right hand held high above his head. 'Do not move,' Augustine menaced. With his left hand, he took the door handle from the man's grip, leaving Alex to slip underneath his brother's arm and inside. Augustine quickly followed, slamming the door behind him and locking it. The man was now outside, rattling the handle furiously and pounding on the door, demanding to be let back in.

For a few seconds, Augustine and Alex saw nothing as their eyes adjusted to the gloom inside. The smell though, hit them immediately. It was the smell of dark, of damp, of decay. It hung heavily in the air, a choking, stale mix of sweat and urine, of faeces and rotting food. Light never came to this fetid place; the outside was never allowed to intrude. In his blindness, Augustine's fingers found a light switch on the wall and he clicked it. Nothing. He and Alex stood peering into the black.

Gradually, shapes emerged out of the darkness. The house was as filthy inside as out. To their right was a pile of dirty nappies, once left by the door to be taken out by someone who never had. A corridor was also apparent in front of them, littered with garbage. Down both sides of the murky passageway ran a series of doors. No sound came from behind them. The only noise was the rattling door handle from the man outside, and his yelling that they hadn't an appointment.

Augustine stepped down the corridor and opened the first door on the right. Immediately, he was the focus of a dozen pairs of terrified eyes. They were children all, the youngest maybe four, the eldest, he guessed an early teenager, crammed together on thin, blackened mattresses on two beds. Some of the younger children were naked, the others were all barefoot and dressed in rags. One of the smaller boys was chewing on a wooden toy train. He'd taken most of the paint off it. Another child, on the floor next to Augustine, had obviously soiled himself, and was sitting in his mess, his hands in his pants. They all stared at Augustine. 'Is Zaki here?' Augustine asked. The children stared dumbly back at him. Augustine looked more closely at them. They were Naga.

'Brother,' Augustine said in Nagamese, pointing at his own chest.

'Bhai,' one of the older boys answered in understanding, but speaking in Hindi. The boy sat cross-legged at the head of one of the beds. He was Naga, too, but he'd chosen the foreign language to answer. Augustine scanned the room quickly. Zaki wasn't here. He turned and walked out, closing the door. One of the children inside began to cry.

Augustine found Alex in the corridor, he'd been checking the rooms on the left hand side.

'Not there,' Alex said.

'These children are all Naga,' Augustine said. 'How did they end up here?'

'The same way as Zaki, I suppose. Orphans, poor families.'

They continued their sweep of the house. Every room was the same, jammed with children, listless and dirty. None made any sound. They sat unmoving in their squalor, seemingly terrified of any intrusion into the deathly quiet of their rooms. Most looked painfully thin, a few so weak they couldn't even lift their heads when Augustine walked in. They just stared at him, uncomprehending, eyes shiny with sorrow.

Augustine found Zaki in the third room he entered. She was sitting against a wall with her head down when he came in. She looked up with a start at the noise of an intruder.

'Augustine,' Zaki called out, looking at him, almost in confusion. She had never seen the new tattoos on his face before.

In two steps Augustine was upon his sister, sweeping her up into his arms and hugging her. She felt strangely stiff, almost lifeless.

'Come,' Augustine said, 'let's go home.'

He strode out into the corridor. 'Zaki,' Alex said, worry creasing his voice as he emerged from a room further down. 'You're safe.'

'Alex,' she replied, her voice a flat monotone.

'Grab the bat,' Augustine said to his brother, pointing to where he'd left it leaning against the wall. 'We'll go out the front.'

They walked further down the corridor. The front door, they could see now through the gloom, was ahead.

Suddenly, a wooden staircase next to the door was filled with the frame of a sweating, shirtless man. He was overweight, his pants were unbuckled and his belly spilled out over his belt. He wore a neat moustache, and a gold crucifix hung from a chain around his neck. Zaki tensed in Augustine's arms. Her black fingernails dug into her brother's neck, and she turned her face away from the man in front of them.

'I am Pastor John. That is my child, and I order you to put her down.' The man had one arm raised, pointing at Zaki. 'You cannot steal that child.'

Alex didn't bother to threaten the Pastor. The first blow with the bat struck him in the ribs, sending him falling to his knees. Alex rained a second one across his back. The Pastor collapsed onto the floor. Alex raised the bat again, the blade poised above the prone man's skull.

'Enough,' Augustine said. 'Enough.'

Alex threw open the door. The blinding light of day spilled in, highlighted by the dust floating in the air. Zaki shielded her eyes. There was less rubbish in the front yard, but it was still unkempt, littered with the ageing hulks of old cars and bicycles. Importantly, it was unpopulated. Augustine hoped the young man was still at the back door, and that the mountains of rubbish would impede his progress to the front. A narrow path between the piles of garbage led the siblings to the front gate. Augustine passed Zaki to Alex. They needed to get out quickly. Augustine wasn't fearful the police might be called, but he knew that if either of the men from inside reached them, the confrontation would be more violent again.

The keys to the padlocks holding the chains around the gate hung from a hook at the top of the jamb. The second key Augustine tried took, and the chain on the smaller door slid away. The door suddenly swung open. Augustine and Alex, still holding Zaki, stepped out onto the dusty footpath. The street outside was quiet. Nothing had changed, no one had moved. Nobody had any idea what was going on in that house. Augustine and Alex—still carrying his sister—walked off up the street.

The first auto they found, Augustine flagged down, telling the driver as they swung in they wanted the train station 'and quickly'. Zaki still hadn't spoken since those first two words of recognition inside the house. As a little girl at home, she'd been endlessly talkative; as the youngest, she was often left to her own devices, and she'd babble away in conversation with herself. Now she sat silently, her arms still around Alex's neck, but not talking, not looking at either of them. She just stared out into the street.

'Zaki,' Augustine said. 'Zaki?' he asked, trying to get her attention. 'Are you okay?'

Zaki nodded but didn't speak.

'Are you sure?'

She nodded again. Augustine stroked her hair. She flinched, almost in instinct, at his first touch. But she didn't protest. Augustine spoke softly to her. 'It's okay, it's me, Augustine. We're going home.'

Her eyes relaxed a little. But Augustine could see the tension in her arms. The fingers she held clasped around Alex's neck were digging into her own hands, her fingernails breaking the skin.

◈◈◈

A police station stood across the road from the train station. Augustine told Alex and Zaki to wait on the platform while he walked over. The train was due in four minutes. It would take them to Delhi, and from there, they'd find a way home. Four minutes was time enough. Augustine marched into the station, past the waiting queue that spilled out the door. He walked straight to its front, where he found the officer he'd met on the train, now in uniform with a sergeant's stripes on his shoulders, manning the front desk.

'Augustine,' he said, 'did you find the place you were looking for?'

'I did,' Augustine said. 'It is here.' He took a piece of paper and a pen from in front of the officer and scrawled down the address on it. 'Now you need to find it, straight away. There are bad things happening there.'

'What sort of bad—?' the officer asked, reaching for his glasses to read the address. But Augustine had already turned to walk out.

❖❖❖

The news broke just after Christmas in Ukhrul. Police had raided the Grace Home for Children and liberated 53 children, most of them Naga, and most from villages nearby to Ukhrul. They were being brought home in two police buses. Their families waited at the bus depot, and Zaki and Augustine walked down together to see the children arrive home. Augustine felt it was important she see that they had been freed as well. They stood at the back of the crowd. Some of the children had parents, others were orphans like Zaki, with extended family waiting. The children were from poor families who lived on the fringes of villages: the vulnerable, the persuadable. The relatives spoke in hushed tones as they waited. They each told the same story: they'd been promised their boys and girls would be cared for in a Christian home, fed well, and given a good education. But everyone had read what was now in the newspapers, and the mothers sobbed over every awful detail.

Police had described the conditions at Grace Home as some of the worst they'd ever seen. There were no working toilets when police went in, children lay in their own filth for days, infected and ill. One child was found sucking on a water tap, despite the fact it was broken and had no water. The children were fed a thin porridge once a day, police said. No vegetables. No meat. They were never allowed outside, or to make noise. Most of them had rickets from malnutrition and lack of exposure to the sun. The education their parents were promised did not exist, and many of the older children, who'd lived inside and in silence for years, had forgotten much of their native language. When they'd been allowed to talk, they'd been forced to speak only Hindi.

In the bus depot square, one father read aloud from a newspaper, voice shaking with rage: 'Doctors examined the girls and found more than half of them had sexually transmitted diseases. The youngest girl with gonorrhoea was nine. Pastor John Jacob is in custody, and will face hundreds of charges, according to police. Children had died in his care, and, as well as abusing children himself, it was believed he was running a sex trafficking operation, smuggling girls to brothels as far away as Mumbai.'

The two police buses pulled in together, their wheels raising a cloud of dust that settled on the anxious crowd. Mothers surged forward to surround the vehicles, their palms pressed plaintively at the doors and at the windows. As each child haltingly stepped down from the buses, they were swept up into the arms of a sobbing relative. One by one, each tearful reunion added to the ocean of anguish. Crying filled the square for more than an hour as child after child filed off. The buses were empty now. Yet some parents stood waiting still. Waiting. Waiting. There were no more children. Was there another bus yet to arrive? They were sure their child was in that home. They'd gone away with other children whom they had just seen returned, but their child was not here. Where were they? In the fading twilight, as the other families began to make their way home for dinner, half a dozen mothers were left standing alone, confused and too frightened to speak. It was dark before they could find the strength to turn to walk home. And Augustine could see, watching from the periphery, it broke them to do it. To walk away from that sad little square was to give up hope of ever seeing their child again.

Zaki moved back into the family house on the hill. But, for all the time Augustine was back, she never spoke. Not about what had happened at the home, not about anything. She was polite and well-behaved. But she never spoke. Never played. Never smiled. Augustine would watch her, lost in quiet solitude, staring off into space, even as the cacophony of Shimray family life at Christmas time babbled all around her. Late at night, when everybody else was asleep, Augustine would walk up from Sechumhang to find Zaki sitting quietly on the back stoop. He tried to talk to her, but she wouldn't, or couldn't, respond. She would just look up at the stars, tears in her eyes.

'She is a sad girl,' Augustine said to his *Ayi* one day.

'She is back in Rajasthan in that man's house,' *Ayi* said. 'The girl she was is back there still. Perhaps with time she will come back to us.'

Augustine nodded.

'Augustine,' *Ayi* said, reaching out for his arm. 'Augustine, I am sorry for what happened to her. We are all sorry. We thought we were doing the right thing. We wanted what was best for her. I wish now we could undo it. I wish now we had chased them away.'

Augustine blamed himself. Zaki would not have been sent away had he not left Ukhrul, not left the family.

◊◊◊

The sound is back. It has floated in and out of their consciousness all morning, but now that they've stopped, and their breathing has calmed, they can hear it clearly in the still air. 'Hooo-yaaaa, Heeeeyyy-yaaaa,' Call and response. Over and over again. The pitch of the war cry hasn't altered, but it has, now, a new urgency. Augustine can picture the men in pursuit: stripped shirtless, padding through the jungle at a half-run, consuming underfoot the kilometres that separate them from their prey. When the front tracker tires, another will take his position to maintain the pace, and the new leader will take up the cry. 'Hooo-yaaaa, Heeeeyyy-yaaaa,' the call. 'Hooo-yaaaa, Heeeeyyy-yaaaa,' the reply. On they press, drawing nearer, minute by minute.

The men are already much closer now. Augustine and Akala can hear it. The men are in the valley below, how far, Augustine can't tell, but they have the track, of that he is certain. They are coming. 'We need to keep climbing,' he says. 'We need to move fast.' The chant has affected him, he can feel it. There is desperation in his voice now, his heart pounds in his chest. He looks down at his hands. They shake in fear, fear of what will happen if they are caught. But that terror is only marginally more confronting than the fear of what will happen if they do make it, if they can escape ahead of the marauding pack. Augustine looks at Akala and sees the same tensions wrought across her face. There is no way out now.

They climb. Akala and Augustine reach the edge of the tree line as the sun reaches its zenith above their heads. There is no shade anymore, and the rock face they stand before is uncomfortably hot in the direct light. Augustine runs his hand over the stone's coarse surface and gazes up. Sukhayap. The cliff stretches away, seemingly straight up, beyond the range of his vision. The summit is up there, but, from here, he has no way of knowing how far, and the scarp offers no obvious way beyond a few craggy handholds. There will be nothing to save them should they fall. Only the floor of the forest below.

They climb. Slowly. Augustine leads, with Akala right behind, seeking out the handholds and the narrow ledges where they can uncomfortably stand a minute or two in the harsh sun, catching their breath. Augustine feels exposed here on the bare rock face, and he is sure those pursuing, if afforded a glimpse of the cliff through the forest, will be able to see them, to monitor contentedly their piecemeal progress. The men, too, will know that they have nowhere left to run.

Small trees grow improbably from the rock face, gnarled hardwoods that cling grimly to their hostile habitat. But the trees are strong, and Akala and Augustine use them to pull themselves up. Where the stretch to the nearest handhold is too far for Akala to reach, Augustine ties his shawl to the trunks, and Akala uses the makeshift rope to drag herself upwards. The effort is supremely tiring. Akala's arms quiver with fatigue, and her hands, wet with sweat, can barely grip.

Augustine spies a jagged crevice running at an angle up the side of the crag. Akala and he inch their way along and up, wearing their hands raw on the coarse stone. Akala's fingers are bleeding. Augustine has sliced his right knee open, and the wound is weeping. Neither stops for their injuries. But on a small ledge where they can stand together, Augustine suggests they rest momentarily. 'No, keep climbing,' Akala says forcefully. 'We have to keep going.' His panic has wounded him, but it has inspired a fortitude in her. She is firm and deliberate. She takes his shaking hand, hers is steady. 'Augustine,' she says, 'we cannot let them catch us. Please keep going.' Akala stares into his eyes: 'for me'.

He turns to keep climbing.

The war cry of the chasing pack, for hours in and out of their hearing, is now a constant reminder of what lies below. The sound grows steadily louder. It reverberates off the rock walls of the narrow gorge below and rings in their ears. 'Hooo-yaaaa, Heeeeyyy-yaaaa, Hooo-yaaaa, Heeeeyyy-yaaaa'. It mocks them and the futility of their plan to escape. 'Hooo-yaaaa, Heeeeyyy-yaaaa, Hooo-yaaaa, Heeeeyyy-yaaaa.'

THE HORNBILL

Augustine left Ukhrul in the new year, leaving what remained of the money from his father's land with his *Ayi*, not for her, but with instructions that it be used by the family to care for Zaki: for anything she needed, but for her education especially. He wanted her in school; she would be safe there, and the money would make sure she could stay all the way through.

But upon returning to Delhi, Augustine could not shake thoughts of Ukhrul. At night he found himself dreaming of the hills around his home, and of hunting trips with his father. He didn't know whether he was just concerned for Zaki—he had taken to calling once a week: brief, stilted conversations, just to see that she was okay—or whether he felt a deeper disquiet. But he heard his *Ayi*'s prophecy in his ears: 'You must promise you will return, that you will come back to your people, and back to your place'. And he heard, too, the voice of his uncle, Simeon's portent cast almost as a threat: 'Know this: you won't be away forever. These hills will call you back. I'll see you again in these mountains.'

The city could no longer hold Augustine. He began to visit Ukhrul more regularly now, every couple of months, and often by himself if Alex was working. In the capital, Augustine drifted between jobs—with his manager's patient acquiescence, he worked at the café irregularly, or he DJ-ed. He even tried working as a salesman in a friend's clothes shop—but all of it was simply a means to an end. He used the lengthening gaps between employment to return to his village; he could feel himself being drawn home, pulled by the dual forces of family and fate. His *Ayi*'s prophecy, and his promise that he would return was, by degrees, coming true. He could see his path led back there now. But back to what? He had sold his land, and the house on the hill held too many memories, too raw. He could not go back there. Not yet.

Yet, each time, leaving his village was more difficult. With every visit his grandmother looked a little more frail, and each time, she clung a little longer to him when she said goodbye. Each time, that embrace was harder for him to break.

◈◈◈

Augustine was home in May, sitting with his *Ayi* at her house at Sechumhang, when she told him over dinner. 'Augustine,' she said to him, looking up from her bowl of rice and chicken and *yongbah*. 'I need you to do something for me.'

'Of course, *Ayi*,' Augustine replied.

'I need you to take over this house,' she said, staring up at the ceiling and at the dark, unvarnished walls. This was the home she'd seen built from the forest, where she'd raised a family and lived a life, where she'd known happiness and grief, heartbreak and love. This was all she had. But she knew it was time. Her words were prosaic, belying their import and the sorrow beneath.

'It is too difficult for me at my age. In the wintertime it is too cold for me now. And in the summer, when the fires come, it is too dangerous.'

Augustine looked at his *Ayi*, and she put her hand out to his.

'It's your time, Augustine.'

He saw what she was trying to do, and he understood the generosity of her offer. This was the home her husband had built for her, it was the place where she'd made and stored the memories of a lifetime. This house would bring Augustine back to Ukhrul, and not empty-handed. He could return to a place of his own, free from the haunting remembrances of the family home at the top of the hill.

'Thank you, *Ayi*. Of course, I will be honoured to look after your home,' Augustine chose his words carefully. 'When I am in Ukhrul I will live in this house, and I will care for it. But I think I will live in Delhi sometimes too. I am not ready to move back here yet, and Alex is in that city too.'

'That's fine, Augustine,' his grandmother said. She seemed content not to let the perfect be the enemy of the good. 'This place will draw you home soon enough.'

Augustine was as good as his word, and *Ayi* as sound as her prediction. Sechumhang, for all its isolation, its contrast to hyper-crowded Delhi, felt increasingly like home to him. When he was back, Augustine found himself easily slipping into the rhythm of life in the country. Living without electricity, he rose and slept with the sun. He grew potatoes and taro and cooked his meals on the fire. He washed in the river at the bottom of the hill. He felt healthier out of Delhi's smog and traffic, and away from the ghee-laden plainlands food of the capital. In the afternoons, he would take long walks to see Simeon at the paddy fields. His uncle welcomed him with chai or rice beer, depending on the time of day. They talked of the weather and the crops and the land.

But something was different now. There was an unspoken tension between Augustine and his uncle. Both men felt it. Simeon's commitment to familial duty, to 'doing right', had become an obsession. He talked constantly of 'honouring the family'. Augustine had the impression that Simeon felt coerced into some wrongdoing in buying his brother's land from his nephew, that he'd been a reluctant, browbeaten partner in something shameful. It was nothing he said, only the way in which he talked. As obliquely as he could, Augustine sought to assure his uncle that what had transpired was okay, and that he was comfortable having sold the land. Although a part of Augustine felt a pang of regret—he missed the fields, missed knowing they were his, missed the connection they brought him to his father—he was at peace now with the transaction.

249

From his quiet home at Sechumhang, Augustine walked up the hill to sit in the rear pews of church with Mun, his minister uncle, the man whose sorry duty it had been to bring the horror of Luke's addiction careering into their family's existence all those years ago. It was Mun, late that night, who'd had to tell Liko that her husband was a junkie. Augustine, then a child, had sat unseen in the shadows, and overheard. With both Luke and Liko gone, that night felt like another lifetime to Augustine.

Now, Augustine and Mun sat together as the afternoon sun poured in—a kaleidoscope of colours through the stained-glass windows. They gazed at the high vaulted ceiling, alone in the massive space, and they talked about life in the city, about Augustine's plans for the future, about family. They spoke unhurriedly.

'Things are not right between Simeon and I,' Augustine proffered. Mun nodded thoughtfully. He never answered immediately.

'Have you considered that perhaps it is not with you, that he is angry?' Mun said, deliberately but gently.

'Of course, he is. I hear it in the way he talks to me.'

'I hear it, too. But I don't think his anger is with you.'

'I don't understand.'

'The sins of the father are visited upon the son, the Bible says. I think Simeon is angry with your father, and you are being blamed for your Dad's failings.'

'Why?'

'Why is he angry? I think Simeon feels your father had all the opportunities in life, being the eldest, and he threw them all away. But your father had obligations, too, to raise his family, to look after the Shimray lands, and he ignored those as well. Simeon feels he has been unfairly burdened with Luke's responsibilities, and he takes it out on you.'

'That's not fair,' Augustine said, angry with the misdirected wrath of his uncle. He bounced a clenched fist off his knee.

'It is fair on no one,' Mun replied. 'It is not fair on you, but it is not fair on Simeon either. Perhaps try to see it from his point of view.'

'But he doesn't see it from mine.' Augustine grew defensive, of his father's memory, and of his own innocence.

'No, he doesn't see it from your point of view,' Mun agreed. 'He cannot yet, and maybe not ever. He is angry.'

Sometimes Mun came down the hill to see Augustine too. He arrived one afternoon at Sechumhang bearing a paper bag full of *heingar*, the hard, sweet discs of coconut and sugar Augustine had loved as a child. The pair sat on the back stoop noisily eating them. They talked easily of the news of the town, but Augustine knew that was not why Mun had come to see him. Always, with these conversations, there was a purpose. Mun would challenge Augustine, but kindly, in a pastoral way.

Finally, Mun asked: 'What are you looking for, Augustine? What do you want?' He had sensed Augustine's nagging sense of dislocation. His nephew was back in the hills of his homeland, he was amongst his people, but still, something was not right.

'I don't know, uncle,' Augustine finally replied. 'I will let you know when I find it.' They both laughed, and Mun punched Augustine playfully on the arm.

Barely twenty metres from the back stoop at Sechumhang stood an ancient mahogany tree, its hardwood branches bowed with age. As Augustine and Mun spoke, a hornbill flew in and quietly sat on a branch. It had its head turned and it stared at the men as they talked, one sharp, black eye never moving from the pair. The men were transfixed by its flowing movements, the grace of the enormous bird. Augustine spoke first, quietly, and without ever taking his eyes from the hornbill. 'Do you remember the story of Yarho?' he asked his uncle. From the corner of his eye, Augustine could see Mun nodding.

'The boy who became a hornbill,' Mun said. 'Your father used to tell that story.'

'That's right,' Augustine said. 'The boy who became a bird.'

Mun and Augustine kept watching the hornbill. The bird was perfectly still. Then, without apparent catalyst, it arched its wings, raising them at the side of its body in preparation for flight. Still the bird was watching them. Still they watched it. The bird leapt effortlessly into the air. With two graceful beats, it soared into the sky, above the trees, and was lost from their vision.

◈◈◈

They climb. Augustine has no idea how far they have ascended, or how much further they have to go. The cliff face stretches beyond the end of his vision above. As he stretches out across the rock face, he, for the briefest moment, looks down. Instantly, he is overwhelmed by blind panic. The forest floor, so far below it looks almost unreal, spins in his vision. Frozen in fear, he clings, paralysed, to the cliff. A fall is certain death. One slip, one loose rock, one handgrip that doesn't hold, one mistake will kill him. Will kill them. From this distance, the forest has lost its hard edges. It is silken green below, yielding and gentle. Augustine can't move. He is stuck, halfway up Sukhayap, pinned against the mountain, too afraid to climb up, unable to step down. His body courses with adrenalin. His arms shake uncontrollably, but his feet won't move. One minute passes... two. *This will all be over*, he thinks, *if I just... let... go.*

'Augustine!' Akala's voice cuts through his panic. He turns to look at her. She is standing on a narrow ledge a couple of metres below. 'Augustine,' she says, 'we have to keep going'. He nods, and the words have their desired effect. His breathing calms. Slowly, he lifts his right foot in search of the next foothold; he finds it and jams his shoe in. He stretches out for a handhold and finds it secure. He drags himself to the next small mantle, and collapses in relief.

They climb. Slowly, slowly, clawing their way upwards, metre by metre, handhold by handhold, until they stand at the edge of a shelf with no way left to go. From here, there is only smooth rock sweeping upwards in every direction. There is a broader ledge, perhaps three and half metres above them, a full metre beyond Augustine's furthest stretch. From there they can reach the brow of the mountain, and the summit of the cliff. They are nearly at Sukhayap. But there is no way to reach it, the path is blocked here. Augustine retreats a few metres back down, looking for another way up. There is nothing, so he looks down further again. And freezes.

He is looking down at a score of small, scurrying bodies, stretched across the cliff face. Barely 40 metres below, steadily climbing, are the men of their villages in their pursuit. Augustine's uncle leads them. There is a quiet assurance in the way the men climb. They know they have their target cornered, that there is nowhere left for them to run. All they need do is keep on the trail, for there is no escape from here. The chant is ceaseless, and ever more menacing. 'Hooo-yaaaa, Heeeeyyy-yaaaa, Hooo-yaaaa, Heeeeyyy-yaaaa'. Simeon is climbing quickly but carefully, picking the same route as Augustine and Akala took, from handhold to handhold, as directly as he can climb. Augustine stares down at his uncle. Suddenly, Simeon looks up and their eyes meet.

'Aaaaaaaooooooooowwwwwww,' Simeon lets out a blood-curdling cry, his eyes boring straight into Augustine's. They both hold the stare as the entire chasing group responds in concert: 'Aaaaaaaooooooooow-wwwwww'. The men know immediately what the cry means. The prey has been spotted. It will soon be theirs.

NIDO

The café at Shahpur Jat was bulldozed so Augustine was suddenly without a job. A week earlier, the manager had received a formal notice to vacate, which he casually ignored, just as he had the dozens that had come before it. But then, on a quiet Monday morning, a dust-covered truck bearing a digger arrived at the front door to demolish the building.

Everybody knew about the development proposal that had been submitted for the block that housed the cafe. But the proposal had sat on a city *babu*'s desk for a decade and nothing had happened. Notices to vacate had arrived and been disregarded for years, because no one believed construction would ever start. But this time was different. Somewhere in the byzantine bureaucracy a way was cleared, money was found—likely changed hands—and the 'first-class, premium-luxury' development, according to a sign the truck driver hammered into the dirt of the footpath, was underway.

The café was still open when the bulldozer arrived. Augustine and the other staff frantically cleared the place, shutting off the water and gas, and pulling out the furniture as the workmen readied their machines. The final few chairs were still being dragged out as the first wrecker went in. Augustine sat across the street with his colleagues, perched on the chairs from the café and surrounded

254

by piles of crockery and cutlery, old posters and rolled-up carpets, watching the place crumble. In a few hours it was gone.

Afterwards, Delhi felt like an increasingly hostile place to live. It had never been particularly welcoming to Augustine, but now, it felt as if the capital's forbearance for the thousands of outsiders who streamed in every week was exhausted. There was no catalyst for the rising tide of intolerance, but Augustine and Alex both felt it. Nido noticed it, too: a subterranean resistance to their presence that occasionally broke through to the surface in ugly confrontation. Despite his academic reputation, Nido was frozen out of elections for student council at university. 'Not for your kind,' he was told when he went to nominate.

In December, things got worse, and the fragile tableau of Delhi as a multicultural, multi-ethnic crucible was exposed for the facade it was. The crime was exceptional, and it was ordinary. On a cold Sunday night, a twenty-three-year-old woman, a student at Jawaharlal Nehru University, boarded an off-duty bus at the stop outside Munirka. Most nights in Delhi, these buses ran the technically-illegal-but-tacitly-condoned out-of-hours routes. It was *jugaad*, a sly fix for Delhi's intractable transport problems. Everybody knew about the 'night buses' that ran off the books, but things were easier with them than without, so nobody stopped them.

This bus was different. The six men on board, including the driver, knew each other, and had collectively decided upon an act of unspeakable savagery. The woman was attacked as soon as the doors were locked and the bus had edged its way back into the traffic. The men drew the curtains on the windows to make sure nobody could see. For an hour, the woman was bashed, gang raped and brutalised with an iron bar before the men threw her, naked and unconscious, from the still-moving bus onto the road. She died 12 days later in a foreign hospital, from the unspeakable injuries they inflicted.

Her murder was international news. The attack's sheer brutality, and the utter contempt the perpetrators showed for the life of their victim, stunned India and appalled the rest of the world even more. Gang rapes happened every day in India. They happened in the cities and in the villages, to old women and to children. They were so common they were barely news; perhaps a few paragraphs on an inside page of a newspaper, but people hardly noticed. This was different. This victim was different. She was low-caste, but she was clever. Her father had sold all his land so they could move to Delhi and she could go to university. She was 'aspirational India', the bedtime story that parents told their children at night because they wanted to believe it themselves: 'If you study hard, if you work hard, you can be a "success".' Now that dream was shattered. The girl who died represented all that was good about India. Her attackers who lived stood for all that was wrong with the country.

India turned in on itself, contorted in an anguished search of the national soul. And it did not like what it found. Suddenly, there were reporters from *The New York Times* asking questions in Munirka, and the BBC was filming at the bus stop. Thundering editorials about India's 'culture of violence against women' dominated world headlines for weeks, and massive street protests in the capital brought the army onto the streets armed with water cannons. Public outrage roiled for weeks undiminished. Unconcerned by any obligation to the separation of powers, the government promised the death penalty for the perpetrators. India raged at itself.

Those living in Munirka could see the reprisal coming. Stung by criticism of their constant indifference to attacks on women, Delhi police quickly rounded up their suspects—half a dozen migrant workers who lived in slums across South Delhi. They were friends and they'd been 'having a party' they told police, drinking and listening to music, when they decided they could have more fun. They stole the keys to a bus one of them drove during the day, and with more booze on board, set off on their sadistic expedition. None of the men lived in Munirka, but they were migrants, too, from Rajasthan and Uttar Pradesh, and the suburb from where, by chance, they'd launched their attack was tarred by association.

Police came through Munirka and shut down the sly grog shops and roughed up the local teenagers, just to be seen to be doing something. There was imposed an informal, but strictly-enforced curfew. The residents of Munirka knew nothing about the crime, but it had its origin in their neighbourhood, so they were somehow at fault. The narrative of the ill-bred jaat wreaking havoc across the city gained new currency amongst Delhi's chattering classes. 'They don't know how to behave once they are away from their villages. They are not civilised,' Augustine heard one high-caste commentator opine on TV, to widespread concurrence.

Hostility in Delhi towards 'other' Indians from outside the capital, always a latent undercurrent, became an open, festering wound. Over the next year, things steadily deteriorated; there were fewer and fewer pockets of acceptance now. The view of outsiders as vulgar troublemakers gained legitimacy across the city. Vigilantes who took matters into their own hands, brutally beating migrant workers whom they suspected of some crime, were celebrated in the media for 'cleaning up the city'. Delhiwallahs openly alleged that migrants were responsible for all of the city's problems: the violence against women, the overcrowding, the power shortages, the lack of water. An indifferent city turned unfriendly, then more oppressive by the day. Augustine was spat on from passing cars as he walked. If he was on the street at night, he was stopped and frisked by police, interrogated as to where he'd been and with whom: guilty unless and until he could prove his innocence. But Augustine was determined he would not be cowed. In his contrary way, the more trouble being an outsider brought him, the more baldly he was determined to show it. To others, the Naga hornbill feather in Augustine's hair was a target above his head. To him, it was a badge of honour.

His grandmother called and urged him to come home. 'You need to be with your people and to see your country.' Augustine and Alex had not planned to go home for Christmas, but, at their *Ayi's* urging, they left Delhi on December 20. Nido came too. 'People like us are not welcome in Delhi now,' he said. The three boys caught the train to Dimapur, where they spent a night with Nido's family, back in their old neighbourhood. Early the next morning, the two brothers caught the slow bus to Ukhrul.

At home, Augustine stayed down at Sechumhang again—his absence from the family home no longer questioned. Alex stayed in the house on the hill, but he spent increasing amounts of time in the quiet with his brother. In the new year, Nido went back to Delhi.

He had papers to write and needed the library. Alex went too. His boss wanted him back in the shop. Uncompelled by work or any other commitment, Augustine decided to stay in the forest a few weeks longer. 'Delhi is too angry right now,' he told his brother.

Still, Delhi's roiling hostility was able to find Augustine, even at home. It was January 26. Republic Day. Augustine never felt more dissociated from India than on the day his country celebrated its nationhood. On a friend's TV, he watched the army's march-past down Rajpath in Delhi, a bellicose demonstration of India's military might. On the back of a truck was a missile: 'capable of depositing a nuclear warhead anywhere in Pakistan' the TV announcer exclaimed, his voice swelling with pride at the thought of unleashing such irreparable chaos. The missile was painted with an Indian flag. It was called Agni. Fire.

Augustine's phone chimed in his pocket. The text from Alex read: 'Call me. I can't reach you. It's Nido.'

Augustine walked out of the house, searching for better phone reception. He couldn't call Alex, but he was able to send a text: 'What happened? Is he all right?'

The reply was one word. 'No.'

Augustine ran to the top of the hill and frantically tried to call. His fifth attempt went through, with a click his brother's voice came on the line.

'I'm sorry Augustine,' Alex cried down the phone. 'I'm so sorry.'

'Tell me, tell me what happened,' Augustine said, panicked now by his brother's distress.

Alex struggled to speak in between sobs. His words tumbled out on top of each other in short staccato sentences. 'Lajpat… Nido went there. To the market. To visit someone. But then…' Alex's voice was a howl now. Augustine had been stunned into silence at his end of the phone. He wanted to say something, the right words to make this all okay again, to undo whatever this was. But he could think of nothing.

'Augustine, are you there?' Alex asked.

'I'm here,' Augustine said. 'Where did Nido go?'

'Lajpat… to Lajpat Nagar,' Alex said.

Augustine knew the place, a dozen neighbourhoods along the ring road from Munirka. It was a polyglot refuge from war, a mix of old Punjabi families who'd come, fleeing the violence of Partition; Bengali widows who arrived in the aftermath of Bangladesh's bloody battle for independence; and Afghans escaping the seemingly endless conflict in their country. For the most part, the suburb juggled its competing worldviews amicably enough. Always though, there was a quiet tension. Alex was sobbing down the phone.

'What happened at Lajpat Nagar?' Augustine asked, forcing his voice to remain steady as the panic rose in his chest,.

'I don't really know,' Alex was speaking more fluently now, but too quickly, at a pace Augustine could barely understand. 'I went down to the market and talked to some old men who had a stall and they said they saw it but the police won't talk to me, so I don't know if there's an investigation or what happened...' Here, Alex paused to draw breath.

'Saw what, Alex?' Augustine interrupted him. He was firm now. 'What happened?'

'Nido... they beat him.'

As best Alex could piece the story together—he was careful with whom he spoke, so as not to cause further trouble—Nido was looking for a university friend's house, and had stopped at a paneer shop to ask the two Haryanvi boys behind the counter for directions. Instead of helping, the boys abused Nido, teasing him about his birthmark and insulting him about being a 'chinky', a foreigner who wasn't a proper Indian. In anger, Nido, slammed the glass counter of their shop with his fist, smashing it. The police were called, and demanded Nido pay an exorbitant sum for the damage. He acquiesced, he couldn't hope for the police to be on his side, but once the officers left—taking their cut of the payment—the boys in the shop wouldn't let Nido leave. They had their own justice to mete out, and they knew the police would not return. Out the front of their shop, and unworried by the attention of passers-by, they beat Nido, pounding his face with their fists until it was decided by someone in the crowd that the smaller boy had had enough. An old Pashtun pulled the assailants off Nido as he lay in the dust. *'Bas,'* he said in Hindi, 'enough'.

'But one of the boys,' Alex said, more calmly now, 'he got one more kick in. Right to the side of Nido's head. That's what the men at the stall told me.'

Augustine did not interrupt his brother.

'Nido had blood coming from his lip and his head, but he was all right,' Alex said. 'He caught the train home to college and went to bed. He told his roommates he had a headache.'

'So what happened?'

'No one knows. He just never woke up. Augustine,' Alex spoke quietly, slowly now, 'Nido is dead.'

Augustine was silent a whole minute. Then the sobs came, tearing through his chest in waves. He dropped the phone, and fell to his knees, wailing with his head in his hands.

Except to those who knew him, Nido's death was unexceptional. It was, at best, a few lines in tomorrow's newspaper, perhaps alongside a comment from a north-east politician arguing the attack was racially motivated. But that would be all. There would be no outcry, no TV crews, no demonstrations or citizens seized to rid the city of the violence which blighted it. The attackers would escape any penalty and the world would forget. Augustine stood at the top of the hill and sobbed for his friend. But he wept not only for Nido, he wept for his family and for himself and for Alex. He mourned the loss of life, and the extraordinary potential wasted. Nido had always been the brilliant one. 'The chosen one,' Luke had called him all those years ago. Luke had been wrong, Nido was not the chosen one, he was marked for death. But to Augustine, Nido's death felt like an attack on all of them. He felt diminished too. Nido was a reminder of his own inconsequence in a place where he'd never belong. Augustine made a decision. He called Alex back.

'I'm not going back,' he said.

'What?'

'I'm not going back to Delhi. When you come up, could you bring my things on the train? I am going to stay in Ukhrul. This is where I should be.'

Augustine hung up the phone. He knew he was being unfair. He understood his hasty announcement was major news to Alex as well, and it left his little brother with an invidious choice. They'd always done everything together. But Augustine knew he could not go back to the capital. He could not make himself board the bus that would take him to that place. Since his first demoralising visit with his dying mother to that uncaring hospital, the city and he had always been on uneasy terms. Now they would be on none.

A week later, Alex arrived home. He'd accompanied Nido's body on the train to Dimapur. Augustine had come to the city too, to wait at the train station, and Alex stumbled into his brother's arms from the rear carriage, where he'd sat with the coffin. He was in tears; too many hours staring at that impassive wooden box. Augustine cried, too, as the railwaymen carried Nido's coffin to the waiting hearse. Augustine and Alex walked to the stricken, silent Horam family home, where they paid their respects and were prevailed upon to stay. Nido's mother made them beds in the front room. They lay awake in front of the TV they used to watch as kids, now silent and covered in the corner.

'Where do you think you go?' Alex said quietly, staring towards the ceiling through the darkness.

'What?' Augustine asked, not following.

'When you die, what happens to you?'

'I think Nido is in Kazeiram,' Augustine said.

'Really?' Alex drew himself up to his elbows and looked across at his brother. 'Do you believe in that stuff?'

'That stuff?' Augustine shot back. 'Of course, I believe in it.'

Augustine realised he'd been unfairly terse with his little brother. Lying on his back and staring at the ceiling still, he softened his tone, and drew Alex into his confidence. 'I never told you, but I went to Kazeiram once.'

'What?'

'I saw Dad.'

'What? When?'

'The morning Mum died.'

'You saw Dad? Did you speak to him? What was it like?' Alex's questions tumbled out.

'I don't know,' Augustine replied. 'It was... it was just like talking to Dad. Only it was Dad when he was young, before he got sick.'

'And what did he say?'

'Nothing much. He didn't speak much, but it was Dad's old voice, like when we were kids. He just said that we would be okay, you and me and Maitonphi and Zaki. That we'd be all right.' Augustine's candour only went so far. He felt uncomfortable lying to his brother, but he knew Luke's declaration about a 'chosen one' would only inspire more questions from Alex, and more awkwardness from him. Augustine hated to think what his father would think about Nido's death. Nido was that chosen one, Luke had always believed. And now he was gone. Now he was in Kazeiram too. Augustine wondered whether he could visit Nido in Kazeiram. What would he ask?

'Are you sure you weren't hallucinating—you weren't dreaming?' Alex pressed his brother.

'You don't have to believe in Kazeiram, but I know it exists. I've been there,' Augustine said with finality. He rolled over in bed, away from his brother, to face the TV in the corner. The brothers lay in silence. Augustine willed for a tiredness, but it was reluctant to come. He wanted to be asleep, not staring at this insensible great box, a reminder of his childhood spent with Nido, and now as silent as he was.

Augustine knew Alex had more questions, but there was nothing more to be said. He knew his brother didn't see the world the same way he did. What was real for Augustine was myth for his brother. Alex had grown up in the same house surrounded by the same stories, the same history, but perhaps as the second son, and two years younger, he had not had the same paternal inculcation as his elder brother. Perhaps it was because the stories were not his to carry on. Alex couldn't believe in Kazeiram until he had been there. And he couldn't go there unless he believed.

He felt the gulf that had emerged now between he and his brother. Lying in the dark he willed for Alex to believe too. The person he was closest to in the world, couldn't see that world the way he did. But Augustine appreciated, too, how great a leap he was asking his brother to make. To Augustine there was no distinction, no boundary between the world he and his brother lived in and that of the gods and the spirits of the dead. All of it was reality.

Augustine lived in a world where boys turned into birds, and the dead could be spoken to. He believed that songs and feasts would bring good rains and plentiful harvests, and that goddesses lived on the summits of mountains, dissembling into human form whenever they chose. He had no problem reconciling the 'real' world with the spiritual, because they were one and the same. There was no line. It was different for the younger Shimray. Augustine believed, Alex understood. Sleep was slow to come.

The Shimray brothers left Dimapur on the bus the next afternoon after Nido's funeral, arriving back in Ukhrul in the middle of the night. It was too late for Augustine to walk down the hill in the darkness to Sechumhang, so the brothers stayed the night in the family home at the top of the hill. They'd not spent a night together in that place for a long time. But Augustine couldn't stay. Before breakfast the next morning, he gathered together all that he owned. Alex had brought his brother's possessions back from Delhi in two striped carrier bags, knotted with string. Augustine would take them down to Sechumhang; that was his home now. From bed, Alex watched his brother quietly pack and walk out of the house. He was awake, but he let Augustine leave unchallenged.

'Goodbye Alex,' Augustine said, quietly acknowledging his sibling as he left.

A week after Nido's funeral, Alex walked down to Sechumhang, a handful of younger cousins in tow. They carried bulbous empty pots under their arms. Augustine was sitting on the stoop, looking down the valley. 'Come with us,' Alex said, stopping to talk to his brother for the first time since they'd returned to Ukhrul. 'We have to collect water from the river, but we are going to the place where you can swim, where the women from Tiya wash their clothes.' Augustine knew the spot. He'd not visited there for a long time. 'I'll come,' he said, standing, and silently following the gaggle already ahead, noisily wending its way downhill.

❖❖❖

From the bank, Augustine dived into the dark river, feeling the sting of the cold water against his face, and the current pulling him towards the fast-flowing middle. He felt for the river bottom with his feet and stood up, running his hands through his hair. For the first time since Nido's death, the weight of his grief for his friend felt endurable, a wound that, while raw still, he knew would one day heal. Nido's death didn't have to mean the end of his life too.

Alex appeared beside Augustine in the river, standing firm against the fast-flowing water that eddied and swirled as it ran into and around their bodies. They were joined by the others, the younger cousins who didn't swim well and who'd made less confident entries, but were now making a sport out of tackling each other into steadily deeper water. Soon the quiet run of the river was overwhelmed by the shouts and splashes of half a dozen bodies. Alex joined in, but Augustine stayed at the periphery of the games. And that's when he saw her, walking carefully down the switchbacks of the hill path opposite, to the riverbank where she crouched at the water's edge. On her back she carried clothes in a heavy *sop*, held by a woven strap that ran across her forehead and pulled her chin upwards. Augustine thought it made her look proud. He couldn't take his eyes from the girl. But she didn't look across the river at him.

Part Three

SUKHAYAP

SUKHAYAP

Augustine is panicked now. Simeon has sighted them. There is no way for them to turn, nowhere for them to hide. They are stranded on the cliff face as their pursuers draw inexorably closer. This is where it will end.

Augustine turns and hastily pulls at a vine that grows in a crack in the side of the rock near his feet. It's long, much longer than he expects, and he pulls out its full length. He scrambles back up to Akala. He doesn't need to tell Akala about their pursuers. She heard. She knows. Augustine makes a loop at the end of the vine and launches it at the ledge above them. There is a small nub of rock just above the nearside of the platform he is aiming for. He is praying the vine will be strong enough, for it is all they have. The first two throws miss. The chant grows louder again beneath them. The sighting of the prey has enthused their pursuers. The third throw takes, and Augustine pulls the vine taut. It feels strong.

'You first,' he says, turning to Akala. 'If the vine can hold you, it is more likely to hold me. And if it can't hold you… I am here to catch you.' He allows himself a smile and Akala laughs. Their situation is hopeless: the chant ringing in their ears is reminder of that. Akala pulls on the vine. Slowly, she begins to pull herself up the sheer rock face, feet on the cliff, her bodyweight supported by the vine. It is only a few short, final metres, but she winces in pain as the gnarled vine digs into her hands.

266

Halfway now. Akala starts to sway dangerously as she draws closer, a combination of the wind catching her against the exposed rock face, and her fatigue. She can't hold her body still against the momentum. Finally, as the arc of her swing brings her closest to the ledge, she throws herself at the shelf. Her fingers grasp only the very edge, but her grip holds, and, achingly slowly, she pulls herself up. She has made it. Sukhayap Cliff is just above her. But he is still below.

Augustine takes the swinging vine and slowly leans his weight onto it. He starts his feet up the rock face, searching for a spot to grip. He releases his right hand from the vine to grasp higher when he hears the crack. Suddenly the world is all sky and rock and sky and rock, all tumbling, all indecipherable, all spinning.

'AUGUSTINE!!!' he hears Akala's voice through the chaos. His mind, for the briefest instant, is clear. He is falling. He throws out his left hand. It finds rock. He grabs at it, a hold, and he feels the weight of his falling body jolt through his shoulder. He looks down to see the vine tumbling to the forest floor below, bouncing off the rock as it plummets. But he is falling no more.

'AUGUSTINE!!!' Akala's voice again. Panicked still. He is hanging by his left hand, holding onto the ledge where, moments before, he was standing. Below his feet now there is nothing for a hundred metres. He can't stop staring down. His body swings as he hangs in space. It is almost peaceful. 'Augustine.' He looks up to see Akala, crouched on her ledge looking down to him. 'Please, Augustine. I need you here.'

Slowly, he begins the task of pulling himself back up. He seems to have exhausted his supply of adrenalin, because the shaking in his arms is gone now. The fear which paralysed him has been replaced by a dogged belief. He knows what it is to fall. Now he will know what it is to climb. He finds a hold with his right hand on the same ledge, and wearily pulls himself back to where he stood before. Akala is still above him, crouched on the ledge he must somehow reach. She looks down.

The span of sheer rock between them appears unbridgeable. Akala holds her hand out, stretching her fingers towards Augustine in a vain attempt to breach the gulf. It only makes her appear more remote. But Augustine can see now, a tiny crack in the rock, one he hadn't noticed before. It is barely five centimetres long, running perpendicular to the two ledges, halfway between. He stretches to run his fingers over the fissure.

Withdrawing his *dao* from its sheath and holding its handle in his right hand, he powerfully stabs the blade at the rock face. He misses the crack and it jars his arm. The second stab is on target, and the blade jams into the crack, sticking out from the rock face at a haphazard angle. It's still too loose. He takes a small rock from by his feet, and using the stone as a hammer, pounds the knife into the cliff face. It has to hold his weight. Millimetre by millimetre, the blade wedges deeper into the rock. He gingerly tests its strength. The chanting below is a steady rumbling.

The blade is wedged as deeply as it will go, and Augustine discards the rock. If the *dao* holds, he can join Akala above, he can make it to Sukhayap. If it fails, he will fall again, this time all the way down. He feels certain he has tested fortune enough.

The end of the handle still oscillates faintly. All of Augustine's faith rests in the steel blade his father forged in the fire at their home at the top of the hill, all of those years ago. He reaches up with his left hand and grips the cold metal. The sharpened edge of the blade finds the grooves of his fingers. He wraps his right hand around his left and slowly, begins to pull himself up, feet skating across the coarse rock face.

It holds. Augustine feels the bite of the blade as it slices into his hand. Blood runs between his fingers and down his arms, pulsing with the beat of his heart. But he feels no pain. His head is level with the blade now and, still, the knife has not shifted. He pulls himself higher still. The knife cuts deeper into his hand as he slowly rotates his grip. He looks up, and he is close. Akala is near now, still crouched, her eyes huge with worry. Augustine—for a moment—pauses, the knife at chest height, his body hanging in space, feet lost in the air, searching for contact. Then, as forcefully as his tired arms allow, he heaves his body upwards, throwing his right hand at the rock on which Akala is knelt. His hand finds its edge and grips it. In an instant, all of Augustine's weight is hanging from that arm. The blood-soaked knife is behind him, quavering with the release of the pressure on it. He finds a hold for his left hand on the ledge, and the coarse rock grinds into his wounds. His feet find the rock face, and he pulls himself up, collapsing into Akala's arms, waves of relief shuddering through his body.

With Akala's help, Augustine rises for the final short climb to the summit. But then he turns and peers back over the ledge at the knife, stuck impassively into the stone. He kneels, and then, lying on his stomach, he stretches an arm towards the blade, in the hope he might retrieve it. He promised his father he would never lose it, and he does not want to break his vow now, so close to the peak. But he is not close. Even hanging half his body over the ledge, it is still far from his grasping fingers. The *dao* will have to stay. Its work is done.

The brow of the mountain is flatter, and Akala and Augustine walk easily towards the summit. But suddenly, after their haste, neither is anxious to set foot on the top. From there, there is no returning. There are still a few hours of daylight left, and they slow their progress. An untrodden path through a narrow crevasse will, they can see, deposit them at the precipice. They don't want to be there yet, but they walk on.

At its narrowest point, the channel through which they walk is barely a metre wide. The stone walls rise imposingly on either side. Augustine runs his worn fingers across the surface of the rock, feeling the coarse grain. He wants to feel everything now. A calm has settled upon him. His senses feel heightened, alert to all the information he can absorb. He stops walking. To his left, at head height, is a dramatic fissure in the limestone wall. It runs deep into the belly of the stone, lost to the darkness after four or five metres. The cleft is nearly his height again. Large enough for a person. Large enough for two. He puts his hands on the lip of the hollow and pulls himself up, offering a hand to Akala, who climbs up alongside him.

'This is their grotto,' Augustine says.

'Shishio and Hatang's?'

'Shishio and Hatang's. This is where they lay together.'

The back of the chamber is pitch dark. From his pocket Augustine withdraws his phone. He has carried it all the way across Nagaland, switched off, but he turns it on now. There is no risk. They are far beyond the reach of any signal. Augustine shines the light from the phone's screen into the nothingness, and the hazy glow finds the rear wall. He scans the cave, the light's weak beam skittering across the rock. Suddenly, it catches the glint of metal. He brings the light to rest on an object stood in the most distant corner of the cave. Standing against the wall is a Naga *dao*.

He crawls towards the knife, holding the light out, fixed upon it. Akala follows. He doesn't touch it at first, but simply stares at the ageing blade and the worn handle, bound with thin vine just as the one his father gave him was. He thinks of his own *dao* jammed, exposed, in the rock. The men would not have reached his knife yet. But they would soon. They would pull the blade from the rock and hurl it from the cliff, to be consumed forever by the forest below. His memory, and his father's, discarded together.

Augustine doesn't touch the *dao* in the cave, but looks past it, to words etched into the smoothest part of the wall. In crude capital letters, clearly carved with the knife before them, are three words: SHISHIO HATANG. Akala traces her fingers over the rough characters. Augustine picks up the dao, and sits cross-legged before the wall. Carefully, with the worn point of the blade, he carves their tribute alongside. It may never be seen; the men in such febrile pursuit of them may never care to stop to look here. But Augustine wants their names to live on as long as these have. AUGUSTINE AKALA.

Akala grabs Augustine and kisses him hard, almost in desperation, on the lips. They have little time left. She runs her hands through his hair, and lifts his shirt over his shoulders and traces her fingertips down his chest. Augustine lays Akala down on his shawl on the floor of the cave, and lies down beside her. Underneath her loose black top, his hands caress her hipbones, and the soft curve of her breasts. He kisses the nape of her neck and her lips. The cave is alive to the sound of their passion. Outside, there is no noise. There is no movement.

In the quiet that follows, they lie silent, listening for the chants of those who pursue them. But no sound reaches into the cave. The world outside does not exist. Not while they lie here together. They drift towards sleep.

❖❖❖

Akala emerges first from their half-slumber. It has been less than an hour, but it feels longer. The light outside has softened. 'Augustine,' she says gently, 'it's time'. He slowly draws himself up to sit. He begins to fold his clothes, placing them in a neat pile at the end of the grotto, and laying his red Tangkhul shawl on top.

'You're not getting dressed?' Akala asks. She is seated against the wall of the grotto, her naked body covered by her shawl.

'We won't need these where we are going.'

She nods in assent and rises to do the same. The order of the two neat piles they leave betrays the chaos of their final few days. Akala and Augustine climb down from the grotto and stand, together, for their final, brief ascent. Augustine takes Akala's hornbill feather from where it sits on the stone and affixes it in her hair, standing straight up from the back of her head. He hands her his feather, and she does the same for him. Save for their plumage, they are naked as they walk the final few metres to the precipice.

They stand now, side by side, at the very edge of the cliff. At this ultimate place, a profound calm has settled upon them. They can hear still the chant of the men chasing, and, if they chose to peer down below, they can even see them. The men are strung out along the cliff face, arms outstretched, their sinewy bodies, slick with sweat, pressed against the rock. But Augustine and Akala barely bother to monitor their progress; the men do not worry them now. They cannot catch them, or harm them. Augustine and Akala have reached where they need to be.

Instead, they look out, over the green lands of the Naga, and the path through the river valleys they have travelled. In the far distance, they can see Shirui Peak, dominant over all.

It is snowing on Shirui.

From its very peak to the river basin below, the mountain is carpeted in white lilies. They see the blooms, spilling down the eastern flank towards Augustine's village of Ukhrul, but too—for the first time they have ever known—blanketing the western side all the way to Akala's home in Tiya.

They stare at their two villages, bathed together in the golden light of the last of the afternoon sun. The Goddess of Shirui Peak has united their people.

They stand, still, side by side at the very edge of the cliff. Augustine cannot hold back the tears now as he and Akala gaze, transfixed, upon their homes. But from the corner of his eye, he sees a beatific smile play, ever so faintly, upon Akala's lips.

'You,' he says softly, in the sudden revelation of understanding. She nods.

Akala thrusts her hand confidently towards Augustine's: fingers spread, searching. Standing at the precipice, she takes his shaking hand in her steady one.

◈◈◈

The two hornbills soar effortlessly towards me, propelled by an updraft of warm spring air.

The lead bird looks to me as he glides to my altitude, and I recognise his gaze, that urgent searching for assurance, for truth. He looks at me now the way he did those nights, those long nights we sat together and told our histories, and kept alive the stories of our people.

'This way, Augustine,' I say, banking left and higher still, 'I know the way, son.' We fly three abreast, wings barely beating, towards the setting sun. Towards home.

FIN